THE

C000175550

Pᴀɴᴋᴀᴊ Sᴇᴋʜsᴀʀɪᴀ is a researcher, writer, photographer, ~~~~ academic. He has worked extensively in the field of the environment and of wildlife conservation with a particular focus on the Andaman and Nicobar Islands. He has been writing regularly on related issues for the English media since 1998, and is also author of two non-fiction books based in the islands: *Troubled Islands* (2003; a collection of his journalist writings) and *The Jarawa Tribal Reserve Dossier: Cultural and Biological Diversity in the Andaman Islands* (Jt. Editor; 2010).

For the last four years, he has been working on the 'Cultures of Innovation in Nanotechnology Research for Development in India' as part of his doctoral research project in Science and Technology Studies and is currently writing up his dissertation.

He lives in Hyderabad with his wife and four-year-old son.

PRAISE FOR *THE LAST WAVE*

'I enjoyed the book. Its flow and its characters smell right . . . and through them we are made quietly aware of the very complex social web that the Jarawa of the Andamans must negotiate now that they have been "befriended" by the administration.' – Bittu Sahgal, *Sanctuary Asia*

'A book to re-read and treasure.' – Monalisa Jena on Facebook

'A poignant yet engaging tale of a group of tiny islands, which seldom find a worthy note of mention in "mainland India", save for tourism and administrative purposes. Unless you are an anthropologist or an anthropology student, you will hardly get to read a work of literature so soothingly immersed in that unusual milieu.' – *The Financial Express*

'Sekhsaria . . . invests *The Last Wave* with an imaginative spiritual core. The book draws on the wellsprings of life forces; it brings to sharp relief the mindless advance of modernity, contrasting it with a natural order of life.'– Shamik Bag, *The Indian Express*

'A commendable debut . . .' – Ajay Dandekar, *Biblio*

'The author has successfully managed to sew together real life stories to his tale and the combination of fact and fiction on an ecological backdrop forms a rich tapestry which will enrich the knowledge of the readers while keeping them enthralled with its lucidity.' – Sabyasachi Patra, indiawilds.com

'*The Last Wave: An Island Novel* is fascinating for the way it depicts a part of India often ignored in literature.' – southasiabookblog.com

'I also feel that this is an extremely important book for the way in which it entertains readers while giving us insights into different ways of living, and showing us the delight and wealth of being sensitive to and promoting cultures radically different from our own.' – Saaz Aggarwal, blackandwhitefountain.blogspot.in

THE LAST WAVE

An Island Novel

Pankaj Sekhsaria

HarperCollins *Publishers* India

First published in India by
HarperCollins *Publishers* in 2014
A-75, Sector 57, Noida, Uttar Pradesh 201301, India
www.harpercollins.co.in

4 6 8 10 9 7 5 3

P-ISBN: 978-93-5136-191-6
E-ISBN: 978-93-5136-192-3

Typeset in 10/13 Minion Regular at
SÜRYA

Printed and bound at
Saurabh Printers Pvt.Ltd.

To
My parents and Peeyush

Latha and Kabir

The Great Cataclysm

All Andamanese tradition dates back to some great cataclysm which submerged a greater part of the land. The Andamanese say that before this cataclysm they were all one tribe, and spoke the same language, but that after it, the survivors became separated into tribes, their languages gradually differed until at last they became mutually unintelligible as at present . . .

. . . It is quite possible that this tradition may be an account of what occurred when, by subsidence, the Andamans were cut off from the mainland of Arracan, and though geologists are slow to allow of sudden convulsions, yet it is certain that the subsidence, whether sudden or gradual did take place. A general gradual subsidence, ending in a severe earthquake which lowered a large tract of land a few feet, and thus submerged a considerable area, might be sufficient to account for this tradition.

It is curious that, though there are no wild beasts larger than a pig at the Andamans now (excepting reptiles and marine mammals), the Andamanese state that large and fierce beasts, as well as many aborigines, were drowned in the cataclysm; and, even in the Little Andaman the people have names for animals which they cannot describe, but evidently have traditions of . . .

. . . Whatever value we may attach to these legends, however, one thing seems certain, viz., that the Andamanese have inhabited these islands in their present state for a period which can only be considered by thousands of years, and they antedate any history or record preserved among these peoples . . .

'A History of our Relations with the Andamanese'
MV Portman, Fellow of the University of Calcutta
Officer in charge of the Andamanese, 1899

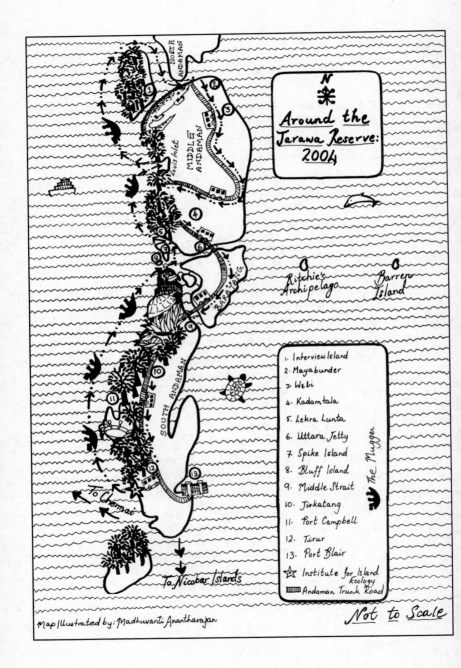

CONTENTS

PROLOGUE

Harish peered into the mouth of the creek as they approached it. The creek, so pretty and welcoming by day, had acquired a completely different feel at night; the waxy green of the mangroves had now turned pitch-black. Dense, uninviting, its earlier enticements replaced by an ominous darkness. The mangrove revealed nothing of what lay beyond. The sky, juxtaposed, offered relief – studded with a million twinkling pinpricks, little windows to gaze into and see through to the other side of the great heavens.

Reality was replicated perfectly in its reflection. The mangroves were revealed as a dark wall on the surface of the water along the banks of the creek. In the middle was the grey silver of the sky above, and the lines that separated these reflections receded like a giant V into the distance of the creek. If a guiding star was to be plucked from the night sky and placed in a creek, it would be the illusory tip of this always receding V, forever at the centre of the channel of water – focus on it and you were never lost.

But they were not navigating the creek for the fun of it, Harish, Seema, crocodile man and institute director, David; and their most local of guides, Uncle Pame. This survey was to span the western coast of the South and Middle Andaman Islands – and they were actively looking for crocodiles. The inflatable moved at a steady pace, with David at its tip, staring intently into the night. He sat for a while and then switched on his torch. The powerful beam of light cut sharply through the dark and fell on the water's edge to create a little pool of diffused yellow. It sallied back and forth, as David willed it, went off and then came on again on the opposite bank. This went on for a few minutes.

As they moved deeper into the mangroves, the creek became progressively narrower and the banks started closing in. The tip of the V was now closer, but still receding, always just out of reach in the brooding darkness.

David flicked the torch on again and directed its beam to the right. Suddenly, he gesticulated in a wild, animated manner. Uncle got the message immediately. The inflatable slowed down considerably and Uncle angled it to the right. Seema and Harish directed their attention to the new pool of yellow light that had come to rest on a little bunch of mangled mangrove roots and floating debris. They were about forty feet from the creek bank; the pool of light remained stuck where it was. David indicated again with his right hand. Uncle killed the motor completely and picked up the oar. Seema and Harish felt the tension, straining their necks as they scoured the pool of light that David now held steadfast.

David seemed to be in his element, completely focused, his gaze locked with something out there. 'Glowing coals,' he muttered in a muffled voice. 'Look for the glowing coals.'

For a moment it made no sense. Then, all at once, it was clearly visible. Right at the centre of their attention, in the mangled debris, separated from each other by only a few inches, were two small dots of brilliant red: the eyes of the monarch of the mangrove creek. The animal appeared transfixed, blinded by the concentrated beam of powerful light fixated on it. Seema and Harish also watched, transfixed, as Uncle rowed onward in complete silence. The only sound now was of the swishing oar.

'Small croc. Young one, about three feet long,' David said softly, as if he could read the questions in the ignorant minds. 'The distance between the glowing coals . . .'

The animal lay completely still even as the boat moved closer, its eyes and snout just visible above the surface of the water. David and

Uncle were obviously not scared; they had done this a number of times before. For Harish who was sitting at the tip of the inflatable, however, this was completely new. He instinctively slid back a little, nervous.

'Are we not getting too close?' The tremble in his voice was evident, the question barely audible. 'Aren't we?' Seema asked too.

'Don't worry,' David assured them, 'there is no danger at all.'

Just then the tip of their boat, now not more than ten feet from their quarry and still gliding, gently hit the mangled branches within which the crocodile's eyes glowed like burning embers. This disturbed the creature, and as four pairs of human eyes watched, one pair of crocodile eyes dipped into safety under a gently rippling sheath of dark water.

David had been poised like the spring wound up in a watch. Now, as he freed himself from his crouch, the strain eased visibly. Seema and Harish too felt the knot of fear and excitement loosening in their stomach.

They paused for a few moments in silence as they recollected and recomposed themselves. The tension eased and David signalled to Uncle again. The engine came on with a gentle whirr, and as Uncle turned the accelator, the inflatable zoomed deeper into the creek. About ten minutes passed in silence, then David moved his torch in a clockwise circle. It was time to turn back. No pair of glowing coals was seen again.

'When I first surveyed this creek seven years ago,' David finally spoke, 'it was full of crocs. It was amazing how many you could see in a single night. It used to be great fun but not anymore. This creek has now been trashed. Completely trashed. Too many people, too much encroachment. Only the first wall of the mangroves now stands. Everything beyond has been converted to paddy fields and plantations. Little left for the crocodiles,' he shook his head vigorously.

'But it's not like this in the creeks of the Jarawa Reserve,' he continued, 'as you will get to see in the next few days.'

BOOK ONE

1

HARISH COMES TO THE ISLANDS

Harish Kumar had been on the Andaman Islands for only a few months now. This was not a long time, but Harish could already sense that life was going to be very different here on from what it had been so far.

He was always seen as one full of potential and promise, but he had never been an achiever – remaining always on the threshold of success, never able to cross over. Initially this hadn't bothered Harish. But in recent years, it had started to. Self-doubt hung around him now like a millstone, pulling him down and deep. What did he have to show for his thirty-one years? What was he doing with his life?

Invariably, memory would take him back to the 'gang of four' in school, in his hometown of Hyderabad. He was the cleverest, the 'zyada hooshar', of them. He consistently scored more marks than his friends, but he also never topped. He was always second or third in class, always within striking range. The two who always pipped him to the top were either of two girls: Namrata or Ankita. For the boys in his class and the 'gang of four' in particular, this was an affront to their schoolboy traditions. Girls couldn't be allowed to keep beating them. Things had to be set right – and Harish was their best bet. They'd keep egging him on to get just those many more marks in the next exam to save their izzat. 'You bugger,' his friends would shout at him every time as exams approached, 'Kuchh kar! Do something!'

'Pucca,' he would assure them every time. 'This time, pucca.' He knew and they knew, it was never going to be.

Even back then, there were too many distractions for Harish to focus single-mindedly on studies and exams. He was an avid reader of mystery books, having completed the usual trajectory of boys his age: starting with Enid Blyton's Famous Five, moving on to Hardy Boys, and progressing a little later to Sherlock Holmes. But the book that was by far his favourite was one none of his classmates or neighbours had even heard of. A friend of his father's, who knew of Harish's interest in books and passion for mystery, had sent him the book from Bombay. Unsure at first if a mystery in translation from the vernacular would prove worthy, Harish was soon captivated – reading the book from cover to cover over the weekend and in the process missing out on most of his homework. *The Elephanta Caves Mystery* was the English translation of Bapu Deshpande's very popular Marathi book for children.

Harish had particularly liked the lead character, Shyam, a brilliant young man in his late teens with a personality hued with many shades of grey. He had started off guiding tourists around the ancient caves of Elephanta Island and then graduated, in collaboration with fellow guides, to petty thieving from the very tourists they guided. In the process, he stumbled upon a network of smugglers that was using the island and the tourists as a conduit to move drugs and other contraband to the city of Bombay. His conscience was pricked and he masterminded an operation, with his fellow guides, that busted the network and had the kingpin arrested.

The Elephanta Caves Mystery had been a bestseller in Marathi, but was barely noticed outside Maharashtra, in spite of the English translation. Harish didn't tell anyone what he was doing that weekend; the last thing he wanted was to be caught reading a downmarket mystery book by some local author.

No matter what they were doing, the gang of four had always hit it off. These were friendships they sustained into their teens and now their thirties, when at least two of them had begun growing paunches that were signs, pretty much, of worldly success. Shamik had always scored the lowest marks amongst the four at school, but had gone on to become a cost accountant and then a chartered accountant with top all-India rankings. He was now one of the most respected financial analysts in the country. With offices in Chennai, Bangalore, Pune and Hyderabad, his company had an annual turnover of nearly fifty crore rupees. He was what they called well settled: wealthy and married, with a darling of a two-year-old brat and a second child on the way.

Then there was Prasad, whose poems Harish had never thought to be any good. He had, despite this, encouraged Prasad to write, and had always read and commented on his writings. He was, perhaps, the only person to have witnessed the outcome of Prasad's early forays into poetry. Prasad was now the editor of one of India's fastest growing news magazines, *InFocus*. He had also published two collections of poetry, the first of which had been dedicated, in a magnanimous gesture on the part of the poet, 'to a school friend, who was always interested'.

The third member of the gang was Ashok, who had made it big in the United States. After struggling through his graduation in Mechanical Engineering – he had taken six years to complete the four-year course – he'd managed to be at the right place at the right time. The software boom was happening and he had managed to do what he called 'one of those software courses in one of those software training institutes'. Then he landed an unexpected job with Magnum Computers Limited, one of India's first computer giants, doing the first six months at their headquarters in Chennai before moving to Philadelphia. Here he settled in beautifully: he had acquired an American twang in one month and a Hispanic ladylove in another. When he announced he was getting married to this lady, three years older than him, his family had had multiple convulsions. But, to everyone's surprise and relief, things had turned out well. Ashok was on his way to becoming a father and getting a green card at about the same time. Emails from him, and these were frequent, always brought a smile to Harish's face. 'Sala gora,' he would exclaim to himself. Harish was never envious of the success his friends had achieved, being genuinely happy for them. Neither did he ever wish to be in their shoes. 'That's their life,' he'd tell himself, 'and I have to make mine.' But, of late, the difference between doing what one wanted and achieving wordly success started to weigh on his mind.

He couldn't even be sure that he had done his best. He'd completed his BA in Literature and had then done odd jobs. For the first few months he worked as an instructor at Hobby English Classes, teaching the language to beginners such as rural migrants and middle-class, middle-aged women. Then he worked as a freelance translator for an online news portal, and for a couple of months after that as a sales boy in a bookstore in Banjara Hills. Finally, he had settled into a decent job as a manager at a printing press – only to fall desperately in love, a few months in, with the graphic designer of one of their regular clients, a prominent publisher of coffee-table books. Harish had proposed to Usha in a few weeks and it had taken her a few more to agree. She had wanted some more time before getting married, but everything worked out seamlessly and they were swiftly united. The following few months looked to the outside world like nothing but complete marital bliss. That bliss had lasted about a year.

With time, Usha began to get increasingly irritated by Harish's easy-going, even lackadaisical, approach to life. She wanted more for him and for herself. She wanted him to move up the career ladder, she wanted him to socialize more, she wanted him to accompany her to the parties she loved. Harish couldn't bring himself to do any of that; he was happy with what he had. Usha's irritation turned to constant nagging, then haranguing. Fed up, Harish began to retaliate by objecting to Usha's lifestyle. Till then he had had no problem with it at all; now she was partying too much, drinking too hard, spending too much time with other men. A showdown was inevitable and the undoing was so rapid that everyone was caught by surprise. A little less than three years after they had been wedded, the world had it that it was all over.

Harish was shattered. 'Would I have been different if mom were still with us?' he had asked his father in one of his bleakest moments – the day after he had told him that Usha had finally walked out, and that his marriage was, at last, over. He had not meant it, but he knew that instant that something very important had snapped inside his father. It had been the wrong question to ask. He was a man who had brought up his only child alone, with every affection and care, trying hard to protect him from the unpleasant legacy of his own marriage; Harish's mother had herself walked out of their marriage when Harish was only six years old. A couple of years later, she had died, in an unfortunate road accident. Father had lived with son like he would with a friend, and the friend was now holding him responsible for what had gone wrong. 'Would I have been different if mom were still with us?' Harish had asked him.

Even in that state, Harish knew how unfair this was: Usha was the one decision his father had vehemently opposed. They had fought bitterly about her, even abusively. 'Trust me Harish,' his father had argued in vain, 'this is the wrong decision. She inhabits a very different world and you will not be able to cope. I don't want you to go through the same thing that I did.'

Harish was too blindly in love to listen, and his father had no choice but to give in and consent to the match. However, as a father-in-law, he was gracious and accommodating, trying to be as much a friend to Usha as he had been to his own son. But that nasty feeling that something was wrong never went away.

Now a failure in love as well, Harish was not quite sure how to cope. He wanted to take a break for a while, be by himself, recoup. But how would he earn a living while doing this?

The opportunity came a few months later when his old friend Prasad came to town for a business meeting. He agreed to stay on for an extra day so that the two of them could meet and spend some time together. They sat by the Hussain Sagar under the distant gaze of the standing Buddha, discussing the potential course afforded by Harish's future options.

'It was unfair, Harish,' Prasad sympathized with his friend, 'but you have to move on. What's over is over. It is likely,' he suggested, 'that I might be going to Port Blair soon. If you like, you can come along with me. In any case, I need someone to help me with the stories I intend to explore for *InFocus* when I am there. You can come along on a short-term contract for the magazine and then perhaps even stay on for a few months. We'll see about that when we get there.'

Harish was unsure of himself and what he wanted to do. He was also doubtful that he would manage all by himself in a new place so far away. He'd said no, but coaxed on by his friend, he had finally agreed to go along.

His father too had nudged him along, aware that a change of place would help. 'Don't think you are running away,' he had offered as a final piece of parting advice. 'You can run away from people and from places, but never run from yourself. Going away was something I could not do. I had you, both as a responsibility and a reason to carry on. Life has been worthwhile because of you. Yours is a more difficult struggle, because you have to find yourself within. I hope you will forgive me.'

'What's that, Dad?' Harish had hugged his father hard, trying to disguise his emotions and his regret. 'I'll be okay. Will see you soon.'

This was how Harish had landed in the Andaman Islands in November 2003 and set off, almost immediately, though unwittingly, on another tumultuous journey. Their final destination had been the Institute for Island Ecology (IIE), located about 20 kms outside Port Blair. The director of the Institute, Dr David Baskaran, was a very good friend of an uncle of Prasad's. Over time, Prasad had gotten to know him well and their friendship had grown. Prasad had been to the Institute on a couple of occasions in the past already, first on a reporting assignment and then on a small holiday with his wife and son.

This time, there was a buzz in the news circles about certain new developments related to the 'dangerous' Jarawa people of the Andaman Islands, and the possibility of a couple of breaking stories was something that excited the journalist in Prasad considerably.

The Institute was like nothing Harish had ever seen before, or even expected, certainly not in such a remote place as this. Spread over more than two acres of land, it occupied a little rocky outcrop located a small distance from the edge of the ocean. Towards the southern side of the campus was a small patch of mangroves. Beyond that and towards the right, the land climbed up a gentle slope to a little plateau that had a beautiful view of the small bay.

At the entrance of the campus was one of the most beautiful wooden buildings Harish had ever set eyes upon. It was a recent construction – he couldn't believe that such a simple and elegant wooden structure could still be crafted. The building was a two-storied wooden structure built on concrete stilts. The ground floor contained a huge hall that was the venue for meetings and seminars. The floor on top had computers and workspaces for the researchers, as well as a small library, a very specialized one that was considered one of the best for books on and about the islands.

Located at some distance to the right of this building was a row of five small bamboo huts, also built on concrete stilts. These were the living spaces for visitors and the scientists who worked here; one of these would soon become home for Harish.

Between the kitchen and the main building was the 'quadrangle', a largish square paved with rough stone, with a thatched roof, a small table and a few chairs. This was where researchers and visitors gathered every night, after dinner, to chat late into the night. The islands were the thread that bound these discussions together, their diversity and range decided by the nature of those who assembled. A wide variety of people had passed through this place: anthropologists and historians; the middle-level Port Blair bureaucrat who came here regularly, lured by the company and the evening drinks; and occasionally, mainland journalists like Prasad who landed up as much for the company as for possible story ideas to justify their trip to the islands.

The rest would largely be clubbed under the category of field biologists – the dominant crowd here. There was the mercurial Dr Ravi Sankaran, one of the country's finest ornithologists, who had made an international name studying the little-known birds of these islands. His was the first comprehensive study of the endemic Nicobari megapode, a bird that scrapes together a mound of earth and decaying matter for a nest in the low-lying coastal forests in the Nicobar Islands, and then the edible nest swiftlet that builds its nest in dark, inaccessible caves with nothing but its own saliva.

Whenever Sankaran was at the Institute, conversations would inevitably turn to birds, like they would to snakes when Gokul Mehta was around. Mehta was a man obsessed with snakes; the deadlier and more venomous it was, the greater the challenge and thrill. Unlike Sankaran for whom the study of birds was as much passion as profession, snakes were a hobby for Mehta. The only hint of what his actual profession was, lay in the thick gold chain that hung around his neck and an equally thick gold bracelet that circled his wrist. Mehta belonged to a rich goldsmith family and had inherited one of the biggest jewellery chains in Mumbai's famed Zaveri Bazaar. He sold gold and gold ornaments for eleven months a year. In July, when the monsoons slammed his part of the world, he would pack his bags and embark on his annual, month-long pilgrimage to these islands – to the also rain-soaked, but far more interesting, slushy, leech- and mosquito-filled forests through which he trekked to bag, pickle and study snakes. His interest in the discussions in the quadrangle was aroused only when snakes, or at the very least, reptiles and amphibians were discussed. Nothing else ever seemed to excite him. If he stayed on, it was only by virtue of his innate politeness.

There were women too, though only occasionally. There was one who had studied bats and owls, another, tourism in the islands and a third, a young American marine biologist, who had almost drowned while studying coral reefs in the Mahatma Gandhi Marine National Park in Wandoor. The latest among the visitors was Seema Chandran, a Port Blair girl who had recently returned to the islands for her Ph.D.

Finally, there was also the staff.

The abiding presence here was that of Uncle Pame, the old Karen man from Webi, near Mayabundar on Middle Andaman Island. The Karen were a small community of people that had been first brought to the islands from Burma more than eight decades ago, and Webi was the first settlement that they had created on arrival. A majority of this community of a few thousand, Uncle Pame's large extended family included, continued to live in Webi. Unlike most of his generation, however, Uncle had moved out to explore the larger world. He was the first man David had recruited when the Institute came into being. An islander in the truest sense of the word, Uncle was in many ways the local guide and expert, knowledgeable about both the oceans and the forests in an unparalleled manner. A calm, quiet man with a dreamy look, he would often be found sitting in the quadrangle alongside the researchers. His face was like a sheet of paper, except for a broad protrusion that passed for a nose. The two cheekbones stood out sharply, framing two narrow slits of dark eyes that were almost lost in that big round face.

Combined with a constant look of languor, the eyes gave him a mysterious, unfathomable appearance. It was impossible to look at Uncle's face and say what was on his mind. Unobtrusive and apparently unconcerned with what was going on about him, Uncle would sit at the table in the quadrangle with his peg of whisky or rum or whatever the drink of the evening was and listen intently, staring aimlessly into the space in front of him. For any person who was new to the setting, it would appear as though Uncle saw, heard or registered nothing; that he was floating on his drink in a world entirely his own. But those who had been around longer, even for a week, knew that was not true. Uncle spoke rarely, but his comments – suffused as they were with wit, astuteness and wisdom – said more than the most voluble among their company.

Harish took an instant liking to this old Karen man.

2

THE LOCAL BORNS

Earlier that year, just a little before her twenty-seventh birthday, Seema Chandran finally made her first trip back to the islands. After spending four years at Delhi University, where she had completed her Masters in Anthropology, she had now registered there for her Ph.D. on 'The Socio-economic Evolution of the Andaman's Local Borns'.

'Local Borns in the Andamans? What kind of people are these?' the head of the Department of Anthropology and her prospective guide had asked her when she first proposed the theme. 'If you want to work in the Andamans,' he had argued, 'why don't you look at those incredibly enigmatic set of people there – the Onge, the Great Andamanese, or even the Jarawa? Researchers and students from all over the world would give anything just to access the islands and these groups and for you, Seema, they are in your backyard.' She had considered these possibilities earlier, and considered them again now, but could not convince herself of the need to change the subject of her research.

Everyone who saw her proposal – other professors, colleagues and friends – found the topic intriguing, and Seema was happy to provide an explanation: 'I want to study my own community,' she would say with pride, 'I am an Andaman Local Born.'

The Andaman Local Borns were, indeed, a unique people, the

owners of an unlikely identity born from a combination of the strange circumstances of their origin and the compulsions of their evolution. Seema's genealogy was a good example, and a typical one. It began with her great great grandparents, Syed Iqbal and Lalita.

Syed Iqbal had been lodged in Port Blair's famously infamous Cellular Jail around 1925 – not, as many believed, for his part in India's freedom struggle, but for the murder of a policeman in his village near Lahore. With one stroke of his machete, he had chopped off the head of the man who had raped his younger sister, who, traumatized, had committed suicide by slitting her wrist. During his trial, Syed had willfully admitted to his crime, breaking down twice while talking about his sister. This was a revenge killing, complicated by the fact that his victim was a policeman, a government servant. It would have to be the death penalty. Considering, however, the nature of the assault on his sister and his own willful admission, Syed was allowed his life. He would be sent across the seas to the Andaman Islands, to Kalapani.

Saddened as he was by the turn of his fate, memories of his sister and his affection for Dhanno, the dhobi's daughter who lived in the adjoining quarter in his village, Syed was a trouble-free convict. He was deeply and secretly in love with Dhanno; it was Syed's hope that once he finished his term in prison, he would return to his village and resume life from where he had been forced to leave off. This was never to be.

About three years into his term, he received a letter from his ageing father that completely broke his heart. His mother had died of a strange illness, and Dhanno was getting married. The letter had reached him more than three months after it had been written; ironically, just a day before the wedding. Syed wondered why, out of so many things in the world, his father had chosen to write to him about Dhanno's wedding. It had, perhaps, not been such a well-kept secret after all. Syed had, if he was to be honest to himself, known all along that he was hoping for the impossible. For a Muslim, and one convicted of a crime such as his, he knew he had little chance of actually marrying Dhanno. The flame of hope, however, had continued to flicker in his heart. Not anymore. The day he read his father's letter was also the day he decided that he would never go back to the land where he was born; he was clear that his fate willed him to live here. Meanwhile, his good behaviour in prison resulted in the commuting of his sentence. His release was a little less than six months away, and he was coming to terms with his changed circumstances when he began to notice Lalita.

Young, vivacious, with lovely eyes and thick, long hair, Lalita had not been in the jail for too long. Though much smaller in terms of numbers, the Cellular Jail had its fair share of female convicts, most of whom had, in fact, been involved in some form of anti-empire political activity.

The attraction was mutual. Syed was not conventionally handsome, but it was his brooding, lost look that had drawn her to him. Each looked forward to the hour every evening when the male and female prisoners with relatively clear track records were allowed some space and free time, with the possibility of mingling.

Nudged by his fellow inmates, Syed made the first tentative move. 'My name is Syed Iqbal,' he began, in a tone that was hesitant and unsure, 'You have very beautiful hair.'

Lalita laughed a full-throated, lively laugh. 'My name is Lalita,' she had said, 'and I like you too, even though you don't have very good hair.'

Syed laughed in nervous embarrassment.

'I hear you are here for the murder of a policeman,' she continued in a tone that had now become stern.

'Yes, you're right,' he was caught off guard, 'but . . . but . . .'

'That's why I am here too . . .' she guffawed, and laughed another full-throated laugh, adding, 'We'll make a good pair. What do you think?'

Ignoring the stunned look on his face, she went on to explain the details of the incident that had brought her here. Lalita had been part of a small group of young men and women who had stormed a local police station near Bhopal in the middle of the night and set it ablaze. The building had been gutted and three of the men on duty had suffered serious burns. One succumbed subsequently. The two in the group who were identified as leaders had been sentenced to death by hanging. The rest, including Lalita, were sent to Kalapani to cool their heels. 'And,' she concluded, 'what you did to that policeman was absolutely correct. I would have also slit his throat if I were you.'

Their attraction quickly moved to a deeper involvement and they were regularly allowed more free time and privacy by the prison staff than was officially permitted. It was a relationship that was acknowledged and accepted by all around, and there was a general mood of celebration when it was announced, five months later, that Lalita was pregnant with Syed's child. In this far away, distant land, many such men and women found companionship, love and passion, oblivious to considerations of age, class, caste or religion. The marriage of Lalita and Syed Iqbal was solemnized inside the prison itself and two months later, man, wife and unborn child were released and given an acre of land to start life anew. This child was Seema's great grandfather, and there were about 3,000 others like him who had been born in similar circumstances; born locally – 'the local borns'.

There were many like Syed and Lalita, whose fate forced them to break all that bound them to their past and to start as a new set of people. The Muslim man, who could have only dreamt of taking a Hindu wife in Lahore, was encouraged wholeheartedly by the people now around him to marry Lalita. Back home in the towns and villages they had come from, their families would have howled like rabid dogs for Syed's blood. They would perhaps do just the same if Lalita and Syed returned now. But this was some place else.

This was the Andamans in the 1920s, an excitingly important decade where new flavours from elsewhere were being added to the stew all the time – the Moplahs from the Malabar who came to the islands after their rebellion against the British; the wandering Bhantus from the fertile Gangetic plains, forced to flee as they were being implicated and regularly persecuted for being thugs and dacoits; and even a sizeable number of families from Buddhist Burma.

Officers of the Empire, as always, were busy with a host of their own activities: missions to remote parts of these islands, attempts to establish contact with the dangerous natives of the dense forests and elaborate expeditions for botanical and zoological studies. One official had even helped organize the local borns into the Local Borns' Association.

At the same time, the Great Indian Railway project on the mainland and demands of the British Navy meant that timber extraction in the rich forests on the islands grew rapidly and a need arose to induct new labour and expertise into the Forest Department. The rulers looked in both directions to get their work-force from – the thickly forested Chhota Nagpur Plateau on mainland India in the west and the famous teak forests of Burma in the east. The Church was forever willing to oblige the empire, and it soon became the recruiting ground for those to be brought to the islands with promises of plenty and prosperity. The Mundas, Oraons and Santhals were recruited through the Church in Ranchi, and came, ingenuously, to be called the 'Ranchis' in the islands. The Karens, Christians from the Baptist Mission, too were brought in from Bassein in Burma under the supervision of the Reverend Father Lugyi and the leadership, in fact, of Uncle Pame's father.

Not surprisingly, when the decade of the twenties slid into the next one, nearly thirty different languages were being spoken by the 20,000-odd people inhabiting the Andamans – Urdu, Hindi, Bengali, Tamil, Andamanese, Telugu, Malayalam, Burmese, even Pashto. The islands had truly become a cultural melting point.

Over time, customs and rituals fused. Some were lost completely, while others were created anew, hybridizing rapidly with Darwinian enthusiasm, creating a new community that kept growing newer as the decades marched on.

The Moplas, the Bhantus, the Bengalis, the Karens, the Local Borns had all, individually or together, been put away and forgotten as irrelevant deposits of the colonial project – a forgetfulness that Seema had an intuitive discomfort with. These identities had not only charted the trajectories of the islands, they had shaped the very contours of the land – rich stories and enduring legacies. Yet, those pasts were considered barely significant?

The relatively classless and secular community of the Local Borns had grown in number and continued to maintain its original character right till Seema's time. Nearly 40,000 strong now, they formed an important part of the island's population and claimed the islands to be both their land of birth and action – janam and karam. The islands, for them, were home.

Many of Seema's generation were now moving to the mainland. They were very aware of their origins, of what might have been called the illegitimate conception of her own great grandfather. But this did not matter. There was no shame in their history. Instead, there was pride that they had shaped the islands, that they were the pioneers. Many, however, did not know what to do on the islands, finding it too small and constrained, and having moved out, were determined to stay away.

Like others of her generation, Seema too wanted to explore the world and had stepped out. Unlike most of them, however, she was equally interested in their own history, her history – the stories of the people and the place she belonged to. Hers became a reverse focus, a re-inverted lens. For her it didn't seem right that the Andamans merited only a few paragraphs in an Indian history and merely footnotes in the British one. There was more, much more to these islands and the islanders.

This interest also forced her to look beyond the local borns. 'If we are the local borns,' she wondered, 'should not the Jarawas, the Onge, the Great Andamanese, be considered the "first borns"?' While the vintage of her own people did not extend beyond a century, that of the first borns hailed from so far back in the past that it had not even been fully acknowledged or identified yet.

Recent genetic work – the genotype, haplotype kind of thing – had indicated that these people had been here for anywhere between 20,000 and 60,000 years. Seema had been both excited and troubled when this research first came to her notice at the university. She had felt excitement about the limitless possibilities; one of the first genetic studies had been carried out on samples of Great Andamanese hair stored in a museum collection in far away Europe, ancient DNA it was called. The findings were concrete evidence that their inhabitation of these islands existed much deeper into the past than believed.

What bothered her, however, was an issue of ethics: biological samples were now being taken from these people without their knowledge of the larger implications. It was a dilemma Seema couldn't resolve; she decided to let it be.

There had been earlier influences too. An avid reader, Seema was a frequent visitor during her school days, to that unrecognized gem of her city – the State Library in Port Blair. She had discovered this treasure trove with the help of the assistant librarian, the genial Mrs Fatima Bose, a rotund, quietly efficient old lady who agonized immensely about how little the citizens of Port Blair cared for books. She would complain about this to anyone who was interested in listening to her, and often this would be Seema. Initially, it would irritate Seema, but she soon came to like Mrs Bose, and their common love for books slowly strengthened their bond.

Mrs Bose's biggest complaint was against her own boss, the chief librarian, who rarely visited the library. He was a politically well-connected man who believed he had better things to do than supervise a library no one visited.

'He knows as much about books,' Mrs Bose once confided to Seema, 'as a buffalo knows about stars.' She placed her hand on her mouth to muffle her loud guffawing, 'Bu ... ffa ... lo ...' she repeated slowly and deliberately, and Seema exploded into uncontrollable giggles. 'But don't tell anyone I said this,' she said in a tone full of conspiracy as they quickly walked out, Seema laughing. Mrs Bose became Fatima for Seema that evening, and a deep friendship was formed.

If truth be told, Mrs Bose was actually happy that her boss did not come visiting and also that he allowed her full control over the library. It allowed her the freedom to be and to work the way she wanted. A young, keen reader was a rarity in her space, however, and she treated Seema with great care and affection. Seema spent many hours browsing through the books in the Andaman and Nicobar section of the library. On occasion, Mrs Bose would even allow her, against the rules, to take books home if she wanted to make notes.

One such book was the century-old *Researches on Ptolemy's Geography of Eastern Asia (Further India and Indo-Malay Archipelago)* – more than 2,000 pages of finely printed words authored by Colonel G.E. Gerini and published jointly by the Royal Asiatic Society and Royal Geographical Society.

Mrs Bose had told her a bit about Ptolemy – of how this man had mapped the entire world nearly 2,000 years ago, the challenges he had faced, of his travels, his passion and the great book that he had put together. Seema had listened, transfixed, and her concluding analysis was succinct and to the point. 'This Ptolemy must have been crazy,' she said affectionately, like she was referring to some favourite granduncle, 'and this Gerini, I am sure, was crazier. How can people think of doing such things, Fatima?'

Roughly fifty pages had been devoted in Gerini's book to the

Andaman and Nicobar Islands, and she had promptly photocopied that section for her own personal collection. She was amazed by Gerini's argument that Bazakata in Ptolemy's maps was, in fact, the Andaman Islands and the naked people here that Ptolemy referred to as the Aginnatai, were in fact the Jarawa, the Onge and the Great Andamanese – the Negrito people. Ptolemy's Khaline, Gerini noted, was probably present day Car Nicobar, and Agathodiamonos, the island that Ptolemy had placed on the equator, the island of Great Nicobar.

Gerini had drawn intricate connections between Chinese, Siamese, Tamil and Sanskrit words, even to Pali, to draw his conclusions. He had referred to the Jataka tales, studied the Burmese script, looked at Chinese historical literature, examined the journals of more recent British travellers and a huge deal more to account for what he said. Gerini's interpretations and conclusions fascinated Seema. She was in awe of his scholarship.

Another important influence was Seema's distant uncle – Butterfly Uncle, who occasionally visited the islands from Bangalore, to study rainforest butterflies. He had grown very fond of Seema and spotted, early on, her interest in and potential for scholarship on the islands. They corresponded regularly, and whenever he came across books, articles or writings about the islands, he would promptly mail them to her.

By the time she completed high school, Seema had a rare collection of books on the islands that included many she understood only partially, and a few she did not understand at all, among them, *Above the Forest, A Study of Andamanese Ethnoanemology, Cosmology and Power of Ritual* by Vishvajit Pandya. It was a prized possession, an autographed copy, gifted by the author himself, when he visited her home with Butterfly Uncle.

'This book is about Vishvajit's stay with the Onge of Little Andaman Island, about their lives and their beliefs,' Butterfly Uncle explained as Seema beamed at her new gift. Though an islander herself, she had never been to Little Andaman, which was only a six-hour ship ride, south of Port Blair. Neither, as far as she knew, had anyone else from her immediate family. And yet, here was this man, coming from so far away to study the people of the forests there.

'So, Uncle,' she had asked Dr Pandya, 'they are not junglees then?'

'No,' he had emphasized. 'They are junglees. It depends on what we mean. Those living in the forests, in the jungles, are junglees – like those living in villages are villagers, or those living in Delhi are Delhiwallahs or those living in Australia are Australians. But by junglees, if we mean savages, uncivilized people, that they are not.' He had paused. 'Certainly not.'

It had also worried her immensely that the entire population of the Onge people was only about a hundred. 'You're joking, Uncle,' she said when Pandya had told her this. 'That's half the population that lives in this colony. There are more dogs in Port Blair than that,' she had exclaimed, and felt immensely and immediately embarrassed at her inadvertent comparison.

Pandya had explained a little to her about the Onges, how their population had fallen, how, from being masters of the Little Andaman Island and the forests there, they had been reduced to second-class citizens. 'It's very sad, actually,' he had concluded in a gloomy tone. 'Maybe you will want to study more about them when you grow up.'

Viswajit Pandya was just the kind of 'undesirable influence' Seema's mother would curse later in life, when her daughter started to make the kind of choices she made. First, wanting to study for so long; then that she wanted to do it far away in the mainland; further that it was neither medicine, commerce, nor management, not even engineering that she was interested in, but some god-forsaken subject like anthropology. 'What subject is this? Study local borns for what?' she had asked exasperatedly. 'We are all here. And these Onges and Jarawas? You've lost your mind! I knew it the first time I had seen that Pandya – all these silly ideas – I'm sure you got them all from him!' But it was clear to her that Seema could not be stopped.

Fortunately for the girl, her father supported her completely, respecting the urge of scholarship even if he didn't entirely understand it himself.

Having reconciled themselves to their daughter's choices, Seema's parents were now looking forward to having her back in the islands with them after a long while.

3

SEEMA'S RETURN

Seema's research upon her return home had begun with an unexpectedly exciting discovery. This was the story of the Aniket settlement in Port Blair. It was here that Seema had been born and where she had grown up – so integral a part of her life that Seema had never stopped to think about it. Aniket, however, had not existed forever. The story of how it had come to be was special and a rather beautiful one. For Seema it was, in some ways, taking off from where she had gotten with Gerini's Researches on Ptolemy's Geography of Eastern Asia. There was one big difference, however. Gerini's stories were available in black-and-white: indelible, printed words that you could see and show others. The story that Ahmed Mia told Seema too was made up of words, but these had floated away in the wind the moment he had uttered them, imprinted only in the memories of those who heard it.

The one acre of land that Syed Iqbal and Lalita had been given to restart their lives could best be described as being nowhere – some place that didn't yet exist, had no context, location, or identity. It was somewhere out there, a few kilometers from the jail, amidst the mighty rainforest. In those initial years, other couples too had been given similar plots of land. The situation soon became unmanageable, which, in turn, brought the deeply religious and god-fearing Lt. Albert William into the picture.

A junior officer of the penal administration, Albert was given the responsibility of organizing and planning two settlements for the convicts and the 'nowhere land' that had been allotted to them. William was a friendly officer and, unlike many of his colleagues in the islands, came to be loved by the local population. He, the convicts from the jail who were employed here as labour and others, like Syed Iqbal and Lalita who were now free, worked day and night to clear the mighty forests, construct houses, lay out the roads and create basic infrastructure.

As the work on these settlements gained momentum, as 'nowhere' was slowly transformed to 'somewhere' – a tangible place with character and an identity – William suffered a great personal tragedy. An undiagnosed fever engulfed his two daughters, Annie and Kate, twins, a little less than three years old. Within a few days the girls had succumbed and were buried in the cemetery on Ross Island, located just across the channel of sea from Port Blair. There was nothing they could have done, and yet, the couple could not forgive themselves.

William and his wife, Jane, had the option of returning to the mainland or even to England. To leave their first borns behind in this manner, however, would have been for them a greater sin than letting them die. They chose to stay on, absorbing themselves in the work at hand, working shoulder to shoulder with the others here, toiling tirelessly with their bare hands, seeking forgiveness and redemption.

The new islanders soon had an opportunity to repay the debt and express their gratitude; when the first twenty families were to formally occupy their homes, they decided to name their settlement in the memory of the departed little souls; one was to be Annie, the other Kate. The Williams were overwhelmed, crying with joy, gratitude and sorrow. This, perhaps, was the forgiveness that they had been seeking. Strange, indeed, were the ways of the lord.

'We are extremely grateful for this honour,' Albert William explained, 'but we cannot accept this. It would not be right. We do not wish to impose ourselves on so many new lives and futures.'

For those beginning these new lives, this was not an imposition. It was a choice they had willingly made. It was Lalita who spoke on behalf of all who had gathered, 'Mr and Mrs Williams, you are making a mistake. We are not asking for your consent. We are merely informing you. We have made the decision and you are not at liberty to change it. Our settlements will be known as Annie and Kate.' She spoke with firmness, yet her words were gentle, filled with fond affection. And so it was decided.

Over time, the settlements grew substantially, moving towards the crest of the ridge that separated them. The twenty families each grew in due course to forty, and then quickly to a hundred. Outsiders too came and settled here, drawn by the twin lures of perennial fresh water and good cultivable land. In another twenty years, the ridge was also completely occupied and Annie could no longer be differentiated from Kate. The Williams and almost all of their generation passed away, but a small puja continued to be performed on the death anniversary of the two girls.

With time, the physical boundaries between Annie and Kate blurred even more; now these were not two settlements, but one single place people started referring to as Annie-aur-Kate. In due course the conjunction also perished. Annie and Kate were themselves forgotten, and there were no more ceremonies on their death anniversary. Smoothly, like the natural confluence of streams that turn into a larger flow, their destinies, identities and existence merged, just as they had with the very earth of the islands. The two settlements of Annie and Kate became one, the vernacular Aniket – the name for the wanderer, the one without a home.

Seema could hardly believe the story, but it had to be true because it came from the grand old Ahmed Mia. He was the last remaining amongst those in Aniket who had actually seen the Williams. He had only been a few years old then, but his memory of the couple was clear and vivid.

Seema had known Ahmed Mia since she was a child and he had always been fond of her. It had never crossed her mind till now that he might have things to say that she might want to know.

'How many more such stories are there in Port Blair? What have you been doing all these years, Ahmed Mia? Why don't you do something about these stories?' she asked exasperated, 'Do you want to take all these to your grave with you?'

'Grave?' he smiled a sad toothless smile. 'My time will come too.'

'Ahhh! That's not what I meant Ahmed Mia.'

'Can anything or anyone escape that?' he went on. 'A man takes nothing but himself to the grave. But,' he said turning to Seema, an earnest and even confused look on his face, 'tell me beti, who is interested in the islands, in what happened here? In people like me? And,' he paused for a moment, 'and, do you know how many people have asked me about this in the last forty years?' He paused again, before answering his own question. 'One.' His finger was pointed at her, 'You! Where were you all these years?'

'I am too old now. If I had known you were interested, I would have put them down. But tell me, really, is anyone interested?'

'But, Ahmed Mia,' Seema tried answering, 'someone's interest does not decide the significance of these things. It may not matter to others, but does it not matter to us? To you? Should it not? Is this not like a line in stone, as real as the bones of Annie and Kate? Nobody sees it, but that doesn't mean it doesn't exist. Nothing can erase it – rain or wind or shine.'

Ahmed Mia burst out laughing, 'Ay,' he got up with a sense of mock urgency, 'I need to go and see your father. Have to ask him what he's created. You've surely got a lot of that Lalita's blood in you. You've become a philosopher my little one.'

Then, just as suddenly, he stopped laughing. 'Maybe, beti,' he said, 'it's too late. What was being done all these years?' It could have been a question to Seema, but more likely he was seeking answers from himself.

'Do something Seema,' he said, after a pause. 'Make a trip to Ross Island. You know the old cemetery there, by that crumbling church building. Check the corner near that big banyan tree. That is where Annie and Kate were buried. William saheb had put two identical gravestones there. Those might still be there – you'll know then that this story of Aniket is true. The proof exists.'

'You are proof enough, Ahmed Mia,' said Seema. 'I'll sit with you. You tell me everything that happened and I will take it all down.'

But Ahmed Mia had been right when he had said it was too late. He made a peaceful departure the very next afternoon, during his regular mid-day nap. Seema too had been right. He took all he knew with him to his grave.

Seema's homecoming was, from the beginning, a mixed bag of discovery and loss: losing Ahmed Mia forever, but just after rediscovering him, and through him, new nooks and recesses, entire hidden passages of a lavishly rich history.

Delhi had been exciting but it could never be Port Blair. Delhi was a huge sprawl, soot-laden and suffocating, growing amoeba-like into land that extended infinitely on all sides. Port Blair was still small and compact, easily negotiable, eminently manageable, fresh and airy in a way that only small seaside towns can be. It urged you to breathe deeper and harder.

Seema knew its little paths and corners better than she knew the lines on her palms. The Mountbatten Cinema with its wooden pillars and old world charm; the saw mill at Chatham where she had become addicted to the smells of freshly sawn timber; Foreshore Road from where ships could be seen entering the harbour as if in a 70 mm wide-screen movie; the marine workshops at Phoenix Bay where history could be held in your hands (her most prized find there was a 1931 lantern from a dismantled ship of German origin); the view of Ross Island from atop Cellular Jail; Japanese World War II bunkers that stood all over like forgotten sentinels; Port Blair's own Marine Drive that went on and on till it reached Corbyn's Cove at the other end.

Homecomings allow an experience of change that is denied to those who never leave. Port Blair had changed significantly in the years Seema was away. It was like a little brat of a city now, discovering simultaneously the pains and the pleasures of growing up, forcing similar discoveries on those who cared for and lived with it; particularly for those who returned. It was far more crowded and chaotic than Seema remembered. There was an increasing restlessness – more vehicles, more speed, more movement, more action, more desire and greater ambition. The nights were longer, the shops bigger, the noises louder and the roads narrower. Garbage now accumulated on street corners and on the roads; dogs had multiplied in direct proportion to the spread of the dirt and filth (Port Blair had seen more cases of dog bites in the last three years than in the preceding thirty); previously unknown entities called beggars and pickpockets had begun plying their trade in the bazaar; street urchins now openly defecated in the overflowing British-era drains and traffic jams were a regular feature in Aberdeen Bazaar. Traffic snarls in Port Blair? Yes, all this and more in just a few years.

Old wooden Mountbatten Cinema was about to go and a steel and glass structure of a shopping mall was to come up in its place. The old wooden State Secretariat had gone too; everything was being replaced by monsters of the modern age, concrete replacing timber with a rapidity that would soon send termites out of business.

It was the state of the library, however, that saddened Seema the most. Fatima had had to take early retirement due to her failing health. Her boss, the chief librarian, had become an even more important politician and had even less time for an insignificant thing like a library. A replacement hadn't been found for Fatima, and the library had quietly fallen to ruin. 'What difference one dedicated person can make,' she thought to herself, 'and what trauma it will be for Fatima to come here again.'

Seema had been banking on the State Library to guide her through the initial days of her reading and research. The other problem was the absence of almost any published material on the local borns. Hardly anything had been written about these people and what little there was, was scattered and would need to be collated. She would need to begin further back in the past than she had thought.

The more ambiguous and difficult pulse to put a finger on, however, was the sense of the present. There would be others like Ahmed Mia, but his loss was crucial and also personal. His questions about relevance and a lack of interest were bothering Seema, and she sensed a deeper significance in these concerns.

The Local Borns' Association, with a membership that ran into thousands, had been the most active organization in these islands. Now it was mainly the older generation – not more than a few hundred – that identified with it, and their number too was falling rapidly. Initial discussions with some of them had thrown up a number of unexpected issues, even a sense of disquiet. These were the people who prided themselves on making the islands what they were. They were supposed to be the pioneers, but little of that spirit was now visible to Seema. Nowhere did she see the enthusiasm and vitality the community had been known for. Their very identity seemed under question now.

'Nobody is interested,' Krishna Raj, the Association's secretary droned to Seema, his manner so matter-of-fact that she couldn't be angry even though she wanted to be. 'Perhaps,' he said, 'we are not significant anymore.'

The irony was stark. If distance and time provide an opportunity of objectivity, they also often ensure a loss of contact with reality. Seema couldn't be sure which was true in her case. She had found unacceptable the insignificance imposed on these islands and the islanders by others, but what was she to do now? Krishna Raj himself was saying they were insignificant. He was much more aggrieved inside than he appeared to be, she was sure. All she needed to do was scratch the veneer a bit and it all came tumbling out.

'History?' he asked. 'You are interested in the history? That won't go away anywhere. But do you know there is no future for us? We are a people with a history, but no future. Look at this.' He pulled out a flimsy, yellow-coloured sheet of paper from the file on his table. 'This came just last week. Samaresh Basu's been circulating this in Mayabundar and the Diglipur area.'

'Samaresh Basu?' Seema asked, staring at the Bengali on the pamphlet in front of her.

'You don't know Samaresh Basu? He is one of the most powerful politicians in the northern part of the islands. He's been here for forty years and you know what the bastard is doing?' His face was flushed with an angry excitement as he picked up the pamphlet and thrust it towards Seema, "I am sorry, lady. Please forgive my language . . . He's saying, that all encroachers on forest land should be given three acres of land each. You know who these people are?'

Seema nodded her head.

'These are people who have come to the islands during the last ten years, maybe less, and Basu is more worried about them. You know why? It's the bloody votes. He is creating a bloody vote bank. The elections are approaching, and this is the main card he is playing this time. I was born on the islands, and I never got more than a couple of acres. But Basu – and he's not alone – none of them will demand anything for us.' Krishna Raj was livid, his frail body trembling. 'That's why I say we are not significant anymore. See what the world has come to. Follow the law and be doomed. Go ahead, break the law, encroach fearlessly and be rewarded. They will have more land in five years than I have had in fifty. I was a fool all these years to have not encroached. All of us were fools. All the local borns. Me, Lobo, that Ahmed who died the other day, your father. See this,' he pulled out a small book, and turned to a page marked with a bookmark. 'These are Census figures,' he pointed his finger at the table on a page that had certainly seen much use. 'In 1951, the population of the Andaman district was only about 19,000 people, a majority of whom were local born. I am one of those counted in that Census. Today, this number has increased to more than 250,000.'

Krishna Raj paused for a while, taking in a deep breath and a sip of water. 'Arre, I'm sorry. Forgot to ask. You'll have some tea?'

'No. I'm okay.'

'No. It's not okay. Chotu, chai. Jaldi,' he called out loudly through the window by his desk. 'See,' he said a little apologetically, turning again to Seema, 'these things get me really angry. My doctor has warned me to be careful, not to get very excited. I'll pop it otherwise, he says,' he laughed, nodding his head. 'So what was I saying . . . Yes, the population, how the population here has grown. Yes . . . all these people, these 250,000 were not born here. Most of them have come from outside, from the mainland – labourers, traders, petty businessmen. Then they moved deeper to find land to encroach upon and godfathers like Basu to protect them. It's like an incoming tide that keeps rising, a tide that now refuses to turn back.' The old man's right hand went from his chest to his neck. 'Rising . . . and rising and we are all being swamped.'

He was now nodding his head vigorously, trying hard to shake away a reality that would simply not go away.

'No, we are not being swamped,' he corrected himself emphatically. 'We *have* already been swamped into insignificance and I don't know anymore what can be done.'

4

THE JARAWA

That first night at the institute, Harish had one of the most interesting dinners he could remember having in a long time. The food was basic: dal, roti, rice and one simple potato-and-onion sabzi. It was the long discussion that Prasad had with David as they ate and then stayed on chatting that had been captivating. The only other person present that evening was Uncle Pame. It was David who actually did most of the talking, being both director of the Institute and a well-informed specialist.

David was primarily a reptile man, particularly interested in crocs and monitor lizards. He also had a finger on the pulse of the islands, the many developments that went on amongst its people. This intelligence included local and small-town politics and the petty gossip that David's elaborate network of unofficial informers regularly updated him with.

His extensive surveys had convinced him that the best croc habitats in the islands now lay only in the mangroves and creeks of the Jarawa Reserve. The Jarawa Reserve was, he believed, one of the biggest anomalies in the islands and a uniquely positive one. It was a thin sliver of thickly forested land on South and Middle Andaman islands, five kilometers wide on an average and running north to south for about 200 kilometres. This was one of the last frontiers still standing; forests that hid innumerable mysteries within, forests that had remained, even in today's day and age, unexplored by the outside world, forests that were home to the Jarawa.

David did not need to go into the many subtle and complex aspects of the Jarawa: their unknown origin; of how they had come to be here in the first place; their historical relations, interactions and animosities with the Great Andamanese, the other original people of the islands; the timber extraction operations that were started in Jarawa forests in the 1970s and the Bush Police camps that were set up along the forest fringes; the settlement here of thousands of migrant families from mainland India; the construction of the Andaman Trunk Road through the heart of Jarawa territory; the settlers who had been killed by the arrows of the Jarawa; the administration's attempts to befriend them along the coast; Bhaktawar Singh's success in establishing first contact with the Jarawa. All this and much more, Prasad already knew. He had written widely about these, and David went straight to what was current.

'A paradigm shift appears to have taken place in the outlook and perception of the Jarawas,' David began. 'For the first time in recent history, they are coming out of the forests, into the settlements on the fringes, particularly in and around Kadamtala, unarmed.' He paused for a moment, to allow what he had just said to sink in. 'Unarmed in broad daylight!' he stressed emphatically. 'Can you believe that? No more of those armed, fleeting, midnight raids, when no one knew where they came from and in what direction they went; no more arrows, no more animosity. The enduring modern myth of the implacable junglee, the unfriendly inhabitant of the dark deep forests, the hostile, violent Jarawa is shattered. Shattered forever. It's astonishing.' David paused. 'Astonishing!' He had this habit of repeating words for emphasis.

'The reaction of the settlers has been hysterical. The moment the Jarawas appear, the settlements empty out. So far, only young Jarawa men have been coming to the settlements in small numbers. But the moment they enter, there is panic. People either lock themselves up in their houses, or run away. All that they find missing when they return are a few metal utensils and bananas and coconuts if any were lying around. No resistance has been offered to the Jarawas so far, so they've been coming and going as they please, on an average once in three days. You realize this, Prasad,' David's voice became sombre and serious, 'this is a historical historical moment, the implications of which will be far-reaching.' He reflected for a moment on what he had just said. 'We don't know what this could mean. I fear for the worst and for this we need to see what happened to the Great Andamanese and the Onge; how the loss of their hostility was their first step on the road to annihilation.'

'Annihilation, David? Harish interjected. 'That's a really strong word. And why do you think this change has taken place?' 'We don't yet fully know why,' David replied, 'but the most obvious one, the immediate catalyst, has been this young Jarawa boy, Tanumei.'

Prasad pulled out his diary, pen ready.

'This happened in March earlier this year, a couple of nights before Holi. Like they often did on full moon nights, a band of Jarawas came to the houses in the small settlement of Phooltala on the southern fringe of Kadamtala. Like always, they were swift and efficient, and moved on quickly after collecting some bananas from the gardens of a few houses. A very normal course of action – but with one significant twist in the tale.'

The interest of visitors had peaked and they were all keyed up to get the rest of the story. David's next words then came as quite the anti-climax. 'I don't really know the full details of what happened. We'll hear it tomorrow from the horse's mouth. There is near Kadamtala a fisherman named Pintu, a distant cousin of our cook, Montu. He knows the whole story. He was a key player, and Montu has already informed him that we are going there tomorrow. We'll take the five o'clock bus in the morning; should be there before noon, and there is always an outside chance that we might actually

encounter on the Andaman Trunk Road some of these Jarawa boys
I was just talking about.'

The journey next morning, was uneventful, except for a minor
breakdown the bus suffered. It was noon by the time David, Prasad
and Harish arrived in Kadamtala. One of the little boys hanging
around at the teashop near the bus stop offered to take them to
Pintu's house, and they went straight over after leaving their bags at
the government guesthouse they'd be staying at.

Pintu was a short, squattish man with a large forehead that
appeared even larger because he was balding. His protruding belly
reminded Harish of one of those Russian Matryoshka dolls. His
smile was pleasant, and he was clearly pleased to have important
guests visiting him from the mainland, insisting and ensuring they
ate well.

Lunch over, the story continued from where David had left off
the previous night; Prasad's diary was finally in use.

It was early in the morning after that night's raid by the Jarawas
and Pintu was headed to his boat, which was anchored in a small
creek amidst thick mangroves, a little distance from the village.

'That is when I saw this smallish dark figure in the distance,' Pintu
started, in voluble Hindi. 'At first it seemed like a wild pig and it
looked like a rather odd place for it to be in. I thought it ran away,
but then it seemed to be standing still. I thought my eyes were
deceiving me. You see, I know these forests well, but they are like a
maze. Even I get lost sometimes.' He paused for a moment. 'I think
I am moving in one direction, but I end up headed in another.
Sometimes I know I am headed in the wrong direction, but I am not
able to turn away – my mind seems to be telling me something,
some other power appears to hold me in a trance and take me in
another direction. These forests are full of mysterious things, and
unknown paths. One cannot be sure of the spirits, or even the

Jarawa. Actually, the Jarawa themselves are like the spirits of the forests; quiet and fast. Very quiet, very fast.'

He paused again, trying to find the right words. 'Like arrows. Like shadows that disappear when you turn around, like the wind that blows in the forest unseen; only the rustle of the leaves tells you it has gone by . . . Whenever I go into these mangroves and the forests on those hills,' he pointed in the distance, 'I feel I am watched. Every time. There is nobody around, but I feel I am being watched. I go there because I like the forest, and I believe they know that too.'

'They?' David interjected.

'The spirits, the Jarawas. See, I don't mean harm. I am never scared, I don't feel threatened, and so nothing has ever happened to me till today. But that morning I was unsure of things. I decided to ignore that shadowy figure and turned around to return home.' Pintu closed his eyes as if trying to recreate in his mind the image of the spirit that morning. 'Yet, when I started to walk, it was in the direction of the shadowy figure. Then I heard a human sound, the sound of sobbing. Someone seemed to be crying. It could not be a spirit, I reasoned. Spirits don't cry.' Pintu's eyes were still closed, his voice hushed.

'I continued to walk in that direction. And I couldn't believe what I saw. Sitting there, not very far from where I stood, was a Jarawa teenager – naked like a new-born baby, dark like the amavasya sky at night. He was leaning against a tree trunk, his right leg tucked under his left, which had been straightened out. He was bent over a little and clutching his left thigh with both hands. There was a pained look on his face, and his tears had created two clear lines as they flowed down his dark cheeks. He seemed to have been crying for quite a while.' Pintu opened his eyes to look at his audience. 'I was taken aback. Didn't know what to do. He had not noticed yet, but turned just then and looked at me. I saw fear erupt in his eyes, like a volcano. He tried to get up, but the moment he moved his left foot, he screamed, gripping his left thigh even more tightly. He screamed not in pain, but agony. I realized that he had hurt his foot. He was, probably, one of those boys who had come the previous night to Shyamalda's house. While making their exit, he had probably tripped in the tangle of the mangrove roots and fallen exactly where he was still sitting. But the Jarawas are not the kind to leave behind their people. Why had they left him behind like this?' Pintu's question, more to himself than his visitors, was enveloped in gentle lament.

'For a moment, I suddenly became intensely aware of the huge forest around me. Were the other Jarawas somewhere in the vicinity, hiding, watching? Were they waiting to take back their boy? What if they saw me so close to him? Would they think I meant harm and attack me? Should I leave? I stopped and looked all around me, not that I could have seen much. You can't see the Jarawa in these forests, you can only feel their presence, and that too only if you know the forests well.

'The boy was still about ten feet from where I was. I wanted to go up to him, but he was very very scared, just as our people are scared of the Jarawas; only the situation was reversed now. I had to assure him that I meant no harm, I realized. I stood still for a while, thinking. I had no idea how long he had been lying here. What would I have wanted if I was him? Water, I realized, and maybe something to eat. I pulled out the bottle of water from my bag. I opened the bottle and drank a little, trying to help him figure out what it was. His face relaxed. He seemed to realize I meant no harm. I stepped forward and handed him the bottle. He eagerly gulped the little water that remained in the bottle and returned it to me. He seemed more reassured now.

Our settlement is not too far away, and I decided to go back to get help for the boy. He had to be extracted from here too, because he clearly needed medical help. He seemed to have instantly read my thoughts because just as I was about to turn to leave, he pursed his lips, widened his eyes and gently shook his head. Don't go, he was telling me. I tried to assure him with my gestures that I would return.

'I rushed back and got home in less than ten minutes. It was locked. I was not expected back home so early. My wife and Bubul, my son, had probably gone to the bazaar. I wondered whether I should first go to the Primary Health Centre (PHC) or to the police. I ran to the medical center, which our medical officer, Dr Bandopadhyay Babu, was just entering. I told him what I had seen. First, he refused to believe me. I think he was scared. He would be expected to go into the forests to look for this Jarawa boy, and maybe even bring him back. What if the Jarawas attacked? He didn't say it, but I know this was the question on his mind. He agreed to come with me finally, but said it would be subject to permission and help from the police. The Tribal Welfare officer would also have to be informed.'

Pintu paused.

'See, the Tribal Welfare officer is my old friend, Shyam, and he agreed easily. He knew it was his job. He said he'd come but "We need some police protection," he insisted, "just in case the Jarawas come back and attack." We headed straight to the police.

'That harami SHO Halder,' Pintu now took off on a tangent, 'was not at the police station.' It was clearly a subject close to his heart and his guests did not interrupt. 'God save us from policemen like him – not interested in anybody but their own well-being. He's made a small fortune on the side. That murder case involving Rama in the neighbouring village last year? He just let off those Telgi fishermen who had killed Rama. Someone was saying he took 5,000 rupees for that. You won't believe this, but that bitch, Rama's wife, is in Halder's bed every other night. I don't understand these women. What do they see in a guy like him? Maybe he threatens them, maybe they have no choice . . . but he's got a new woman in bed almost every six months. His poor wife! And you know where I found the harami?'

He veered back to his original story. 'He was in the tea-shop in the bazaar, chatting away with my wife. I explained to Halder why I was looking for him. "Those junglees . . . their women, have those big big things, " he said, winking at me and cupping his palms in front of his chest. "You've seen some no?" Now, tell me, does he need to talk like that with my wife right there, next to us? She quickly got up, pulled Bubul up with her, and left.

'"They should all be killed – madarchod sare," he continued once my wife was gone, "They've made life miserable for me. Who asked them to come to the village last night? Did they take my permission? Now if some harami has broken a bone in the forest, it is not my problem. I have work to do. I was just going to the thana anyway. I can't come. "

'"Okay," I told him, "the doctor and the tribal welfare officer and I are going anyway. You know that if the doctor and the tribal welfare officer ask for help in any Jarawa case, you can't say no. We'll go and if anything happens, it will be your responsibility." Now Halder had no choice. He got up reluctantly, muttering abuses under his breath. He was bloody scared.'

There was a smirk of satisfaction on Pintu's face, recalling the small battle he'd won against a man whom he clearly detested.

'So, there we all were – the doctor, Shyam, myself, two attendants carrying a small stretcher, Halder and two constables carrying guns – all headed out on a very important mission. And quickly, as if out of thin air, a whole bunch of onlookers had also collected. Soon, this huge procession started off into the forest, where, I had told everyone I had seen an injured young Jarawa boy sitting by the trunk of a mangrove tree. We passed my house, the fallow paddy fields that lay beyond, and took the path,' he pointed it out with his finger, 'that I take every day to go to my boat. That is when panic suddenly gripped me.' Pintu spontaneously clenched his fists. 'Had I actually seen the Jarawa boy? Would he still be there? Had I been deceived by the magic of the forest? Would I become the laughing stock of my entire village? And you won't believe it, this is exactly what happened.'

In his mind, Pintu was back in the forest, confused, standing again before the entire village. It showed on his face. 'I have lived in this house since I was a child, and have roamed these forests ever since I remember. Even when no one ventured in, because of the fear of the forests and the junglees, I would go. I know the forest,' Pintu stressed, 'but that morning when I went back with Bandopadhyay Babu, Halder, Shyam and all the others, it was like walking back into a maze. I thought I knew where the boy was and headed straight there, but I realized I was moving in another direction.'

Pintu threw both his arms in the air in frustration and continued slowly. 'I was confused, but how could I let that show on my face? I stopped for a while. All eyes,' – his right hand slowly swept a small arc in front of him – 'were staring at me expectantly. I didn't quite know what to do, which direction to head. I was sure I had seen the boy. I had even given him water to drink. I thought I'd turn around, retrace my steps and then restart. Start looking for the boy again. However, just as I turned, I heard him again; his sobs. I will never forget that sound. I turned to my left and there he was, about fifty metres away, sitting exactly where I had left him, resting against the trunk of the mangrove tree.' Pintu paused. He looked at his visitors with a huge, relieved smile. The visitors smiled back in anticipation, and he continued.

'I headed towards the tree. The crowd that was following behind, excited but silent, had also seen him. They all froze where they were standing; each one of them, Shyam, Bandopadhyay Babu, that harami Halder as well. I was now walking alone towards the injured boy. His left leg was still stretched out and his pain seemed to have increased. I reached into my bag and pulled out the three bananas that I had picked up for him. He slowly stretched his hand out, took the bananas and then indicated he wanted water. I handed him my bottle again and he took a sip. He peeled the banana slowly, pushed his head back against the tree and bit into the fruit.

'All this while and it was not more than a couple of minutes, the

entire crowd stood its distance, straining their necks, trying to see
what was happening. The younger ones had climbed onto the trees
to get a better view. I turned towards Shyam and Halder and
motioned to them to come over. There was a now an audible buzz as
the excitement of the crowd began to spill over, like milk on the boil.
One of the constables tried to hold back the crowd; the other one
walked immediately behind Halder, whose hand was already on the
pistol in his belt. Actually, it had been there since the moment we
had started from the village. That harami was scared.

'Now, this Jarawa boy too seemed to realize what was happening.
He turned to see everyone, including this big moustached constable
with a huge gun, surging towards him. Fear gripped the poor boy.
He started to cry again, a torrent of tears now flowing down his
cheeks. I felt sorry for him. He couldn't run, couldn't fight! I tried
hard to assure him that he would not be harmed, but all my
gesticulating was futile. The crowd had closed in and everyone was
staring at the boy as if . . . as if he was a museum piece from another
world. This was probably the first time many of them were seeing a
Jarawa, and that too, so close. Were they really naked? Did they have
curly hair? Was their skin as smooth as wax? Do some of them really
have fangs? How do ghosts breathe? The Jarawas had till then only
been like the fleeting shadows of the dark nights. All shadows are the
same, aren't they? Mine and yours,' he said pointing to David, 'and
yours and yours,' he pointed to Harish and then to Prasad. 'And can
you ever catch a shadow? But here he was, this boy, like a shadow
transformed into the real thing, into a human being of flesh and
blood. People stood and stared curiously, trying to make sense of a
myth that we have all been living with for so many years. A myth
with a form, a shadow with weight. There are many stories in the
villages about who the Jarawa really are. Yes, stories. All stories,
because we didn't know better. There are as many such stories along
these forests as there are villages of the settlers. Villages where the
Jarawas would come, where they still come . . .' Pintu realized he
had slid away from the story he was telling.

'I reached out my hand and gently placed it on the boy's shoulder, trying to reassure him. It was a strange experience, touching a human being like one of us and yet so different; a people we have believed are almost not human. He had two hands, two legs, two ears and two eyes just like us. He was breathing like us, he had been crying like we do. They say Jarawa can spit and kill. They say their saliva is poisonous, but I have never believed that anyway. In the little time I had been with him, he had expressed and experienced the same emotions and feelings that I or my son would have. I was sure he was hoping his family was there with him. What else would one want?

'He flinched when I touched his shoulder. I could feel his helplessness and fear and I could see him resign himself to his fate. What could he have done anyway? What could anyone have done? He was gently lifted onto the stretcher and we headed back to the PHC in the village. He was taken in and as we all waited, Bandopadhyay Babu checked the boy. He was alright, except that he had broken the ankle of his left foot, multiple fractures. I was right; he would have to be shifted to Port Blair immediately.

'And then it was like a big flood that hit us all. There was huge activity. We understood that all the departments – Medical, Tribal Welfare, Police, PWD – had informed their bosses in Port Blair. Apparently, even the Lt Governor's office had been told about the boy. Instructions had come that the Jarawa boy was to be treated very carefully. The ambulance was readied and within an hour, the Jarawa boy on the stretcher, Bandopadhyay Babu, Shyam and one of the police constables headed to Port Blair.

'For a few days after that, the Jarawa boy was the hot topic of discussion. There was a lurking fear that the Jarawas would come looking for him; that they would attack in the belief that this village had swallowed one of theirs.

'Fortunately, nothing of the kind happened. The discussions about the Jarawa boy, about the incident, his rescue, all eventually died down. It was mentioned only occasionally, if at all. Surprisingly, the Jarawas too stopped coming. Completely. As if they had decided to abandon our villages. Nobody knows what happened.'

Pintu had been speaking for quite a while. He stopped and took a deep breath. 'That was March,' he repeated with a sigh, 'this now is November. And I must tell you, the world of the Jarawas has changed.'

David broke in with a smile, 'Pintu, did Tanumei, this Jarawa boy, not come back? Did you not see him again? Montu was here the other day and he told me about your meeting when he returned.'

'Oh, he did?' Pintu replied, with evident embarrassment. 'Yes, of course, that was about three months ago, in August. Actually, it was the 29th of August, a Thursday, if I remember it right. See, I don't really know what happened in Port Blair when Tanumei was there. Have heard a bit from here and there, but I can't be sure. He apparently became very fond of watching television programs, started wearing shorts and shirts, and I was told he was also taken around Port Blair in a VIP's white ambassador. He was a VIP there, baba, and must have had a good time. No,' he corrected himself with an immediate after thought, 'maybe he did not have a good time. When a villager like me gets disoriented in a place like Port Blair, I can only imagine what a simple boy of the forest like Tanumei must have felt. We heard that he was soon telling the doctors that he wanted to go back to the forests. I don't know what actually happened there, so can't say for sure. What happened here, I know. That Tanumei fellow,' he said with mock indignation, 'made me the laughing stock of the entire village.'

'Why? What actually happened?' David prodded again.

Pintu started reluctantly, 'Tanumei returned to Kadamtala a star. We had heard stories of how he now knew at least some of our own ways; the black man learning from the brown. Everyone here wanted to see how he looked now. Had he changed? Did he behave any different? To tell you the truth,' there was a seriousness in Pintu's tone now, 'I was a little worried. Would he remember me? What would he remember me for? Was I not responsible for him being taken away?' He paused for a brief moment. 'Anyway, Tanumei was already in the PHC when I learnt he was back. There was an atmosphere of gaiety when I reached there. People were milling in and out of the PHC like it was a mela, and there was a kind of good feeling in the air. The moment I reached, however, there was a sudden hush, you know, like something had been planned. I grew a little suspicious as I entered. Tanumei was sitting right there and he recognized me immediately. There was a big smile on his face, which turned into a mischievous grin. It had all been planned,' Pintu nodded his head in disbelief, 'and then everything went silent as Tanumei began with complete confidence and innocence: "Main Tanumei. Tumhara naam kya?"'

'Such good Hindi from a Jarawa boy! I was taken completely by surprise. I didn't know what to say. "Pi, Pi . . . " my name was stuck in my own throat.' Pintu's eyes lit up with the recalled mirth of that afternoon.

'"Pin . . . Pintu," I stammered, sending the whole room into a boisterous laughing fit. And that Tanumei fellow? He was rolling on the floor in mirth. "Pintu! Mera naam Pintu," I finally said, settled down on the chair and burst out laughing myself.' David, Prasad and Harish were laughing now, at Pintu's enactment and his little Russian doll tummy that jiggled in front of him in small amplitude. He began again, but now in a tone that had gone suddenly sombre.

'So, that was it. The time for Tanumei's final journey back home had come. The doctor from Port Blair, Tanumei and myself; the police held back everyone else this time, headed back into the mangroves where we had first met. You know something?' Pintu asked softly, as if talking to himself, 'Tanumei was a caged bird finding freedom again. There was the smile of liberation on his face and a spring in his step. We will never know what it means,' Pintu looked straight at his guests, 'because only after you have been in prison will you know the joy of freedom. We reached what I now call the Tanumei tree and stopped there in silence for a few moments. Then Tanumei turned right and began to walk towards the hills and the forests not very far away. We followed for a while and then stopped. Tanumei continued on his own, stopped and looked back. He smiled, waved and then, turning around set off purposefully in the direction of home. Six months away in a strange place is a long time, don't you think?' Pintu's question was directed at no one in particular. 'Even as I watched, that dark figure merged with the formless shapes of that giant tapestry.' Pintu was speaking with deep reverence now. 'Like a wisp of fragile smoke, he dissolved into that ancient forest. I heard some strange whisperings and,' Pintu's eyes closed again and there were a few moments of silence, 'just then, as if in acknowledgement, a gentle breeze went rippling through.' He opened his eyes and smiled at his guests. 'I know you won't believe me, but that gentle breeze told me something that no one will understand, not even me. When no one saw the crashing tree inside the mighty forest, what hope is there for the leaf that drifts silently down from its giant canopy, for the snake that slides effortlessly on the forest floor, for a creature of wing and feather that sings a melodious melody somewhere in between?'

The visitors were quite taken in by Pintu's lyrical proclamations. The story was as fascinating as Pintu's manner of telling it. The journalist in Prasad had quickly discounted the last bits, but he knew better than to interrupt. He was taken aback when the storyteller turned and looked straight at him. 'I may not make sense, but trust me,' he took a deep breath as he continued, 'because that breeze warned me – a big storm is on its way!'

5

TANUMEI'S RETURN

The period immediately after Tanumei merged back into the giant forests was a strangely anxious one. Jarawa raids, part of the lives of the settlers for over a decade had now stopped. This was an unusual quiet, an edgy calm in the villages and settlements that dotted the forest fringes. There was no saying what was brewing deep in the hearts and forests of the Jarawas. These were, after all, people who could shoot an arrow straight into your heart even under the canopy of a dark rainforest. There was an uneasy feeling that something was about to happen.

It did, about a month later, when Tanumei re-emerged. He came back not alone, but with a group of young Jarawa boys like himself. They made their appearance suddenly one morning at Uttara Jetty, just a couple of kilometres down the road from Phooltala. The wheel had begun to turn.

Uttara was a small jetty that existed only because of the Andaman Trunk Road. Located amongst thick mangroves, it was meant only for small boats and, more importantly, the vehicle ferries. Vehicles travelling from Mayabundar in the north to Port Blair could not go further than Uttara. Here, a huge creek separated Middle Andaman Island from Baratang, and vehicles and buses had to drive onto a ferry that went back and forth across the creek like a slow-moving piston.

Through the day, there would only be a small smattering of people at the jetty. There were a couple of shacks selling knick-knacks, a few village urchins who loitered aimlessly around, occasionally fishing in the creek, and a couple of perennial drunks sprawled at impossible angles inside the tiny passenger hall. For the past few months, waiting with them was a thoughtful old brown cow, and a couple of goats would also often plant themselves underneath the concrete benches that skirted the perimeter. The only time when there was activity at Uttara was when the buses from the north arrived and waited for the ferry from the other side. Passengers would get off for a stretch or a glass of tea. The men in the bus would, of course, need to relieve themselves all at once.

It was here that the Jarawa boys, all of them in their early teens, had emerged that morning, their arrival announced by the fear-filled scream of a bus passenger watering the trees behind the passenger hall. 'Jarawaaaa!' he had screamed, leaving his job half done, turning around and running for the safety of the passenger hall. Nobody in the hall, however, heard him; their ears and attention were held by the loud commentary spewing out from a radio in the corner:

'Shoaib Akhtar runs in to bowl the last ball of this eighth over. Can Sachin Tendulkar do it now? This has been an incredible innings . . . Akhtar comes in, right arm over the wicket. This ball is slightly short, outside the off stump and . . .' a huge uproar erupted from the radio '. . . it's gone.' The commentator was panting as if he was running the runs himself. 'What a masterful innings – and that is another century for the master blaster, the one and only Sachin Tendulkar.'

The commentator was shouting, the gathered crowd of listeners had erupted in a joyous roar of their own, and together they drowned out the fear-filled scream of the man amongst the trees. A few had noticed him running wildly, hands fluttering like a kite in the wind. They thought he had gathered the significance of Sachin Tendulkar's century and was not able to contain his excitement. When the Jarawas ambled in tentatively behind him a few moments later, the radio was swiftly flicked off and all other sound also died a crisp, spontaneous death. Now suddenly, even the chirping of sparrows on the ceiling above was clearly audible.

Jarawas outside the forests? In broad daylight? Unarmed? Their arrival sent a wave of panic and fear into Phooltala and even Kadamtala in just a few minutes. They were unarmed, but they were Jarawas. They could not be trusted. After many months of lying dormant, they might have returned with a plan. Maybe this was an advance party; maybe they had hidden their bows and arrows in the mangroves close by. Maybe their entire band was hiding in the vicinity, waiting for the signal, for the right moment, to launch their attack.

The junglees of these forests were entirely capable of this, of plotting and planning, scheming and scheduling. Many, many years ago, a century and a half ago, the Great Andamanese, those other dark co-inhabitants of these dark forests, had orchestrated an incident that demonstrated just this; one that everyone still spoke of. There was also the still-intriguing story of Dudhnath Tiwari, convict 286 of the Penal settlement of the Andamans.

Dudhnath Tiwari, Sepoy, 14th Regiment, Bengal Native Infantry. Location: Jhelum, in the Punjab. Year: 1857. Nobody knew if he had actually fired a single shot from his musket – of the same make, incidentally, that the famous Mangal Pandey had shot his British officer with. It didn't matter. The Great Indian Sepoy Mutiny, that this catalysed, had spread like wildfire but had been doused out eventually. Within a few months, a few hundred mutineers, Dudhnath Tiwari included, were sent for their misdemeanours to the Andaman Islands, to Kalapani, the dreaded black waters – the kingdom of deadly diseases, of torture at British hands or a swift-arrow death at the hands of the fierce, naked denizens of a dangerous forest. In April 1858, Dudhnath and ninety other convicts had decided to take on their fate and escaped from incarceration, hoping to make it to Burma. Somehow.

Fate did them in. All they encountered were endless coastlines, unfriendly forests, incurable fevers or the arrows of the original inhabitants. None but one survived – Dudhnath Tiwari. The very people who had injured him with their arrows – one had pierced his right thigh, the other his left shoulder – had saved his life. Just why they did that will remain forever unexplained. The injured Dudhnath was adopted by the Great Andamanese. He was nursed and fed by them till he regained his health and his spirits. He became one of them – hunting, fishing, living the lives that they lived, following rituals they followed, imbibing spirits they imbibed. In little more than a year, he had married two Great Andamanese women and even fathered a child. Then fate threw the dice once again.

Dudhnath heard of an impending Great Andamanese assault on the British and on their settlement at Aberdeen. The mutineer joined the battle, but from the other end; he left his benefactors the night before the attack and sought out their enemy. The British were warned and thereby saved. Dudhnath Tiwari's action was highly appreciated and he was pardoned for having helped the British save Aberdeen. He returned to mainland India a few months later and disappeared in the vast expanse of the northern plains.

Versions of history walk different paths in remembering what had happened in Aberdeen. For some it was an insignificant attack, a foolish attempt on part of the locals, a localized version perhaps of the failed sepoy mutiny that had brought Dudhnath here in the first place. Others remember it as the great 'Battle of Aberdeen', the glorious fight of the Andamanese, worthy of being memorialized in a stone inscription that stands in Port Blair to this present day: 'This monument is built in the memory of those Andamanese aborigines who bravely fought the Battle of Aberdeen in May 1859 against the oppressive and retaliatory policy of the British regime.' They had lost only because they had been cheated. Dudhnath Tiwari's treachery, this lot argues, changed the course of history in these islands; the British would have otherwise been comprehensively routed from here.

If the Great Andamanese could have plotted such an elaborate scheme against the British then, surely the Jarawas could do it today?

Those at Uttara that morning had no cause to worry, though. The Jarawa boys were themselves very tentative; scared and unsure of what to expect. Only Tanumei exuded some confidence. He had, after all, lived in this outside world, even if only briefly.

Soon a crowd gathered and the police had to intervene to keep it at a reasonable distance from the six Jarawa boys that had settled themselves in the shade by the passenger hall. Nobody knew what was to be done. The Tribal Welfare Officer, meanwhile, had also reached the spot. Some bananas were brought in and handed over to the boys. Pintu and his boat were also called for. The boys had to be dropped back into the forests, and Pintu would be the best person to navigate the creeks for this.

Something similar happened four days later – only the group was a larger one this time. This soon became a regular occurrence. In another month, the average size of the group that gathered from the forests increased to twenty and they would move out into the villages every other day. Tanumei was always there, leading the group out; a Jarawa bachelors' party with a free run of the place. They started to come and go as they liked, taking bananas and coconuts from the villages as they wanted, entering houses when they found them open and showing aggressive defiance when stopped. Rapidly, the Jarawas had become a nuisance.

The occasional nightly Jarawa raids that used to take place before the Tanumei incident were remembered now, in light of this continued interference, as benign. It had only been a few months since Tanumei first appeared, but the world seemed to have been upturned all over again. The fear of the Jarawa was still there, but it was draining away quickly; being replaced now by a mixture of resentment and impatience. A new chapter was emerging in the complicated relationship between the Jarawas and the settlers of these islands.

This was the mounting impatience that David had brought Prasad and Harish into – the cusp of the storm that came at the end of Pintu's captivating story. The last Jarawa raid had occurred less than a week prior to their visit to Pintu.

An opinion was now emerging in the villages that nothing had actually changed, that the junglees knew only one way of being; only that bows and arrows had been replaced by more brazenness, that Tanumei was being ungrateful. Pintu continued, however, to believe otherwise. For him there was a qualitative difference – this was like real warriors now taking to thuggery and petty dadagiri, not fighting a real war anymore. And this was only the beginning.

'Tanumei has taken it upon himself,' – Pintu moved with a confident flourish to the conclusion of his story, which had gone on late into the evening – 'to lead his own people out, and we can't say for sure what will happen now.'

6

JARAWAS AT THE JETTY

The plan now was for Prasad to take the first bus next morning to Rangat in the north. He wanted to take in the landscape and speak to people to get a wider perspective and quotes for his story. David and Harish were to do the same, but in the opposite direction. They were to walk down to Uttara jetty, take the ferry across and then, perhaps, take a short bus ride further down the Andaman Trunk Road. They wanted to see the places along the road where the Jarawas were emerging from the forest, and meet some of the settlers as well.

It was early in the morning, with their minds were still full of Pintu's Jarawa and Tanumei story of the earlier evening, when Harish and David started towards the jetty. There was a flurry of activity and vehicles there. At the jetty, they saw a swarm of people lined along the water's edge, all staring at the other bank of the creek in the distance. A large bunch of young boys had even clambered onto the roof of the passenger hall to get a better view. It was clear that something was happening on the other side, but no one knew exactly what.

Harish and David squeezed through. The crowd that they were part of now was reasonably large – at least 150 people – but also uncharacteristically quiet. There wasn't the loud, bustling din that is normally associated with such gatherings – just strained whispers.

'What happened?' Harish asked the profusely sweating young man standing next to him.

'Jarawas,' he hissed without turning his head. His gaze was locked in the distance.

'Yes, but what happened?'

'We'll soon know,' he said.

On the other side of the creek was a huge gathering of Jarawas and the dead body of an Andaman Public Works Department (APWD) worker they had killed the earlier night. The details were unclear, but for the crowd that had gathered, it was an indication that things had not changed much after all. The Jarawas were ungrateful, the same dastardly junglees they had always been. Anger was simmering.

In a short while, a boat could be seen leaving from the other bank and moving towards where the crowd had gathered. As the boat neared, two policemen in khaki became visible. Harish also recognized Pintu, who was steering the boat.

'They are bringing the body,' someone from atop the passenger hall shouted.

A tense hush descended as the boat neared and stopped alongside the jetty. On a makeshift stretcher in the boat lay the body, shrouded in white. A garland created a white oval on one side and a few flowers lay scattered at the other end. The police constable waiting on the jetty jumped onto the boat to help. Together, they lifted the body to bring it ashore.

The anger of the people on the jetty was palpable. 'Harami!' someone screamed.

'Those junglees, saale Jarawas!' shouted someone else.

'Kill them,' someone else shouted.

Everyone broke out into vociferous abuse, a din so loud that nothing else could be heard. The crowd was slowly turning into a mob, with blood on its mind.

'We won't let you bring the body,' another voice boomed.

'We won't let you bring the body,' the crowd echoed in unison.

'First get the Jarawas who did this . . . Saale harami!'

A huge crowd of disparate souls was thinking like one, asking the same questions: Who was the man who had been killed? How had he died? Which of the Jarawas were responsible for this?

The policemen grew worried. The situation was rapidly spinning out of control. They put the body back down in the boat, and one of them raised his hands and gestured to the crowd to quieten down.

'Listen!' he screamed at the top of his voice, clapping and waving his hands to get some attention. No one was listening. The crowd had slowly shuffled even closer to the edge – there was pushing and heckling, and the constables standing on the jetty, their lathis stretched in front of them, were just about managing to keep the surging crowd at bay.

Pintu had been sitting at the end of the boat all this while, watching the crowd grow increasingly restive. Now, he got up. Like the policeman, he too raised both his hands, gesturing to the crowd to calm down. This seemed to have some impact.

'Listen,' he shouted, pointing to the policeman. 'Listen to what he has to say.'

'Yes, yes. Okay . . .' a voice came from the crowd, 'what is it?'

'First thing . . .' the policeman sensed an opportunity and screamed at the top of his voice. 'The Jarawas . . .' he finally caught the attention of the crowd. He paused and then started again. 'First thing. The Jarawas did not kill Rajib babu.'

'Rajib babu?' The question went coursing through the crowd.

'Yes,' the policeman continued. 'This is Rajib babu,' he said pointing to the body lying at his feet. 'May God give peace to his soul, and,' he stopped to ensure emphasis, 'the Jarawas did not kill him.'

A chirping murmur arose from among the crowd as people tried to figure out who had misinformed them doubly. The Jarawas had not killed the man, and he was not a PWD worker.

'You all know Rajib babu,' the policeman took off his cap and scratched his head in visible relief. 'His body was found a few kilometres from the jetty.' The cap went back on his head as he pointed to the other side. 'God alone knows when and how he got there, but it was probably around midnight. We all know how much he drank. He was more drunk last night than he normally is, and some people from Adajig had seen him swaying uncontrollably by the road. He was run over by a PWD truck just before sunrise.'

'Oooooooo . . .' The crowd exclaimed in choreographed unison and the tension released like steam hissing out of a pressure cooker.

'Can't really blame the truck driver,' the policeman continued, his finger pointing to the truck that stood across the creek, 'but we've taken him in for interrogation anyway. Now, please move,' he said as he jumped out from the boat, 'and let us get on with our work.'

The crowd parted and Rajib babu's body was laid on the jetty. The policeman quickly jumped back into Pintu's boat. The job was only half done. On the other side, there was this large group of Jarawas that still had to be dealt with. They were only making one of their now regular trips to the world outside of the forest, but each such trip was moving everything and everyone, one unpredictable step at a time, towards the sharper end of an escalating restlessness. Was this now the edge?

Pintu had noticed Harish and David, and beckoned to them to jump into his boat. The policeman showed his stern disapproval, but in the present circumstances Pintu could not be refused; he had just saved the day.

'I told you, did I not, that a storm was coming?' Pintu said with a satisfied smile as his guests hopped in and the boat took off for the other side.

For two days now, Harish had constantly been hearing about the Jarawas. Now, on this other side here, suddenly and unexpectedly, they were before his very eyes: the Jarawas, the 'other', the 'them', the dark people of the dark forests, the darkest night in human form, teeth shining the white of a rain-washed moon.

The men and women were all naked. Most of the women had

leaves and red thread tied around their waist. Intricate shell jewellery hung around the necks of the younger women and others wore a headband of delicate red and white flowers. The boys too wore a headband of red thread. Chest guards made from tree bark and decorated with symmetrical lines and intricate designs covered some of their torsos.

The world that Harish had just come from couldn't have been further away from the one he was presently in. Harish was stunned. 'How can both be real? At the same time?' he wondered.

Here was a flurry of activity and complete confusion. The roadside vendors were selling paan, biscuits, cigarettes, sukha and tea, among other things. The PWD truck that had killed Rajib Samaddar was parked nearby. A passenger bus of the State Transport Service had just arrived from Port Blair, and was waiting for the vehicle ferry. Normally, the entire load of passengers would have been out, but the presence of the Jarawas ensured that a significant number simply waited inside, nervousness written all over their countenances. For many inside the bus, this was their first view of the Jarawas. Eyes filled with interest and apprehension peered from behind the bars of the bus windows. A little boy who poked his head a little further out was quickly pulled in by his mother. No risks could be taken. For these people, the Jarawas were as much myth as the ghosts or the gods inhabiting the unknown forests of their own imagination.

There were others too at the jetty that morning, those whose fields, plantations and households had been raided by the Jarawas in recent months. There were some like Pintu who had been deep into the dense forests of the Jarawas, and there were also those who had been at the forefront of this conflict in the past many years. They knew the forests well, had regularly and illegally entered the Jarawa forests, poached deer and pigs, and collected honey.

Among the Jarawas, a majority were making their first visit outside their forest homes, the first tentative steps, perhaps, of a bold new journey. These were the Jarawa eyes that brimmed with apprehension and curiosity about an unfamiliar world. Five of the younger lot had climbed onto the open back of the PWD truck. A few had clambered into the passenger bus, some were on top of it and others were interestedly staring at what the paanwallah was doing. Two young Jarawa men stood out in the group. One had a policeman's khaki shorts around his waist and a black baseball cap on his head. The other looked rather incongruous, even absurd, sporting a pair of white – now soiled – VIP underwear, which stood out in stark contrast against the ebony of his skin.

The women, meanwhile, sat quietly in the shade of the passenger waiting hall, looking around, their eyes making intermittent 180-degree sweeps of the world in front of them.

Here was a strange, unprecedented roadside meeting of two worlds living side by side, yet separated by huge legacies of history, distrust and fear.

It occurred to Harish that the guy in the khaki shorts had to be Tanumei. His demeanour, his confidence, but most importantly, his familiarity with the other world stood out. The Jarawa boy went up to the policeman who was in command and saluted him jokingly. This was Pintu's 'harami', SHO Halder. The two exchanged a few words and then he went back to his people to communicate what Halder had said. He also chatted and laughed with the roadside vendors, whom he seemed to know well.

Pintu, meanwhile, walked up to stand beside Harish and David. Harish was right.

'That is Tanumei,' Pintu pointed to the Jarawa youth in khaki shorts. 'It's like the difference between night and day,' he said shaking his head, 'Tanumei then and Tanumei now, difficult to believe.'

Harish tried a quick count of the Jarawa – sixty-five, probably sixty-eight, maybe seventy.

David too was astounded. 'Seventy-two,' he exclaimed, looking at Harish. He had been making his own count. 'If Census estimates are to be believed, this is nearly a quarter of the entire Jarawa population. Never before have they been seen in such large numbers in one single place. This is a significant happening, Harish,' he said as he walked towards the passenger hall to see what was happening there.

Tanumei had seen Pintu's hand pointing in his direction, and had immediately walked over, a toothy grin revealing the most perfect set of teeth Harish had ever seen. 'Ay madarchod,' he gently tapped Pintu's shoulder, 'Kaisa?' he gestured with his hand. 'Sukha hai?'

Pintu recoiled, both at Tanumei's language as also this crude demand for tobacco.

Harish was also taken aback. 'Where has he picked up such language? Does he even know what it means?'

Tanumei did not understand the disapproving looks on the faces before him. This is how people here greeted each other. It was the perfectly normal thing to do.

'Sukha kyun?' Harish raised his hands in interrogation.

Just then, a little scuffle broke out to one side and Tanumei went rushing across.

One of the young men from the bus, dressed in tight jeans and a flaming orange shirt, had been standing in a corner and staring lecherously at a Jarawa woman. Harish had noticed him earlier. He had inched closer to her and brushed his right hand 'accidentally' against her bare bottom. She had retaliated, pushing the man away; he had lost his balance and toppled over. People from both sides rushed towards the man, and quick tension filled the air. This was a thin fuse waiting to go off at short notice. Two policemen ran across, waving their lathis, and quickly herded the Jarawas into the passenger hall.

Harish quickly pulled out his look-and-shoot camera that Prasad had insisted he take with him. He had taken only a few pictures when the policemen objected and Harish was forced to put it away.

'Let's go,' the bus conductor said. He quit staring at the naked women, stopped scratching his crotch and beckoned to his passengers. 'Let's go,' he called out again, prodded by the police, who didn't want any trouble. The ferry had also arrived and the truck driver had carefully driven into the flat-bottomed vessel. Now there was just enough space for the bus, which was driven in to fit so perfectly, it looked like a crane had lifted it and placed it there. The remaining passengers climbed into the ferry, leaving behind only the Jarawas, the few policemen, Pintu, his guests from the mainland, the vendors and a few hanger-ons from the nearby settlement.

Nobody knew what the Jarawas had come out for. There needn't have been a reason. All they were asking for today were coconuts and bananas; they were adamant that they would not leave without these. These were the basic messages that Tanumei had been interlocuting between Halder and his own people. Some of these discussions were going on when Pintu, who had been called over to the other side of the creek a while ago, returned with three women in his boat. Two of these were clearly Bengali, and another most likely Tamil. They had been sent for by SHO Halder.

'Why would this man,' Harish thought to himself, 'send for these women in all this confusion and potential trouble?'

The thin, round-faced lady in the sari was off the boat first. The second one, the lady in the pink kurta bore a striking resemblance to Halder and was clearly related to him. The third was the largest of the three, and also the most subdued. She walked behind the other two women and stood meekly to one side. Pintu came over and stood with Harish and David.

'What's happening?' David asked. 'Who are these women?'

'Halder's wife, Halder's sister and that is constable Ramaswamy's wife.'

Hierarchy among the men had with natural ease been transferred to the women too. Halder's wife scurried to her husband with a small cardboard box in hand and an agitated, 'what have you called us here for?' look. The attention of the small motley crowd at the jetty was now all centred on the SHO, Ramaswamy and the women who had just arrived.

They watched Halder speak to his wife, gesturing to her to relax. He then appeared to explain what he had called them for. In only a minute, the lady seemed pacified; she nodded her head and there was even a faint smile on her face.

Halder sent Ramaswamy into the passenger hall and stood smugly beside his wife. It was a big breakthrough he appeared to have engineered, but the small crowd gathered here still had no clue what this was about. They watched in eager anticipation.

Ramaswamy returned shortly with Tanumei, followed by a Jarawa woman with a little one at her right breast. The incongruity was stark as Halder's wife and the Jarawa woman stood in front of each other for a few quiet, uneasy moments.

Then the Bengali woman reached for the right hand of her Jarawa counterpart, who transferred her baby to her left hip to allow for that. The baby started to bawl immediately: the heat perhaps, maybe hunger, maybe both. The Jarawa woman rocked the baby, which, to everyone's relief quietened down quickly.

Halder's wife now opened the cardboard box she had brought along and pulled out a bunch of red and green glass bangles. So this is what she was to do! The intrigued crowd finally understood what was happening. As for Halder's wife, the gratification showed in her eyes. Here was a woman who was what a woman should not be: a woman not conscious of her body and her nakedness, who had no lajja, no shame. Haldar's wife held up the Jarawa woman's right hand, picked up a bunch of bangles and slipped them effortlessly over the dark bare wrist.

Harish felt the wrongness of this hit his gut. 'What the hell do they think they are doing?' he asked no one in particular.

Pintu promptly turned his head towards Harish, a confused look on his face. 'Why,' he quizzed, 'what's wrong? Is she not a woman? Does she not have a child with her? We are all Indians, aren't we?'

Halder's wife then brushed a little sindoor from the parting of her own hair and placed a small dot on the forehead of the Jarawa woman. It was now the turn of Halder's sister. She picked out a few bangles from the box and like her sister-in-law, slipped them over the Jarawa woman's right wrist. Ramaswamy's wife had nothing in particular to do. She stood there, uncomfortable and uninterested. It was her job to stand behind the others and this she had performed satisfactorily. As Halder's wife watched her sister-in-law in action, she suddenly felt she wanted to do more – to ensure the modesty, the lajja, of the Jarawa woman, wrap a sari around her, perhaps, or at least cover her naked breasts with a chunni. She also realized, however, that this was only the first encounter and that only so much could be done this time. Another chance would, hopefully, come soon.

Their tasks done, the three women returned in the boat they had come in, and the Jarawa woman went back to the passenger hall she had been called from. The looks on the faces of the Jarawa women now betrayed nothing but complete amusement. They listened to the clink of the glass with excitement. Then someone else shook the bangled wrist. First they started to giggle and soon were laughing loud and carefree.

It was at this point that Harish noticed that one tall Jarawa man, standing to one side, had been intently registering everything that had been going on with an indecipherable look. Harish had seen him earlier, but it was only now that he noticed the aggressive disapproval in those intense eyes. He was clearly the oldest of the Jarawa men in the gathering, but had chosen not to act, not even to instruct. He stood leaning against the wall, inspecting the scene – observing, studiously assimilating everything that was happening around him. He was like a rubber band pulled and held taut; unpredictable, but ready to act, brimming with potential energy, but extremely vulnerable at the same time. A release now would mean an explosive outburst; stretching a little more would mean a permanent snapping, and this finely tuned control captivated Harish.

Harish stood at a small remove, gazing at the man. He was trying to decipher the look in those intense eyes, when, in an unexpected moment, that gaze locked with Harish's own. It knocked Harish back with an intensity more raw than a street fighter's well-directed punch. It was a potent mixture of anger, pride and concern. Harish could bear that look only for a moment.

He lowered his eyes in retreat and glanced towards David. Instinctively, he looked back again and found he was still being scrutinized. The other gaze had not moved at all. He felt he was being singled out for something. Shaken, he stepped back and walked away towards the water's edge, where a boat loaded with bananas and coconuts for the Jarawas had finally arrived.

Lost inside, within a huge load of nuts, were a group of new people. The mien of officialdom dripped off their faces like saliva from a dog thrilled at the possibility of a good bone. This was an All India Radio team on its way back from an assignment in Rangat; they had arrived in the midst of a situation that was an unprecedented opportunity.

Bytes. Jarawa sound bytes! What a scoop this would be. A man carrying a backpack and a small, black Sony recorder slung around his neck jumped off the boat. Sleek silver frames rimmed his large eyes, which evidenced their delight. He walked energetically towards Halder.

'My name is Shukla,' he said, reaching out with his right hand to Halder. Halder held the kind of position that Shukla would have contemptuously brushed aside in another situation. But this was the 'other' situation. 'Shukla,' he repeated, 'Arun Shukla.' The grey-haired, middle-aged woman accompanying him wobbled over, 'And this is Madam. From All India Radio.'

Madam, in contrast to Shukla, looked tired and uninterested, a toad yanked out from its aestivating slumber; perhaps just a reaction to the blazing sun, or more likely her way of being, the response to any new idea being to deflate it.

Halder wasn't unaware of his position. In the hierarchy of the administration, the likes of Madam and even Shukla were far above him. He also knew, however, like Shukla did, that this was that situation where the balances were tilted just a wee bit in the other direction. Shukla had said she was Madam. That should have been enough, but Halder was Halder. He didn't mind playing a few games, at least till the balance maintained its tilt. He stood there pretending lack of concern and interest.

'Madam? All India Radio?' Halder knotted his eyebrows.

'This is Madam Jacob, Deputy Director, All India Radio.'

'All India Radio . . .?' Halder's legs were still crossed, his eyebrows knotted in an officious knot.

An irritated Madam Jacob clicked open her handbag and pulled out her Identity Card.

Halder had had his kick. 'No, Madam,' Halder unknotted his eyebrows. The balance regained official non-equilibrium. 'Where is the need for that?' He uncrossed his legs and straightened up. 'Tell me, what can I do for you? What do you wish to do?'

'We want to do some interviews with the Jarawas. It's so hot. Shukla, please give me some water.'

Shukla pulled the bag off his back and pulled out a bottle to hand over to Madam.

'We want to know what the Jarawas feel.' Shukla didn't want to be left out. He plugged in the cable and handed the mike to Madam. Like a sulking child who had finally got her lollipop, Madam revived quickly.

'Ay Ramaswamy,' Halder shouted out, 'get that Tanumei fellow here.' Ramaswamy came quickly back with Tanumei.

'Madam.' Halder looked at Tanumei and pointed to Madam. 'All India Radio. Tanumei, namaste bolo.'

Tanumei said his namaste. Madam looked pleased.

'Bolo, sab theek hai na?' Halder prompted Tanumei just as Shukla put on the recorder.

Madam didn't like leading questions, and the policeman had no business prompting Tanumei in this manner. She looked disapprovingly at Halder and placed a finger on her lips.

She turned back to her quarry, 'Tanumei, thoda apne bare mein bataein. Aap ko kya lagta hai?' Questions had to be open ended, the interviewee had to be helped settle into the interview, made comfortable when speaking about himself.

Tanumei looked a little hassled. 'Namaste,' he said again to Madam, and turned to Halder. He had other more important things on his mind. 'Woh, bhenchod, narial, kela lao na.'

Madam's eyes exploded in shock. Shukla squirmed. Halder just about managed to conceal his wild amusement. The interview was over even before it had begun. There were no sound bytes to get here!

As if on cue, a couple of small Jarawa boys ran out from the passenger hall and gleefully dived into the cool waters of the creek. They swam a bit and climbed onto a boat parked by the jetty. Then, suddenly, one of them started off on a loud monosyllable yodel which filled the air with its rhythmic beat. The other boy also joined in and the two quickly reached a crescendo.

Ramaswamy briskly walked towards the boat and jumped in, screaming at the boys to stop. They paid heed to the cop only when he whacked hard the bottom of one, and then of the other. They stopped instantly, faces crestfallen, not sure what they had done wrong. They were about to get off the boat on the instructions of the policeman when Shukla snatched the mike from Madam and ran across. An idea seemed to have struck him. He jumped onto the boat and thrust his mike into the face of the older of the two boys.

'Gao,' he instructed. If nothing else, the yodelling of the Jarawa boys, at least, could be taken back as a recording of their songs.

The little boy didn't know what it meant. What was he supposed to do? What was this thing that was being shoved into his face? His face creased up with doubt and tears welled up in his eyes. He looked at the mike with fear.

'Gao,' Ramaswamy ordered sternly.

'Gao! Gao!' Shukla continued, desperate not to miss this chance.

He tried the yodel, 'Aisa gao!' He sang out, gesturing to the boy that he should do the same.

Confusion and fear clouded the face of the little boy, and he turned apprehensively to Ramaswamy. Ramaswamy pointed to the mike and tried a gesture he thought communicated the yodel.

The little fellow started again cautiously, softly, eyes fixed on Ramaswamy, tears still trickling down his face. Ramaswamy was pleased with himself. He was getting the Jarawa boy to perform. The boy now pushed up the volume and looked at Shukla, who looked pleased as well and nodded vigorously, smiling.

A relieved half-smile ironed out the creases on the boy's face, and he urged his friend to join. The two boys started in unison, creating a perfect harmonic, and yodelled away with increasing abandon. Shukla beamed. So Ramaswamy beamed. The boys also beamed.

And then, just as suddenly, Shukla decided it was enough. Two full minutes of Jarawa yodel had been put down for posterity, perhaps the first recording of its kind. This was a little coup, and he was very proud of himself.

While Shukla was creating his own little bit of history, the coconuts and bananas were unloaded onto the jetty and the Jarawas were sent for. Two coconuts and a bunch of bananas were given to each and they were directed into Pintu's boat, which could accommodate about half their present number. The remaining were accommodated in a second boat. It was only around two o' clock, a full six hours after the Jarawas had first arrived at the jetty, that they were taken back along the creek waters to be dropped off deep inside their forest home. Their little adventure for the day was finally over.

When they met later that evening, it was an incredible story that Prasad got from Harish and David. There were also the pictures that

Harish had managed to take, and Prasad was loud with his satisfaction and excitement. This was going to be an incredible story – even a cover, perhaps! His day, in comparison had been rather uneventful, though he had gathered some interesting and useful insights into people's perceptions of the Jarawas.

Pintu was uncharacteristically quiet. He smiled reluctantly when Prasad went up to him. 'You were right, Pintu,' he said softly, 'I don't know about that breeze, but the storm you spoke about yesterday is certainly coming.'

Back at the Institute the next day, Prasad and Harish worked furiously at getting their story together. Prasad was leaving in a couple of days and he wanted to get the maximum done before he left. Then the two settled down with David for another long evening of discussion.

'There is a lot under the immediate surface, David,' Harish started. 'We are not even perceiving all of this, leave alone understanding it. There are far too many unanswered questions. Why are the Jarawas coming out of their forest now? What are they thinking? What is happening to their world? What role is Tanumei playing? What do the Jarawas think of the outside world? Where do they see their future going? What is the future?' he rattled them all out in one breath, worried that he would forget something if he paused for even a moment.

'These questions I believe,' David said, mulling for a moment, 'don't have answers, cannot have answers. There is no one who can answer them. The Jarawas are not accessible. Nobody else knows their forest, nobody knows how to find them and nobody knows whether you and I or anybody else is yet welcome inside. But that is not what I mean when I say accessible. Tanumei is standing next to you, but he is not accessible. You saw what happened with that interview thing – that is what I mean. Language, Harish, language and many other barriers and hurdles. Nobody to understand and nobody to answer. Nobody. What do you think Prasad?' he turned to Prasad who had been listening intently.

'That's true,' Prasad said slowly and thoughtfully. 'As a journalist, I have been trying to visualize myself in the position of that radio correspondent. Tough choice. Tough luck. What you might want to do, Harish, is look at the mirror.'

'Mirror?'

'That's what I would do if I had the time. I am thinking aloud, so let's see where this leads us . . . What I am suggesting is . . .' Prasad paused, 'what I mean . . . Ok, let me ask a question. Who best knows the Jarawas, besides themselves, that is?' He paused again. 'It is the people who live in and around the Jarawa forests, right? The Pintus, the residents of the Phooltalas and Kadamtalas, the policemen, the forest workers, the poachers who go in regularly, the fishermen and all those who have lived and are living on the margins of Jarawa existence.'

'Yes?' asked David.

'So?' Harish chimed in.

'So, this is the mirror,' Prasad responded. 'All these people are the many mirrors, each reflecting a small part of what the Jarawas are, of the Jarawa reality. To look at them would be to look at the Jarawas, but through their experiences and their perceptions. To know them would be to know the Jarawa.'

'But,' David asked thoughtfully, 'how real will that image be, Prasad?'

'When we know nothing of the real itself, what can one guarantee of the image? But, you're right David,' Prasad was clearer about what he was saying and liking the sound of it too, 'it will be anamorphic. Multiple anamorphisms. And because it's an image of the real, at one point it will appear regular. It will. It has to. Reality will be reflected as it is, in bits and pieces, scraps of this and that, to be scavenged from the fringes of the Jarawa existence, and put together on a single canvas. You know what I mean?' He looked expectantly at the faces in front of him. They weren't revealing much, so he continued.

'Put simply, all I am saying is this. Get to know the people who live on the fringes of the Jarawa forests and learn about Jarawa existence.' He turned to Harish, his old, dear friend, one for whom he had agonized immensely in recent days. 'Harish,' he said, 'this is something that you could attempt. You should. What do you think David?' he turned his attention to David. 'My sense is that it will be very worthwhile and add very important information about the Jarawas, about their forests and also about the people living around these forests.'

David nodded his head in thoughtful affirmation. Harish too nodded, marvelling at the clarity and articulation of his friend. With one considered swipe, he had cut open a whole swathe of enticing possibilities.

'Anamorphic, Prasad? Multiple anamorphisms!' Harish smiled. 'You bugger, did you ever score more than pass marks in physics in school? Now you sound like you are in line for the bloody Nobel!'

All three burst out laughing.

It had been less than a week since Harish had come to the islands but he was already beginning to feel a huge distance from the world he had left behind. It was like switching movies in the middle – running away from a slow-moving, emotionally charged juncture in one to a racy investigation of an unlikely mystery in another.

The running away was proving to be hugely helpful and he decided he would stay on here for a while longer. Usha was quickly receding into the background, and Harish felt considerably less guilty about the pain he had caused his father. More importantly, he had started to feel that there was something here for him to do; something of his very own that he would want to unravel. What would this be? That was the question he would have to now discover for himself.

7

WHEN HARISH MET SEEMA

By the time Prasad was gone, the skeleton of what Harish had to do had been put together. He had to now work towards putting in the meat: distorted images, scavenged information, scraps from the Jarawa fringes.

Unknown to Harish, Prasad had spoken to David about him, and David was okay with Harish staying on. He had taken a liking to the young man too and he saw value in the work Harish now seemed excited to do.

In the days that followed, Harish settled smoothly into the rhythm of the Institute. He volunteered for regular housekeeping duties and struck up a good relationship with the staff there. He spent a lot of time sitting by the sea, particularly in the mornings, watching the motorized boats bring in their catch after a full night of fishing. Evenings were the time for long meandering walks through the countryside. Occasionally, he would visit the lone tea-shop at the junction and chat aimlessly with the set of other regulars over a glass of tea or a plate of hot samosas. He was slowly immersing himself in the ways of the islanders.

The rest of the time Harish spent, almost invariably, in the Institute library. He looked forward to detailed discussions with David when he had the time. They would discuss what Harish had read of the situation of the Jarawas, the issues at hand and the various ways of structuring his investigations and fieldwork. It was quite clear that the interaction happening on the fringes of the Jarawa territory – between the Jarawas and the thousands of settlers – was in a large measure unknown to the outside world; interactions that anthropologists were not looking at, changes that researchers were not researching and developments that the media – an odd Prasad notwithstanding – were not interested in probing.

The potential was huge. And importantly, the image of the Jarawa as the hostile killer contrasted starkly with the reality, which evidently, was far more complex.

Prasad had indicated the direction Harish should begin in. Not only could the Jarawas be understood through the eyes of the settlers, it would, in fact, be very interesting and important to comprehend these neighbours of the Jarawas themselves. This was a community of people that was constructing its own meaning just at it was trying to grasp and resolve what was happening around them. Comprehending and understanding their struggle could provide one of the critical keys to the mysteries surrounding the Jarawas.

Harish decided he would begin with the settlers living along the Jarawa forests. David helped him to get a sense of the geography: maps were used to broadly identify the boundary of the Jarawa reserve and locate the settler villages along this boundary. The Andaman Trunk Road made things rather simple. To the left of the road as one travelled north from Port Blair was the Jarawa Reserve, the territory demarcated and protected for them. Most of what lay on the other side was outside the reserve. The simplicity of the division hid an intriguing anomaly. Were the Jarawas aware of this boundary? Did they never use the forests on the right of the road? When had the division taken place? How?

In the weeks that followed, many other exciting opportunities also came Harish's way. A turtle biologist came visiting from Orissa, and David and Harish accompanied him to the west coast of Little Andaman and then to Galathea on the Great Nicobar Island in the

extreme south. Here, he was enthralled as he watched giant
leatherback and green sea turtles nest on the soft sands on dark
moonless nights. He then made one exciting trip with Uncle Pame
to the little, castaway island of South Sentinel, famous for large
populations of the giant robber crab. On his return, he boarded one
of the administration boats which took tourists around Barren
Island, the only active volcano here, that had recently started to
spew out smoke and vapour again. Everything was exceeding his
greatest expectations.

Harish wrote a small letter of thanks to Prasad, updating him
about what he was doing, and apprising him that no significant
developments were being reported related to the Jarawas.

He also wrote to his father, another small letter saying that he was
doing well, was in good spirits and inviting him to visit these 'beautiful
and captivating' islands as soon as was possible.

Back in Delhi, Prasad and Harish's cover story on the Jarawa had
been published, and had generated considerable interest all around.
Seema's professor immediately sent her a copy in Port Blair. Pleasantly
surprised to see her islands get such prominent media attention, she
was hoping this would bring the islands alive with discussions about
the changes taking place in the Jarawa universe. In a disappointing
anti-climax, this had not been the case at all.

The Jarawas were still a small, insignificant aspect of the islands. It
was early 2004, and the debate in the islands was already and almost
exclusively focused on national elections that were still a few months
away. It amazed her how these political discussions completely
absorbed and consumed the interest of her tiny islands, whose
contribution, ultimately, was just one member to the parliament.

Seema's initial days upon her return to Port Blair were spent setting things up and making the shift to the Institute, where she would now be spending a substantial amount of her time. There were three reasons that contributed to finally bringing her here. They wove themselves seamlessly into each other. One was the official reason, the other an existential one and the third the most personal.

Firstly, she needed books and research material, because Port Blair had turned up a complete blank. The State Library had been her best bet, but after Fatima had let go of charge, it had nothing substantial to offer. The second reason was an outcome of her homecoming. Seema's mother had initially reigned in her motherly instincts. Then she let them take over – the prospect of Seema's marriage became centrestage. Allusions to her age, the need to get married and to settle down were relentless, first addressed to her directly, then indirectly, then through hints, loud whispers and complaints that she was meant to hear. It was, Seema realized, a situation she could only deal with by getting away. In a small place like Port Blair, which was also home, this was going to be a tough thing to orchestrate. She was willing to sacrifice some of the freedom she had become accustomed to in Delhi, but the constant nagging about marriage, she simply could not bear. The Institute offered her a way out.

Seema had first come to the Institute after having unsuccessfully searched all of Port Blair for *Penal Settlement in Andamans*, noted historian R.C. Majumdar's seminal account of the islands, published in 1975. She was angry that Port Blair cared so little for itself; that it did not have space for a book as important as this. Finding the Institute, its library and the book she was searching for was a huge relief. She would have to come back.

Lodging was available here and this, she realized, was her only means of getting the best of both worlds. If she moved here, she could keep visiting home and at the same time save herself from her mother's constant nagging.

Convincing David was far easier than convincing her family. David Baskaran liked to act big brother to young, enthusiastic and even not-so-enthusiastic researchers working on various aspects of the islands. He realized she could add immense value to his set-up.

In the face of this easy approval, Seema's family also relented. She moved in eagerly and, like Harish, blended quickly and smoothly into the rhythms of the Institute.

The other significant passage that this move had helped Seema make was an intensely personal one. This was Amit Chouhan, a true blue Rajput who was completing his own doctoral work on the palaces and forts of the desert state of Rajasthan. He was the love she had been forced to leave behind in Delhi. She had been in touch with him over the phone since, but this had been erratic and left her dissatisfied. The phone connection at the Institute was even worse than the one at home, but here she had the possibility of receiving his calls and letters without any fear of nosy relatives. This was the first time they had spent so long apart, and she was missing him already. Amongst the first things she did on settling in at the Institute was to write him a short letter, imprinting her new address on it eagerly and pleading to hear from him.

Amit, unlike Seema, was not a great one for letters, but that hadn't stopped Seema from hoping. To her complete surprise then, his first letter arrived within just a few weeks of her move to the Institute.

It was always a thrill for her to hold a freshly received, unopened envelope with 'Seema Chandran' written on it; to wonder what might lie for her inside. She had been an active pen-paller in her school days, and had made many friends through the pen-pal corners that regularly appeared in magazines and newspapers. Over time, her letter-writing had reduced substantially, but living in the islands now, there was going to be no other option.

Amit was her first love and now here she was holding his first letter to her on the islands. Amit had, in this letter, recollected the memories of their first night together – of how he'd been intoxicated by her long tresses, the kisses on his lips, the first sight of her small breasts, the feel of her bare back, the tingling in his fingers as they sculpted her graceful curves, the feeling of his naked body entwined with hers . . .

In her room in the islands now, the memories of that first night of their lovemaking filled Seema's mind and senses with pleasure and desire. Amit had catalysed the blossoming of her passion in a way she did not know she was capable of. She missed him bitterly. The letter in her hand now only heightened her unease, throwing her into deeper desire and guilt-tinted turmoil. What was she doing here, so far from him? Even after he had argued with her in his gentle manner that she should not leave, that they would be too far apart, that he would miss her too much?

'You'll only value me more,' she had replied mischievously, 'I'll be back soon. I can't live without you either.'

This letter from Amit was the first of an unexpected stream. Another arrived two weeks later and then they kept arriving at regular two-week intervals; eight continuous letters – creating a regular rhythm of expectation, arrival and excitement that made Seema's days of research special. The monsoons had set in with their regular frenzy and there was little else that you could actively do outdoors, unless of course, you were a Gokul Mehta, the goldsmith from Mumbai. He had arrived in the islands for his annual rendezvous with the creepy crawlies and moved immediately to the Forest Department Camp on the uninhabited Interview Island.

In the weeks that passed, Seema befriended her co-inhabitants at the Institute. Her energetic, animated manner endeared her to those around her. The liveliness of her personality was tangible in the colourful kurtas she wore; their pinks, reds and blues were matched only by the flashy butterflies that flitted carefree about the Institute grounds, or the scarlet minivets and fairy bluebirds that flew in and out as part of regular mid-day hunting parties.

She had occasional chats with David when he had the time, and long conversations with Harish, who had all the time.

A bare-bodied Harish had been washing his clothes at the tap by the Institute entrance the day Seema arrived. He was alone here that morning; the two devout Christians – Uncle Pame and his nephew – were at church for their Sunday mass, Montu-the-cook was away in Kadamtala for a week and David was in Port Blair for a long planned city weekend.

No one was expected, and Harish wondered who it could be as he saw the taxi enter their lane and pull up a short distance away.

A young woman in a sunflower-yellow kurta alighted and walked straight towards him.

'Hi,' she called out to Harish, waving her hand. 'That's a strong flow of water from that tap! In Port Blair, we are lucky if we have it half as good.'

This very pretty woman, with her confidence and the show of familiarity, caught Harish completely off guard.

'Hi,' she said again as she stretched out her hand to Harish, who was still squatting by the tap. 'You must be Harish?'

He had no clue who she was. The puzzlement on his face was evident.

'David, told me you will be here. I'm Seema . . . you know, Seema Chandran.'

'Oh. Haan, Seema, yes, of course. Seema.' Harish was as flustered as he was embarrassed.

'Ya, just a moment. I'll just be back,' he said as he got up, feeling terribly naked. He scurried away to his room, grabbed the shirt by the door, put it on and rushed back.

'Seema. Yes, of course. Hi,' he tried to regain his composure. 'I'm Harish. But you were supposed to come . . .'

'Yes, yes,' Seema interrupted him, 'supposed to come tomorrow, but I had to run away from my mother. You see,' she said in a tone with mock urgency, 'she wants to get me married now. And if she meets you, I'd be done for. You are a good-looking guy!'

'What?'

'Ayyo, just joking, baba. I'm already hitched.'

Her friendliness was disarming, yet intimidating. With time, however, the initial awkwardness waned, helped in a large measure by Seema's own breeziness. She too liked his quiet, efficient manner, and their acquaintance soon grew into an easy and comfortable friendship.

The rains helped too, keeping them indoors and together. They discovered a number of relevant books, monographs, reports and documents from the Institute's exceptional archives, reading and gathering as much information and perspective as was possible.

Most often, Harish and Seema discussed in great detail the various aspects of what they had set out to do. There was one concern that tied their endeavours together in a very unlikely manner. 'The Local Borns,' Seema summarized Krishna Raj's words to Harish during one of their discussions, 'are being swamped by a tide from the outside that shows no sign of receding.'

Harish's reaction was instinctive and quick. 'If the Local Borns are being swamped,' he asked, 'what hope can be there for the Jarawas?'

'That's true,' Seema had responded thoughtfully, 'we are all being swamped by someone or the other, something or the other, all the time.'

In the meantime, Seema, and his regular letters had become the subject of playful banter at the Institute. Uncle Pame in particular enjoyed teasing this lovely young addition to their community. One evening, as the four of them – Uncle, Seema, David and Harish – sat in the quadrangle sipping tea, he brought out a photograph of his youthful days and placed it before Seema. 'Look at this,' he said, 'I may be old, but I'm surely as good as Amit. You know what they say – when in the islands, look for an islander,' he said flirtingly. 'Don't be far from your man for too long. Men these days, I can tell you . . .'

'No, Uncle,' Seema protested, raising her hand to her forehead, Bollywood style. 'My Amit is not like that.'

They all laughed, as they continued to heckle her.

8

MURDEROUS JARAWAS AGAIN

Island News
October 1, 2004

Murderous Jarawas at It Again

The Jarawas of Tirur appear to be getting bolder with every passing day. While earlier they attacked only villagers, this time, their target has been a policeman. Constable Pillai of Bush Police Camp Tirur No. 1 was killed in a most gruesome manner. His mutilated body was found early on Wednesday morning beside the path that connects the village settlement to the police camp.

Constable Pillai was on leave for three days and was supposed to join duty on the day his body was found. Mr Ram Krishna, who discovered the body early in the morning said, 'The sight of the body with the chopped off hands was a gruesome sight. It has not allowed me to sleep for the last two nights. The Jarawas are becoming a serious problem.'

The police were not willing to make any statement, but said that investigations were on to find out what happened, and that some concerted action will be taken soon. The villagers of Tirur have sent a representation to the Lt. Governor requesting that steps be taken to ensure their security and safety.

The monsoon had just about withdrawn, and the time had come for Harish to begin his fieldwork.

Tirur was a small village situated along the southernmost boundary of the Jarawa forests, created for the settlers who had come in from the mainland during the 1960s. Over the years, it had reported significantly intense levels of conflict and had been one of the prime target of Jarawa attacks.

There prevailed a general belief that the Tirur Jarawas were a different group; a band distinctly different from the one seen at Uttara Jetty a few weeks ago, and that the two groups did not really see eye to eye. More than a hundred kilometres of thick forests separated the two locations and the situation certainly lent itself to this possibility. This, however, was all conjecture. Everything about the Jarawa was conjecture.

Harish decided to let a few days pass before he went to Tirur; he did not want to parachute into what could be a volatile situation in the immediate aftermath of the policeman's killing. If the trip was made later, he felt, things would have settled down and more could be achieved.

The early morning bus to Tirur was all but empty. Harish sat by the window in the third row, deliberately choosing the seat behind an old man wearing a dirty, crumpled kurta. His white dhoti, tied in the typical Bengali fashion, was just as crushed and dirty. He seemed to be a regular and knew the conductor well; they exchanged pleasantries the moment he got on. Once the few passengers had been issued tickets and the bus had started off, the conductor went up to the old man and asked him for some tobacco.

'I forgot mine today,' the conductor remarked as the old man reluctantly pulled out two small packets from the pocket of his kurta and gave them to the conductor – one tobacco, the other lime. The old man's mouth was already stuffed with the mixture that the conductor was now rubbing in his left palm, with the thumb of his right. He popped it into his mouth, returned the two packets to the old man and took his place near the driver.

Harish hung over his seat a little, to talk to the old man. 'You are from Tirur?' he asked gently.

The huge rattle of the bus appeared to have drowned the question. He bent forward a little more and repeated his question, much louder this time, 'Are you from Tirur, dada?'

The old man turned to lean out of the window, spat out a whole load of tobacco that had blocked his tongue and turned to Harish. 'Yes, I am,' he said in a voice that betrayed irritation, 'What is your problem?'

He turned around, leant out the window again and cleared his mouth of the remaining tobacco. 'And you?' he turned back to speak to Harish. 'You've come for the Jarawas? Haven't you? You don't have anything better to do?' Many in the old man's upper row of teeth were missing. The others were all in an advanced state of decay, stained red and even black, evidence of many years of relentless tobacco chewing.

'Yes,' Harish replied, 'I read about what the Jarawas did to that policeman, I forget his name . . .'

'Pillai,' the old man offered, 'that harami. Good that . . .' he stopped mid-sentence, realizing suddenly that he was perhaps saying something that he should not. He cautiously surveyed the people around, hoping that nobody had heard him. Nobody had. The racket the bus was creating was so loud that even a person sitting next to the old man, if there was one, would barely have managed to decipher his words.

'Yes, Pillai died. Poor chap.' The old man changed tacks suddenly and conspicuously. 'And these Jarawas are becoming a big nuisance. Something has to be done about them. Life is becoming increasingly difficult. Cutting off Pillai's hands!' Harish strained his ears to get the words that were almost being drowned out in the rattle of the bus. 'Something like this has never happened before. See how bold they have become . . . First they would only raid our houses . . . and take things away . . . Sometimes they would also shoot with their arrows . . .'

'Shoot what?' Harish was losing the words. He got up and moved into the empty seat by the old man.

'Arrows, baba, arrows. The Jarawas don't have guns yet,' the old man responded sarcastically. 'There are many people in our village who have wounds from Jarawa arrows. But this?' He paused. 'They have never done anything like what they did to Pillai.'

'Then why Pillai?' Harish asked hesitantly. 'What happened in Pillai's case?'

'Why are you so interested in Pillai?' the old man snapped. 'Was he related to you?'

'What? What does this have to do with my family?' Harish spat back, now himself annoyed at the belligerence of the old man. 'Pillai was killed, wasn't he? I did not even remember his name. You were the one who told me. If you don't want to talk, don't talk, but why must you talk like this?'

'Okay, okay!' the old man patted Harish's knee. 'But I'll tell you only at home, not on the bus. Come home with me. Have a cup of tea first.'

Harish smiled. 'If you insist, dada. Sure, thank you.'

'It's okay,' the old man returned a sheepish, toothless grin.

The following fifteen-odd minutes passed without a word. The old man dozed off and Harish peered out at the rice fields and the occasional house that went flying past. The road got progressively bad, the jerks jerkier and the speed of the bus, correspondingly slower.

A small yellow kilometre stone saying 'Tirur – 1 km' went past and soon the bus reached the very end of the road they were driving on. No more tarmac. No more road even, just the forest rising in front of them like a massive wall. It was a dead end; here, the bus would turn around and leave for Port Blair in about twenty minutes.

Harish was intrigued. A thin but clear line divided the two worlds. The land to the left sloped gently down into a huge, shallow depression that was all lush paddy fields. It was like a huge saucer that had been rimmed off towards the right by a tall and impenetrable evergreen forest. A narrow path went right alongside this edge, first down, skirting the fields and then climbing straight up a small hillock that lay at the very edge of the clearing. Here was a reasonably large wooden structure, almost embedded inside the forest, trying to straddle two worlds, and appearing to fit into neither. The building and its location gave it a brooding, even ominous look.

'That,' the old man said, noticing what Harish was gazing at, 'is the Tirur Bush Police Camp No. 1. And that,' he continued, now pointing to the bamboo mud and thatch hut that was closest to where they stood, 'is the house of Ram Krishna.' Harish noticed that all the houses seemed huddled together to the extreme left, trying deliberately as it were, to locate themselves as far away from the tree line as was possible. Ram Krishna's, however, was at the other end, away from the rest, set out as if the village had cast it aside.

The scene otherwise, was typically that of an early morning Indian countryside. Ram Krishna's house emitted white and grey smoke from the fire of the morning's cooking. Two young boys were playing in the courtyard and a couple of cows loitered outside it. A young woman, her head covered with the pallu of her sari, purposefully swept the courtyard, sending up huge whiffs of dust in rhythmic, anti-clockwise arcs.

Somebody inside the house was trying to tune the radio, which went abruptly from what sounded like a Tamil news broadcast to a Hindi film song and then to a Coca Cola jingle. The female voice of a news-reader crackled through: 'This is All India Radio . . .' Before she could say anything further however, she was silenced by the tuner who was still unsure of what he wanted to hear.

The radio had only existed on the periphery of Harish's existence till he had arrived in the islands, but here nothing happened without it – shipping schedules, the weather forecast, music for entertainment, or news from around the world – there was nothing more reliable or accessible than the radio. It was a constant accompaniment to life here.

'You come with me,' the old man said to Harish as he started to walk. 'Have a cup of tea and I'll take you to Ram Krishna's house after that.' The tuner returned to the newsreader: 'The political crisis in Tamil Nadu has deepened with the Chief Minister . . .'

'Ram Krishna, I have a guest for you,' the old man shouted over the crackling airwaves, as he walked past the earthen courtyard wall. 'Taking him for tea. Will bring him here in about half an hour.' The airwaves suddenly went silent again, and a young boy of about twelve came running out. 'Hey Puklu,' the old man did not stop walking, 'time to go to school?'

His house was pretty much like Ram Krishna's: one in a cluster of five, a mud-and-bamboo structure that stood on relatively higher ground amidst the swaying paddy. From the courtyard they stood in, the house looked big and airy, though sparse. It had been built with the bare minimum. The walls had been plastered recently and the faint smell of cow dung and wet mud still hung in the air.

Now that he was home, the old man was visibly more relaxed. 'Sit. See,' he started off, as he rolled out a chatai in the courtyard. 'I came here in 1969, from what later became Bangladesh. Just my wife and me. We cleared these forests with our own hands, created the fields, directed the water channels and started cultivating paddy,' he said pointing to the fields beyond. 'It was a tough life . . . Minuuu,' he called out suddenly and loudly, 'Minuuu, make two cups of tea. Quickly.'

'Haan! What was I saying?' he turned towards Harish, 'Yes, did the government not know then that there were Jarawas here? Now, if the Jarawas were already living here, why did they give us this piece of land? If someone comes into my fields and starts cultivating, will I not fight back? Look,' he said, pointing to the wall of trees in the distance, 'the Jarawas are like the shadows in the forest. These gently swaying fields here,' he said, now pointing in the other direction, 'were all forests earlier – tall, thick and dark. The Jarawas don't farm. They hunt and collect honey. So . . . when their forest was cut down they must have been very unhappy. In the early days, they would attack us with bows and arrows. Once, two people were also killed. We protested. We told the tehsildar that we cannot live here, that all of us, about fifteen families would move to Port Blair till a solution was found. You give us some protection, or how do we survive?'

He turned around and shouted to Minu again, 'Minuuu, you're making tea, no? Quickly, Beti!'

'That is when Tirur No. 1 – that Bush Police camp was set up there. You saw the building on the hillock? That one. Three policemen with guns were posted there in those days. But do you think they could really have done anything in these dark forests, which were even thicker then? You could never see where the Jarawas were; you could never tell when they would appear and from where.'

'We started keeping dogs to warn us when the Jarawa came. The dogs turned out to be better than these bloody policemen. Even they needed to keep dogs. It was around this time that the police also started to practise blank firing. They would fire three times every night to scare away the Jarawas. One shot at dusk, one again just before midnight and the third at around three in the morning. I think these shots worked well and the Jarawa attacks declined substantially. But mind you, they did not stop. Every night we would worry. Even today we worry; when the Jarawas will come charging upon us, from where, how? You can never be sure about these Jarawas. You never know . . .'

'But Pillai . . .?' Harish took the opportunity of the small pause in the old man's excited monologue.

'Yes,' the old man was not agitated anymore, like he had been in the bus, but his tone still went a little hushed. 'Pillai was a harami. Actually all the policemen these days are . . .' his voice trailed off as a short, stout lady, chewing vigorously, came bustling into the courtyard.

'There you are!' her paan-stained words exploded on the old man. 'Where were you last night? Sleeping on the road again? How many times have I told you to stop drinking? But it's like pouring water over a buffalo's body. And who is this?'

'This is . . .' the old man faltered.

'Harish,' Harish answered for him.

'And you are here,' the lady leant over the courtyard wall and spat out the paan that filled her mouth, 'I presume, because of the Jarawas? You have nothing better to do? They are a headache anyway, and this old man,' she turned again to the old man, 'keeps bringing strangers home every other day. Have you offered him some tea at least?'

'Yes,' replied the old man, 'I've asked Minu. The tea must just be coming.'

'The tea must just be coming,' she screwed her face and repeated sarcastically after him. 'Will it drop from the sky? Have you told Minu? When? Minu is at Lakshmi's. She's on her way, following me. This old man is useless,' she murmured to herself, as she walked in. 'I'm making the tea now,' she screamed from inside. 'Don't let him go.'

The old man looked shaken, as if a sudden powerful gust had hit him from nowhere. 'My wife,' he said sheepishly. 'She's a little hot-headed, but . . .' he didn't really know what to say, 'but she makes very good tea.'

'Bring some biscuits also,' he called out aloud, more to reset the balance than out of actual need.

'You know where Pillai was when he was killed?' the old man returned to the subject of their earlier conversation.

'The news report said that he was on leave for three days and was to join duty the day his body was found,' Harish replied.

'Yes,' the old man lowered his voice again, 'And what was he doing those three days? See, nobody will ever tell you this – Pillai had gone hunting deep inside the forests with two other policemen.'

'How do you know?' Harish asked, surprised.

'How do I know? Arre! See, all these policemen, what do you

think they do with their guns and bullets? Their favourite pastime is to go into the forests hunting for wild pig and deer. And how do I know this? I am an old man now, but there was a time when I too went hunting into the forests with these policemen, even with Pillai.'

Just then a young girl in green salwar kameez and long hair came in. She stopped the moment she saw the two men and then quickly ran inside.

'Minu, my granddaughter,' the old man said affectionately, staring after her for a moment. 'We may not remember, but the Jarawa never forget. Most of the other policemen would go to the forests, hunt deer or wild pig and return. Pillai had other interests too. At least thrice, we heard that he had destroyed some Jarawa huts. He enjoyed doing it and would often boast about this to others. Many months ago, we heard that he had cornered a Jarawa woman in one of their camps after firing in the air and scaring away the others. Can you believe this?' The old man turned his head and spat out in disgust, 'He forced himself on the woman and came back boasting of his manliness. Is it not strange that only Pillai was treated in this manner the other day and nothing was done to the others who had gone with him? See, the Jarawa never forget,' he repeated. 'How they got Pillai I don't know, nobody knows, nobody will know, but they got him somehow and that is what matters. There was no arrow mark on his body either. They killed him brutally. It was difficult to see the body, with the hands cut off at the shoulder. They left the body on the outskirts of the village along with his gun. Look,' his tone changed now and so did the body language, 'we might never become friends with the Jarawas, but I am sure we need not be enemies. Yes, we took their lands, but if we don't disturb them, they'll accept what has happened. It is these bloody policemen. They have the guns to protect us from the junglees, but they are busy creating more trouble for us.'

Minu came out rather shyly this time, a small tray in her hand bearing two glasses of tea and a plate of glucose biscuits.

'Harish babu,' the old man introduced the visitor to his granddaughter. 'Namaste bolo.'

The girl said her namaste, placed the tray on the floor and quickly disappeared inside. The two men sat quietly for a while, munching thoughtfully on the biscuits as they sipped their tea.

The old man had an idea. 'Try and meet the policemen at the Bush Police camp,' he said. 'See what they have to say.'

Tea and biscuits over, Harish took the old man's permission and stepped into the house. He peeped into the kitchen and saw the old lady by the fireplace, combing Minu's hair. Here was the quiet of life on the fringes, between the jungle and civilization that was at the heart of what Harish was trying to understand. Maybe I'd like to live here for a bit, he thought to himself, as he thanked the couple and set out to the police camp, located at the edge of the forest.

The old man's logic seemed plausible, but how much could he be trusted? While the newspaper report that had brought him to Tirur unambiguously held the Jarawa responsible for Pillai's death, the onus had now been shifted entirely to the opposite camp.

The situation in Tirur clearly stood out in stark contrast with what he had seen at Uttara. To Harish, it seemed a direct and obvious reflection of the location of the particular interface. Fewer settlers, no road, no traffic, thick forests. Here in Tirur, the balance seemed as much in favour of the Jarawa as it seemed against them in the interactions at Uttara. The Jarawa version of the story was never going to be known, but surely there was something that he could begin to infer?

'Oy, where are you going?' a rough, loud voice broke into the conversation Harish was having with himself just as he reached the foot of the small hillock. He stopped and looked up ahead. Standing about a hundred feet from him was a bare-bodied policeman in khaki pants, with a balding head and huge handlebar moustache made famous by South India's well-known forest brigand, Veerappan. 'Stand where you are. What do you want?' he asked gruffly.

'I am a researcher,' Harish gave a subdued, intimidated response. 'I wanted to know what happened to Pillai . . .' The instant Harish uttered the man's name he knew he had done himself in.

'That's none of your business,' the policeman barked. 'Who sent you here?'

Harish was scared. Perspiration broke out on his forehead. He tried to compose himself. 'No . . . No one,' he blurted. 'I am researching the forests of the Andamans and have come here for a small survey.' The policeman was not willing to believe him. 'Then why did you ask for Pillai?'

'Forget Pillai,' Harish regained partial composure. 'Can you give me some water?' he tried to undo the damage, starting to walk towards the police camp.

'Stop where you are,' the policeman shouted. 'If you want water, go to that house over there. Don't bother us. We've enough to deal with anyway.'

'See,' Harish said firmly, 'I'm only looking for water to drink. You don't have water in your camp?'

'Don't act smart,' the policeman was beginning to bristle. Hearing the raised voices, meanwhile, a couple of his colleagues emerged from the building.

One of them, wearing a lungi, walked over. 'What do you want?' he asked Harish in a calm, measured tone. 'When he is telling you to turn back, why don't you listen? You can't come up here.'

'I am only asking for water,' Harish was not willing to let up. 'You don't have water in your camp?'

'You can't come up here,' the man in the lungi repeated sternly. 'Get back, or . . .'

'Or . . . or what? Are you threatening me?' Harish felt a rage building.

'Stop arguing,' the first policeman had raised his gun and was pointing it straight at Harish. 'Turn back before I lose my head.'

'You're going to shoot me, are you? What are you scared of?' now

Harish barked, staring straight at them. 'What are you are trying to hide? You've hunted wild pigs in the forest? Have you?' he asked with vehemence. The look on the faces of policemen turned even more menacing, but Harish did not stop. 'I am behaving decently with you and you show me a gun? Am I a villager from Tirur to feel scared of you? I am not. You think you can behave as you want? Is this your property? You just wait and watch,' he turned around and walked purposefully back, bristling, but also pleased with himself for this parting flourish.

As he headed back, he saw that a small crowd had collected by the house of Ram Krishna. They all stood looking in his direction even as he walked briskly towards them. Now, as he neared Ram Krishna's house, he slowed down, conscious of the ruckus he had created, not knowing what to expect next. He was relieved to see that he knew at least one person in that small gathering – the old man he had just had tea with. The two women in the group quickly disappeared into the house as Harish approached, leaving three other men.

The old man introduced Ram Krishna to Harish.

Clad in a soiled dhoti with a gamcha thrown carelessly across his left shoulder, Ram Krishna brought his hands together. 'Namaste,' he said with a faint smile on his face. About six feet tall, with strong shoulders and muscular arms, Ram Krishna looked very much a man of the soil. Harish guessed he must be in his mid-forties.

'Namaste,' Harish replied. 'What is wrong with these guys? Do they always behave like this?' he asked, turning around, half expecting the moustache-bearing policeman to be standing where he was, still pointing the barrel of his gun at him. He was doing exactly that, and Harish quickly turned back as Ram Krishna started to speak.

'These policemen!' he exclaimed with resignation, 'They behave as if they are kings. You know why they didn't allow you to get closer? They must be in the process,' he said matter-of-factly, 'of cutting up the three wild boars they hunted last night.'

The shock on Harish's face was evident. Accusing the policemen of hunting wild pigs had been solely a means of provoking them. He had not known that his arrow had hit bull's eye.

'This is all they do,' Ram Krishna continued, responding to Harish's shocked response. 'It is an open secret. I know because Ramlal was out with them last night.'

'Ramlal?' Harish queried.

'Ramlal. Oh!' Ram Krishna placed his arm on the shoulder of the man standing next to him, 'My younger brother.' Harish exchanged greetings with the man.

'See,' the older brother continued, 'Pillai was the only policeman here who knew the forests well. All the other chaps are rather new to Tirur. That fellow with the big moustache, the one pointing the gun, he is the biggest coward of the lot. He never steps out without his weapon.'

'But why do you go hunting?' Harish turned to Ramlal. 'Is it not dangerous? You could get into trouble.'

Ramlal smiled a faint guilty smile. 'If you go with the policemen, what trouble? The only real fear is from the Jarawa, but then the only people in danger are those like Pillai.'

'Why? Why Pillai?'

'When I go into the forests,' Ramlal responded as if he already knew the question, 'it is only for deer and wild boar. I have never gone anywhere close to a Jarawa settlement. Pillai was different. The Jarawa never forget – they got Pillai at the first opportunity that came their way.'

'Did I not tell you?' the old man who was standing quietly till now, butted in. 'I think Pillai got what he deserved.'

'But what about all those news reports then, of the killings and the brutality of the Jarawa?' Harish now directed his question specifically to Ram Krishna.

The response was a spontaneous one. 'The Jarawas didn't publish that newspaper, did they? Who asks them anyway?'

9

THE LAST HOPE

A contemplative Harish met an uncharacteristically subdued, even brooding, Seema when he got back to the Institute late in the afternoon. He had thought she would be keenly interested in his first-hand version of the Tirur story. Seema, however, was immersed in an Amit-provoked despondency. When Harish returned, he walked into an 'Uncle-cajoling-Seema' session, which seemed to have been going on for a while.

The continuous flow of Amit's letters over the many weeks had left Seema yearning for more; now she was disturbed and upset that none had come for a long time. Maybe, she had thought at first, it's on the way, maybe stuck somewhere in the post, maybe Amit was late by a few days. Five weeks of keen waiting had, however, yielded nothing, and Seema was left feeling dejected, concerned and indignant, all at the same time.

She knew she was being silly, and had tried hard to act normal until she finally lost control; it was a sulking, softly sobbing Seema that Uncle was trying to console.

Uncle was finally playing the role of, well, an uncle. 'Come on Seema,' he said gently, as Harish came and joined them in the quadrangle, 'don't be so upset.' He turned to Harish, 'Tell me Harish, is there any reason for Seema to feel so dejected?'

He turned back to Seema, who was staring at the floor. 'He's not left you and gone, has he? It's only a letter. It must be on its way. How do you know it's not stuck in the post somewhere? And,' he continued, 'you've been lucky. In the last four months you have received . . . how many letters? Four? Six?'

'Eight,' Seema answered softly, guiltily, with sheepishness that did not escape Uncle's sharp eyes.

'Eight!' he threw his hands up in exaggerated protest.

'Eight letters in four months and you are still complaining. Look at me.' Seema lifted her gaze. 'I mean, I've been married for thirty-five years and I have not received these many letters in all these years put together. Not that I miss that old lady too much these days,' he winked and then murmured good-naturedly under his breath, 'I'm sure she's found some other old man.'

The old man's uncharacteristic banter brought a reluctant smile to Seema's lips. 'Women are not like that uncle,' she finally spoke. 'And' she paused for effect, now mocking Uncle, 'I wonder what Aunty actually finds attractive in an old man like you. What do you think?' She turned and smiled at Harish.

'Sure, we must find out,' he said absent-mindedly, his mind still buzzing with all that had happened earlier in the day in Tirur.

This was going to be a day of unexpected developments. Now David returned from town, looking uncharacteristically combative and also triumphant. 'Got it!' he exclaimed, banging a file of papers on the table as he joined them.

These were the permissions for the crocodile survey he had wanted to conduct along the western coast of the South and Middle Andaman Islands – the Jarawa coast as he called it. This was the sixth year of his crocodile surveys of the islands and though he had never been to these parts, he was convinced that some of the most undisturbed habitats in these islands survived here; that the best and most healthy populations of the crocodile were to be found only in the creeks along this Jarawa coast.

The survey trip had been planned for a long time and even the generally patient David had grown restless. His file had been stuck on the table of some middle level officer with a reputation for wanting to make a quick buck on the side. It was David's policy not to bypass the hierarchy of the organization and the process of the system that needed to be followed. So, he had waited for at least two months more than was usually necessary. He had tried hard to argue sense into the officer's head, but this had led nowhere. David had finally decided to confront the guy.

'No more buts sir,' David had declared. 'I have been on these islands for nearly a decade now. My paperwork has always been in place and I have never ever had this problem before. You are harassing the wrong person. I,' he said, finally pulling out the card he didn't really want to use, 'have known director, Tribal Welfare, Mr Chaturvedi, for four years, and he does not yet know of the trouble I am having. If my file does not move from your table by this evening . . .' he paused, menace in his tone, 'believe me, you've had it.' Turning around, he walked out, not waiting to see the expression on the officer's face, leave alone allowing him to explain.

The file had indeed moved that very evening, was in Chaturvedi's office the day after and back in David's hand with the permits granted the very next day. All in three quick days.

Thanks to these weeks of delay, however, Harish and Seema were now both free to join David. He had already assumed that Harish would accompany him, and readily agreed when Seema asked if she could go along too.

David outlined the plan. They were to travel north as far as Interview Island in the Institute's country-made boat, sail past Interview and reach Mayabundar through Austin Strait in a journey that would need about seven to ten days.

'We are going to be literally and completely at sea,' David said, 'and the boat will be home for the entire period. We should be ready to leave in about a week.'

The whole thing sounded exciting to Seema, but doubts were also clearly evident on her face.

'Yes, Seema. Boat will be home. Don't worry. You'll manage. We do it all the time. It'll be fun.'

'Oh sure!' Seema smiled, still doubtful. 'Of course. I'm looking forward to it.'

Harish did not really fancy crocodiles, leave alone going looking for them. What excited him was the fact that the next few days would be spent entirely along the western fringe of the Jarawa Reserve. While the road was the artificial eastern boundary of Jarawa territory, this was the one that nature had created. It was along this coast, he presumed, that the Jarawa lived their life the way they wanted to – without interference from the outside world.

'By the way,' Seema asked, a little tentatively, 'what is a crocodile survey like?'

There was a glint in David's eyes, 'Ah! You'll soon see. I need to test ride our inflatable and the OBM before we take it on our long survey trip. Narrow creeks obviously cannot be negotiated by our big dungi,' he explained. 'Uncle, can we do a run now?'

'Yes David, no problem.'

'And what's an OBM?' Harish asked.

'Oh! Better get used to these terms. It's the outboard motor – the OBM drives the inflatable,' David's chatter grew animated. 'Get ready, men and women. We're going for a spin now.'

David's exultation over the permits and his child-like enthusiasm for the survey were infectious. After a round of tea and an hour's preparation, Uncle and his nephew Popha led David, Harish and Seema through the mangrove forest to the inflatable.

All of them, except Popha, climbed in and the inflatable zoomed towards the creek, just a short distance away on the other side of the bay.

The creek was alive, in a lustrous, waxy green typical of mangrove forests. It was wide and the gentle breeze created small ripples on the clear blue of the reflected sky. Uncle turned the accelerator, and the inflatable was almost flying across the still surface of the creek waters. A short distance in, the creek branched into two. David indicated that Uncle take the left arm, and Seema could see an arc of water being created behind them as Uncle curved the boat into the channel at high speed. The inflatable banked considerably, and then settled down as the stretch straightened out.

David sat in front, at the apex of the inflatable's V. He pulled down his baseball cap to keep it from flying away. He crouched a little, and closely inspected the banks of the creek as they flew past. Harish sat just behind, marvelling at the greenness of the mangroves, looking at David every once in a while and wondering how he would see a crocodile if they kept moving at such speed.

A snow-coloured egret took off from the other bank, disturbed by the creature cutting through the water at a significant clip. A small kingfisher was next: the translucent blue of its back flashed sharply as it rose from the branch it was sitting on and took off in the opposite direction.

Harish turned around to look at it, and his eyes were drawn to Seema who was sitting beside Uncle at the rear. She had untied her dark, lustrous hair so it streamed behind her. Her eyes were closed and her face lifted up to the air, exhilaration lighting up her entire aspect.

A fine spray came streaming up as Uncle went even faster. It hit Harish's face, then Seema's. She opened her eyes, saw Harish looking at her and smiled. He smiled embarrassedly, self-consciously and turned his eyes to what Uncle was doing.

Uncle was sitting to the left with the rudder and accelerator in his right hand. His wrist turned slowly, and Harish could feel the boat slowing down a bit. He turned to David, who was still looking ahead but now moving his right hand in a slow but deliberate clockwise motion. The inflatable slowed down further, turned an angle of 180 degrees and headed back in the direction they had just come from. All this time David had not looked behind at Uncle even once – a finely tuned sign language had been working perfectly between the two.

When David finally turned to Uncle, the two of them exchanged a quick, short smile. They were obviously enjoying themselves.

David then turned to the other two with a mischievous smile. 'So . . .' he queried with a nod of his head, 'Crocodile surveys are fun and fast, aren't they?' Then he murmured to no one in particular: 'The inflatable's working fine. We'll come back tonight.'

'Tonight?' Seema and Harish blurted out in unison.

'But David,' Seema queried suspiciously, 'what kind of a survey will you carry out in the night? What will you get to see?'

'You'll find out.' David had no intention of revealing much, 'Unless you are scared and . . .'

'No, no.' Seema didn't allow David to continue. She had no clue of what was in store for the night, but neither was she going to let such an intriguing opportunity slip by.

A little after dinner that night, the four set out again. They walked through the mangrove forest in a single file, led by Uncle. David brought up the rear, flashing his torch occasionally to indicate the way in the dark. Not that Uncle really needed direction. This was for him a well-trodden path and even in the darkness he knew intuitively where to put his foot next.

The inflatable had been pulled on shore and was tied to the trunk of a mangrove tree. The four dragged it a small distance into the shallow water. David climbed in first, followed by Harish, then Seema and finally Uncle.

Uncle started the OBM, revved it up and took off, with David shouting 'jabo' like a battle-cry. This was the Karen word for 'let's go', something Harish and Seema would hear many times in the days to come.

For David, these night time boat-runs in the creeks were the highlight of his work. He was addicted to the adrenalin this brought, just as he was mesmerized every time he saw the glowing coals of a pair of crocodile eyes. This was a majestic animal, the undisputed monarch of the mangrove creeks, which had survived everything that evolution had thrown at it. A crocodile gliding smoothly, stealthily through inter-tidal waters was the tiger softly, silently stalking deer on a leaf-littered forest floor, was the majestic griffon soaring unbounded in the blue heavens. The crocodile evoked in David an emotion he could only explain as primordial. 'It does something to me, I can't explain,' he'd say every time he was asked 'Why crocs?'

For David, the real star of the show was the female crocodile, the first of whom he had encountered in his second year in the islands. They'd been monitoring a crocodile nest in the very creek they were surveying that night. It had been a relentless monsoon and they had seen many crocodile nests that season. There was one female they were following particularly closely as she put together a mound of leaf, soil and detritus for her nest and laid her eggs. They'd even been aggressively attacked by her on a couple of occasions, following which they constructed a small machan from which to continue the observations.

One afternoon, about three months after the eggs had been laid, David thought he heard squeaks from the direction of the crocodile nest. Slowly they got louder and more numerous – the eggs were hatching; the little ones would be out soon.

He could only marvel at the tenderness and sensitivity with which that huge animal was dealing with her little ones. She scrambled up to the nest and started to excavate it. The hatchlings started to emerge slowly. David could even see the mother croc gently rolling some of the eggs in her mouth to assist the hatching. As the foot-long hatchlings scurried about, their nine-footer of a mother gingerly picked them up in her mighty jaws and ferried them to the water's edge.

These were the same jaws that had created havoc in the nesting season the following monsoon. Robert Minj from the neighbouring Ranchi Basti and Ram Charan, who had just come to the islands from the mainland, were attacked and killed with one snap of her powerful jaws. The mother crocodile was only protecting her nest and her eggs. But this was too big a crime. There was a huge hue and cry over the man-eating crocodile and the forest department had been forced to send in someone to shoot down the animal.

That was a watershed year. A large group of migrants from mainland India had been allotted the forestland beside these creeks for their houses and for agriculture. Slowly, this wave of humans and their settlements had penetrated deeper and deeper, trashing the forests as David often said, and destroying prime croc habitat. Conflict was inevitable and the eventual loser evident. Many were killed legally by the forest department gun, or illegally by the noose and machete of the recent settlers. This became a pattern in all the areas right up to the Jarawa Reserve, and David could see the impact almost immediately. Creeks where they counted tens of large crocs every survey now showed up essentially empty. An odd one would be spotted once in a few days, but it was never even half the size of the mother croc David had taken a personal liking to. The Jarawa Reserve was indeed the last hope.

10

AN UNLIKELY STORM

Back in her room after their night survey, Seema decided that she would wait no longer for Amit's letter and try to somehow speak to him. She requested Harish's help, and the two drove into town on the Institute motorcycle a little after lunch the following day.

Harish dropped Seema at Satguru's Telephone Booth and suggested they meet in an hour's time at Island Sweets on the opposite side of the road. He would go and buy a few things he needed while Seema spoke to Amit.

Getting through was not very easy, and when she finally managed after about ten minutes of trying, it was Rajesh who answered her call. Rajesh and Amit were colleagues and close friends. They had been sharing a house for many years, and Rajesh had become a good friend of Seema's as well.

'Amit's out. He'll be back in half-an-hour,' was all he said. Seema was speaking to him after a rather long time, but there was no friendly banter. 'Can you call then?' he asked, disconnecting the phone without waiting for a response.

'That's strange,' Seema thought as she walked to the post office, just down the road. She bought some envelopes and some stamps and posted her latest letter to Amit. She sipped a glass of tea at the junction and then ducked into the small bookstore nearby, flipping through its small selection of magazines and buying a couple of the latest ones.

She strolled back to Satguru's, and this time the call went through immediately. Amit's hello across the line melted inside her like delicious ice cream.

'Hi! Love, how are you?' she exclaimed, loud in her enthusiasm. 'Hi Amit,' she lowered her voice, noticing the strange stares directed at her. She was finding it hard to contain her excitement. 'I miss you. Why have you stopped writing to me? I've been waiting for your letters. Did you get mine? I've sent you three long ones in the last week.' Everything came flying out like birds finally released from a small cramped cage. 'I'm really missing you. How are you? What have you been doing?'

She stopped and waited. A long pause was all she got in response. Long. Silent. Disconcerting.

'What happened?' It fell upon Seema to break the silence. 'You're not going to say anything?'

'No, nothing,' a tired, disinterested answer came through finally.

'What's the matter Amit? Is something wrong?'

'No, not really . . . I'm a little tired. I've been quite busy the last few days.'

Pause. Then reluctantly again, 'Something very important . . .' There was another long pause.

There was something to Amit's voice and tone that was not right. It made Seema very uncomfortable. He had never sounded like this before.

'Why? What happened? Is everything okay? You've not written to me for so many days. I desperately wait for your letters, Amit!'

'Yes. No . . . did you not get my letter? I sent one, a week . . . no, fifteen days ago.'

'You're not telling me something, Amit.'

'Seema, a lot has been happening. I've written to you . . .' his voice trailed off. 'In fact,' he resumed as if he had suddenly remembered something important, 'it's an important letter. Yes, I sent it about ten days ago.'

'Amit, what's the matter?' There was desperation in Seema's voice. 'What's in the letter?' she asked, pleading.

'No. Nothing Seema. You'll receive the letter. You'll know then . . . I must go. I have something important to finish now.'

He disconnected abruptly.

Seema felt numb. She dialled the number again, and he answered immediately.

'Amit, Seema again. Is everything okay, Amit?' she asked softly. 'Are you hiding something from me?'

'Let's not talk now Seema, I'm a little caught up. You'll get my letter, okay? Bye.'

He disconnected without waiting, and Seema didn't have the heart to try again.

She stood against the wall of the small cubicle, staring aimlessly at the small fan whirring at her from above. A tap on the cubicle door sounded so loud, it seemed to knock at her head itself. She replaced the handset, pushed open the door and walked out.

'Madam, madam,' a young boy came running after her, 'Paisa, paisa.'

She regained her senses and paid the owner, who was staring at her with disapproval.

Seema now walked across to Island Sweets and sank into the plastic chair placed by the entrance. She gulped down a glass of water, then another, trying hard to sort things out in her head, even as she ordered a glass of tea. Why was Amit behaving like this? Why did he not want to talk to her? Even Rajesh sounded so strange today. And that letter that should be reaching her soon . . .? For a moment she wondered if she really wanted the letter, any letter from Amit. What was it that she felt so scared of? Was she over-reacting? Maybe she had caught him at a very bad time. He sounded preoccupied. Perhaps he was worried about something. Maybe the matter was of no relevance to her and he didn't want to cause her any worry.

But she was worried. He sounded so different. Why did he not want to talk to her? What is there in that letter? The circle of questions and concerns began all over again. She felt lost and completely unanchored.

When Harish arrived, Seema didn't register him. It was only when another glass of tea was placed on the table before her that she looked up. Hers was still full and now cold.

'Oh,' she said, surprised to see Harish staring at her. 'When did you come?' she asked, a little embarrassed. 'Oh, your tea has also come.'

'What's the matter, Seema? You're looking like a ghost.'

'Nothing . . . nothing is the matter,' she tried to pretend.

'Did you speak to Amit? Is everything okay?' Harish asked gently.

'Yes. Yes . . .' she stammered. 'I spoke to Amit. Everything is fine . . .' She buried her face in her hands, trying to hide the tears that were welling up in her eyes. 'Everything is not okay, Harish. I don't know,' she began to sob. 'I'm scared, Harish. Amit sounded like a stranger. He didn't want to speak to me. I don't want to receive his letter.'

'What letter, Seema? Did he say something?'

'Harish, I don't want to receive his letter. I'm scared, Harish.'

This was beyond Harish. He had not known Seema for too long. He knew little about her personal life, even less, actually nothing, about Amit. He felt bad seeing her so troubled, but he realized there was little he could do.

They sat in silence for a while, until a small boy came along to clear away the glasses. 'Let's leave, Seema,' Harish said at last.

Halfway back to the Institute, the sky changed unexpectedly. A grey curtain of thick clouds blocked out the sparkling blue of the afternoon and a sharp spell of rain came thundering down. The two had to take shelter for more than an hour under the awning of a roadside shop, and even when they decided to finally leave, the rain gods hadn't given up fully. The clouds helped dusk roll in faster, and

Harish drove slowly and carefully back in the soft drizzle that bathed them gently.

They went straight to their respective rooms, deciding to meet up for dinner half an hour later. Chapattis and potato sabzi were already on the table, and hot rice and dal were just being brought in as David walked in with a couple of newspapers and a bunch of letters that had arrived earlier in the day. Harish spotted one for Seema that was from Amit and deliberately slipped it to the bottom of the pile. He then turned his attention to the newspaper, and had just turned it around to the sports page, when Uncle and Seema joined them at the table.

'Hello,' said Uncle, in his accustomed drone. Harish hoped he would not remember, but how could he not? 'So did you speak to Amit? What does your man have to say?'

'Yes, I did,' Seema responded, 'He didn't say much today. I'm hungry . . .'

There was an awkward silence for a while as the four served themselves. Seema got herself some rice and then poured some dal. 'Anyone for pickle?' she asked as she stood up to get the bottle from the small cupboard in the corner.

'Oh, there's today's mail,' Seema said, seeing the pile of letters lying on the table. 'Uncle, please pass me the bundle.'

'Why,' Uncle said teasingly, 'Are you going to get Amit's letter today?'

'Just give it, Uncle,' Harish snapped.

Uncle handed it over, taken aback at Harish's uncharacteristic terseness.

'Oh. There it is.' Seema sighed as she put her spoon down and gently caressed the envelope before tearing it open and pulling out the sheet of paper.

Harish was gripped by a great sense of worry. He tried to look disinterested, but failed. He looked at Seema furtively.

Seema unfolded the paper, and placed it by her plate. She picked up another spoonful of rice and put it in her mouth as she started reading.

> *Dear Seema,*
> *Do you remember what I had told you about Shalaka?*
> *Seema, Shalaka has come back into my life . . .*

Seema felt a violent fissure inside her. Even as Harish watched, her eyes grew wide in obvious shock. She stopped chewing, her mouth still. She sat motionless, staring at the piece of paper before her. Then the bubble popped, the emotion disappearing from her face like a drop of water touched by the flame of a flickering candle. Even as she sat there, she crumpled – crushed under the weight of the letter in front of her.

The other two men at the table finally gathered something was drastically wrong.

'Seema. Seema!' Uncle called out.

She closed her mouth and picked up her spoon, as if to begin to eat again.

'Seema,' Uncle called again, 'What's the matter? Are you okay?'

She hadn't heard.

'Sorry . . .' she blurted out, still staring at the letter, which she finally picked up and clutched to her side. 'But I must go.' She got up and ran back to her room.

Here, she continued with the rest of it.

> *Shalaka says going away was a big mistake. She says she wants*
> *to come back. She says she still loves me and wants to marry me.*
> *I had thought I had moved on, that I had grown, that there*
> *was nothing that I felt for her anymore. I have spent the last*
> *week with her, and nothing seems to have changed. It is fresh*
> *like the first time I had met her. I've told you about all that had*
> *happened. I had really thought it was over, but who knows the*
> *ways of the heart. She has come back like a gale of wind, exactly*
> *the way she came into my life the first time around, exactly as*
> *you captured my heart. I think I am still in love with her.*

How I wish you had not gone away. I would have never even thought of meeting her if you were with me. The last few days have been very difficult. I feel completely torn. I want you, Seema, but Shalaka is truly back into my life. Things had gone wrong between us, but there is something that never dies and that is love.

'Love?'

Seema was beginning to feel sick, a little nauseated. 'I don't want to know this. Why is he telling me all this?' She got up from the chair, stumbled across to her bed and lay down.

Shalaka had pretty much dissolved from my canvas. Believe me, she had. But it seems now that I was still somewhere within hers. She was very apologetic when she came back. She said she had made a big mistake and wants to be back with me now. She wants me back, Seema. I have thought about it a lot – for the last many days, that's all I have been doing.

I love you deeply and I want you to know that. But, Seema, I can't let Shalaka go this time. I value your love . We can always remain friends.

With lots of love,
Yours,
Amit

This letter minced no words, it allowed no soft landings. Seema's heart sank. In a sense, the letter was exactly like the conversation she'd had earlier in the day. Short. Abrupt. Unconcerned. Cruel. The finality in Amit's letter was the perfect consort to the tentativeness in his afternoon voice. Everything snapped so correctly and instantly into place, Seema saw no space left for her to manoeuvre.

Like a tiny leaf in a careless wind, her hands started to tremble, threatening to snap and blow away in front of her very eyes. She tried stopping them as she got up from her bed. 'Stop. Stop . . .' she pleaded gently, as she dropped the letter onto the table, collapsed into the chair and clasped its arms. She felt weighed down under a sheath of bulky, humid air that hovered thick around her. She was breathing fast, almost panting. Her mind had stilled, drained now of all thought and ideas.

She felt a desperate need to talk to Amit. 'If I could talk to him just once, I would convince him. He loves me, but wants her. He can't do this. God! Why did I leave him and come to this god-forsaken place?'

'Amit . . .' words of longing escaped her lips, 'don't do this to me . . .' Tears flowed, ceaselessly. 'Amit . . .' she sobbed, 'Amit, I love you. Amit, you can't do this.'

Prodded by David and Uncle, Harish walked hesitatingly to Seema's room a few minutes later. The door of her room was ajar. Harish peered in cautiously. He could just about see Seema, sitting at the table with her back to the door. Her sobbing was loud and continuous. He stood there for a moment, not sure what to do. Stepping forward, he gently pushed the door open. It creaked loudly, but Seema didn't move. Harish tapped on the door gently after a few moments, and waited for a little while more.

'Seema,' he called out softly. 'Seemaaa . . .'

She finally seemed to have registered his presence. Her body stiffened as she got up and turned around in one movement. 'Harish,' she stumbled forward, crying unceasingly. 'Harish . . . my world . . .' words came forth with great difficulty, as she sank to her knees and buried her face in her arms.

'My God!' Harish exclaimed. He went up to Seema, crouching before her and gently holding her shoulders.

He needed a moment to gather his own wits.

'Seema,' he tried to steady his own voice. 'Stop crying,' he said softly. 'Please, get up.'

Seema pulled herself up, and sat down on the bed.

Harish picked up the bottle of water from the table and handed it to her. 'Stop crying. Tell me what happened.'

Seema's sobbing subsided as she took a small sip of water. She pointed to the letter on the table. 'Read it,' she mumbled between her sobs. 'Please!'

Harish hesitatingly picked up the letter. The edges where Seema had held it were damp, and in a few other places drops of moisture had smudged the words of the ink pen's elegant inscriptions.

Reluctantly, he began reading it, looking up every now and then at Seema, who stared fixedly at him.

Harish didn't know what to say. 'This must be difficult, Seema,' he said finally, as he put the letter back on the table. It's not a nice place at all to be in. I can understand.' There was a small silence and then Harish spoke again 'Is there something I can do?'

Even these few words were hugely comforting. Seema stopped crying and regained her composure

'I'm sorry, Harish. Thanks,' she said self consciously, gathering her hair together and tying it up. 'I'll be okay.'

They sat quietly in the room for a while and then Harish coaxed Seema to finish her abandoned meal. They walked back to the dining hall, where he heated up the food for her.

Seema put a spoonful of food into her mouth and exhaled a small sigh.

She looked at Harish, who was pretending to be leafing through a magazine. He looked at her and smiled. A weary, grateful smile escaped her own lips and then she ate quietly, some aspect of her old energy seeming to trickle back onto her fatigued face.

'How quickly your situation can change,' Harish thought to himself. 'And how small the steps are on the road back to recovery.'

He walked Seema back to her room, where she collapsed on the bed, sleep quickly taking over her exhausted existence.

Harish had no such luck. Memories of Usha came flooding back, crowding his mind. 'Why is everything so fragile? Why does life keep changing like that?' These were the last thoughts he was conscious of before sleep finally overcame him as well.

BOOK TWO

11

FLEETING MEMORIES

At the Institute, the work on getting the dungi ready for the survey began in earnest. A few tasks remained, and Uncle announced that it would be ready in about five days. In the meantime, Harish had shared Seema's story with David and Uncle. Seema knew that they knew about her grief, and felt deeply indebted for the space that they allowed her, and for their care and concern.

David, however, was caught in a fix of his own. He felt responsible for Seema, and protective too. He did not want to leave her behind by herself, and yet he was not sure she wished to accompany them right now. The survey, he thought, would help by means of the experiences and challenges it always threw up for those who undertook it. It would be a completely new endeavour for Seema, teaching her many things and perhaps also keeping her mind and emotions occupied. More importantly, he couldn't delay the survey for he had managed the permit with much difficulty and it was valid for only a month. He decided it would be carried out as scheduled.

Meanwhile, Seema, broken as she felt, had managed to assemble a semblance of her normal self. She was now worried that David and Uncle would suggest that she stay back. The one thing that she was sure about was the survey, and she was damned if they were going to leave her behind.

'Seema,' David asked tentatively, 'are you coming for the survey?'

'Yes, David. Of course.'

As it turned out, neither party had needed convincing.

'Oh good! Get ready for an adventure then,' David said, laughing.

The vessel was fully ready in four days. Christened Mugger after David's pet passion, the dungi was a new acquisition for the Institute and perfect for the work to be undertaken. It was deep-sea worthy, and its nominal draught ensured at the same time that it could negotiate shallow coral reef areas and enter mangrove creeks with ease. The dungi was an incredible piece of Karen skill and craftsmanship – efficient and sturdy, yet simple. It had multiple local names too: Karen dungi, in recognition of the community that created these; engine dungi as it was now powered by a diesel engine; and bonga dungi, because the hull of the boat was a dugout made from a specially chosen log, the bonga, of a tropical tree. The Karen name for it was khlee, but it was rarely used by anyone.

Uncle, his nephew and chief assistant Popha, and others at the Institute worked hard to get Mugger ready for the survey. Final preparations now included stocking up provisions.

Early on the fifth day, the staff of the Institute were seen going up and down loading the dungi, bearing all that was needed for the trip. There were cans of diesel, kerosene and drinking water, a sack of rice, two smaller sacks (one filled with onions and potatoes and the other with dal), a bag full of packets of masalas (salt, sugar, red chilli powder, turmeric), pickles, matchboxes, two bottles of refined groundnut oil, a bundle of firewood, two large aluminium vessels for cooking, two aluminium kettles, some plates, glasses and spoons, small lanterns, torches and two boxes of cells for the torches. There were several sheets of plastic and a second tool kit, in addition to one that always lay in the dungi.

'It's like setting up a new house,' Seema exclaimed as she sat at the dining table sipping tea, watching the men go back and forth.

David was engrossed in ensuring they had everything they needed. Once they set out, they would be miles away from any kind of help. Nothing could be left to chance.

'Everything seems to be in place, but there is something that I am forgetting . . .' he murmured to himself even as he, Seema and Harish prepared to leave, walking over to the dungi with their respective haversacks on their backs. Uncle and Popha were already there, waiting for them.

David had carefully run through his checklist with Uncle. Everything was in order. Life jackets were the last entry in that master checklist.

It was just as David was boarding the dungi that he suddenly remembered it: 'Ah. The maps! This is something I always forget. I had taken them out last night and they are lying on the table in my room.'

Popha jumped out of the dungi and was back in a few minutes with a large, plastic-wrapped roll.

They were finally ready to go. Harish climbed into the dungi, followed by Seema. She did a quick survey of the entire set-up. Mugger was a largish vessel, about fifty feet in length and ten feet at its widest. Right along the edge of the vessel, nailed into its sides were flat slats of timber, two feet wide – benches that served as seats during the day and bunks at night. The front end of the boat tapered gracefully towards the bow, and a crudely crafted iron anchor tied at the end of a long yellow nylon rope lay on the deck planks here. A cane framework had been created over the dungi and two huge sheets of thick blue plastic were being tied across it to create a roof.

Everything was tucked away under the benches on either side. Harish, Seema and David shoved their haversacks under the benches, and Uncle came over to cover them with a sheet of plastic. What both Seema and Harish found amusing was that the inflatable that they had zoomed around in a few nights ago had been lifted as a single piece, and placed at the front end of the dungi. It fitted in snugly, as if it had been configured exactly for the space in which it now lay. The dungi, which had appeared rather compact and not very big from the outside, now seemed like a rather large vessel.

The rear end of the vessel was equally interesting. At its extreme end, just before the rudder, was another little canopy, this one for those who manoeuvred the boat. Just ahead and occupying pride of place, about four fifths of the way down the back of the dungi, were the two Kirloskars: huge, greasy, green diesel engines secured with heavy bolts on a specially laid foundation at the bottom of the boat. The engines were sturdy, relatively inexpensive and easy-to-maintain contraptions that boatmen in the islands swore by. For the Kirloskars, engineering giants based in the western region of mainland India, these engines and the Andaman Islands were unlikely winners – this was where they had sold the maximum number of units in the last five years.

Competition in the form of the Chinese Jiansu engine had made its appearance, however. It was a much better machine in that it was less noisy, better damped against vibration and much faster. Everyone in the Andamans knew about them, thanks to the many Burmese, Thai and Indonesian fishing boats that the Jiansus powered into these waters for very productive though illegal fishing. The higher cost of the Jiansu, small as the gap was, had proved the new engine's stumbling block, and for that reason alone the Kirloskars were still holding out in these islands.

'Jabo!' Uncle and David screamed in unison as Popha cranked up one of the Kirloskars now. It came alive with a sputtering sound, and its plume of dark, diesely smoke coloured the sky a dirty grey. The wind blew it straight into Harish's face, nauseating him mildly as the vessel set out onto the placid waters of the small bay.

David was seated next to Uncle, while Harish had already moved to the front of the boat and sat on the bow plank at its very tip. Seema walked over and sat next to him just as Popha cranked up the second Kirloskar. The engines created such a din out in the ocean that it was almost impossible to hear one's own voice – it was the only thing that marred an otherwise perfect setting.

The gentle mist of the morning had cleared and a little fishing boat was just about visible on the horizon. A moist, invigorating breeze caressed the faces of the occupants of the dungi as it simultaneously cut through the waters below and the air above. The sea itself was calm – a sheet of thick, fluid glass so clear you could see down to the very bottom of the yet shallow ocean floor.

The dungi was moving forward with purposeful linearity, the water below bobbed up and down, and patches of colourful coral in all sorts of shapes, sizes and forms passed quickly by. Tropical fish, big and small, painted as if by a child exuberant with a newly discovered palette, darted in and out of the coral architecture, some in groups and others in solitary explorations. It took a few moments for Seema's untrained eyes to settle into the ocean's complex rhythms.

Harish and Seema were both bent on either side of the dungi, peering intently, enthralled by the wonders passing below them. They looked up at each other, shared excited smiles and quickly turned back to the waters, like little children, not wanting to miss even an instant of this visual treat.

Their eyes were immediately drawn to a smooth, linear movement in the depths ahead. For a moment it looked like the shadow of their own vessel. In the next moment it was a mystery transformed. Out of the literal blue, unaware and oblivious of the mysteries and love it inspires in the humans it shares the world with, a dolphin emerged from the deep and swam alongside Seema for a few seconds.

'Dolphin!' she shrieked.

Nothing could have prepared her for this moment. The dolphin skimmed along just under the surface of the water, keeping pace with the Kirloskars. The morning light passed through the waves, making abstract white patterns on the darker body of infinite elegance. The beautiful creature swam along for a short while with silken grace, and then broke through the water surface, emerging for a few moments. Gliding along in the country boat, Seema was within touching distance. She only just resisted her desire to reach out and caress the glistening animal.

The dolphin continued to swim with them, propelling itself effortlessly over the shoals of tropical fish and the coral. Then, with an imperceptible twitch of its tail, like an accomplished ballerina at the height of her performance, the dolphin switched to the other side of the dungi and swam alongside Harish for a while. Harish was no less ecstatic – only his nature did not allow him Seema's liberal expressions. He watched transfixed as the dolphin emerged again from the water for a few fleeting moments, dived back in and then disappeared from view just as quickly as it had appeared.

For Seema and Harish, these fleeting moments felt like forever, but the three men at the back of the vessel had not even registered them. Uncle, David and Popha sat unconcerned, oblivious to the epiphanies being experienced up front. Coral, fish, turtles, dolphins, jellyfish – these were a regular part of their privileged lives as residents of the islands and as mariners in one of the world's richest and most pristine ocean waters.

Uncle pulled out a packet of bidis from his pocket and handed it over to David. David took one and passed it on to Popha, who in turn pulled out two, one for himself and the other for the pilot of the boat. Pilot – that is what Uncle was referred to when in charge of the boat. This was the tradition in the islands here. There was another one too. The pilot never lit his own bidi when at the helm.

David pulled out his lighter and lit Uncle's bidi, then his own and then Popha's. The three inhaled deeply and puffed out smoke in whatever contemplative silence could be found amidst the racket-making Kirloskars, now firing away at maximum capacity. This was a journey they had undertaken many times in the past. It still held its thrill, but of a different kind – that of re-reading a masterpiece that had gone yellow and dog-eared with years of scrutiny.

In a few minutes, the dungi had exited the sheltered waters of the bay. The ocean floor dropped quickly away and was soon invisible. The water turned a dark blue, bordering on black; now a dark carpet, revealing nothing of what lay beneath its immediate surface.

The boat moved in a straight line, parallel to the coast of the island landmass. They passed by a silver beach that the ocean waves lapped at softly, then a rocky cliff that the waves collided against powerfully, a patch of littoral forest where the crowns of the trees had been wind-combed in one direction like modern punk mops, a creek that split the landmass effortlessly open, only to dissolve further inland, followed by another silver beach, more littoral forests, rocky cliffs, then another silver beach and a creek again. Beyond this interface of land and water rose a green wall of primeval origin: a virgin tropical rainforest holding up the skies with delicate solidity.

As the boat continued its journey north, the steadily climbing tropical sun became unbearable, particularly to the two who sat without shade at the front. The waves too had come into play. Freed from the clutches of the enclosed bay, they danced larger and bigger as the dungi entered even more unsheltered waters. The dungi pitched increasingly and the movement was further amplified for Harish and Seema as they were sitting at the very tip. Seema held fast to the side of the boat with one hand for a while, and as the boat jerked hard, instinctively clutched Harish's arm with the other. She hadn't realized this and when she did, she pulled it back immediately, her face flushed.

The pitching and the heat were making it impossible to continue sitting here. Seema was forced to hold Harish's arm again as she stood up, then quickly grabbed the cane framework and literally tumbled back to the middle of the boat. Here she settled herself on the bench, under the blue tarpaulin.

She was feeling a little dizzy from the heat. The shade provided some respite, but the vibrations of the boat started to get to her now. So powerful and unrelenting was the engine's throbbing that nothing in the dungi was unaffected. Some of the things, including the heavy bags of potatoes and rice, had slowly slid from under the benches to the middle of the dungi. A can of water fell to its side and the life jackets that had been left on the bench had vibrated to its very edge.

Every bone and joint in Seema's body seemed to be vibrating vigorously, sending tiny, irritating sensations rapidly up her system – inexplicably and distressingly, to the tip of her nose. It was right below her eyes, yet she could do nothing. It demanded to be itched. She responded promptly, but the promise of relief, if any, was only illusory. She tried holding her nose tip, rubbing it gently, even splashing a palm full of water on it. Nothing helped. The only real solution was to either get off the boat or stop it, neither of which, she knew, was feasible.

David had walked over and Seema asked if he knew what she should do. David burst out laughing. 'Boatman's . . . sorry. Boatwoman's itch. It happens. You'll get used to it. Try taking a nap.' Seema was not in the least amused.

Harish could see how miserable Seema was. He bent over and pulled out his sleeping bag from his haversack. He handed it to Seema, suggesting that she pull out hers as well. 'Now sit on one,' he shouted, over the din, 'and place the other one against your back.' Seema did as instructed. 'Shock absorbers,' he screamed.

A considerably improved Seema took in a sip of water, adjusted the makeshift shock absorbers under her and lay down on her side. In a couple of minutes she had dozed off into an uncomfortable sleep. Harish lay down himself and closed his eyes, but even an uncomfortable sleep would not oblige him. He continued to lie on his back, eyes open, staring at the blue tarpaulin flapping above, wondering what the next two weeks on this boat would bring.

The men at the rear, in comparison, were perfectly at home. Popha was snoozing peacefully, and David, having returned to the back, had pulled his bright red baseball cap over his eyes and appeared to have dozed off as well. Uncle sat motionless, staring unblinkingly ahead. He lit up another bidi, and his right hand went back to the rudder. The others were sleeping, so the pilot had no choice but to light his own this one time.

Soon, they were sweeping past Constance Bay where the Jarawa Reserve actually began. They passed a number of smaller bays, beaches and rocky outcrops, and continued without a stop for a couple of hours. Then came the first change of direction; east into Port Campbell, port of first call.

Port Campbell was a huge labyrinth of water channels, creeks, mangrove forests and smaller islands located in the heart of Jarawa land. The forests all around were thick and lush and the waters of the bay were considered very good fishing grounds. The fear of the Jarawa threat here was very significant, yet the catch of a couple of days could be so bountiful that fisherfolk were forever willing to take the risk.

The Port Campbell that Mugger chugged into, however, was desolate. There was no other vessel here. Uncle cut the engines and joined Popha as the two poled the dungi along with the long bamboo it always carried. They manoeuvred it into a calmer, sheltered part of the bay and dropped anchor after ensuring that the distance from the shore was enough to deter the Jarawas from attempting a night-time ambush.

Seema had a more immediate problem. Very reluctantly, she approached David.

'David,' she started, hesitantly, 'How does one . . . erm . . . take a dump here?'

'It's simple,' he answered matter-of-factly, 'at the back of the dungi.'

'At the back, David? Where?' She paused. 'How?'

'Oh!' he exclaimed. 'What kind of an island girl are you? Come. I'll show you.'

'Show me? What David?'

'Arre, what do you mean what? The big job? Isn't that what you just asked me?'

'Yes, but show me?'

David burst out laughing. 'What do you think I am going to show you? Come, come, don't worry.'

Uncle and Popha had realized what was happening, and Seema saw the amused smiles on both their faces just before they quickly turned their gaze elsewhere.

'Come with me before it's too late,' David prompted again, laughing.

They walked to the stern that jutted out below the super structure of the boat and where the rudder had been fixed. There it was, about three feet below the main framework of the boat – a wide-ish step about three feet in length – the toilet of a Karen dungi of the Andaman Islands. 'This is where you have to sit,' David explained to Seema pointing his finger. Her response was an embarrassed and incredulous 'here?' look.

'That's how it's done. We all do it. And hold on to that pole of the rudder when you sit,' David continued with a chuckle, 'otherwise, you too might fall into the water with a lot else.'

Seema grinned sheepishly as David climbed back up and then returned with a sheet of cloth, which served as temporary curtain. She squatted, hugely aware of how flimsy this privacy was, but relaxing because she was well below the eye-level of the others in the boat. The wall of cloth covered her on one side – but on the other, she sat exposed to the entire world. Fortunately, there was no one here today who would be watching.

12

ON THE WINGS OF SILENCE

Port Campbell's significance went deep into the past. In March 1942, with the theatre of the Second World War firmly located in the east, the Japanese had taken complete control of the Andaman & Nicobar Islands. In March of the following year, the Civil Administration, the Miniseibu, took charge of the islands from the Gunsheisho, the Military Administration. Later that year, in a development that took the Japanese completely by surprise, the Allies conducted a series of air raids, knocking off vital Japanese defence installations in Port Blair with deadly precision. The accuracy of the campaign was so pointed that there could be no doubt it was the outcome of seriously successful espionage.

The explanation lay in a secret mission under the leadership of Denis McCarthy, the Superintendent of Port Blair Police, who had in a far-sighted move, been evacuated just before the Japanese invaded. Code-named Operation Baldhead, the mission had successfully brought a Dutch submarine into Port Campbell in 1942, followed by another that sneaked in a few months later. The two had landed four commando missions in the dense forests here, and these had then infiltrated the civilian areas bordering Port Blair to gather intelligence. This had been possible entirely due to the support of a few forest labourers, believed – though this was never confirmed – to have included a couple of Ranchis and Karens and also the last of the remaining Great Andamanese who knew every nook and corner of the vast forests. The latter, most importantly, had provided the commandoes with much needed assistance in the forests: places to rest for the night, information about sources of fresh water, very welcome tobacco and even the occasional snatch of opium.

For the Great Andamanese, the most numerous of the Andaman indigenes, the significance of this Port Campbell went even deeper. It had been home forever and had continued as their stronghold till contact with the British and disease initiated the process of their almost complete extermination in the period leading up to the second world war. Estimated at anywhere between five and eight thousand people when the British set up their colony in the islands in 1858, the Great Andamanese were left with a population of under a hundred individuals when the Japanese came visiting less than a century later.

One account of how this came to be was M. V. Portman's 1899 classic about the islands and its islanders, which Harish had perused in fascination and horror. Portman had described in detail the impact of the 1877 epidemic of measles, the worst to hit the Great Andamanese. At least half the Andamanese population in the Great Andaman islands had died and Port Campbell was among the areas worst hit. Portman's was a bleak, chilling record of what had happened to an entire people. It read almost like a dispatch from the war front:

> At the Viper Home – 71 Andamanese were attacked and 6 died. Of the syphilitic patients, 43 were attacked and 10 died. Of the visitors in hospital, 77 were attacked and 37 died. Self-treated in the jungle, say, 350 attacked and 56 died.

The final prognosis, as it were, came in another report published by Portman a little more than a decade later.

> . . . All the people on Rutland and Port Campbell are dead, and very few remain in the South Andaman and the

Archipelago. The children do not survive in the very few births which do occur, and the present generation may be considered as the last of the aborigines of the Great Andaman ...

There couldn't have been a greater irony – the Great Andamanese were on the verge of an extinction they didn't know was coming; their own battles had long been lost, and here, in the middle of the twentieth century they were collaborating with their annihilators, the British, in fighting a war for a world they had no clue about.

Harish had discussed Portman's account with Seema in great detail during their discussions at the Institute. 'If this happened to the Great Andamanese,' he had asked her, 'could this also not happen to the Jarawa? Are they not just as vulnerable?'

'It's certainly possible,' Seema had replied thoughtfully. 'When small, nomadic, forest-dwelling populations come in contact with sedentary, high density populations, there is always the chance that they will be infected with diseases that might be common in the settled communities.' She had paused for a moment and then continued, 'Measles is a classic example, but you know Harish, what's very surprising is that the Andamans and the Andamanese never featured in whatever little we studied at university. Australia yes, Fiji yes, Amazonia yes, but the Andamans? Never. And,' she had become even more thoughtful, 'from the little I know and understand, the present Jarawa–settler interface is exactly this – the developments at Kadamtala that you witnessed, the interactions in Tirur, God alone knows what else is going on – it could be a time-bomb waiting to explode. The fuse perhaps has already been lit.'

It was time for the first meal on board and Popha got into action, ducking under the bench Harish occupied and dragging out the vessel of rice he had cooked early in the morning, before setting out. This was to be eaten with sugar or salt, and there was pickle too.

Harish, the only vegetarian on board had no choice but to go for the ubiquitous mango pickle of a well-known brand from the mainland. The others didn't think twice as they went for the Nappi, the special Karen prawn pickle Popha had prepared himself.

This was the barest of meals, yet each of them ate with the acute concentration possible only of the extremely hungry. Fifteen minutes later, the mounds of rice were all devoured and Popha was ducking below the seat to stow it all away again.

Lunch done, Popha lit a bidi and handed it to David. He then lit one for himself and retreated to join Uncle at the back end of the dungi, where the old man had already lit his own, contentedly drawing in the first puff and blowing it out.

There were still a few hours before sundown, and they could have travelled further into the creek. David, however, decided otherwise; many hours of continuously negotiating the dungi had left Uncle exhausted. He needed to rest.

Portman's account and the discussions with Seema came back to Harish as he sat, watching the forests intently. 'Do you recollect, Seema?' he asked after a while, 'Portman's account of what happened to the Great Andamanese here in Port Campbell?

'I know Harish. I've been thinking of that too. It's a strange experience to be sitting here and recollecting all that happened to those people.'

The hours before sunset passed slowly. There was no more conversation among the people in the boat as they enjoyed the respite from the engines; each one alternately smoking a bidi, dozing off into a light sleep or staring contemplatively at the calm waters of the bay. Unconsciously, each sat from the other at roughly equal intervals; five independent universes within fifty feet of wooden architecture. The only sound was that of the lapping waves, the flapping of the boat cover in the gentle wind and the occasional splash of water as a fish on the surface dived with alacrity in response to some imagined danger or tempting food.

The sun's own journey to its slumber was as deliberate as it was colourful: the yellow orb slowly turning orange, then red and then sliding seamlessly over and beyond to the other side. Darkness began to throw its cover over the dome of the earth, and as it did, it seemed to dissolve these independent universes. Just as the lonely occupants were stirring out of their meditations, thinking of what to do next, it began.

Riding the darkness and the silence, announcing the takeover of the advancing night, rising from somewhere deep in the surrounding dark forests, came the high-pitched, haunting yodel of the Jarawa. It wasn't loud, but it was clear, with the mysterious quality of a very real dream. The pace was gentle to begin with, the beat unhurried. Then, in measured steps, it began to increase, picking up pace in slow notches, and rising quickly to the high-pitched crescendo of a fast, foot-tapping rhythm.

This continued for a while and then it died abruptly, like the sharp snapping of a delicate thread. In those few moments, the silence re-surfaced clear and crisp, a glowing, starry spread on a sheet of night-coloured paper. And then after a few moments, suddenly, it took off again, precisely at the pitch and peak it had just been abandoned.

The five in the boat sat mesmerised as they listened to the ancient rhythm. Harish had heard this one before, from the little boys at the jetty, when the mike had been thrust in their bewildered faces with orders to 'sing'. David recognized it too. It sounded the same, and yet it was different, very different.

Harish was struck afresh by the significance of this place. Here he was, the outsider, now in the heart of the ancient land of an ancient people. He felt a deep sense of wonder at the life of the Jarawa. 'It must be extremely tough,' he thought to himself, 'and yet it seems so simple – just the elements and the people.'

'I once wanted to spend my entire life in these forests,' Uncle said as he came and sat down next to Harish, pointing in the direction the Jarawa sounds had come from.

'What? You've been in these forests, Uncle? When? Do you know what they are saying? What do they mean?' He looked expectantly at the old man, whose face seemed to reflect, as it always did, a chronic, unchanging disinterest. At the same time, however, Harish noticed a difference. There was a wistful twitch in his steady gaze – an expression that Harish could only understand as emotion, a sense of wonder, even longing. The old man had travelled into an entirely different world.

'Don't know,' Uncle replied laconically, lost deep in the forests and in the silence that the sound of the Jarawas had just lapsed into.

The silence was not to last for long; broken now by an altogether different music and rhythm – the soft sound of human sobs as they drifted in from the front end of the boat. In the midst of this primeval world, Seema was encountering her own emotions anew. Harish walked up and sat on the bow plank next to her.

'You okay?' he asked gently.

'Yes, thanks,' she wiped her tears with the sleeve of her kurta. 'I'm sorry. Really sorry.' She went across to the rest of the company. 'I'm sorry Uncle. Sorry David. I'll be okay.'

Smiling understandingly, the two men managed to convince Seema to join them for a spin in the inflatable. What better way than this to cheer someone up and the threesome were soon zooming away into the dark night in their search for more crocs.

Harish, meanwhile, watched quietly as Popha began preparations for dinner. A small mound of flattened mud, about six inches high and two feet in diameter, lay on the floor of the boat. The three stones that had been loaded onto the boat formed an equilateral triangle on the pile of mud, and Popha adjusted their positions a little to support the big aluminium vessel he had placed on them. He then pulled out a few twigs from the bundle they had brought along and pushed them under the vessel. Harish had seen this simple stove on earlier journeys, but every time he saw it being put together and performing its functions, he could only marvel.

Popha sprinkled a few drops of kerosene onto the twigs and threw in a lighted matchstick. The kerosene flared up instantly and collapsed just as quickly. It was enough, however, to light up the smaller twigs. He fanned the flames and set the rice, dal and potatoes to cook.

Eighteen-year-old Popha was the only son of Uncle's youngest sister. A shy young man, he kept to himself most of the time. He worked hard and efficiently and spoke little, even to his Uncle. His life found little intersection with those of Harish and Seema's and rarely, if ever, did he allow space for conversation. Harish had tried often, but the nephew was quite like his Uncle, mostly quiet and unreachable. Harish tried once again.

'Uncle told me,' Harish started, as Popha pushed in a couple of larger twigs into the fire, 'you always topped in school?'

Popha smiled a shy smile, but didn't say anything.

'You didn't want to continue?' Harish prodded further.

'School was so boring,' Popha finally replied, the shy smile still on his face. 'This is life,' he swung his arms around, 'isn't it? How can that be better than this?'

Harish thought they could finally have a conversation, but before he could say anything else, the mildly embarrassed Popha got up and quickly retreated to the back of the dungi. He emerged only upon hearing the excited chatter from the inflatable when it returned after a while.

David was triumphant. 'Seven big, two small,' he said thumping the air with his fist. 'I told you, na, the mangroves and creeks here are something else. It's incredible. Incredible.' David's excitement was palpable. 'If this is how many crocodiles we see in less than a night, I can't even imagine what the entire system here holds.'

Dinner was served shortly afterwards, and consumed with enthusiasm only marginally less than that of the afternoon. Action now moved to the middle of the boat, that had now become a bedroom. Bedsheets and sleeping bags were pulled out from underneath the benches and rolled out on top of them. The kerosene wicks that had lit up the dungi with their flickering flames were put out and the five lay down – the end of a rich but tiring first day.

The boat rocked gently and a gentle breeze blew in from the west. Popha and Uncle quickly dropped off into their respective slumbers. Seema looked at her watch. It was only half past seven. In Delhi, where she had been only a few months ago, the night would have just about begun – sound, lights, traffic, shopping and partying about to commence. Not long ago, it had all been an integral part of her life. Now it all seemed so far way. Here, in a lonely boat in the land of the Jarawa that was also the land of her birth, a fascinating day was coming to an end and a tired Seema soon drifted off into a deep slumber.

David, meanwhile, switched on his head torch, pulled out his pen and began jotting down his diary notes. Harish lay on his side, watching him for some time. The vigorous scratching of pen on paper was clearly audible in the still night, and it was the last sound he registered before he drifted off, wondering what it was that David noted so assiduously in his diary.

Harish slept so soundly he was the last one to get up the next morning. Popha was at the front of the dungi and the kettle was on the boil already. The other four had been up for a while and all ready. Harish splashed himself fully awake and quickly disappeared to the back of the boat. He returned to Popha's refreshing ginger tea, followed by a hot Maggi noodles breakfast. This was topped off with another cup of steaming tea and they were all set to take off again.

Popha pulled up the anchor, cranked the Kirloskars alive and moved to the front of the dungi to help navigate it out into open waters.

They moved a considerable distance away from the coast, then turned right and headed towards the north once again. Hundreds of black-naped terns flew past them in the opposite direction. The black half-collar at the back of their necks stood out starkly against the snow-white of the rest of the body. A few of them would suddenly stop mid-air, hover a while and dive down into the water like a bullet from a gun. Invariably, they would come up with a little fish in their beaks and move off towards the coast to consume the fruits of their labour.

About two hours later, a small mass of white and green – located not very far from the coast that they had been moving down – sailed into view. David rolled out the maps that he had brought along and pointed out that they had just passed Cape Bluff. What they now saw before them was the small pin-head on the map that went by the name of Bluff Island.

Bluff, along with the much larger Spike Island lying immediately to its north and east, was located right between the main islands of South and Middle Andaman and was lodged in the collective memory of the people here with Jarawa, junglee and blood imprinted all over it.

It was certainly a pretty island – small, considerably flat and clothed in uniform stands of the littoral sea mohwa, also known as the bullet-wood tree for the hardness of its timber. The waters were shallow, but deep enough for boats to approach and hit land with ease. Bluff was a convenient staging point for fisherfolk who could head eastwards from here for rich and productive fishing and for the hunters who could head west into the forests of Spike in pursuit of honey, wild pigs and venison. Often the fisherman was a hunter too, and a place like this allowed a double bonanza. The risks were clearly worth taking.

Like the intruders, the Jarawa too collected honey and hunted wild pig and monitor lizard in the forests of Spike. The quarry of the two groups of hunters was the same and the pursuit brought them face-to-face more than occasionally. When they did, the encounters were bloody and both sides often had to carry back the bodies of more than just their original quarry.

Bluff had begun to show up prominently in conflict records in the 1980s, but that was only the tip of the iceberg. The most recent report of a Jarawa attack on fishermen here was only a fortnight old. This area was not far from Kadamtala, where the Tanumei incident had just occurred, but the situation here was more like in the forests near Tirur; an intense tension and a continued hostility still endured.

'Why, is it,' Harish asked David, 'that these hunters and fishermen keep coming here even when there is so much risk? Can nothing be done to stop these intruders? Not only is it unfair on the Jarawa, it also leads to conflict, doesn't it?'

'You are right Harish,' David agreed, 'but who is going to bell the cat? It's the same story – what you saw at Tirur. Do you know who these guys are?'

'You mean those who come here?'

'Yes! You know the leader? He doesn't come fishing anymore, but he's the big one. You've seen Biswas Super Store in town, haven't you? How do you think he made his crores? He didn't even have a proper house fifteen years ago.'

'Nooooo!' Harish's exclamation was long. 'You mean he's made all his money from the Jarawa area. Illegally?'

'Uncle knows him very well,' David continued. 'They used to fish together. The guy has immense risk-taking capacities. He would regularly venture into places others would never dare to enter, like Bluff Island, like Spike, like the forests of Port Campbell. Shark fishing, diving for shell and sea cucumber, hunting turtles in the shallow waters, wild pig in the forests and more than the occasional crocodile. These crocodile skins fetch a huge price in the international leather market, and Biswas has at least three channels to smuggle them out of here.'

'Really?'

'It is difficult to stop people from being drawn to these riches. Biswas has so much money now he doesn't need any more. But there is greed and there is need. You've seen the people around the Institute, haven't you? I won't say they are poor, but then life is not easy either. Half of them work for Biswas in his teams that keep coming here. We have to accept that these forests and these crystal waters here,' he swung his hands around him, 'have huge resources locked up inside.'

'But David,' Seema said, 'the Jarawa need it. It's for them first.'

'Isn't that right?' Harish concurred. 'The first claim has to be that of the Jarawa?'

'No, no!' David responded with alarm. 'I am not saying even for a moment that it is not their's, but whom am I saying this to? The Jarawa Reserve exists only on paper. It is important to realize this. Nobody knows how many intrusions are made on a daily basis, even along the Andaman Trunk Road. When the road that can be easily patrolled, is not, who is going to check such a huge and indented coastline and the innumerably large number of bays and creeks that lie within? Even if they wanted to, there was nothing they could do. It's a different matter, altogether,' he concluded with a small sigh, 'they want to do nothing at all.'

Uncle had navigated the boat past Bluff Island and into a wide channel to the right. 'If we keep going straight,' David explained, 'we'll reach the jetty at Uttara where we had witnessed that tamasha a few days ago. It's not really far from here.'

'So,' Seema asked, 'is that where we are headed now?'

'No,' David responded, 'we enter the creek system, turn left and finally park ourselves near Lekra Lunta for the night.'

'Lekra Lunta?' Harish queried. 'That is a strange name, but it sounds familiar.'

'Of course it would be familiar,' David responded. 'I'm sure you've been reading about it. See, I don't know much about the contact missions with the Jarawa, but it was at Lekra Lunta where it all began more than three decades ago. It was here that the team led by the famous policeman, Bhaktawar Singh, is said to have first befriended the Jarawa. You must have read about it. There is some disagreement, though. Some people say that the real credit for the success should go to someone else; I forget the name.' He paused for a while trying hard to recollect. 'It will come to me. Anyway, Lekra Lunta is where the ice is supposed to have been broken. The contact parties of the administration were basically a bunch of jokers who came in from the sea and dropped gifts – coconuts, plastic items, red cloth . . .' There was creeping contempt in David's voice, 'It didn't happen immediately, this friendship. Initially, the Jarawa on the coast always showered these visitors with their arrows. Then it slowly changed. First they started accepting the gifts, and in due course, members of the party also started landing on the beach to intermingle and interact with the Jarawas. These were major breakthroughs that happened sometime in the seventies, I think, in some ways similar to what happened with Tanumei at Kadamtala – tectonic shifts in a community's relationship with another. Maybe,' he added as an afterthought, 'maybe, what had been sown then is now being reaped in Kadamtala. And there is Tripathy I must tell you about. Remind me when we get to Lekra Lunta.'

The dungi continued in a straight line for a short while and then turned along an arc to the left, finally entering a wide channel that opened straight ahead into the sea. As the vessel moved to the middle of the channel, David indicated for the engines to be cut. The dungi drifted for a while and finally became still as Popha threw in the anchor.

The banks on either side of this channel were clothed in thick mangroves. As the channel moved towards its mouth, it grew increasingly devoid of vegetation. There were no mud banks for the mangroves to colonize and the land beyond was rocky and steep, offering little opportunity for trees to lay roots. It became progressively narrow and in the best illustration of the bottleneck was narrowest at the point it exited into the sea.

'There,' said David pointing to the bottleneck, 'where the sea enters this channel is Lekra Lunta.'

'And,' Seema prompted David, 'Tripathy? You were going to tell us about Tripathy, David.'

'Yes, Anil Tripathy. The two of you must meet him when we return to the Institute. Remind me and we will invite him for a meal one day. I too have not met him for a long time myself. Anil is an anthropologist. Well,' he corrected himself, 'he was an anthropologist working with the Tribal Welfare Department – the only guy, I would say, with any bloody spine. He went on many of these contact jamborees. Yes, that is what he called them – jamborees.'

Seema and Harish were all ears.

'And you know what else he told me? "David, if there is one thing that screwed up the Jarawa, it was these contact parties. These were indeed parties where the main aim of the men who came – women hardly joined these teams, you know – was to have fun and to make contact with the Jarawa women, literally. They'd boast of how many women they had touched and where . . . it was disgusting." You know how Tripathy described the gift dropping and the thing about friendship? It really hit me in my gut.

'"What friendship David?" he said, "You drop gifts and they pick them up. It's like throwing grain and then waiting to snare the birds. The Jarawas got snared, David. They lost their freedom. Forever."'

'Hmm,' Harish mumbled thoughtfully.

'That's scary,' Seema added.

'You must meet him,' David continued, 'he is one of those rare people who could have made a huge difference to the Jarawas if he was allowed to. But he is a bastard too – gave up without fighting – not for himself, not for the Jarawas. And that's what I tell him, that he is a bastard. A poor little bastard who was screwed by everyone because he dared to speak the truth and stand up for what he believed was right. He tried, you know, he really tried. He not only questioned the logic and the need for these contact missions, he was also the original whistle blower. He'd uncovered two financial scams in the procurement of these gifts for the Jarawa missions, and had also reported two of his colleagues for this touching and groping of the Jarawa women. An enquiry was called for and word was simultaneously leaked that it was all Tripathy's doing.' There was a rare anger in David's words and also regret. 'They ganged up against him like a pack of dogs on a hunt – hounded him, humiliated him publicly. The system that should have stood by him was the one that let him down. It sucks. When Tripathy couldn't do anything, tough chance anyone else can.'

13

TWO INTRUDERS

The search for crocodiles began again next morning after tea and a light breakfast. Uncle stayed behind in the dungi this time as the other four set off to explore the huge maze of creeks that beckoned to David from all around. He had taken control of the rudder and directed the inflatable into a side channel to the right. They moved for a few minutes and then came to the edge of what appeared to be a much-frequented area. A path led through the mangrove forest into a clearing that was visible even from the water's edge.

David pointed along the path that Seema had just noticed. 'You asked me about intrusions yesterday, but look at this – Ranchi Basti, an encroachment in what is called the heart of Jarawa land. It's been here for years, everybody knows about it and yet it continues to exist. Seema, I suggest you take Popha and go in. See what you can find out. Don't worry,' he responded to the concern on her face, 'there won't be any problem, and Popha's with you anyway. I'll take Harish for a spin and catch up with my crocs. Let's meet again in a couple of hours.'

Seema jumped out of the inflatable and set off behind Popha. This was an intriguing settlement. If David was indeed right and there was no reason he would not be, how the hell did it get here in the first place? And how had it been allowed to remain?

They had been walking for only a couple of minutes, when they saw two men approaching them aggressively. 'Who are you? What are you doing here?' The younger of the two asked sternly. 'How did you get here?'

'We . . . we are here for a survey. Survey . . .' Seema was taken completely by surprise, 'of, crocodiles,' she stammered. 'Our team has gone into the creek. We got off to see the basti. Can I get some water?'

The two men continued to look at them suspiciously. 'I know the crocodile survey team,' the shorter, darker and older of the two men remarked, 'but I have never seen you before?'

'We have come with David. Dr David Baskaran.'

'Oh, so you are with David babu,' the name had an instant calming effect on the two men. 'Is Uncle there too? And you?' he turned to Popha, 'You are from Webi no? I have seen you before. You are . . . you are . . .'

'Popha. Uncle's nephew.'

'Ah see, I told you. I have seen you somewhere before. See,' he turned his attention now to Seema, 'David babu knows our problem. What to do, the Forest Department and the patwari keep telling us that we will have to go away. We get worried when any new person comes in here. My name is Felix and this is my nephew Nelson. Come, come,' he led Seema and Popha along the forest path that led into a large clearing that was their settlement. They walked a couple of hundred metres more and stopped by the first house. 'You wanted water, no?'

Seema sat on the small bench outside the house as Felix went in and Nelson disappeared into the forest beyond. This was a neat little village. There were two rows of ten houses each on either side of a short narrow path but there weren't too many people to be seen. A few children were running around, the radio blared from a couple of houses and on a bench similar to the one she was sitting on, Seema saw three old men at the other end of the settlement. Beyond was a small shallow valley that had all been converted to farmland. She counted eight people – six men and two women, working there. To the left, one could make out the creek by the presence of the mangroves that curved around the land like a girdle. To the right the farms extended to the edge of what was a huge wall of rainforest trees.

Felix walked out with two glasses and a tumbler of water. He was bare-bodied, and like all those who laboured on the land, his body was chiselled. He gave Seema and Popha the water and disappeared again into his house. 'I'll just be back,' he shouted from inside and returned in a moment with a green file that had clearly seen a lot of use.

'See,' he said, opening the file and pointing to the laminated paper that lay at the very top. It was obviously an important document. 'My land patta. Official papers proving that the land is mine,' he said pointing to the east. 'That field on the edge of the forest with the scarecrow – that one. Extending from there to that little stream,' his arm went around. 'All that land is mine – a little more than an acre. This is the paper of that land,' he hit the sheet emphatically with the back of his palm, 'and now they say they will take it away.'

Seema was puzzled. If this was Jarawa territory, legally a part of the Jarawa Reserve, how could that piece of paper be a land entitlement?

Felix flipped over his land entitlement. The next page had a photo stuck on it – the usual studio portrait of a family with the Taj Mahal painted in the background. Sitting on a cane chair in the photo was a lady in a blue sari, head covered, a prominent sindoor mark showing on her forehead and an angelic baby in her arms. Standing behind her and staring sternly into the camera was a much younger Felix.

'That is my son,' Felix said pointing to the baby in her arms, 'now eight years old. He was born in this house. How can they say we have to leave?'

'Leave?' Seema asked. 'Why do you have to leave? Who has asked you to leave?'

'That's what I am saying. David babu knows our problem.' He now turned to the end of the file. 'Look at this, madam.' He thrust the file into Seema's hands.

'And what is this?'

'Eviction notice madam. They say this is Jarawa territory and we have to leave.'

'Oh!'

'Were they sleeping all this while? You know who brought us here? We came here more than twenty years ago as forest labour; fifteen Ranchi boys, including myself. We created this settlement with our sweat and blood. We cleared the forest, prepared the fields, constructed our houses; they even gave us the pattas. If this is Jarawa Reserve, did they not know it then? Maybe this was Jarawa territory. *Was*,' he stressed. 'But *now*, it is ours. This is our land.' There was deeper emphasis and also anger. 'How can one live like this? Earlier, for all these years we had to fight the Jarawas.'

He turned his right shoulder to Seema and pointed to what must have once been a deep and nasty gash. 'Jarawa arrow.'

He got up and turned around, showing Seema another scar on his left thigh. 'Jarawa arrow.'

He sat down. 'It was not easy but we built our lives. Now, after so many years, the Jarawas don't attack anymore – we are even friends. And we have to leave? Is this fair? Where will we go? Where will we get such land? What about our children? Here, I at least get something to eat from the fields.'

'Friends with the Jarawas, did you say?' Seema asked with interest. 'You were friends with the Jarawas?'

Felix clarified. 'Not friends like very great pals, but we do know each other well. There is no more fighting between us like there used to be. If we are allowed to continue here, we'll even become good friends – we can even make these junglees humans. We'll civilize them. That is what the government also wants now, isn't it? Then let us do it! We *can* do it. We can help the government do it. Tell me,' he was extremely confident of what he was saying, 'who knows the Jarawas better than us? We have been living with them, here, like this, for so many years. See, in other areas, these fellows, these Jarawas are still aggressive, but when they come here, they know who the boss is. They listen to us. They know how to behave. Everybody says that the Jarawas are dangerous, but here, the last attack, this scar on my thigh, this was five years ago. They even come and take rice from us now.'

'Really?' Seema was quite surprised.

'See,' Felix changed tack a little, 'all these people come from the mainland and spend sometime in Port Blair, go for a drive on that Andaman Trunk Road and speak to God knows whom. Then they behave as if they know everything about the Jarawa.'

'Hmm. Okay,' she said, 'so what is the real story about them then?'

Now Felix found himself unexpectedly caught on the back foot. 'No, see,' he tried to gather himself, 'I am not educated like these researchers. Like you. So I can't say everything for sure, but we are living here? Isn't that true?'

'No, no. You're right,' Seema tried to put Felix at ease. 'I agree that people coming from the outside don't know everything.'

'Okay,' Felix continued, 'they say the Jarawas eat only from the forest and the sea. Now how can I believe that? For at least the last, let me see . . .' he looked down at his fingers and did a count, 'two, three, four . . . for at least four years now, we have been giving them cooked rice for which they come here regularly.'

'Really?' Seema could hardly believe what she was hearing.

'This is the problem. Nobody believes when we say this. We don't have those expensive cameras and everything else that people like you carry along. I don't have photos to show you, so it's up to you to believe me or not. Is it really so surprising?' Felix asked, a little agitated. 'I'll be honest – I sometimes go into the forests and get some honey or even kill a wild pig. In a similar manner, don't you think that the Jarawa would be interested in coming and seeing what we do and what we eat? Why should that surprise anybody? Don't people go to their neighbours for all kinds of things?'

'That,' Seema nodded her head, 'is a valid point.'

'Honey,' Felix started off now on a completely different path. 'Do you know how the Jarawa gather honey?'

'No. Nobody told me,' Seema replied, turning around to ask Popha if he knew. There would be no answer – Popha had dozed off into a comfortable snooze.

'Nobody told you,' Felix said with obvious pride, 'because nobody knows. I'm telling you – all this talk about Jarawas this and Jarawas that, Jarawas live like this and Jarawas do that, is only talk. Empty talk. We know because we live here, and now they want to throw us out. If –'

'Hmmm!' Seema interrupted quickly, realizing Felix was heading off on a tangent again, 'Honey. So how do they extract honey?'

'Oh sorry! But I must tell you, this is a fascinating way of getting out the honey.'

Meanwhile, David and Harish too had stumbled upon the unexpected. They had moved ahead after dropping off Seema and Popha, turned left into a big channel, then immediately right and finally left again into a much narrower creek. The inflatable was moving ahead at a gentle pace, and David was carefully scouring the banks for signs of crocs.

'Looks like we have company,' he said, a little surprised, pointing to another dungi at the far end of the creek, 'and what could this be doing here?'

Something looked amiss. David looked a little concerned, and Harish decided to wait before asking anything. The dungi was much smaller, but very much like their own. As David brought their inflatable alongside, he recognised it instantly. 'That bastard Shiva again,' he cursed. 'Wonder what he's up to this time?'

'What is it David? Some problem?' Harish finally asked.

'I'll tell you. Come, let's get off first. This dungi parked here means something fishy's going on.'

Harish jumped off and then gingerly walked into the mangroves along a small narrow path that was just about visible. He reached higher ground and waited as David tethered the inflatable to a mangrove branch and negotiated the slush to join him. Now David took the lead and Harish followed.

They had not gone far when they heard human chattering. The two stopped and listened, concentrating. The sounds were coming through clearly – there were at least three people, and one was speaking Hindi with a distinctly European accent.

David nodded his head in dismay and anger. 'That bastard is at it again.'

Shortly, they came to the edge of a small natural clearing that was occupied by two small tents – one light brown and another just behind that was light green in colour. The rustle of human feet appeared to have alerted the three voices that now fell silent.

A head popped out from the brown tent. It peered at them for a while, and quickly a body followed behind it. This was a bare-bodied man with a round face, Chaplinesque moustache and dark long hair that reached his shoulders. He stood meekly before David, like a school child caught in the middle of a classroom prank. He crossed his hands behind his back, looked fleetingly at David, and then looked away at his tent as a second man now emerged. He was much shorter, but more muscular. They must have been about the same age, but this fellow was balding significantly, and the mark of an old wound ran prominently above his right eyebrow. A toothy, guilty grin filled his small face the moment he saw David. He also stood up next to his compatriot, crossed his hands behind him and lowered his eyes in wilful admission of his own culpability. It was a rather comical sight: two fully grown men standing sheepishly before a rather indignant-looking David. Harish just about managed to prevent a chuckle.

David was not amused in the least. He hadn't said a word, but it was obvious that he was angry. David, Harish realised, was not looking at the two men standing before him. He kept staring at the tent. A third head eventually appeared – a white man in perhaps his mid-forties, also bare-bodied, with a bidi glowing between his lips. His blonde hair appeared a little unkempt and a small stubble on his cheeks implied that he had been out a few days now.

It was only when he stood up that one realized how big and well built he was. David was not a short man, but even he appeared dwarfed in comparison.

'Hi! I'm Michael Ross,' he said, smiling self-consciously and extending his hand towards David. 'From London – photo-journalist on assignment with The Bangkok Mail.'

David's arms remained tightly knotted across his chest. 'What are you doing here?' he asked sternly.

The white man looked liked he had been punched suddenly, but he spoke firmly. 'And who, may I ask, are you to ask me?'

Harish could see a steely rage building up inside David, who now turned to the other two.

'Shiva,' he asked sternly, 'permit hai?' He waited for an answer he knew wouldn't come. Couldn't come. 'Shiva, tell him who I am,' he said turning back to the Englishman.

Shiva also turned to Michael Ross. 'Sir, David! Scientist. Researcher. Knowing many islands very well. Many years.'

'Oh! Mr Baskaran! Dr David Baskaran? Have heard a lot about you. What a pleasure to meet you sir. Looking for crocs, I presume,' Michael Ross extended his hand again in greeting.

'And you are presumably here,' David was not interested in any pleasantries, 'to get fucking pictures of naked Jarawa women?'

David wasn't loud, but his voice was trembling with the effort he was making to control his rage. Harish was shocked. He had never heard David speak like this before. Was this going to get ugly?

'Mind your language, mister,' Ross said in a measured tone.

'Listen,' David said, glaring at him, 'you'd better leave now! You have no fucking idea who I am. I'll get you into prison. You don't even have permission to get to this place, and you ask me who I am?'

Michael Ross was not the type to be easily deterred. 'Whoever you are, do *you* have the permits to get here? And I am an accredited journalist – it's my business to go everywhere.'

'You bastard,' David exploded. 'Why don't you take pictures of your naked women, in your bloody country and splash them on the front pages of your newspapers?'

This was more than what Michael Ross would tolerate. He took an aggressive step towards David, and would have surely punched him had Harish and Shiva not quickly jumped between the two.

'Let him, Harish. Let me see what he does. I have seen enough of these guys – so-called journalists with no fucking scruples. Do you know, it's against the law of the land for you to be here?' he glared at the Englishman. 'You, Michael Ross, you bloody Britishers screwed these people – now what are you taking pictures for? The people . . .'

Michael Ross wouldn't let him complete. 'Look who's talking. Who is screwing the Jarawas now? Actually screwing them? For a thousand quid – your fellow Indians,' he turned to Shiva and the other man, 'will get you two nights with a Jarawa woman. Britishers don't come and screw them. Your fellow fucking Indians do. Don't tell me you don't know this.' Michael Ross was now barking with indignation.

'We'll deal with our people,' David snapped back. 'You get the fuck out of here first, or I'm warning you, you'll be in trouble.'

He turned to Shiva. 'You're finished, Shiva. I had warned you. How many have you brought after that Frenchman? Bloody goras!'

He looked at the other fellow. 'Asit, you'll never learn, will you?

Poaching and cheating is in your blood? You've forgotten the hammering the police gave you last time. You told me, didn't you, that it would be the last?'

'What to do?' Asit started apologetically. 'Need some money no? There . . .'

'Now explain to the police,' David interrupted him, and turned again to Shiva. 'I don't know, Shiva, if this guy will understand but you sure do. Leave now and I mean it!'

Felix had now grown animated as he told Seema of the Jarawa honey method. He lowered his voice in a way that was both dramatic and full of conspiracy. Seema found Felix's manner more than mildly hilarious, and worked hard to prevent a smile from escaping her lips. She did not want to short circuit Felix at this point.

He explained in detail how the Jarawa used the leaves of a plant called tomale, the juice of which worked as a bee-intoxicant. 'After applying the juice to their bare bodies, they scamper up huge trees like monkeys did back in my village in Jharkhand. Tomale juice has an unbelievable effect on the bees. They get drowsy and tipsy, exactly like our Mathew uncle,' Felix chuckled, 'gets high on aunty's handia. You see,' he looked at Seema, with an excited look in his eyes, 'the bees lose all their aggression and all orientation. They are all around you, but they don't sting. You can easily get all the honey you want. It is a simple and efficient method and completely risk-free. I don't think,' he emphasized, 'anyone in the world extracts honey in such a fantastic manner. In some matters these Jarawas are ustads.' The admiration was evident in his tone. 'Real ustads. Sometimes I wonder how they know so much. Who taught them all these things? And you know,' he continued with pride, 'they even taught me. I can extract honey just like the Jarawa themselves, and I am even better than some of them now,' he concluded with a wink.

'That I must say,' Seema smiled, 'is amazing.'

'What am I telling you, Madam?' Felix quickly took off as he was wont to do. 'We have been living here for so many years. You live here with me for three years and you will also learn. God alone knows what else the Jarawas have knowledge of. They don't take our medicines even. They know everything about the forest. It's like their bazaar, but here everything comes for free.' He sighed as if to signal he was finally done, but then suddenly started off again. 'Arre, I forgot in all this talking,' he said, getting up. 'I'll just be back.' He went into his house and came back with a small plastic bottle filled with a golden-coloured fluid. 'Pure honey, from the land of the Jarawa. The best honey in the world. Give it to David babu also!' he said, thrusting the bottle into Seema's hands.

'No,' Seema tried to resist. 'It's okay. I don't want it.'

Felix insisted. 'I know what you are thinking. I agree this is honey from the land of the Jarawa, but this is the honey that I have collected myself.

'Please take it,' Felix pleaded, leaving Seema with no choice.

'Thank you,' she said taking the bottle, 'but Felix, can you tell me something about this Tanumei as well? What is his story? You know him?'

'Tanumei? Everyone is talking about that Tanumei, his fracture and all that. We always knew him and his band – absolute rascals. They live just behind this hill, only two hours walk from here. He returned from Port Blair and started behaving like a hero; maybe they showed him too many of our films there. He came here a few months ago with a group of four and asked for rice. He wanted the aluminium vessel too. "I want the degchi," he kept saying and even tried to snatch it. We thrashed him nicely.'

'Thrashed him,' Seema asked with a start, 'and they didn't do anything?'

'Not that we beat him up or anything,' Felix realized suddenly that he may be asking for trouble. Had he not said enough already? 'I mean, we had to be aggressive ourselves to prevent him from taking away our vessel. See,' he continued, now trying deliberately to move the conversation to safer ground, 'the Jarawas are slowly getting civilized and we can help if we are allowed to remain here. We are already living peacefully together. Like good neighbours,' he emphasized, to reinforce the point that he had made a short while ago.

'But Felix,' Seema said, deciding now to take charge of the conversation, 'the Jarawa are the people of the forests, aren't they? They have lived here for thousands of years – before you came here, before anyone was here, even before the British. They should be allowed to live the way they want to. There is nothing wrong with that?'

Felix was sharp. 'I agree . . . sorry what is your name. I completely forgot to ask'

'Seema.'

'You're right Seemaji. Absolutely right. But you can't talk about the Jarawa anymore without talking about us. Now the administration is trying to teach them agriculture.'

'Really? Who says?' Seema interrupted.

'See, that is the problem,' Felix replied, 'Ask David babu to show you what is happening in Lekra Lunta. It's not very far away. Here the Tribal Welfare Department has created a full plantation of coconut and banana for the Jarawa. If they should be allowed to live their original lives, why this? If the administration and the Tribal Welfare Department does all this, it's okay, if we do farming here and are also willing to teach the Jarawa that is not okay? Why? And now they also want to throw us out.'

That dangling sword of eviction kept returning to the conversation.

'If you can help in some way . . .' Felix's tone changed. He looked expectantly at Seema, making her extremely uncomfortable and self-conscious. 'We are in Jarawa territory – that's true,' he admitted, 'but what will happen to us? See, if you can tell something to the administration. You are educated people, and they will listen to you. See, we also want the good for the Jarawas. We will help them in whatever way we can. We can also help the administration in any way they want. They can even take some of our land for plantations for the Jarawas. No problem, but . . .'

'But what will you do if the Administration insists?'

'Then what can we do, Seemaji?' resignation and sadness weighed heavy in his tone. 'We'll have to go. What else?'

'Who knows what our destiny will be. Maybe, we won't be here when you come around for the next survey?'

The other interaction, meanwhile, had intensified. Shiva had gone pale in the face of David's relentless attack.

'Michael sir,' he spoke in broken English, 'we go now.'

'But . . .' Michael tried to reason.

'No but, sir.' Shiva wouldn't let him. 'We go now. All money return. Big trouble come. Came already sir . . .' He turned now to David. 'Sorry sir, but please let us go. Really really last time. When you are going back? I'm coming to the Institute to see you. I am bringing Michael also – nice guy sir.'

Shiva paused, waiting for some response. 'Okay, okay,' he quickly corrected himself, 'I am not bringing him. Coming alone only. Michael,' he turned back to the Englishman, 'we go now.'

He beckoned to Asit and quickly disappeared into the tent.

Michael stood in his place, extremely upset. Only after Shiva had called for him twice did he turn around and go back in.

David waited, watching Shiva and his client dismantle their tents, load their stuff into the dungi and leave. Not a word more was spoken, except those between Shiva and Asit and that too only to figure out the logistics of the packing.

Once they were packed, David and Michael locked eyes one last time. David stood his ground, and Michael Ross left in a huff. This had been an uneven match from the very beginning. This was David's territory – the Englishman didn't really have a chance.

'Who do these guys think they are?' David started off, once the intruders were gone, 'This is not the first time it's happened. Two years ago, there was this French guy, also a photo-journalist, who had come to the Institute. He told me he was interested in wildlife, forests and the tribal people on the islands. He was good,' David paused, 'but only as a photographer. He showed me some of his pictures from the Sarawak forests and they were really good. Actually stunning.'

Harish was all ears.

'He was desperate to get into these forests, to get some Jarawa pictures. I suspect that he made a promise to some publication that he would do it – maybe he'd even taken a big advance. I was categorical, telling him he wouldn't get permission, that he should not try even. He was unwilling to listen. You know what the guy did? "David," he told me, "See I need to get those Jarawa pictures – at any cost. I can pay you and the Institute any amount if you help me get in there."'

'Really?' Harish finally spoke.

'Exactly. I couldn't believe it myself. Did he think I was a pimp or something? I was really angry, but not as much as I was today,' David shrugged. 'I asked him to leave immediately.'

'And then?'

'Yes, and then to my shock and horror, three months later, I get this packet in the post from France, from this guy, Henri . . . something or the other – I don't remember. Inside was a six-page colour pull-out – a centre-spread from some French magazine with fifteen pictures of the Jarawas. This Henri guy was taking his revenge. There was no need for him to send me that feature, but it was good that he did. It got me wild. A disproportionately large number, ten of the fifteen pictures, if I remember right, featured women. It was nauseating – clearly, many of the Jarawa women had been asked to pose. The corniest was a wide-angled picture of a well-proportioned Jarawa woman reclining in the crystal waters of the coast, her head resting on her hand, her breasts thrusting into the camera. He'd obviously got her to do it. Shameless voyeurism, complete vulgarity. I found out later what the caption said. "An innocent creature of mother nature, on the virgin coast of the Andaman Islands." What was he doing? Trying to create that noble, untainted savage? Can it really get worse? What a bastard!'

'David!' Harish didn't really know what to say.

'No, Harish, listen. Remind me to show you the feature when we get back and you'll see what I mean. It's worse than those pictures of naked Jarawa women that are sold and bought openly in the Port Blair bazaar. There are no pretensions here. At least it is honest. And there's more – in that set of fifteen pictures, there was one small one that featured the photographer himself. It had obviously been taken by the person who had accompanied him there. There was this white man in the middle with his arms around a Jarawa man on his left and a woman on his right. And you know what? A black band had been deliberately placed across his eyes, blanking out his identity. Such cowardice. Now you tell me . . .'

Harish was quiet. He had nothing to say.

'And there was a biographical note at the end of that feature,' David continued, 'that Henri whatever was an award-winning photo-journalist who had not only risked potential attack by the dangerous Jarawas, but also taken his chances with the Indian law to get these pictures. Do they have such contempt for their own laws as well?'

'And who was this other person who might have taken this Henri in there?' Harish asked, intrigued.

'That is what I wanted to find out and I did. That Michael whom we just met, what was the last name?'

'Ross,' Harish prompted.

'Yes. You know Harish, that Ross – he's also right and that's the tragedy. What's the point of shouting at and fighting his type when those who make it happen are your own people. When the rot is within, why blame the outsider? When I saw that French photo feature – I was so enraged that I went straight to Ranjit. I don't go to him often, but he's a good friend.'

'Ranjit . . .?'

'S. Ranjit, the intelligence chap. The Intelligence Bureau fellow in Port Blair. I have got to introduce him to you as well. We'll do it when we are in Port Blair next. It didn't take too long to find out. It was Shiva who had organized that trip for the Frenchman. Ranjit gave Shiva a good shouting. I was there. He was even threatened with jail if found doing this again. Shiva promised it was the last. Never again, he had said with tears in his eyes. He seemed terrified. Maybe he was, but obviously it's worn off. I don't see him stopping. It's good money – the curse of the white man's wealth. The bloody exchange rate! You know,' he said, more thoughtful now, 'the Japanese, even the Americans, the others with a lot of money don't seem too interested in stuff like this. Hardly ever seen any of them. It's largely these Europeans, still carrying their white man's burden, aren't they?'

'David,' Harish interrupted tentatively, recalling what Ross had said, 'What about the two nights with the Jarawa women. Is that true? Is that really happening? Where?'

'I have only heard about it once before,' David said with resignation. 'Never thought it was true, but maybe I am wrong. I was told it happens at some points along the road – it's difficult this side, but you never know.'

'But why would the Jarawa women agree? What about their community?' Harish was really troubled. 'How does one make sense of this?'

'What can I say, Harish?' David sounded irritated and angry again, burdened, it seemed, with more than he could deal with. 'You know what my problem is? I get involved with too many things. Is it my bloody job to keep tabs on Shiva and fight with that Michael Ross? Am I the only one worried about these forests and the Jarawas? Why can't I just fucking stick to surveying my crocs and turtles?

Don't I have enough on my plate already?' He was now speaking as much to himself as he was to Harish. 'I think I was too nasty. Do I have the right to be angry like that? I didn't behave well with that Michael fellow, did I Harish? What do you think?'

David's questions caught Harish completely by surprise. He had, in fact, drilled to the very bottom of Harish's own unarticulated discomfort.

'I don't know David,' was all he could offer. 'What can I say?'.

David and Harish returned to pick up Popha and Seema. Seema's excitement over her time with Felix was immediately clouded by the sombre silence David and Harish brought with them. She was bubbling over, but decided to wait till a little later.

Popha had stepped into the inflatable, and Seema was just jumping in when her left foot slipped on the bank of the creek and slid along on the greasy surface. David's quick reflexes ensured she didn't fall over into the water.

'You okay?' David asked, as he grabbed her hands.

'My ankle . . .' she grimaced as she hobbled into the inflatable.

'You're okay?' David asked again as the four men now helped her to climb back into the dungi.

'It's hurting, but I should be okay. I think I'll take a painkiller,' she replied, pulling out a packet of medicines from her bag.

'So,' Uncle decided to finally get the conversation going. He had noticed the other dungi leave a short while ago. 'You had company? What was Shiva's dungi doing in there?'

Harish narrated the story as he had witnessed it. David sat by quietly, spent, looking increasingly embarrassed as he listened to the tale of his exploits.

'I need to learn to control myself,' he admitted, nodding his head. 'Otherwise I am going to get into deep trouble some day.'

Uncle was also nodding his head, but in dismay. 'No, David,' he said, 'it was the right thing you did. And that Shiva – he's the one asking for trouble.' He then turned to Seema. 'What about you Seema?'

Popha brought the tea that Uncle had prepared while they had been away, and Seema took a sip as she started.

'We met Felix,' she said, turning to David. 'He seemed very fond of you, David. And we learnt some very interesting things about their settlement, the Jarawas, about Tanumei, of how they collect honey. See, he even gave me this bottle.'

'So he's told you the honey story too?' Uncle asked. 'Actually, he's well known here for the honey he gets. He's very good in the forests . . . Good chap, this Felix.'

'You know him well, Uncle?' Seema asked.

'Yes. Very nice chap. I didn't know he was back. Only a few weeks ago he was in Kadamtala and before that in Port Blair, trying to get some official paper work done. Poor chap. His wife died of malaria. I've told him so many times to leave this goddamned place and go elsewhere – where there is some civilization. But he just doesn't listen. If he had been anywhere close to even a small town, his wife would have been alive today.'

'Oh,' Seema said, 'he did show me a photo of his wife and child, but didn't tell me anything. But why doesn't he leave? It's clearly not an easy place to live in.'

'It's understandable, isn't it Seema?' Uncle said taking a sip while the others listened in silence. 'Twenty years and more is a long time. His father used to work in the forest camp near Webi. They spent so much time and labour creating this basti. It is difficult to just leave. I know what it takes to create land from the forest. The land will give you your food, but not before it takes your blood and sweat. You won't understand – these are the pains of those who live by the land.'

The effect of the medicine that Seema had popped had worn off and her ankle, now swollen up, began to hurt. It showed on her face.

'This needs some looking at,' David said with brotherly concern and boss-like finality. 'We're lucky we are here. Kadamtala is not too far down this creek, and I think we should go and see a doctor.'

'But the survey, David?' Seema was concerned she was impeding the man's work.

'I'll go with her,' Harish offered. 'You carry on.'

David was in a serious bind. This had been a difficult survey to get going, and now he was the only person who could accompany Seema. Sending Popha was out of the question, and Harish was too new to the place to manage by himself in case Seema's problem worsened. Uncle could have escorted her, but that would leave nobody to pilot the boat. Not only that – no one knew the Jarawa creeks and waters like Uncle did, and without him there would be no survey. Popha was there to assist and David decided he would let them take control of this part of the journey.

'No,' David said as he made up his mind, 'I will go with her. There is no other option. The three of you carry on. We'll meet in Mayabundar in a couple of days. See how her ankle is swelling up – a doctor needs to check this out immediately. And I'll be there on the return leg of the survey, in any case. What do you say, Uncle?'

'That's fine, David. Whatever you say.'

This was Seema's last breakfast on board, and she was distinctly unhappy that she had to leave. Her ankle, however, was throbbing with pain and she was grateful that some medical help was close at hand. Mugger was soon rattling along the water channel that would take them to the jetty at Uttara. Here David and Seema hired an auto rickshaw to the PHC in Kadamtala, the same PHC Tanumei had been brought to with a broken foot many, many months ago. Dr Bandopadhyay, the only doctor at the PHC was out in the field, so Seema had no choice but to be admitted and await his return.

The first day went by and there was still no sign of the doctor.

Neither did anybody seem to have a clue of his whereabouts. Seema tried asking the nurse a couple of times, but all she got was a shrug. She had reached the end of her patience by the afternoon of the second day. That is when Pintu finally brought some information.

'You always come at a very interesting time, David babu,' he started. 'I've just found out, Bandopadhyay babu was away deep in the forests of the Jarawa Reserve. He is on his way back and should be here in about an hour.'

'What has he been doing?' Seema asked, irritated. 'Why doesn't anybody know anything?'

'I don't know for sure,' Pintu replied, 'but we heard that some Jarawas have come down with fever – some kind of rash because of the heat. He had gone to check that. Maybe you can ask him when he is back.'

Dr Bandopadhyay had a reputation for being a sincere and hard-working man, a doctor who was passionately committed to his profession and his patients. He was at the PHC within a few minutes of returning from the field, and came immediately to check on Seema. He was a middle-aged man with hair that was still mostly black. He wore thick, plastic-rimmed glasses that he kept pushing up the bridge of his nose every now and then. 'I am very sorry,' paan-flavoured words tumbled out in a rounded Bengali accent. 'Something very important and urgent, you see.'

He inspected Seema's ankle. 'There is an inflammation. It is quite bad. We'll get an X-ray done and let's see then.' Every time he spoke, the room filled up with the sweet flavour of what he was chewing. 'And Dr David, I am very glad to meet you finally. I have a few other patients to check on, and will come back to see you a little later.'

He returned later in the afternoon. 'The X-ray does not show anything,' he said handing the envelope to Seema, 'but I would advice you to stay on for another day. It will take some time for the inflammation and the pain to come down further.'

'Do I have to?' Seema said, with a disappointed look on her face.

'I think you must,' the doctor said firmly.

'I agree,' David added, turning to Dr Bandopadhyay. 'If you don't mind,' he asked politely, 'can I ask what took you so suddenly into the Jarawa Reserve.'

'See, I can't say much,' the doctor replied, with visible reluctance, 'but there were reports of fever among some Jarawa boys. I needed to check on that. I think we will be bringing two of them here in the next couple of days.'

'Is it a serious matter, doctor?' David asked again.

'I don't think so. We will investigate further once they are here. And now if you will excuse me.'

14

OLD MEMORIES,
STRENGTHENED BONDS

Mugger had, after dropping Seema and David at Uttara jetty, returned along the same route. In a short while, they were exiting the narrow channel past the precise point called Lekra Lunta, and as they did, Uncle guided the dungi closer to land and slowed down considerably to allow Harish a closer look.

Just beyond the water's edge was a patch of raised flat land, a biggish plateau marked by the huge thatched canopy of a Jarawa communal dwelling. The roof of the perfectly circular structure sloped almost all the way down to the ground. Harish estimated the construction to be at least forty feet in diameter. It had a neat look to it, and was certainly the product of a lot of labour and considerable skill. It did not seem, however, to be in great shape and had clearly not been in use for a very long time. The roof had collapsed in a couple of places and the jungle bush had begun the process of its reclamation. Beyond it, the land gently sloped upwards for quite a distance before it finally disappeared into the forest.

This gentle slope was not barren. It was, like Felix had told Seema, a not very old plantation of coconut and areca – official, administrative efforts at teaching the Jarawas the ways of the civilized human being.

The dungi entered more open waters as they moved further from the coast and once again Uncle turned it to the north. A short while later Harish thought he noticed some movement on the coast, far away. Five tiny dots of black stood out on the white sparkling beach, moving in unison towards Lekra Lunta. He turned to Uncle and pointed towards the coast. 'Jarawas?' he asked, screaming over the rattling engines, barely able to conceal his excitement. Uncle smiled, nodding his head in affirmation even as they continued towards Louis Inlet, the last major creek system scheduled for David's croc survey.

They entered Louis Inlet in a bit, and Popha cut the engines. The coast near the inlet was rocky. The land on the left bank went up a sharp gradient right from the water's edge and then flattened out a bit. Here, about a hundred feet up the cliff, in a decidedly picturesque setting, was the Bush Police outpost they needed to visit.

As the dungi approached the water's edge, Uncle picked up the plastic packet that held copies of their permits and beckoned to Harish to join him. As they waded ashore through the thigh-deep water, Popha poled the dungi back in deeper and threw in the anchor.

They walked up for a short while and reached a narrow stream of fresh water that descended rapidly down the incline they had just climbed. They walked along for a couple of minutes and now the stream opened out into a small, palm-fringed pool.

Uncle stood silently for a few moments, staring at the placid blue water. Harish felt like he was witnessing a deeply significant personal ritual. Uncle bent down, scooped up a handful of water and splashed it on his face. He cupped his palms again and scooped up some more, this time to drink. He then sat down on a small log of wood that had been smoothened through years of continued use. A few moments later, he smiled at Harish, a sad, resigned smile.

'This, Harish,' he started off in his regular deadpan manner, 'is where the Jarawas killed my Abba and Amma many, many years ago.'

Harish's jaw dropped. The simplicity and suddenness of the

revelation left him stunned. He didn't know how to react, what to say. His mouth opened, but no words came out.

'Today, I am seventy-three,' Uncle continued, 'and that was about my father's age then.' He went back to staring at the water before them, withdrawing quickly into a quiet, private world.

Harish regained his composure and sat down on the other edge of the log. The story came out shortly – and slowly.

'A group of four, Abba, Amma, a cousin and I had come to Louis Inlet for fishing. It was my third visit, and no one knew how many times Abba and Amma had been here. Even they didn't remember. It had been a proud coming of age when Abba first asked me to join them on this trip. These are rich fishing grounds today. They were even richer then and the Karens came regularly. We occasionally dived here for shell and also went hunting for wild pigs and monitor lizards in the forests. We would row from Webi to here, fish for a couple of days and then row back for an entire day. It was hard work, but fun and worth the effort – one never went back empty-handed.

'On that day, we had stopped at the mouth of the inlet, very close to where our dungi has been parked today. This stream was the best and most easily accessible source of water. It was Abba who decided that day that we'd come up and get some for ourselves. The two of them – Amma and Abba – came up this slope just the way we did today. I followed along with my cousin, but we had needed just that much more time to tie up the boat. It was just as we were hurrying up this slope after them, that we heard loud shouts. Jarawa sounds.' Uncle paused and shut his eyes. He was silent for a very long time. 'Then there were two screams,' he opened his eyes and turned to Harish, 'Abba and then Amma. The old man's assumption, or was it a calculation, was all wrong.

'It was a costly mistake. A very costly mistake. Abba knew these forests very well. People in the village used to say he could smell the Jarawas from a distance. It was always safe going to the forests with him. Maybe his time had come . . .' Uncle's words were twitching with emotion. 'Luckily for us – or were we the unlucky ones? – the Jarawas had not seen me and my cousin. We were not very far, and I still don't know how they missed us. We crouched by a small bush some distance down this slope, trembling. Even today, a chill runs down my spine when I think about that day. We waited for a while, terrified that any movement or sound would give us away. We heard a shuffling sound that went on for sometime. When it stopped, we turned around and raced down the slope, jumped into the dungi and rowed quickly away from land. In the middle of the creek, surrounded on all sides by water – I had never felt safer before. I don't know what Abba was thinking that day. It was like the Jarawas were waiting for him, and yet he had no clue. The two of us waited till the late hours of the afternoon. Then, terribly anxious, we came back. We had to check, but what if we were also attacked? Slowly and quietly, we climbed back, wary of any movement or sound. We turned left and reached the stream, half expecting a Jarawa arrow to pierce our own hearts. We walked up to this log here,' Uncle tapped the log the two of them were sitting on, 'holding hands, still trembling with fear. On that stone over there,' he now pointed to a largish boulder that was also smooth with many years of use, 'we saw something that I will never forget – marks of blood that seemed to have just dried. What a way to die! Even their bodies were not found.'

Uncle nodded, his eyes moist.

'Three months later, I came back all alone with Abba's old gun. I came up to this pool and waited in the forests along the edge, on the other side there. It was on the afternoon of the second day that I saw a group of five Jarawas approach the pool. I steadied myself, took aim and blasted the man at the front with my first shot. The others scattered like feathers in a strong wind. That very moment, I also promised myself and the Jarawas that I would never come to their forests with a gun again. I never have.'

Harish was dumbfounded. Uncle seemed to him in this moment

like a little child who needed assurance that all was okay. And what
forbearance. So much had happened, yet Harish had only seen
respect for the Jarawa in Uncle's eyes and manner.

They sat by the pool of water for a while, then walked up to the
police outpost, got their permits checked and returned to the dungi,
all in complete silence. The boat was then moved deeper into the
more sheltered waters of another mangrove maze and the anchor
was thrown in for another night.

'Can I ask you something, Uncle?' Harish asked finally, tentatively.

Uncle smiled and nodded.

'There are many things I want to know,' Harish started, 'but first
tell me, really, what do you think of the Jarawas? They killed your
parents and . . .'

'I knew you would ask me this,' Uncle interrupted him. 'Yes it's
true, but you know, the Jarawas are a proud people. They have
dignity, they are the real people of the forests . . . they deserve
respect. This is their home. If you came stealing and plundering into
my house, what kind of man would I be if I let you in without
fighting?'

'But, Uncle, then why come stealing, hunting and fishing at all in
these forests and these waters?'

'I agree, Harish, but don't we have to live too? When people
become greedy like that Biswas, I agree, that cannot be accepted. But
for every Biswas, there are a hundred like my father. Then and now.
These are people who barely manage to scratch up a living.'

Uncle paused, and Harish waited.

'Harish, the Jarawa are called junglee, but show me one man or
woman who knows the jungle better than them. Things have changed
all around the Jarawa, but in many ways the Jarawa have remained
the same. I have known them and others like them for many, many
years now. You know, when I was still a boy, maybe about fourteen
or fifteen years old, the Japanese had come to these islands. They

seemed first to be people like us – smooth fair skin, small eyes, high cheekbones, strong and muscular – so much so that small children thought they were the cousins of our parents and our aunts and uncles. Initially, we were all excited because we thought that people like us would treat us like they treated their own. I too had thought the same. But how wrong we were! People can be like each other in many ways – it's how you live and how you fight that counts. That is why I say that the people closest to the Jarawas of the Andamans are the Karen on the Andamans – men and women who have made their lives with their bare hands. The Jarawas fight only for what is rightfully theirs, and in this they will not yield an inch. It was my first big lesson in life. I am told there was a big war for the world at that time, and that is how the Japanese found our islands. They reached all over, even to Webi. They treated us as if we were their slaves. One night they burst into our house with guns and took away Abba and my brother. I don't know where they took them and why. My brother never came back, and Abba came back a completely changed man – broken in both body and spirit. There was a limp in his left foot, and he was no more the jovial and light-hearted man I had known him to be. I never asked him anything and he told me only one thing: "Be very careful of these people." It was not just Abba and my brother – similar things happened to many of us. I was very, very angry and I decided I had to do something. I don't know if you will believe me, Harish.'

Harish held his breath and his excitement. 'What could it be? What more, Uncle?' he thought to himself.

'A message started doing the rounds those days,' Uncle continued, 'that help was needed to get the Japanese out, and there was need for someone who knew the forests. There was this British officer who came in an underwater boat . . .'

Harish could hardly believe what he was hearing. 'McCarthy! Uncle, you are talking about McCarthy?'

'Yes,' Uncle replied, a trifle surprised. 'Yes, McCarthy sahib. You know about him?'

'What could I know, Uncle?' Harish could barely contain his excitement, 'Did you know him, Uncle? You met him?'

'Yes, McCarthy sahib and some white soldiers, had come into Port Campbell in that underwater boat of theirs. They wanted help to move through the forests to reach Port Blair, or at least close by to get information on what the Japanese were doing and . . .'

'And,' Harish's excitement was now bubbling over, 'you were one of those who helped them, that little known Operation Baldhead? Does anybody know about this, Uncle?'

'There were the three of us,' Uncle didn't directly respond to Harish's question, 'two Ranchis – Robert and Mahato – and me. Robert died only last year. Mahato is still there, he lives in Rangat with his grandson. Our job was to help the British soldiers. We often went as far as what are now the villages of Wimberlygunj and Ferrargunj, but the soldiers never left the forests. The three of us would sneak out one by one and meet certain key people in the basti there. They would give us an envelope that we carried back to the soldiers. Immediately we would all move back deep into the forests.

'The only other people we met in the forests then were these few Great Andamanese and occasionally, the Jarawa. The Jarawas never bothered anybody in those days, and with the Great Andamanese we all became good friends. They would either be dead drunk or high on opium, but also very useful. They knew everything there was to know about the forests. It was tough living, but those were great days – fun and adventure, some opium, some risk and also the value of doing something meaningful for my own people.'

Uncle seemed intoxicated with the pleasures of those powerful memories, and even as Harish looked on, he had wilfully slipped into their familiar embrace.

Harish was reminded of their recent night in Port Campbell as they listened to the sounds of the Jarawas. 'I once wanted to spend my entire life in these forests,' were Uncle's wistful words. Men like Uncle, Harish realized, had actually lived lives that someone like him could never even dream of.

15

'AY TAKHWA'

The sun was well up in the sky the next morning when Uncle finally decided that they should go out to do what they were here for. Uncle and Harish zoomed off in the inflatable and were soon navigating another complex maze of mangrove forests and crocodile creeks. The sun was blazing in the sky above, but it felt like the inflatable was cruising through a cool, dark tunnel as the mangroves closed in above the narrow channels. Streaks of light streamed through, creating a playful patchwork of dark and light on the creek's rippling surface.

There was something new every time they ventured out, but here they had company that was without comparison; the ruddy kingfisher – every feather on that creature's body was a deep brooding saffron. Every time it took off, it resembled a glowing ember on wings that lit up the dark canopy of the mangrove it inhabited. This particular creek was full of these birds – just like it was full of crocodiles.

Uncle and Harish soon came across an exceptionally huge creature – at least ten feet in length, a hulk of a monster that lay basking on an exposed mud bank. Uncle had slowly guided the inflatable in its direction, and even though they had closed in considerably, it budged not an inch. This one was not going to back out, wouldn't take refuge of the waters, as is the habit of crocodiles. It held its ground and for once Uncle thought better than to approach it beyond a certain distance.

Getting close to crocodiles gave men like Uncle a primeval thrill. Many in the Karen community, particularly those of Uncle's generation, had regularly hunted these animals from their rowboats using spears and rope. They had done it by themselves, and they had done it with the Thais, the Indonesians and the Burmese who visited regularly in the past to get the creatures. The event itself was sport, the meat was food, the fat medicine and the hide a good source of income. The creeks were unending, the mangroves thick and crocodile numbers rich. For people who lived only by the land and the sea, everything was fair game and the crocodile was no exception. Over time, however, this had changed. Large mangrove areas were cut down and coupled with continued hunting had caused a serious decline in crocodile populations. At the same time, laws to protect 'wildlife' were being put in place by people in faraway New Delhi. Almost overnight, the crocodile became forbidden quarry.

For the first few years the Karens did not even know that they could not hunt the crocodile anymore. Neither that they couldn't dive for shell, trap birds or hunt deer and wild pig. Perfectly acceptable and long-standing livelihood pursuits suddenly became illegal. Hunting became poaching, and getting food and income a criminal activity. The act was the same, its implications frighteningly different. From hard-working people eking out a living from the land and the waters, the community had now come to be branded a band of poachers.

The initial, occasional run-ins with the law and its keepers soon turned to a minor deluge. The Karens couldn't figure out why they were being stopped. No one had taken the trouble to explain the changed situation and laws to them. Uncle himself had been caught in these situations. Eventually, experience taught them that something had changed, that there was a new law and that they could not do certain things that they had taken for granted in the past.

Hunting, as a consequence, came down significantly over time. The younger generation did not particularly miss this lifestyle, but many of the older lot did. That is why Uncle and some of the other oldies loved so much to accompany David and other researchers when they went out in the field. Here was a legitimized way in which they could enjoy the thrills of their youth.

In many ways, it had been a mutually beneficial collaboration. Researchers like David needed people like the Karen. In a difficult place like the islands, someone even marginally less capable, courageous or informed would be a liability. Had it not been for Uncle and some others like him there was no chance that David, his institute and its research could have survived, let alone thrived.

Now, Uncle guided the boat away from the ten-footer, and they moved further ahead along the length of the creek. They had not gone very far, when in a channel to the right they saw another small dungi. It was similar to Mugger, but also distinctly different. Uncle quickly turned into the channel and cut the engine of the inflatable. They glided quietly towards the stationary boat and were still some distance away when they heard a sudden burst of noise from inside the mangroves. Uncle and Harish were taken by surprise, and as they looked in the direction, they saw four to five men, scattering aimlessly like partridges flushed from the undergrowth.

'Ay takhwa!' Uncle called out loudly. Takhwa in the language of the Karen meant cousin, and it was, Uncle knew, something these men would understand. His voice went booming through the green and then the mangrove absorbed it quickly, muffling it like a silencer would. He waited a couple of seconds then called out again 'Ay takhwa!' following this up immediately with a few loud sentences in what Harish recognized was the language of the Karen. He'd heard it often enough when Uncle and Popha spoke to each other, but there wasn't a word he could understand. Uncle's call, meanwhile, had its effect. The sound of men running in the mangrove slush stopped, and Karen like faces emerged tentatively from behind the trees.

These were, in fact, Uncle's own people, not the Karen of Webi where Uncle lived, but Karen from faraway Burma, from where Uncle and all his predecessors had come to settle in these islands many decades ago.

This was another aspect of the islands that was known and yet not known. These men who came in with impunity from the neighbouring countries were spoken of as 'international poachers', with all the connotations this held – of a well-organized syndicate, even a cross-border mafia. The reality, for those who knew about it, was anything but this.

Burmese Karen, like this particular group, were regularly encountered in the creeks of the most remote and inaccessible parts of these islands, and none more so than the territories of the feared Jarawa. These Karen were not people from the famous hill lands, where a bitter struggle for a homeland was going on, but from the lowlands of Bassein, much closer to Rangoon – also victims of politics in a country held in the tight tentacles of the military junta. Their poverty had left them with little choice but to run the full gamut of risks. The Andaman waters and forests, particularly those in the Jarawa territory, were still rich and teeming with game of all variety. If they managed to get here, there was some chance of making a decent living.

They had to first negotiate the mighty Irrawady Delta, perhaps the toughest part of the endeavour. There were the elements of nature to deal with; there was the police and also the military surveillance, both Burmese and Chinese. In recent times, Twantay at the mouth of the Irrawady had become the base of the feared Liberation Tigers of Tamil Eelam, and if encountered, the Karens would pay a price to them as well. The river was best navigated in the day, the surveillance best eluded at night. In the balance it was the river they trusted more, so most journeys were undertaken under the cover of darkness. First landfall, if the delta was successfully cleared, was Landfall Island, the northernmost of the Andaman group. From here, there were two routes for the taking. One went east to the extinct volcano island of Narcondum, then south, past the Ritchie's archipelago along its eastern side and then west again to the west coast of the island of Little Andaman. Some stayed here, and others ventured even further, risking the wrath of the ten-degree channel to the Nicobar Islands – taking greater risks, but if successful, also returning with greater rewards and riches.

The other route was the one this present dungi had taken, coming along the west of Landfall Island, hugging the coast, taking shelter and making best use of the inlets and creeks of many North Andaman Island, then Middle Andaman – where they were presently located – then South Andaman Island onwards to Rutland, and occasionally, further south to Little Andaman as well. It helped them hugely that there were almost no settlements along this coast and they could have a free run. In more ways than one, the Jarawas were the unlikely benefactors of these people.

There were no records of the run-ins these Burmese had with the Jarawas. There were the anecdotal accounts of fierce battles, but these could never be authenticated. The state agencies, including the Intelligence Bureau, did not keep such records. The only records they had were of the successful and well-publicized encounters when they had managed to apprehend some of the intruders. Putting on paper the other visits that they had managed to get information and intelligence of, but could do nothing about, would be more than a tacit admission that international boundaries were being penetrated regularly and blatantly by foreign nationals. The record sheets were kept clean and everyone went home happy and to a good night's sleep. This was why the photo-feature of the Jarawas by the French photographer had created a huge ruckus; many were made to answer questions. The system had broken down, ironically, because the offender had provided evidence of his offence. An indelible record had been created, and the smooth logic of the past had been pushed onto a dangerously slippery slope.

In the recent past, those like these Karen from Burma came to the Andaman waters mainly for fishing. Now they had then taken to diving for shell and for sea cucumber. During the day, the groups would take shelter deep in the dark creeks, perfectly hidden from the occasional aerial sorties of Coast Guard helicopters and the patrols of their ships. They would move out only under the cover of darkness and return well before the sun ascended the next morning.

The curvature of this particular creek as it turned to where the Burma dungi was parked had hidden the inflatable till it was rather late. When they finally realised that they had visitors in an inflatable very much like that of the Coast Guard, the intruders had scattered through the mangrove. Now, hearing the reassuring sound of their own language, they emerged slowly and walked tentatively towards the visiting party.

Uncle continued talking, further reassuring them and successfully engaging them in conversation. There were four young guys – the oldest must have been in his early twenties. Two of them didn't have their shirts on. The other two wore what could be best described as tattered rags. Their hair was dishevelled, a stubble of many days was visible on their chins and their arms and feet were caked in a thick layer of brown mud. They looked tired, even desolate, their wretchedness accentuated by the tension writ large on their faces. Being caught now and here, after all the effort and the risk, in what was considered the safest part of the voyage, would have indeed been a travesty.

Their hope showed in the tentative half-smiles that came as they spoke their native tongue. Maybe they had not been busted after all.

The inflatable now stood beside the Burmese dungi and Uncle drew Harish's attention to it. It was to Mugger what Uncle was to these other men – distant cousins. It was a specimen of great craftsmanship, and like the dungis made by the Andaman Karens, it too had a dugout for its hull. At the far end was a compressor and a single Chinese Jiansu engine.

'Look at this.' Harish was not sure whether Uncle was referring to the entire boat or just the engine. 'What a boat!' he continued. 'What skill. I wish I could lay my hands on one of these. And see that engine.' Harish saw, but could make nothing of it. He understood nothing of these matters. Uncle's eyes were, however, beaming with admiration and with envy. 'It's incredibly smooth and powerful,' he continued. 'You won't believe how silent it is. These Chinese are amazing.'

He turned to the men on land and spoke, presumably complimenting them on their boat or engine, most likely both. They nodded in vigorous affirmation and broke out into an energetic chatter amongst themselves.

Harish surveyed the scene. Just a little beyond the first line of trees was a small, temporary wooden table with a fire burning under it. The table-top was a grid of thin twigs about five feet from the ground and roughly the same in length and breadth. A couple of ankle-length canvas boots hung from their laces at one end, drying. One edge of the table was occupied by a shirt that had also been laid out to dry and on the opposite side was an assortment of utensils – a few plates, a couple of cups, some spoons and a tea kettle.

The rest of the surface was occupied by brown, flattened, rubbery strips roughly two inches across – the sea cucumbers. They would be collected by the hundreds, dried and then carried back in gunny-sacks wrapped in sheets of plastic.

After chatting for a bit, Uncle decided it was time to leave. He told Harish later that he had wanted to talk to them a little longer, but did not want to unsettle them or make them suspicious.

Back in Mugger, they had just settled down to sipping the tea that Popha had prepared, when two small boats came rowing in from the other side, passed them and entered the very creek system from which they had just exited. They could have easily approached the dungi, exchanged a few words and then proceeded on their way. They didn't, and Harish was intrigued.

'They are going to the Burmese,' Uncle explained confidently. 'Did you notice the big pumpkin inside the first one? Do you realise it is not possible for these outsiders to be here for so many days and not have some interaction with the locals?'

'The locals?'

'Need to find out, but it's most probably some Bengali or Ranchi settlers from the settlements further up this side of the creek. It's a well set-up system, and has been around since the first Bengalis came here. They provide them with water, vegetables and grain, depending on how long they stay. A part of the catch is given in return. It works perfectly.'

'And the police?'

'As if they don't know. They are all on the bloody take. The local chaps know it all but deliberately turn a blind eye. It's only when it comes to the notice of the seniors that there is trouble and some action gets taken.'

The rowboats had gone gliding by gracefully, and it was not long before one of them returned.

'Ay dada!' Popha called out at Uncle's prodding.

The boat turned, and inched towards them rather reluctantly.

'Looking for crabs,' a bony little fellow wrapped in a lungi of blue and white squares offered an explanation that had not been sought. 'Bad time. Difficult to get anything,' he said, trying to ensure that the conversation and the questioning did not enter uncomfortable territory. In the boat was a big plastic bucket that was empty. Lying besides the bucket was the locally crafted contraption for extracting crabs – a wooden handle, a foot long, attached to a much longer iron rod that had been rounded off towards the end like a hook.

'Can we get some crab?' Uncle asked half-jokingly, trying to ease their tension. 'Where are the crabs?' The man in the front replied. 'We hardly get anything these days.'

'What are you doing here?' the second man at the other end of the small boat asked in a high-pitched, irritated tone. He was much older and even thinner than his companion. He sat, crouched and shrivelled, at the end of the boat. His bones stuck out prominently from beneath his skin. 'How long will you be here?'

'Not very long,' Uncle responded. 'Maybe one more day. We are looking for crocodiles. Research team!'

'Ah! Okay!' the younger man exhaled a gasp of relief.

'Crocodiles?' the old man barked, still irritated and now even more suspicious. 'What for?'

'Arre, leave it no, dada!' the younger man screeched at the old man. 'What is your problem? Don't bother, babu.' He looked up at Harish with an apologetic smile on his face. 'Let's go now. Okay babu,' he turned the boat and started rowing vigorously.

Everyone was on the move here, if not actually on the run.

It was now a little after the sun had retired for the day. The three were sitting quietly in the gently rocking boat, when Popha pointed out again in the direction of the creek.

There was a small linear movement against the increasing darkness of the mangroves in the background. The Burma dungi was emerging slowly, chugging quietly, a thin plume of silent smoke in its wake. Having been spotted earlier in the day, they appeared to have decided that it was time to move on.

Harish realized now what Uncle meant about the silence of the Chinese engine – it emitted only a gentle whisper. The boat first turned left into the opening of Louis Inlet and receded slowly into the western horizon. After a while, it turned left and headed for safer fishing grounds further south. Harish kept looking for as long as he could. 'They must be cursing their luck,' he thought.

The night turned cold, and the three men retreated to their respective sleeping spaces after their regular on-board meal of rice and dal. In a while, Harish found himself completely awake. He checked his watch. Midnight. He had slept only four hours, yet he felt alive and refreshed.

He took a sip of water, slipped out of his sleeping bag, walked to the front of the dungi, peed into the ocean, returned and slipped back in again. The second session of sleep was about as long as the first one because when he found himself awake and looking at his watch again, the smaller hand had just gone past four.

Harish sat up and looked at the dark line of mangroves from where the sun would rise shortly. The night had started to fade away and the stars had begun dissolving in the sky as it turned from black to an inky blue, melting further into an even lighter shade as the moments slipped by. 'Is sunrise the moment the curve of the sun-orb first peeps out above the horizon?' he thought. 'Or is it now already, when the tinge of morning light is making its first appearance?'

He looked in the other direction to see how the sky was faring on the earth's western flank on this cold, crisp morning. The sight captivated him. There was no water, there was no horizon and there was no sky. There was only a soft curtain of ethereal mist – a milky, mysterious, malleable white that blended the elements into a harmonious whole. And yet if someone had asked Harish what he saw at that moment, he would have unhesitatingly answered, 'Nothing.' A painting that revealed nothing, neither shape, nor colour, not even the stroke of the painter's brush.

Then, even as Harish watched, it appeared like an embellishment. The frame had been so created that Harish's eyes were effortlessly drawn to the object that emerged onto this canvas. This was, Harish realised, a masterpiece still under creation. He peered for a while trying to make out what it was. It seemed to get closer to him at a slow, steady pace and then he suddenly recognized it. The Burma dungi that had disappeared into the twilight a night ago was reappearing in the twilight of the morning – hazy, shadowy, like the very lives of the Burmese Karen themselves – scratching out a living from the twilight zone of multiple, forbidden worlds.

'How different can all of our worlds be?' Harish thought to himself. 'How do I compare the world of these people, or even that of Uncle's and Popha's with mine? And the Jarawas?' he wondered.

In the brief moment that Harish concentrated on the small moving object and his own floating mind, the backdrop in the canvas changed. The Burma dungi was now moving in a clearly defined world – the mist had dispersed, the water had appeared, the horizon was where it always is and the blue of the sky was getting sharper by the moment. It was more day than night, but it was still the twilight zone. The dungi entered the bay, retracing its route of the earlier evening, emitting that same whisper, the same plume of silent white smoke. It chugged along for a while, and even as Harish was watching, disappeared into the mangrove creek they had left only the previous evening.

16

FLOWER POWER

Later that morning, Mugger and its occupants made the final run past Interview Island and onwards to Panighat, deep inside Austin Strait. The dungi would be parked here while its occupants headed for Webi, the old Karen settlement created by the first people the British had brought over from Burma. The road from Panighat led to a T-junction on the main road. To go to Mayabundar, the administrative headquarters of Middle Andaman, you turned left. To go to Webi, you turned right and then onto a nondescript road that branched off at an angle to the left about three kilometres away.

Webi was not small, but the way it was laid out and its distance from the main road hid the village from view. The name, literally the 'hidden village', was apt, but it wasn't clear if it had been planned as such, or this was just one of history's strange coincidences.

Popha helped Uncle and Harish unload their personal bags from the dungi into one of the ubiquitous yellow-and-black Ambassador taxis that appeared to be waiting just for them. Before alighting from the dungi, Uncle had changed out of his discoloured old field clothes. He looked neat, in his light green T-shirt, smart blue shorts and the sports shoes that had come on in place of his rubber chappals. The tarred road stopped at a point just inside Webi, and the taxi dropped them off here; they would have to walk the rest to get to Uncle's house. With their bags on their respective backs, they started off on foot, Uncle in the lead as usual.

Harish noticed a different aspect to Uncle as he walked ahead, possessions swaying behind him. Perhaps he could see him better in these clothes; or it was the memory of the histories he had recently revisited. Uncle's age now seemed to weigh upon him. His body bent over, the convex curve of his bowed legs, the distinctly wobbly trot, the unhurried pace at which he went forth: the seventy-three years Uncle said he had lived, showed clearly today.

The men climbed up a gentle slope, walked past a couple of beautiful old wooden houses, and up to the church of Webi. This too was a delicate wooden structure, groaning under the weight of its age and clearly in need of urgent repairs. Popha said his good-byes here and cheerfully headed home. Uncle and Harish continued straight past the church and onto a log bridge that forded a small stream. They carried on through a patchwork of fields swaying with the emerald of a paddy almost ready to be harvested. In some fields that lay fallow, cows grazed peacefully and drongos, those dark glossy birds with long forked tails, made many quick sorties in search of unfortunate insects.

Uncle Pame's house was at the foot of a small hill at the extreme end of the settlement. It was a typical wooden Karen house, built on stilts using the finest timber. All Karen houses were built like this – a carryover from their lives in Burma, where houses on stilts were the best protection again the large herds of wild elephants that roamed those forests. It helped here too, particularly in preventing snakes, frogs and insects from crawling in when the ground became slushy after the frequent tropical thunderstorms that slashed these islands. The walls of the house, both internal and external, were made of bamboo matting and the roof was of corrugated tin sheeting. This was the one significant change witnessed in Karen houses of recent years. It was also an indication of the relative wealth of the family. Those who could afford it went for the tin sheeting; those who couldn't had to fall back on their labour and the thatch they collected from the forests to lay their roofs.

What Harish really liked was the feel of the lower floor. Just behind the steep staircase that led into the house, hung a striking wooden swing. It was about five feet in length, a log hollowed out like it is for a dugout canoe and polished smooth with many years of continued use.

Beyond the swing were three huge baskets, nearly five feet high with a diameter of about three feet, woven bamboo meant to store the paddy from the fields of the family. They were covered by sheets of tin, and on one of them, an air gun lay casually, a weight to keep the sheets down.

'Use it to hunt some birds,' Uncle said sheepishly, as Harish looked at the gun and then at Uncle. 'But only occasionally,' he added quickly.

A little distance from the baskets lay a huge sow with six little pink piglets suckling away feverishly. The sow raised her head to check on the new arrivals, then returned to maternal bliss. Hens ran around the courtyard with their young chicks in tow and two howling dogs stood chained to the bamboo fencing in the corner.

All of Uncle's five children had settled in the islands, but only one had continued to live here in Webi. One son was in the police, the other was a teacher at a school in Mayabundar, while the third, the youngest son, managed the farming of the three acres of land they owned here. Both his daughters were married – one lived in Port Blair and the other in Rangat, where their husbands had permanent government jobs.

Uncle's wife, Aunty Pame, had a reputation in Webi for being as colourful a personality as Uncle was. She was a good shot with the gun herself, and was also known to be an excellent swimmer. The two made a good pair, one of the most popular in the Karen community. There was a discernable sparkle in her eyes as she caught sight of Uncle now.

'Hey, old woman,' Uncle said teasingly, 'still waiting for me, or you found some other old man?'

'Hm,' she admonished him, 'behave yourself. We have a guest.'

'Namaste,' she said, turning to Harish. She bent over a little in greeting, and reached out to hold Harish's hands gently. 'Welcome to Webi. You must be hungry.'

Everyone had had lunch, but she quickly cooked up some rice and dal for the two men.

The new arrivals then took a welcome cold water bath, and Uncle decided to retire for the afternoon. Harish just about managed to resist the temptation of the beautiful swing; he had to go and meet Dr Sreekumar Kutty, the man with the strange reputation of being a 'subversive botanist'. Uncle called for his grandson, and issued directions to take Harish to Kutty's office.

The two walked the fifteen minutes to the head of the road, then found an auto rickshaw for the fifteen-minute ride to Mayabundar. Uncle's grandson took him directly to Kutty's office, leaving only when Harish assured him he would have no problem finding his way back on his own.

The Mayabundar local office of the Botanical Survey of India – another old, elegant wooden structure that threatened to blow away in every storm – was essentially a one-man operation. Harish knocked on the partly open door with a name-plate of the occupant on it, pushed it gently and peeped in.

This was a small room with a scattered feel to it. In the middle was an old wooden table covered with herbarium sheets, files, books and other papers. There was a computer to one side, and a new-looking grey table lamp to the other. On the floor was an extension board that connected these to the power source on the wall. A wire dangled carelessly from here, and on a hook beside the switch-board hung a calendar that was two months behind schedule. Against the wall on the left stood a green-coloured metal cupboard whose colour had been scraped out in a number of places, while the opposite wall had an elegant wooden cabinet with shelves stacked to the brim with herbarium sheets. On a small table near Kutty's chair was a partly covered glass of water and two small glasses of tea – one empty, the other steaming.

'Hello Dr Kutty,' he said introducing himself, 'I work with Dr David Baskaran at the Institute for Island Ecology.' As Harish stepped into the room, he was enveloped by the mild aroma of old, yellowing cellulose and a glue of unknown vintage. Many of these herbarium sheets were decades old, and this aroma that emanated from them seemed to wrap the occupant of the room and everything around him in a fragile, translucent bubble of nostalgia. These priceless sheets were now disintegrating into dust; decimated by neglect and the elements: humidity, and in particular, the successive generations of silverfish that had had an unrestricted run of the place till Kutty had arrived.

Kutty was both thrilled and saddened to discover this treasure trove, and had spent many hours pouring over these sheets when he had first been sent here a few months ago. His passion for plants and his work were well known. People generally thought him a little crazy, someone who cared for nothing but plants and herbarium sheets. He looked the part of the 'mad scientist' too: a bony, tall man with a sharp nose and a scalp like a recently denuded forest – cleaned out, but with small bushes and brush still attempting purchase. Stubbled chin, crumpled clothes, often barefoot, or in worn-out rubber chappals. He cooked his own food, exercised regularly and kept pretty much to himself most of the time.

He looked unworldly, but only to those who didn't know him. For those he was close to, there was no one as friendly, warm or wise as Kutty, or SK as he was generally called. Nothing, in fact, was more important to him than his family: his wife Amrita, who appreciated and supported him in the pursuit of his passion, and a young, eight-year-old daughter, Tripti, whom he adored.

He had come to Mayabundar all by himself because Amrita could not leave her school-teacher's job, and more importantly, for the sake of Tripti's schooling. It was a difficult move that would not have been possible but for Amrita's unstinting support and belief in her husband. For SK, it was not the shift to Mayabundar that had been difficult, but the reason for it. SK was an unlikely subversive, banished from Port Blair to Mayabundar on a punishment posting. A nerdy botanist who asked too many difficult questions, he was being punished for doing his job too well.

Now, far away from all of that, Harish could rely on David's name to allow him access to Kutty; in the fringe circles of botanists, wildlifers, zoologists, snake people and such like, David's name was like a master key that allowed quick entry.

'Sorry for dropping in just like that,' Harish continued. 'I was wondering if you had some time. David had suggested I meet you. He mentioned –'

Dr Kutty cut in enthusiastically: 'Oh, hi! And don't call me Dr Kutty. SK's just fine. That's what everyone calls me anyway. You are Harish, aren't you? The guy studying the fringe areas of this so-called Jarawa Reserve? So how's it going?'

'No,' he tried to hide the surprise in his voice, 'not really studying. Just –'

'Where's David?' SK interrupted again.

'Should be here in a day or two. We dropped them at Kadamtala. I wanted to know –' Harish tried to come straight to the point.

'Yeah. See, actually there was not much that I did,' Kutty responded again without waiting for Harish to complete, 'and I ended up getting more credit and therefore into greater trouble than I actually deserved. Actually,' he said, pulling out a file from a drawer in his table and handing it to Harish, 'this is what it is all about. Read the highlighted parts while I organize some tea for you.' He handed Harish the file and stepped out of the room.

Harish opened the file. It bore only a few sheets, pages from what looked like a more extensive report:

REPORT OF THE PROJECT FOR FORMULATING
A LAND EVALUATION SURVEY OF
ANDAMAN AND NICOBAR ISLANDS

By Satish and Shanthi Nair
Department of Environment, Government of India, 1983

He turned the first page and began to read the parts highlighted in a
fluorescent green. Some lines in the highlighted section appeared to
have been highlighted further; underlined in the neat grey of a
pencil. Harish read slowly and carefully as he tried to make sense of
the technical and scientific language the report was liberally littered
with.

He thought he had got a sense of what it was about, but began a
second reading just to be completely sure. SK walked in with a glass
of tea and placed it before Harish.

'Thanks,' Harish said as he took a sip and handed the file back to
SK, a big question on his face.

'Come on,' SK chided Harish, 'it's not all that difficult. See,' he
said, settling back into the chair behind his desk, 'I told you, I didn't
do much. This report – it is about what is called the Andaman
Canopy Lifting Shelterwood System, followed here by the Forest
Department for nearly half a century.'

'And what is it?'

'If you really ask me, it's all gobbledegook.' He laughed a small,
exasperated laugh. 'See, I've never understood what it is. It's the
scientific system that the Forest Department here says it follows for
timber extraction. If you ask me further, I would say it's the murder
of the natural system that exists in the forests here.'

'And why would you say that?'

'Actually, that's not a new theory, and I am not the only guy
saying it,' he said, tapping the file in his hands. 'More than twenty
years ago, the Nairs had already said it in a Government of India
report – this one. See what it says.'

He turned open the file and read aloud: 'By the canopy lifting system, the entire floral composition is altered and more gregarious stands of select species are encouraged to grow . . . This method is not congenial for species conservation in an evergreen biotope.'

He looked up at Harish. 'It's all in here. It can't be said more clearly,' he tapped the file again and went back to reading from it: 'The entire evergreen forest cover of these islands is changing to deciduous because of this management practice . . . For about twenty species of timber value, a forest of infinitesimally greater value and diversity has been lost sight of . . .'

He lifted his gaze and looked again at Harish.

'See, what's basically happening is that the evergreen forest here is slowly changing. It is becoming' he paused, 'actually, it's being forced to become deciduous, more like a forest in Central India on the mainland – it's becoming dryer, more brown, and with that, the associated forms of small plants and animals are also changing, even disappearing. The converse can also happen. In fact, it's clearly happening.'

'The converse? And what is that?'

'It's a scientific principle; certain plant and animal forms that are not found here or have only a nominal presence become more dominant when the character of the forest changes. It's not immediately evident, but you only need to scratch the surface a little and you'll find out. It's tragic, really tragic and it's so real – I see it all around myself. We are losing a priceless forest. Little remains of what used to be the famous tropical evergreen forests of these islands – and all this is being done as scientific! This is timber extraction, and that is the long and short of it. It's not science, it's certainly not scientific – this fancy sounding Andaman Canopy Lifting Shelterwood System.'

SK had become quite animated. This was a subject he felt very strongly about and it showed. 'I am saying that at the very least, we should be honest. You want timber? Say you want timber – cut the forests saying you want timber – don't parade it as scientific. Please.'

'But then –'

'But then why does it happen?' SK interrupted Harish again. 'That's what you want to ask, right?' He shut the file and pursed his lips. 'I wish I knew. That is what I am trying to find out. Can you believe that nobody here knew of this report – a 1983 report of the Department of Environment of the Government of India and nobody knew about it? First they denied its existence, then expressed ignorance, and when I finally showed it to them, they said this is only a report – not a scientific paper. "Prove it scientifically," they demanded. It might have been a costly mistake. I tried to explain that what the report said was evidently visible all around. In science, I was told, nothing is evident, everything requires evidence, and they had evidence that their gobbledegook was science. I was told the Andaman Canopy Lifting Shelterwood System is a scientific system, is properly worked out, and existed in the Forest Working Plans for more than half a century.'

SK was bracing for a showdown, and Harish could see it in his manner and his words. 'Repeating a lie does not make it a truth,' SK stressed every word, 'not for half a century, not forever. If it's not the truth it's not the truth. I persisted and that's when I started to get into trouble.

'"Why are you getting involved in unnecessary things?" My boss called me to his room one day and gently asked. "You are here to study plants; you are being paid to do certain things, and you're doing well, Sreekumar. Stick to what you are supposed to do. Go out in the field. Write papers. Why are you getting into matters that you are not meant to?"

'This took the wind out of my sails and sent me soaring at the same time. Dr S.M. Pal, my boss, a legendary botanist, one of my heroes, calls and tells me I should not get involved in unnecessary things? What a sad day that was. I lost respect for the man instantly. He knew about this, about the report and the irreversible changes that had happened in these forests. He knew it all, but didn't have the guts to stand up and say what was right. The tragedy was, he was not going to let me do it either.'

'And the orchid, Dr Kutty? Sorry, SK, what about that orchid thing?' Harish asked.

'You seem to know a lot, young man,' SK was evidently surprised. 'David must have told you about this. My work on PT had already begun by then – even before I discovered this report on this Canopy Lifting System.'

'PT?'

'Oh! Sorry! The name's a little complicated so I just made it easier – *papilionanthe teres* – PT – my orchid,' he said with obvious pride. 'It's also called *vanda teres*, but I prefer to call it PT. See, flowers brought me to botany. Flowers fascinated me from childhood, and when I learnt that I could be forever in their company and also make a living, I knew exactly what I had to do with my life. With time, of course, my botanical horizons expanded, and I came to be interested in other aspects of plants that were equally fascinating. But, that's another story. See . . . I first noticed PT on my second or perhaps third visit to the northern islands. I noticed the flower all along the Andaman Trunk Road from Port Blair right up to Mayabundar here. Those days, I used to come here for the routine field surveys that my office was conducting.'

He opened a photo album lying on his table and showed Harish the first picture. 'A nice pretty pink. Beautiful flower, isn't it? Like all orchids are. PT is very common. You can't miss it. Along certain stretches of the Andaman Trunk Road, entire trees are covered in its pink hue. It was actually this profusion that first drew my attention to the flower. See,' he closed the album and looked up at Harish, 'there is one very important ecological characteristic of PT that is extremely relevant here. It needs to receive direct sunlight to bloom. Let alone the flower, even the plant will not grow in the shade. It's out and out a sunlight-loving plant. It's what can be called an ecological indicator.

'On one of my following trips, this was a bus journey more than a year ago, I noticed something even more striking – something that really set me off. It was true that the flower could be seen all along, but there was also a very curious division along certain lengths of the Andaman Trunk Road. For long stretches, the flower was seen only on one side of the road. Forests on the other side were completely devoid of its pink beauty.

'It was actually quite stark, two different worlds separated by only a ten-metre-wide tarred road. I looked at the Working Plans of the Forest Department, and should have I been surprised? The overlap was striking. Forests where I was seeing PT now had seen extensive timber extraction over the years. This might interest you – the other side of the road, where there wasn't a sign of the flower – was the Jarawa Reserve, and there the Forest Department has never been allowed to enter. There seemed to be a clear connection between logging in the past and the pink flowers I was seeing. It sounds too easy, so simple, it's almost bizarre. But it's true – cent per cent true.

'I then studied the Working Plan carefully and identified two different categories of land areas – one in Baratang, where the Forest Department had conducted large-scale logging operations, and the other inside the Jarawa Reserve, the untouched pristine, evergreen forests that once clothed every inch of these islands. I surveyed these patches and did a simple scientific exercise of assessing and estimating the presence of PT in each of them. The outcome was stunning.'

'So,' Harish asked, 'maximum orchids in the extracted forests, and almost none in the unlogged forests?'

'No. Not almost none. Absolutely none.' SK stressed. 'Not a single in the original, undisturbed forests. You've seen some of these forests now. The canopy of an unaltered rainforest closes above like an umbrella – not a scrap of light can get through. PT does not have a chance of establishing itself here. It never has and never will grow in an undisturbed forest in these islands. They wanted scientific evidence. Here it was. I then further refined my survey, and made it more complex to eliminate other factors that could be playing an influencing role. Another month of surveying in the same areas, and the same result. In such an enquiry, one can never say that such and such is the only reason, but it became clear that the most important influencing factor was the character of the forest. There could be no doubt about that.'

He pulled out another file. 'These are the final tabulated findings. Baratang was particularly striking. If you drive beyond the mud volcano in Baratang, you pass through a badly degraded natural forest interspersed with row after endless row of exotic teak, flimsy stands that extend as far as the eye can see – planted many years ago as a commercial enterprise, now huge failures. Pristine forests converted to plantations of trees that have no place here. They don't belong here and the quality of the tree shows. It's an apology of a teak tree, even an insult to a tree that is nothing less than magnificent in the habitat where it belongs. But not here! Those forests, if you can even call them that, have a dead feeling about them. The brown of the trees, particularly in the dry season, seems to merge with the brown of the soil that was once rich with humus and life. Now it is completely eroded, dead and sterile. This is where PT flourishes, even running riot in an eerie manner; hundreds of these delicate, pink flowers swaying gently, very beautiful, but it's like an offering at a funeral. That part of Baratang is like a furnace, and the villagers there have a serious water problem. It's not just the forests that suffer, people do too – the entire hydrology of the area changes . . . See, I'm going off again on another track. But it's all linked, you know.'

'So what happened then? Your findings were still not accepted?'

'No they weren't. They were still not scientific enough. "Doesn't show anything, Sreekumar." This was my boss, Pal, again. What the Forest Department did was worse. "What is Dr. Kutty trying to prove anyway and why? What is his real interest?" Yadav, the head of the Forest Department started asking publicly.

'Now, what vested interest could I have? I only wanted them to accept the truth; that the forests were indeed changing character. I didn't want anything more, but I realized in the process that I was challenging the very basis of the Forest Department's existence – it's entire history and, even more importantly, the future. The department had been created for logging, and they'd justified it all along by claiming it was scientific. Now everything stood questioned. It isn't a simple matter. Is it?' SK's tone finally reflected some resignation.

'But,' he perked up instantly, 'I am not going to give up. Now I have even more incredible evidence, and this is something no one can disprove. To show that, I need the computer, and for that we need electricity, which does not come visiting till late in the evening. Can we keep it for tomorrow? We can go to the field in the morning and we'll check out the other stuff when we are back.'

'Perfect,' Harish responded as he looked at his watch. More than two hours had gone by, but he felt he had walked in only a few minutes ago.

17

THE LAST FRONTIER

Breakfast at Uncle's next morning showcased a new dish for Harish. It was a shallow-fried preparation made of the sticky and heavy variety of rice grown only by the Karens and known in the islands as Burma Rice. It had to be eaten with honey, and Harish quite liked it. He willingly had two pieces, then set off quickly.

SK was waiting in his jeep just down the road. They first travelled on the main tarred road for a while, turned left and then onto a reasonably worn-out track that took them further west. Clusters of small houses made of wood and bamboo, with small home gardens of banana, coconut and areca trees appeared regularly. Extensive flatlands separated one village from another. Most of these lay fallow, and an occasional gust of wind blew up huge clouds of dust even as they drove past.

'All this,' SK screamed, over the sound of his vehicle, 'was prime rainforest when I came here fifteen years ago. Now, it's all gone.' His left hand went out in half a sweep, indicating the nothing he was talking about.

'It all began with those Working Plans and the timber logging we were talking about yesterday. Exactly like termites drilling into a wooden frame, the forestry operations created small inroads into the impregnable forests. Small channels that grew step by step, day by day; channels that slowly sent in people, elephants and trucks and quickly sucked out everything – log by log, tree by tree, forest by forest. They may look impregnable, powerful, un-destroyable – but just see how fragile they really are, how easily they can be decimated.

'It's like opening up a frontier. The labour comes in first, followed very soon by their families. A few families get together and create their temporary shelters. These grow slowly, from shelters to settlements and from a smattering of families to a community of an ever-increasing number of people. Friends move in, the larger family moves in, and before one knows it, the flag comes along.'

'The flag?'

'I mean some petty, small time – and sometimes, the not-so-small time – politician will appear from somewhere and hoist his flag. The journey from impregnable forest to timber camps to temporary settlements, then to a notified forest encroachment, and soon enough, a legalized settlement . . . that's the story of all these villages that we are going past. Everything at the cost of these priceless forests.'

They bumped along the country road at good speed in silence, until Harish asked tentatively: 'And the Jarawas?'

'Yes. The Jarawas. But,' SK replied after a few moments of thought, 'they are a lost cause anyway. It's too late. The day their hostility went, when that Tanumei fellow was taken to Port Blair and brought back – the Jarawas lost it. They stand no chance now. In some ways, it's the process of evolution.'

Harish wanted to continue this discussion, but just then SK turned in a small arc to the left and stopped.

'That is the last settlement here – less than a year old,' he said, pointing to a cluster of small bamboo houses on either side of the road that lay ahead of them. He then pointed to the little gurgling stream that emerged from the forest to the right. 'Water – that's why this settlement is here. Come back in a year's time and you won't be able to recognize it. The flag's not here yet, but I am sure it's on its way. A little in from here, about half a kilometre in, was one of my survey plots. The road used to end exactly where my jeep is parked now. Beyond this was only forest, and one had to walk. It's changed so fast, I can't believe it. There weren't too many of my pink orchids here either. Now look,' he pointed up a tree on the side of the road not very far from where they stood. Four huge bunches of pink flowers swayed gently.

'They're beautiful,' Harish exclaimed, quite taken in by the profusion of pink above him.

'Yes,' SK said as he turned on the engine of his vehicle, 'they are, but they come about at a huge price. Come, let's go.'

From here onwards, a dirt track cut like a tunnel through the thick forest. SK plunged his vehicle through vigorously, now looking completely unlike the relic he appeared to be in his mouldering office back in town. The vehicle rattled even louder, spewing huge quantities of dust, creating a soft, brown funnel in its wake. In just a minute, the two occupants of the vehicle were clothed in a fine, thin sheet, and Harish burst into a bout of loud, dust-induced coughing. SK was unaffected, of course, long accustomed to this routine.

Harish was still coughing when they saw another vehicle – an orange-fronted truck – approaching them.

SK released the accelerator, changed to a lower gear, manoeuvred his jeep to the side and pulled over. The orange-fronted truck went roaring past, raising a large plume of dust that settled on their stationary vehicle in an even thicker shroud of brown.

'What was that?' Harish asked, his words barely breaking through his cough and the dust that was still floating around.

'Oh, you didn't see? It was carrying logs.'

The last bits of dust finally settled down, and SK pulled out a bottle of water from his bag.

'Have some,' he said handing it to Harish. 'It'll help.'

Harish gulped down a quarter of the bottle's contents. 'Thanks,' he said as his coughing subsided a little. 'How much further?'

'Not very much. Five minutes. That's where the latest logging is happening. Should we go?' He had turned the ignition and shifted gears before Harish could respond.

SK drove for a short while and finally pulled up in a small clearing where the motorable road reached its end. There were two small paths that led into the forest from here, one straight ahead and another to the left of where they stood.

'What you see before you,' SK said, pointing ahead, 'is among the last of the ancient rainforests that still remain here, a mysterious unordered world that will soon be no more.'

Harish was as at a complete loss for words and the two men stood silently, surveying the mighty forest before them. Suddenly, a huge thud echoed loud and clear, catching Harish by surprise.

'That,' explained SK, 'is the Forest Department axe at work.'

Trees here were still being cut the old fashioned way. Hard human labour putting iron to timber, knocking it off bit by bit.

'There,' SK pointed into the forest ahead, 'can you see the guy?'

'Which guy?' Harish scanned carefully with his eyes. 'I can't see any . . . Oh! There? Yes, there. I can see him.'

Barely visible in the shadow of that great forest, dwarfed by the huge tree he was knocking at, there he was – a mouse of a man nibbling away at a giant rainforest. It was a formidable sight: a tree that went more than a hundred feet into the heavens, buttresses so thick and huge at the base that a human being could build a small dwelling within them.

And the man with the axe? There were two, perched about twenty feet up the tree trunk on a makeshift scaffolding, just above the point where the buttresses merged into the straight, ashen trunk.

Harish could just about make out as the arm and the axe came around from behind the man's back, traversing nearly hundred degrees of movement in complete silence.

'Thud.' The axe hit the wood and the forest echoed loudly.

The axe came back. 'Thud.' 'Thud.' 'Thud.' It absorbed every other sound that might have been heard.

Harish's eyes had slowly adjusted to the low level of light and he could now see a huge V-shaped cleavage, gnawed into the trunk of the tree – a fresh, angry wound that would soon consume its victim.

'It's almost done,' SK said.

The two men had now disappeared around the curvature of tree, away from the V they had just created. It was a delicate operation. The V had to be just the right size or the tree would collapse before the little mice had time to get to safety. Too little, and it would remain standing. The difference was a fine one and only those with experience knew when it was just right.

The men quickly scrambled down the scaffolding and scurried towards the visitors. They waved their hands to SK as they came up to him. They turned around, panting and sweating profusely, now waiting for the final downfall, for the tree to start tripping over the wound they had just inflicted. It started a little later, a mild sound that came creaking through, then crackling louder as the tree started to tilt over, then even louder. Finally, the tree snapped completely, a huge crackling sound that went on for much longer than Harish thought it would. The crown of the tree started to fall from the summit of the forest, struggling as it came down, screaming for the others to make way lest they too be destroyed. It hit its first neighbour, slid along its side, shaving clean the branches that came in the way and then knocked into a smaller adjoining tree, smashing its crown. The fall gained speed and momentum and the tree finally collapsed with a thud so powerful that the entire forest reverberated with its sound. Then the ensuing silence, for at least a couple of minutes.

Harish stood still, shocked by the power and the violence of the scene before him.

SK walked up to the tree that only a few moments ago had had the rare privilege of communion with the sky and the clouds. 'The canopy of the rainforest,' he began explaining to the still dazed Harish, 'is one of the last frontiers for botanists. It's an entire world up in the sky and canopy studies have taken off in a big way in places like Latin America and Australia. Orchids, insects, reptiles, amphibians, other plants – there is so much that is new to be found in the canopy up there. Something's being done in our own southern

Western Ghats too but there's nothing here, not even a chance in the near future. The Andamans have some of the finest rainforests anywhere, but jokers like me have to wait for trees to fall like this to get some idea of what is up there. I don't really know what to do. But do you see what I brought you here for? There's not a single PT here. This is recorded as a virgin forest even in the records of the Forest Department, and see what they are doing to it. And you know what?' He paused for effect. 'This is illegal!'

'Illegal? Forest Department? How can it be?' Harish was baffled.

'I too was shocked when I first realised it. It is difficult to believe, but it's illegal because this is Jarawa Reserve. We are inside the boundary of the Jarawa Reserve and this entire timber operation here is illegal. I don't know how this can happen here, but it's true. This time I have such evidence that nobody will be able to refute it. Nobody,' he muttered defiantly again, mostly to himself. 'And I'll explain what I mean when we are back.'

'I've managed to get some fabulous satellite imagery,' SK began, as he settled in front of the computer back at his office. 'It's only a year or so old, and the nice thing is that it's been created by our very own National Remote Sensing Agency. They've only given the outputs to government agencies, and that's how it landed in my lap.'

SK clicked open a file on the desktop titled 'Andaman Islands – Forest Cover' and a colourful image of the islands came alive on the screen.

'I am not going to explain everything to you – it's not needed. The red line you see running from the bottom of the screen to the very top. This one,' he traced the line with his finger, 'this is the famous Andaman Trunk Road. This entire patch of green to the left of the red line is the pristine forest of the Jarawas. Now look at the extensive browns and yellows on the right of this red line – you follow me?'

'Yes,' replied Harish, 'that's quite stark.'

'This brown shows the plantation areas – teak, padauk, coconut, areca, etc. Notice the predominance of that colour in Baratang. This is the island with maximum area under such plantations. Most of the rest, this light yellow all along are the paddy fields. It's amazing, isn't it? It's like the Andaman Islands have been divided into two, split down the middle by the Andaman Trunk Road. The original forests still standing to the left, everything else to the right. The browns,' SK's finger moved to the right of the screen, 'are the areas where PT flourishes. The more the logging activity, the greater is the presence of the orchid. It's as clear as can be. And now look at this.' SK's finger had moved further north. 'I had it checked with a GPS and have marked the point with the black dot – this one here in the patch of green. This is the precise spot west of Mayabundar we just visited, where the trees were being felled today. You can see this is clearly within the notified boundary of the Jarawa Tribal Reserve. There is no denying that the extraction going on there is illegal.'

'This is incredible,' Harish said. 'And what has been the response from the others?'

'I am just waiting. I have just put it all together in a scientific paper – my survey and findings of PT distribution, ecological characteristics of the flower itself, data from the Forest Department Working Plans and this satellite imagery – showing the overlaps and the co-relationship – all with *scientific evidence*,' he finished harshly. 'The good news is that it has just been accepted for publication by *Current Science*, India's leading scientific journal,' he said excitedly, 'and it should be out in the next couple of months. They won't like it, but they can't dispute it either. Pal can't do anything, the Forest Department can't do anything, and the administration will not be able to do anything either. This might sound a little dramatic,' he continued in a more measured tone, 'but in this small success of mine lies hidden a huge tragedy, a much larger failure for all of us. It's a priceless heritage, this ancient forest that we are destroying. I hope that at least now we will leave the untouched bits alone. Very little of it is left anyway – look at this map, less than a quarter of the islands have the evergreen of the rainforests.'

'But SK,' Harish finally moved his gaze from the map, 'I wanted to ask you something when we were driving to the logging site earlier today.'

'Yes, what is it?'

'When you said that the Jarawas were a lost cause and that there was no hope anymore – isn't that being too pessimistic, coming from someone like you. Even unfair?'

'Do you really believe,' SK pursed his lips, 'there is any hope? You've seen the situation yourself; you've been following what's happening. See, till they were hostile, it was fine. Now it's too late.'

'But,' Harish didn't understand, 'too late for what?'

'Too late to allow them to be what they were,' SK explained. 'Their future is like the present of the Great Andamanese and the Onge: if they get into the mainstream, they perish; if they don't, then perish faster. That's the law of nature – evolution. Only the fittest survive.'

'But, SK, what is the mainstream? What will this mainstream allow them anymore? And are they not the fittest? Will you and I be able to survive in these forests if left to ourselves? Do you –'

'Harish,' SK interrupted, 'this is not what I am saying. See, they may not be changing, but everything around them is. That is the crux of the matter. As long as the forest is there, they'll manage, but what when the forests are gone? You saw today what is happening to their forest? And there's more – isn't it? They are changing too, behaving like brats, getting used to tobacco, alcohol, to what have you. Some of their behaviour is repulsive. About a month ago, I was sitting by the road at Middle Strait, sipping tea, waiting for the ferry to take our bus across. This naked little Jarawa fellow came over to me and asked for tobacco. I told him to buzz off and you know what he did – it was disgusting. He held his penis in his hand and went all around me rubbing it against my shirt. Disgusting!'

'But are they responsible for all these changes?' Harish asked again. 'What we are seeing is only a fraction of their behaviour, isn't it?'

'Maybe Harish, but they are changing and I don't see much hope. Till only a few years ago, the situation was different. How do you think this map shows these green forests? Absolutely because of the Jarawa; they just didn't let anyone get in. You think the administration has great love for the forests? It's not because of us that these forests stand; it's in spite of us. We have to be thankful to the Jarawas for the last remaining forest – there is no doubt about that. I know how the settlers here used to fear the Jarawas. But that was then.'

'And now?'

'And now large hunting parties from the settlements are guests of the Jarawas. Do you know they now hunt wild pig in the forests together? Do you know that the Jarawas gather honey, crab and timber for the setters in return for rice and dal and salt? There cannot be much hope. This is only the beginning. Wait and see how rapidly things will change. Mark my words – they'll sell out their land and everything they have.'

'But,' Harish protested, 'that's unfair. It's not their fault, is it? What about us, our responsibility? Shouldn't we be stopping some of these things – why don't we work out some system where we can tell the Jarawas what's good and what's not, help them deal with the changes that are happening. Look at the forest, SK. You yourself just pointed that out. They have saved this forest like no one else could – all the best forests stand only inside the boundaries of the Jarawa Reserve.'

'That is precisely my point, Harish. And the Jarawa Reserve? What Jarawa Reserve are you talking about? What boundaries? These boundaries are only on paper. You know who respects the boundaries? Fools who believe that those lines drawn on paper are important – fools like you and me and my friend, David Baskaran. The Jarawas have no sense of this boundary. How will they know?

And why should they respect the boundaries in any case? It was all their forest; they still believe it to be so.'

'So you accept that?'

'Of course I do. How can that be denied? Don't get me wrong, Harish. I'm talking of the present, not of the past. We were talking of boundaries – the Jarawas may not know what these boundaries are, but do you think the settlers do? Did anyone make an effort to tell them? I've spoken to many people here, and they simply cannot comprehend why they can't go into these forests – these rich forests overflowing with game, honey, bamboo and timber. They can't understand why they should be denied legitimate access to precious resources because of a few naked junglees. I am not saying they are right. I am saying this is the reality, a reality that is greater than lines and boundaries drawn on maps in Port Blair or somewhere else. What is the point of boundaries and territories when they mean nothing?'

SK was speaking with an intensity rooted deep in experience and conviction. 'Leave aside everyone else. When those who created the boundary themselves don't respect it – what Jarawa Reserve are we talking about? The Forest Department logs inside the Jarawa Reserve, policemen go hunting inside the Jarawa Reserve and an entire goddamned road, the Andaman Trunk Road, runs right through it – what boundaries, Harish?' And I'll tell you what will happen if someone did decide to take some action. Who do you think will get the rough end of the stick? It will be that poor forest labour, presently squatting in the forest, who will be caught trying to get some fuel wood or thatch for his wretched hut. Those who got them there, the big players, are never touched. This is what boundaries do.'

'But,' Harish tried to argue, 'that it's happening doesn't mean it's right, is it? And what is illegal, whether it is timber extraction or hunting in these forests, should be stopped immediately.'

'Sounds fine,' SK agreed, 'but tell me how? Who will do it?'

'That's important, but that's a different issue. That boundaries, territories and spaces are violated does not mean we have to accept it. One may not be able to do anything about it, but like I said, that is a different matter.'

'So what will you do? I have all the evidence. I just showed it to you. Now what? What will you do now?'

SK was coming on strongly and Harish was starting to feel uncomfortable with his aggression.

'I am not saying I have the answers. I don't know what needs to be done. These are just thoughts and ideas I am sharing with you. You have a powerful tool in your hands, your science – and you have just put across a powerful picture of the situation on the ground. I am sure we can try and get someone interested, don't you think?'

SK was quiet for a while. Then: 'You say these are thoughts and ideas, that you don't have answers. I'm sorry, but I don't understand, Harish. What is it then that you want to do? Don't get me wrong, but you've been here for many months. What do you want to do? Tell me, what have you been trying to do?'

'That's none of your business,' Harish wanted to shout back. He was not used to being asked this question – not all these years, not now. His father had never asked him, Uncle Pame hadn't asked, even David had not, certainly not like this. Who was SK now to be asking him then?

'David told me when I was at the Institute last time,' SK was not letting go, 'that you were studying the fringe areas of the Jarawa Reserve. What for? What do you seek to achieve? I asked David this, and surprisingly, he didn't have an answer. Very unlike him. You say you don't have answers. Answers to what? What is it that you want to find out? What Harish,' he paused, and his tone softened, 'are the questions you are asking? What *is* your research question?'

This conversation had, all of a sudden, reached another place. Harish felt intimidated and confused. He was thrown completely off balance. He didn't like what he was being asked. He knew he had no answer. 'I am not sure if I know,' he replied slowly after some thought. 'I don't know if I even understand your question.'

A very raw nerve had been touched. It made Harish angry that he had managed so easily to lose sight of something so basic. It didn't show on his face, but it was an extremely agitated Harish who thanked SK and said his goodbyes.

Harish's head churned on his way back. This was the way SK operated, this was why he was so effective, so driven, so much a thorn in the administration's flesh – clear questions seeking clear answers – problem-solving where an answer was not the only thing that mattered; the question was just as important.

'What am I doing here?' This question had come to Harish many times in the past. Now it had taken on an entirely different dimension.

18

ALONE, NOT LONELY ANYMORE

David and Seema had already arrived from Kadamtala when Harish reached Uncle's place.

'There you are,' David said with a smile. 'We just arrived. I was asking Uncle where you were. So how's SK doing?'

'He's fine. Had a very interesting time with him,' Harish hid his agitation under good cheer. 'He's quite a character. Had some great stuff to share and show. How are you? How's Seema? Ah, there she is. How are you?'

Seema was curled up in the sofa in the corner, so much a part of the furniture that Harish had almost missed her.

'Hi!' she said, smiling. 'I'm okay.'

'Fortunately,' David offered, 'there was no fracture. The foot only needs some rest now. That's all. Pintu was asking about you,' David continued, 'and there have been other important developments too.'

David narrated the sequence of events, the bits of information they got from Pintu about the Jarawa illnesses in the forest, and also Dr Bandopadhyay's reluctance to say much about what was happening.

'Hmm. We should certainly check this on our way back.'

'Hmm,' David said with a wry smile on his face. 'You sound very much the journalist now, Harish. Prasad could certainly do with your services.'

'Na, David,' Harish replied. 'Haven't thought about this yet, but I should, shouldn't I?'

The phone rang and Uncle walked across to answer it. He was back within a minute, a bit perplexed and with an extremely apologetic look on his face.

'I don't know what to do, David. I'm really sorry, but . . .' he paused.

All the three visitors turned towards him.

'But . . .' he stammered again.

'Yes, Uncle, but what? Is everything okay?' David asked, a little worried.

'Oh yes. Yes. Everything's okay.'

'But what, Uncle?'

'My daughter called from Rangat. It was not an expected call. I'm really sorry . . . She and her in laws were supposed to come only next week, but they are coming later today.'

'So? What's the problem?'

'They'll be staying here for a couple of days . . . I'm really sorry . . . It was really unexpected . . .'

'Oh! Uncle!' David sounded a trifle exasperated. 'You are such a funny man. Why can't you just say it? We'll move. What's the problem with that? We'll move to the Forest Department guest house. I've stayed there often. You know it.'

'Of course, Uncle,' said Seema. 'How can there be a problem?'

'No, but I am really sorry. This is the first time you and Harish have come to my house and you are unwell too . . .'

'No, Uncle. I'm perfectly fine. Please don't worry,' Seema assured him.

The Forest Department guest house in Mayabundar was another of those elegant old wooden buildings typical of colonial times. Small passages on either side of the large central dining hall led to spacious rooms, full of huge, graceful wooden beds that were at least a century old. David, Harish and Seema now got for themselves one lavish room each of this unexpected luxury.

Located on a huge, rocky cliff overlooking the bay on the east and the two small islands that lay within, it was considered one of the most beautiful and picturesque of all buildings on the islands. Rarely did a weekend pass when the rooms in Mayabundar were not occupied by some visiting dignitary.

There was an intriguing story about how Mayabundar came to get its name. The angle, location and the height of the cliff resulted in the experience of a very mystifying moonrise on some full moon nights. It was not a regular occurrence – not more than half a dozen times a year – but many people claimed to have witnessed it. As one stood on the edge of the cliff and watched the moon rise from the dark ocean, a translucent sheet of soft blue appeared to tinge it for those few initial moments. And no, photographs had not managed to capture it yet – it had to be seen in person, that exhilarating illusion. Maya, meaning illusion, and bundar, meaning harbour – Mayabundar.

The other, more popular story was that of Maya, the mysterious young woman who came here with her father in the 1960s along with the first batch of settlers. She was said to be a woman of enchanting beauty. Young men swooned over her, but no one was ever able to gain her affection, only adding to the allure. Maya went about her daily chores oblivious to the world, and spent her afternoons by the sea, writing and then dropping into the waters those sheets of paper. It was rumoured that these were letters she wrote everyday to the lover she had been forced to leave behind when her family had moved to the islands. Her eyes always had that look of someone lost deep in the memories of the past. People thought she had gone a little crazy. At the same time they also felt a deep sympathy for her loss. In time, a small jetty was constructed here and the place became a minor harbour for ships and fishing vessels. The place soon came to be referred to as the one where Maya sat by the sea – Maya's harbour – Mayabundar. No one knew what finally happened to Maya. Some said she aged gracefully and died peacefully. Some referred to the spate of violent storms one particular year and the many fishing boats that had been blown away, saying she had been among the scores who died then. They believed that Maya's restless spirit still inhabited this space; some old men even claimed they felt her presence every time they went down to the jetty. Others had another, entirely opposite explanation – that there was no such girl, that Maya never existed, that she was just the creation of someone's fertile imagination, adding beauty and mystery to the otherwise drab and difficult migrant's life.

Later that afternoon, the croc survey team had VIP company at the guest house. Justice Harpal Singh, the presiding judge of the Port Blair circuit bench of the Kolkata High court had arrived for his weekend break. He was accompanied by chief conservator of forests, Dr T.L. Yadav, the senior-most forest officer on the islands. Yadav knew David quite well, and when he learnt the latter was around, had sent for him. David had no choice but to oblige.

The others retired for the afternoon. Seema said she would take a short nap and requested that she be woken up in about half an hour. Back in his room, Harish took a quick bath and asked for some tea. As he sat down with the cup, his mind went back to the conversation with SK. 'What are my questions?' he pondered thoughtfully as he slowly sipped his tea. 'If I am not even sure of the questions, what answers am I ever going to get?'

In a while he headed to Seema's room, and knocked softly.

'Come in,' a tired voice called from inside.

'You're awake?' Harish asked, surprised, as he pushed the door open and stepped in.

Seema was sitting on her bed, legs crossed, long hair falling carelessly on her shoulders. There was a look in her eyes he recognized immediately, the same one he had seen the day Amit's last letter for her had arrived. She was now holding that same letter.

'Seema, what is the matter?' He went across and sat down on the bed next to her.

Her gentle sobs filled the room.

'Are you okay?'

'Ha . . . Harish,' she said between sobs, holding the letter up at him, 'why are men like this?'

Harish had heard this refrain before and felt that familiar emotion well up. 'No, Seema,' he wanted to tell her, 'all men are not like that.' He sensed his own anger. 'I am not like that. Men suffer too.'

But he knew Seema would not listen even if he spoke; she could not, not yet. It had only been a week or so, and he understood that she needed time. He had been there himself. He felt for her because a chord had been touched deep inside him. This was an anger he had held deep within.

'Will I get Amit back? I can't live without him,' Seema's lament was soaked in self-pity.

And then Harish finally cracked. He had thought he was over it, that new flesh had grown over his old wounds. Now, in this instant, he realised that his wounds had not healed at all; they were deep and sore. They were still hurting.

'Don't be a fucking fool,' he erupted viciously. 'Look at yourself. Just look at yourself. See what the bastard has done to you and you fucking say you can't live without him?'

The explosion took Seema completely unawares, dissolving, for that moment, the anguish of her lost love.

'What more do you want him to do to you? Isn't this enough?' Harish got up and walked hurriedly back to his room, now livid about having lost his grip over himself.

Seema was bewildered. This was a completely different Harish — everything about him, his language, his demeanour, his loss of control, everything was different. She limped after him.

'Harish?' she knocked on his half-open door, peering in cautiously. He was sitting on his bed, face buried in his hands. Seema stood there for a moment, unsure of what to do or say.

Harish looked up, his angry eyes moist, his face all written over now with apology and regret. 'I'm sorry, Seema, I'm really sorry. I don't know what came over me . . .' He stopped. 'Actually,' he corrected himself, 'you know, I know, but it doesn't matter.' He was speaking more to himself. He paused again, composing himself. 'Come in.'

Seema walked in and settled on the chair by the desk.

'I know this must be extremely painful.' His voice was calmer and more measured now. 'I know you need time, Seema,' he continued, 'but trust me. Don't try. Don't wait. Don't ask him to come back. Don't go back to him . . . Don't.' He spoke with an intense firmness.

'Harish?'

'It's lost, Seema – the innocence of first love. You can't get it back. Certainly not like this,' he was almost pleading. 'Don't try. Please!'

'Harish?' Seema repeated.

'It cannot be anymore. And if you will not let it be, trust me, it will never let you be. It will consume you, will never allow you to find another. Don't make the mistake I made. Don't lose more than what you've already lost. Shamik used to say – don't throw good money after bad. Don't hang on . . .'

'What are you saying, Harish? Mistake? What mistake?' Seema was beginning to see what this might be about.

'You got a letter a few days ago, Seema? A letter that ripped you apart? I saw what it did to you,' he said, getting up. 'I too got a similar letter, a long while ago.' He walked to the cupboard behind Seema and pulled out a neatly folded, though crumpled sheet of paper. 'You know why it's crumpled? I had crumpled and thrown it into the bin. Then I retrieved it, straightened it out and put it away safely. That was the mistake I made. I am still holding on to the letter that did to me then what Amit's letter did to you just the other day.'

He folded it again and slipped it back into the pages of a book that looked like a worn-out old diary. 'She was my life,' Harish sighed. He shrugged off the tears and gathered himself together, 'And one day, after three years of being together, she walked out on me.' He closed his eyes. 'Just like that.'

He paused again. The muscles on his face twitched as he shut his eyes even tighter, trying hard, as it were, to lock in his tears. Seema noticed for the first time his beautiful, finely-shaped almond eyes; the large eyelashes curving upwards, now wet.

'She went off with a close friend of mine only a few months after I had introduced them to each other. How could they do this to me? Usha and me, we had our differences. We even fought viciously sometimes, but that cannot have been the reason. What could I have done?'

In this unlikely setting of Mayabundar, with Seema, whom he hardly knew, Harish wept like he had never wept before. Seema did not know how to console him.

Harish opened his eyes, at last. 'I'm sorry Seema. I'm really sorry. I don't know what's come over me.'

Seema gave him a hesitant but warm smile. 'I'm sorry about what happened, Harish. Tell me if there is anything I can do.'

Harish wiped his face with the corner of the bedsheet he was sitting on. 'You don't know, Seema, what a favour you've done me today,' he said as he picked up his diary and pulled out the crumpled letter again. Then, even as Seema watched, he tore up the letter into small pieces, placing them in the pocket of his shirt. 'I will be forever grateful to you, Seema,' he said, a faint smile appearing at last. 'And to that bastard Amit of yours too. And, you know what, you'll be okay, too,' Harish reached out his hand and held Seema's palm in a friendly, reassuring grip. 'You'll be okay,' he repeated gently, as tears now flowed down Seema's cheeks.

'I'll just be back,' Harish got up and walked out.

'But where are you going? Are you okay? You want me to come along?' she called out after him.

'No, I am fine. I'll be back soon. I have something very important to do. Don't worry, I'm okay.'

Harish walked down the winding road from the guesthouse to the jetty in the bay. A few fishermen's boats bobbed gently in the waters and a couple of women were loading their baskets with the small fish that had been drying through the day. Harish walked to the furthest end of the otherwise empty jetty and settled himself on a small pillar in the corner. White-bellied swiftlets who had nests in their hundreds just underneath darted in and out effortlessly – swooping past and around Harish with masterly grace and a silent flurry of weightless wings. He sat motionless for a while, enjoying the gentle dance of the waves before him. Everything else, including the always-restless breeze, was still today. Harish felt cleansed, like a huge burden had been taken off his chest.

A mild breeze started up just then and blew in from behind. Harish felt someone was standing there. He turned around, but saw nobody. The breeze picked up speed, bouncing and twirling as it gathered momentum. It tousled Harish's hair. The trees on the shore swayed and the waves danced more playfully. With his right hand, Harish took the shredded letter out of his pocket and held it for a moment. Then, he let the pieces go, bit by bit. Each piece rose with the breeze, fluttered off in a random direction and then dropped into the water at a place and time of its own choosing.

As Harish saw Usha's letter flutter in the breeze and then drown in the blue waters, he ended a biting, all-pervasive loneliness. He was not lonely any more. He was only alone.

19

A LIFELINE FOR THE ISLANDS

Harish's outburst had taken the sting out of Seema's own pain, at least for the moment. In the reflection of his turmoil, she had seen her own desolation and the self-pity she had been wallowing in. 'I can't allow myself that,' she said to herself as she went in for a long and leisurely shower. She felt the warmth seep into her naked body, draining the tired feeling and helping her spirits rise. She stepped out feeling much better. She was dressed and towelling her hair dry when David knocked at her door.

'You look good. Looks like you slept well. We need to meet the guests for dinner. Please be there by seven? And where's Harish?'

'Right here,' Harish said, peering in from behind. Its freshly bathed occupant gave him a smile that looked both refreshed and refreshing at the same time.

'You're okay?' she asked Harish.

'Why?' asked David. 'What happened?'

'No, nothing.' The two replied in unison, breaking into embarrassed giggles, and leaving David a little perplexed.

'You guys have been up to something,' he said playfully, shaking a finger at them. 'Anyway guys, we need to join the judge and Yadav. Basu will also be coming.'

'Do we have to?' Harish would have much preferred to be by himself. 'And who is Basu?'

'You don't have to, but it will be nice. I told the judge that you would join us. Just courtesy. Never know when it counts. Nothing to lose. And Basu? Basu is Samaresh Basu.'

'Oh, Samaresh Basu,' Seema said animatedly. 'The former Member of Parliament, isn't he? Krishna Raj of the Local Borns' Association was telling me about him.'

'That's right,' David responded. 'Former MP and a very powerful man. Mayabundar is home for him, and he'll be coming too. If you hurry up, you'll be able to get some time with the judge. He is an interesting person. Because once Basu comes in, we can only be spectators.

The Circuit Bench of the Kolkata High Court had first been brought to Port Blair in the 1960s, to deal with the serious problem the islanders faced in running to Kolkata every time they needed to seek justice. A two-member bench now visited the islands every three weeks and held court for another three weeks. Weekends used to be free and state guests like the judges enjoyed royal treatment, often demanding it in ways reminiscent of colonial times. For the islands, populated in large measure by migrants from the mainland, the babu culture and the mai-baap mentality dominated, permeating all aspects of public life, government and governance here.

The white Ambassador with the red light still evoked a sense of awe in a majority of the population and those in power – the judges, for instance – knew this very well. The bench that came to Port Blair generally had two weekends to enjoy themselves. The luckier ones had three. Itineraries for these three weekends were like fixed menus. It was one weekend to Havelock Island in the special luxury boat that stood on standby for high-profile visitors, the second one either to Little Andaman or Car Nicobar in a chopper and the third one – a 'must do' in recent times – was the one that Justice Harpal Singh had just undertaken: a drive down the Andaman Trunk Road from

Port Blair to Mayabundar. It was the journey, more than the beautiful destination that had become the main motive. A chance meeting with the Jarawa was always possible along this road, and no dignitary who came visiting the islands wanted to miss that opportunity. Justice Singh was no exception and Basu's comment as he walked in confirmed just that.

Seema and Harish had just joined David, Yadav and the judge when the former MP came blustering in – ten minutes before schedule, in fact. He was a tall, thin man in his early sixties, with a broad forehead and long, well-oiled hair that curled up just the right amount at the shoulders. There was a spot of vermillion on his forehead and a carefully carved, pencil-thin moustache extended in a gentle curve under his nose. The moustache had remained unchanged ever since he entered politics many decades ago and it was one of the two things he was well known for in the islands. The second was his unblemished record of personal integrity. He was perhaps the cleanest politician in the islands – a visible oddity in the muck that politics had become. Even his bitterest adversaries admitted that. The same consistency, however, could not be attributed to his politics, where he changed allegiances with rapid regularity. The swing he made before the recent election had been disastrous. He had left the main political parties in the supreme confidence that he would win even as an independent. The move had backfired badly; he'd lost by a whopping margin.

One of the key factors was the changing demographics of the islands, the swamping by the outsiders that Krishna Raj had complained so bitterly about. Basu was seen to be siding with these outsiders in an obvious move at creating a vote bank. This alienated people from his own community and other prominent voter segments like the Local Borns. They had been with him in the past, but voted en masse against his candidature this time. The loss had come as a severe and unexpected shock to Basu, and he had taken off for three months to spend time with his guru and mentor in the hills of Darjeeling in North Bengal.

On his return, he had vowed that he would win the next time around and was in Mayabundar to seek his mother's blessings before launching the first round of his all island trip.

He went straight to Justice Singh. 'Good evening sir,' he said shaking hands. 'Hope you had a good journey.'

'Yes, thank you. How are you doing Mr Basu?'

'Fine, sir, thank you.'

He greeted the others. 'And, sir,' he turned again to the judge as he was taking his seat, 'did you have some good Jarawa sightings?'

'Good Jarawa sightings?' Harish's jaw dropped. He turned to look at Seema and then at David.

'Jarawa sightings – were they wild animals that you sighted on a safari through the forest?' Harish wanted to shout, but held himself back. This was, already, a hell of a roller coaster of a day, and he sensed that the last leg was just about beginning.

'Yes!' the judge replied. 'We saw seven of them. It was interesting – only young boys. Where was it Mr Yadav? Where did we come across that group?'

'Just before Middle Strait, sir.'

'Yes, yes, that's right – near Middle Strait – a little before we took the ferry across the creek. They say they can always be sighted there.'

'Something has to be done about this, sir,' Basu started immediately. 'It's not good. These naked men and women on the road – our women get very embarrassed and it's a bad influence on the young boys, sir.'

'But, sir –' Seema tried to interject.

'Please,' Basu stopped Seema. 'Let me finish first,' he said, turning back to the judge.

'Naked people on the road is not good for us; it is not good for our image. What will the world say? That naked people roam on the roads in India, and the government is not doing anything about it?' Basu's was a well-rehearsed act. 'They live a very miserable life in the forest, sir, – no home, no proper food – moving around from one place to another, digging roots, hunting, fishing. Sir, we need to civilize them. We need to teach them how to live proper lives, wear clothes, make houses, do some agriculture, maybe bagicha, bring them into the mainstream so that they can live life normally, enjoy the benefits of civilization and modernization. So far they were very violent, but now they are changing. That is why they have started to come on the road. We now have a good chance.' This was a politician at his opportunistic best. He had found what he thought was a good opportunity and a good audience. 'Also, they are troubling our people, the settlers, too much now. They come into the houses and bagichas, and take away our food, clothes, utensils, bananas, coconuts and all that. There is no security and nobody can stop them. When someone tried the other day, they threatened him with their bows and arrows. They are becoming a big nuisance and some step has to be taken. In Kadamtala last week, people were very angry – they asked me why I was not doing something about this problem. I have thought of something now, sir, and,' he finally paused as he took a sip of water, 'I am going to propose it to the administration soon, to save these poor Jarawa people and save our people too. I am suggesting, sir, that all the Jarawas – they are only about three hundred of them anyway – should be collected and taken away to some other island. It was done with the Great Andamanese and I am sure it can be done with for the Jarawas as well. We have so many empty islands in the Andamans –'

Seema couldn't take it any more. 'What?' she screamed. 'Do you even know what you are saying, Mr Basu? You want the welfare of the Jarawas or to finish them off?'

The intensity of this objection from unexpected quarters took everyone by surprise; Basu, more than anyone else.

'I didn't say that.' He was quick to go on the offensive again. 'I am saying this for the benefit of the Jarawas. I am not suggesting that they be thrown into the sea; I'm only saying that they should be put on another island. Madam,' he was now staring straight at Seema, 'people like you from the mainland have no idea about island life. What do you know about the islands?'

He had played the wrong string.

'Mr Basu, you assume too much. I am a Local Born. My grandfather came here before you were even born. I know I am half your age,' Seema consciously lowered her pitch, 'and I don't mean to be offensive, but there is a serious problem with what you are saying. I study anthropology and what you have suggested is completely out of step with what the world thinks of human communities like the Jarawa. And sir,' she turned now to Justice Singh, 'these are human communities, the Jarawas – they are not animals to be sighted, like you do in a zoo or a wildlife sanctuary.'

Singh was listening carefully and he nodded thoughtfully. 'I agree. I'm sorry.'

Basu clearly was not. 'But I am not sorry, sir,' he interjected quickly.

Some unknown quantity had upset all his well-laid out plans for the evening. He was not going to let go so easily. 'These Jarawas,' he continued, 'they live like junglees in the forests. That is why I am saying they should be clothed and taught to be civilized. And Madam,' he looked at Seema again, insinuatingly, 'you enjoy watching black men and women walking naked on the road, don't you?'

The provocation was obvious, but Seema resisted.

Harish spoke up. 'The problem then cannot be with the Jarawas. It is with the road and with your people. Mr Basu, your suggestion to move them to another island would amount to forcibly taking their land from them. There is a serious problem with that. The Jarawas were here much before we all came here. This is the forest and the land of the Jarawas. It always was.'

'Yes,' Basu responded, 'I agree. But that is not the case anymore. Now it is our land too, of my people, people who were brought by the government and settled here. For 300 Jarawas, should we be denied the opportunity to make our lives and the future of our children secure? That is not fair and I will not allow that to happen.'

'Does it matter to you then that the Jarawas might be wiped out if your suggestion is implemented? And this road that you are talking about, the Andaman Trunk Road, did we ever ask the Jarawas if they want it through their forests? And do you know, sir,' Harish now turned to Singh, 'the forests inside the Jarawa Reserve, not very far from where we are sitting, are being cut for timber, illegally, by the Forest Department?' He turned back to Basu, 'Are you not going to do something about that, Mr Basu?'

Basu had a quizzical, confused look on his face.

'You don't know this? You are from this town, aren't you, and you are telling us that that you don't know what is happening here?'

Harish had said what he had to and what he said left everyone, including himself, stunned. In the thick silence that followed, his mind went scattering through the ruins he had created. Had he said too much? Was he even sure that it was right? SK was confident, but he could have been wrong, and in any case, what purpose did it serve to blurt it all out?

Justice Singh had been listening to the whole exchange very interestedly, unmindful that he had become a bit player in the scheme that was unfolding. It was for him a little like sitting in court again, listening to opposing parties argue their case. Subconsciously, perhaps, this is what the two parties had started to do as well. The mention of the illegality, however, perked up Singh's eyes. He turned to CCF Yadav.

'Is that right Mr Yadav? Is the Forest Department cutting inside the Jarawa Tribal Reserve?'

'Sir? No sir! I don't know. I mean, can't be sir!' Yadav didn't quite know what had hit him. 'There is no reason why we should be cutting inside the Jarawa forests.' He regained a semblance of his earlier composure and looked sternly at Harish. 'Are you sure of what you are saying? Do you have evidence?'

Harish put on his bravest face. 'I know exactly what I am saying – Jarawa Reserve or no Jarawa Reserve, why should there be any logging on these islands?'

Harish felt an arm press him hard on his left knee. It was David's indication that this was enough.

'And,' Singh said again, 'this thing about the Andaman Trunk Road is also interesting. Does it also pass through the Jarawa Tribal Reserve? Its status under the law could be in question then?'

'But sir,' this was Basu pleading now, as if he was about to lose his case, 'that would be a mere technicality. The road is the lifeline of the islands. You see, it connects three islands and thousands of people. It is crucial for our economic growth – it's a vital defence need . . .'

Singh began to laugh, startling everyone sitting around him. 'I thought I'd get a break from day-long hearings in court, and here I find myself in the middle of another one. Judges,' he shook his head, 'I tell you – they never learn.'

Dinner was an elaborate affair, and Justice Singh ensured the discussion did not enter contentious territory again. Basu took his leave almost immediately afterwards. Harish's outburst had caught him unawares, but the politician in him had immediately sensed an unlikely political opportunity. It had been an unpredictably dramatic evening, but also an unexpectedly good one.

'It was a bad day in more ways than one,' Harish said as Seema, David and he stepped out after dinner.

'No. Why?' Seema appeared to sense the regret Harish was feeling. 'There was absolutely nothing wrong with what we told Basu. What does he think he's suggesting? Move the Jarawas to another island? Are they sheep? Goats? Don't you agree, David? You were quiet all the while.'

'Yes,' he said, 'that's true. But Harish,' he had something far more important on his mind, 'what were you saying about that timber extraction operation? Where did you suddenly get all that information from? If you're not right, believe me, we're screwed. It will be a big goodbye to all my work, projects and surveys with the Forest Department. Yadav's not going to like it.'

'I'm sorry, David. I know I got carried away, but it was getting too much for me to handle.'

'That's alright,' David sounded irritated. 'I didn't ask for an apology. I asked where you got all that information from? How do you know that the Forest Department is logging inside the Jarawa Reserve, or did you make it all up?'

'Make it all up?' Harish felt a little humiliated, but didn't let it show. 'I'm not such an imaginative guy. And why would I lie? I told you I spent the afternoon with Dr Sreekumar Kutty. He showed me all of what I said – in the field and on the maps. I even went to the logging site with him earlier today.'

'SK told you?' David sighed with relief. 'I should have guessed. I would trust him, but it's difficult to believe. Why would the Forest Department take such a risk? How can they be so outrageously foolish – or is there something larger to it? If Yadav does not know it, it's a scandal. If he does, it's a bigger scandal. I must go and check with SK tomorrow.'

He placed his arm on Harish shoulder and squeezed it gently, 'I'm sorry.'

It was late and lights in all the others rooms had gone off. Harish sat by himself under the darkness of the open sky, listening to the waves in the silence of the night and tracing Orion in the crisp sky above. Then suddenly, feeling drained and exhausted he returned to his room and lay down in the bed. As he dozed off, the turbulence of the day started to spill into his dreams, a night of strange sleep . . .

> *David's gentle squeeze on the shoulder*
> *glass bangles on a Jarawa wrist*
> *a colourful map of the Andaman forests*
> *the soft sobs of a distraught Seema*
> . . . snippets flowing by fast, like the cascade of a turbulent stream . . .

Basu gesticulating wildly, silently
an enigmatic smile hidden behind long tresses
Karen youth scattering into the forests like partridges
the Jarawa yodel floating in on a silent night
... memories appearing randomly, rapidly, one after the
other, a cacophony of images ...
a dolphin gliding effortlessly along
glowing coals of a crocodile night
a mike in the face of a young, crying Jarawa
the thousand flurries of swiftlet wings
Michael Ross
... dreams slowly turning to nightmares, suffocated,
suffocating, cries muffled by the weight of darkness ...
a giant gurjan crashing deep inside a dark rainforest
bloodied bodies of an old Karen couple,
Jarawa arrows, then Jarawa bodies
a crumpled letter folded neatly within pages of an old diary
... the dreams go suddenly blank, the cacophony is suddenly
over, a piercing silence ... sleep dissolving into abrupt
consciousness ...

Harish got up with a start, his hands sweaty, lips dry, a thirsty throat,
a pounding heart. He reached for his diary and turned the pages
frantically for the crumpled letter that was not there anymore. *I did
tear it apart. Didn't I? I let the pieces drift into the ocean. I'll never see
it again . . .*

He gulped down a couple of glasses of water, lay down and closed
his eyes again. The illusions that had invaded his dream floated
through his conscious mind as he lay still for a few minutes. Then his
mind also stilled.

A but-of-course smile touched his lips. 'I'll find my question, SK,'
Harish whispered to the empty room, as he saw the semblance of a
destination emerging through all the clutter and confusion that
surrounded him. 'And I'll find the answer too.'

20

A HEAT RASH

Justice Singh left for Port Blair after breakfast the next morning, and David went straight to meet SK. He was sure that Yadav was headed for a few tough days. Justice Singh was likely to ask for some details at least, and there was going to be Samaresh Basu to deal with. For a man whose political fortunes had been on a recent downswing, this was precisely the kind of thing that would do him some good.

Allegations around illegal tree felling, wrongful transactions and black marketing of timber were not uncommon in the islands where timber extraction was the largest single economic activity. The hit rate had been a balanced fifty-fifty. Half the allegations were fabricated, the other half, it often turned out, held varying elements of truth. In all these cases, without exception, the Forest Department that Yadav had been heading for nearly four years now, was innocent until proven guilty and proving the guilt was never easy. This time it would be different.

David knew he was going to have a tough time facing Yadav, even if everything that Harish had said was true. But if there was even an iota of doubt, David knew it was all over for him. He was painfully aware of this paradox. He had been willing till now to stake almost anything for the protection of these forests. He had argued this in the papers he published, in the meetings he regularly had with officials and administrators and in interactions with the many islanders he met in the course of his work. Now, and for the first time in his decade in the islands, he hoped for the opposite. He hoped Harish was right, that SK was right, that the pristine forests of the Jarawas were indeed being chopped down. He felt guilty, hugely guilty, but there was no other way out. It was a simple matter of his survival and that of an institution he had so painstakingly put together. If these forests were not being cut down in the manner Harish had indicated, he would have no option but to pack up and leave the islands. Yadav would ensure that.

He realized shortly that he need not have been so worried. Dr Sreekumar Kutty went over all that he had shown and told Harish just the other day. This was an airtight case. SK knew exactly what he was saying.

There was only one possible chink, a small one, and one that would require confirmation. In these parts of the islands, the actual cutting of the trees was not performed directly by the Forest Department but by contractors. It didn't actually absolve the Forest Department of anything, but it could at least allow for half a layer of protection.

David felt greatly relieved. 'Thank god,' he told himself, his mind flushed with shame and guilt at that relief.

That afternoon, Uncle, David and Popha went back to the Mugger. On the way back to the Institute they would retrace the route of a few days ago and look for crocodiles in other parts of the same creek systems. Seema and Harish set off in the same direction, but by bus along the Andaman Trunk Road. They would spend the night with Pintu in Kadamtala, and then continue further south to Port Blair the next day. Pintu had been informed about their coming, and was waiting at the bus stop.

'Namaste,' he said to Seema, 'how is your foot? And Harish,' he didn't even wait for an answer, 'how are you? Good to see you again. How is it that you all only come at the most interesting times?'

'Why, what happened?'

Pintu turned to Seema now. 'The Jarawas that Bandopadhyay Babu had gone to check in the forest – one of them have just been brought to the PHC.'

'Really!' Seema exclaimed. 'Let's see if we can meet Dr Bandopadhyay. Let's go.'

They picked up their bags, quickly walked to Pintu's home and then to the PHC, where the policemen standing at the entrance had barred all entry. A bunch of about a hundred people had gathered and were trying to push their way through – the excitement was evident.

Seema thrust her way straight through the crowd and reached the policemen.

'Madam, you can't go in.'

'What do you mean, I can't go in? I have to meet the doctor.'

'No, madam. We can't let you. There are orders.'

'Orders? What orders?' She had a way of dealing with situations like this. 'I have to meet the doctor because I was here three days ago with a broken foot. Can't you see I am limping?'

'But . . .'

She had already pushed past the man in khaki. 'And what are you standing there for?' she said, pointing at Harish, 'Come with me.' She looked at policeman and said nonchalantly, 'My husband.'

'Really? I didn't know you were married.' Pintu jabbed his elbow into Harish's ribs. Harish walked through quickly and across to Seema. They went straight to the doctor's cabin.

'Hello, Doctor,' Seema said politely. 'How are you?'

'Hello, Seema,' he said, mildly surprised. 'And how are you?'

'I was passing by, and thought I'd see you,' Seema replied, 'just to get checked.'

'Not needed. Not needed. You are fine.'

'If you say so, doctor. And what is this commotion outside?' Seema asked casually.

'Just curious onlookers – they have nothing better to do anyway. I was telling you about those Jarawa boys. One of them was admitted here last night with high fever.'

He noticed Harish, who had been standing to the side. 'This is . . .?' he asked Seema.

'This is Harish, our colleague at the Institute.'

'Hello, Harish. Please sit.'

'Thank you. Is it serious?' Harish asked, 'This fever?'

'No. I don't think so. We won't keep him here for very long. It is not good for him. I am giving him some medicine and will send them back tomorrow.'

'But,' Seema queried, 'will he be okay?'

'Well, what can I say? See, these are orders from the top – from Port Blair. They don't want the Jarawas here for very long. It's, in any case, not good for them here – they can easily get an infection of some kind. See, I'm not supposed to be telling you all this.'

'You think,' Seema asked tentatively, 'that we can see him?'

'Actually, that would not be allowed, but come, you can have a look quick.'

Seema and Harish quickly followed Dr Bandopadhyay out of his room and stopped at the door of the adjoining ward, which he entered. It held four beds; three were empty and the one farthest away was occupied by a little Jarawa boy, about six years old. He looked extremely tired, had a runny nose and a rash seemed to have appeared on his forehead.

Harish noticed from the corner of his eye that there was someone else in room as well, sitting quietly in the corner to the right. Harish turned to look and recognized him immediately. The same glare pierced through him, the same anger that had knocked him out only a few months ago. This was the same Jarawa man he had exchanged glances with on the afternoon glass bangles had been slipped over a Jarawa wrist.

He was staring straight at Harish, and like before, Harish could lock eyes with him for only a few moments.

'Let's go,' Seema tapped Harish's shoulder as she turned and followed the doctor back into his cabin.

'What do you think it is, Doctor?' Seema asked.

'It is some kind of heat rash, nothing more.' The tone of the answer was a clear indication to the visitors that they should be on their way.

'We should be going,' Seema saw that their time was up. 'And I don't need to worry about anything, Doctor, right?' she asked, for the sake of asking.

'No, no. You are fine, don't worry.'

'I noticed,' Seema said to Harish as they were walking back to Pintu's house. 'Why was that Jarawa guy staring at you so intently? It's almost like he knows you?'

'I don't really know,' Harish replied, a little lost in his own thoughts as he described to her what had happened at the jetty the last time. 'But you know something?' he said with a frown. 'There was a change. That glare was the same and yet it was different. Something seems to have happened . . . I don't know!'

They were now with Pintu who had his own speculations to offer. 'There are two things that would interest you,' he started, 'Tanumei has virtually disappeared . . . No, no,' he saw the concern on the faces of Harish and Seema, 'nothing seems to have happened to him. From what we hear, he is still around, but somewhere deep in the forest with his band. He's not come this side for weeks. No one has seen him for a while now. It is quite baffling.' He paused. 'The other thing is this fever. See,' he said, 'I don't know for sure. They are all from that side – from near Middle Strait. One of the Jarawa group has now set up camp very close to the road, and this is where the news is coming from. This boy in the PHC, he is from that group. I know because I saw the man accompanying him.' Pintu looked at Harish. 'The tall, thin Jarawa fellow with those big, intense eyes. You remember him Harish? He was there last time too, at the jetty'

'Yes. Of course,' Harish replied. 'He was there in the ward today.'

'Oh! Was he? These Jarawas are still quite unpredictable. This Middle Strait group more so. You will even see some of them on your way back. Definitely. They are standing by the road all the time.'

'This is what Basu and Justice Singh were also talking about, isn't it Harish?' Seema was reminded of the conversation of the earlier evening, 'The Jarawas near Middle Strait.'

'Basu?' Pintu asked. 'Samaresh Basu? That crook?'

'Yes,' Harish said, 'we met him in Mayabundar just yesterday.'

'He's like a two-tongued snake. Says two things in the same breath.' Pintu clearly had a strong opinion about the man. 'One never knows what these politicians really mean and how much to trust them. He was here last week and promised in a meeting that he would get the administration to move the Jarawa from here to some other island. Might be a good thing to do, but I wonder what Basu's going to gain from that?'

Early next morning, Harish and Seema boarded one of the many buses that made the daily journey from Kadamtala to Port Blair along the Andaman Trunk Road and through the forests of the Jarawa.

Things had changed considerably in the few months since Harish had made his first trip down this road with David and Prasad to visit Pintu. Barriers had come up on the road at the points where the road actually entered the forests, and from here, vehicles were allowed to proceed only at fixed times and in convoys. The main reason for this was the opportunism of local tourism operators, who had quickly and ingeniously created a new category of tourism in the islands that was now being called 'Jarawa Tourism'. It was advertised widely, on the Internet and in operators' pamphlets. The promotion was blatant, often outrageous: 'See and feel the primitive dark tribe of the Andaman forests' went one catch line; 'A once in a life time opportunity of meeting primitive naked people', read another.

In the few months since it had started, Jarawa Tourism had begun to do roaring business. It had even been included as an integral part of the well-established and increasingly popular 'Enchanting Islands' package. An indication of its popularity was the sharp rise in hiring charges for private vehicles in Port Blair. A smooth system had been worked out with the local police involved as well, ensuring that the visitors experienced the uniqueness that they had been promised. Not only did they get to see the primitive dark people, they also had opportunity to photograph them, be photographed with them; even to do the poor, uncivilized lot a good deed by giving them coconuts, bananas and biscuits. It was only when news started filtering out that tobacco and booze were also being offered that the administration decided to take action. 'Dos and Don'ts' boards came up at the barriers and at a number of other points along the road:

a) Don't break the convoy
b) Don't honk loudly
c) Don't over speed beyond 40 kmph
d) Do not overtake inside the Jarawa Reserve
e) Don't stop anywhere on the Andaman Trunk Road
f) Don't give any eatables to the Jarawas
g) Photography and videography of the Jarawas is strictly prohibited

The convoy system with a mandatory policeman in the first and last vehicles was also put in place. The tour operators, consequently, lost their unfettered freedom, and the tourists now had to be content only with 'seeing' the naked people, and if inclined, chucking food items for them from their moving vehicles.

The bus Seema and Harish were in arrived at the Middle Strait barrier and joined the convoy, the scheduled departure of which was still about twenty minutes away. Their's was the third vehicle in line. The first was an open-backed truck bearing about twenty men, all of whom looked like they were headed for manual labour. Just behind was an orange truck with three huge logs of timber – exactly like the one Harish had seen with SK at the logging site near Mayabundar. In only a few minutes, two tourist vehicles that had come the earlier night and were now headed back to Port Blair lined up behind the bus, and behind them came another bus packed with men and women whose foreheads were smeared with ash and sandalwood. There was loud music and drumming in this bus as they sang loud paeans to Lord Murugan in Tamil. A few more vehicles joined up, and eventually there was a long train of vehicles snaking through the Jarawa forests.

The road beyond the barrier quickly entered thick forest that almost closed over like a tunnel. A few kilometres down the road, the truck in the lead pulled up to the side and the men poured out from all sides like water from an overflowing cup. A part of the road was being repaired here, and this bunch of twenty joined another group that was already at work. Here, as if it was part of an already agreed upon plan, the two tourist vans swiftly overtook the bus Seema and Harish were sitting in. The policeman jumped into the front seat of the first van that sped away quickly. The second tourist van followed speedily and was gone around the bend even as the timber truck, the passenger bus and the other vehicles behind went into first gear and started to move. The singing and chanting from the bus with the pilgrims was clear and there was a loud cheer as it started to roll again. Harish was sitting by a window at the very back of the bus, while Seema sat by the one just ahead.

The bus groaned up a steep incline and then picked up speed as the road levelled out. They had been moving for about ten minutes when Seema noticed some movement among the trees just ahead. A young Jarawa woman with red cloth tied around her head and waist emerged from the roadside forest and started to run with the bus at its very front. The bus slowed down and the girl was now running alongside the driver. Seema pushed her head out through the railings of the window to see what was happening. Harish did the same and just about managed to catch the action. The Jarawa girl had stretched out her right hand towards the driver. A hand appeared from the bus and handed her a small packet. She transferred it to her left hand and stretched out her right hand once again. Another packet was passed on to her. Her hands dropped to her side and she moved away from the edge of the road, gazing intently at the shiny packets in her hand. It was a quick and efficient operation. The bus picked up speed again and left the Jarawa woman behind. It was evident from their shape, size and appearance that these were packets of paan masala and tobacco.

'You saw that?' Harish asked Seema, as they pulled their heads in.

'Yes. This is crazy. The boards, the convoy, it's all meaningless. Paan masala and tobacco to the Jarawas? It will ruin them.'

In a while, the entire convoy again did what it had been clearly instructed not to. It crossed a bridge over a gurgling stream of water and stopped as they negotiated a gentle bend. To be fair, they were forced to stop. They had finally caught up with the two tourist vehicles that had slipped ahead a short while ago. There was a big group of Jarawa here; the prime reason these visitors had undertaken this journey in the first place. The Jarawas had set up camp here only recently, attracted by a good combination of proximity to the road and access to a source of fresh water – the stream that the convoy had just crossed. This was the same group that Pintu had referred to and Justice Singh had also spoken about. All the occupants of the tourists vehicles were now out on the road, feverishly photographing the Jarawa and giving them the bananas and biscuits they had been carrying in the hope of this opportunity.

The look on Seema's face was one of horror, and one that clearly indicated to Harish that something was about to happen.

'What the hell is this?' she fumed under her breath as she fumbled through the luggage-clogged passageway to the exit at the front of the bus. Harish followed. She headed straight for the policeman who sat unconcerned in the vehicle at the very front, chewing a mouthful of paan.

Seema stood glaring at the policeman, gritting her teeth, breathing fire. 'What do you think you are doing?' she shouted loud and angry, yanking the policeman out of his stupor. He looked up and down at Seema, stepped out from the vehicle, took a step forward and went 'Thoo!' The load in his mouth went flying through the air and created a dark, abstract stain as it hit the road with a splash.

'Yes?' he asked unconcerned, as Seema quickly took a small step back.

'Chan . . . dra . . . shek . . . har Kumar,' slowly and deliberately she read his name aloud from the badge on his chest. 'How much money did these guys give you?' She turned her contemptuous look at the driver of the vehicle. 'Both of you are finished,' she said with a bravado that had Harish biting his tongue.

He too was angry, but the absurdity of the situation made him want to laugh – this fuming young woman threatening a rifle-wielding, completely nonplussed policeman and a cowering driver who didn't know what was hitting him. All the others had also realized that something was going on. They stopped what they were doing and turned towards where the action was now taking place.

'Madam –' the policeman began.

'Shut up,' she pounced on him furiously. 'Listen,' her finger was pointed accusingly at him, 'I've got your name and these vehicle numbers. Just watch now.'

The impact was immediate and all those outside, the tourists, the photographers, even Chandrashekhar Kumar, quickly got back into their seats like little obedient children. Seema, however, was not done yet.

'So, sir,' her target now was the middle-aged, balding man who had taken his seat just behind Chandrashekhar Kumar. 'Got good pictures of naked women?' This wasn't a question. 'Big breasts? You like big breasts? You'll frame it and put it alongside your wife's picture, won't you?'

Harish was immediately reminded of their encounter with the

British photographer a few days ago, and of David's account of the French photographer. And he had himself taken Jarawa pictures a few months ago. How would she have reacted, he tried to imagine, if she had seen him with a camera that day at Uttara.

'Seema,' Harish tugged at her kurta sleeve, 'let's go.'

'Perverted bastards! Take such pictures of your wife, and I'll buy them from you,' she barked, still fuming. 'Get going now.'

Seema and Harish were now the recipients of many respectful stares as they boarded the bus and headed to their seats at the very back. Not many people in the islands had the guts to look straight in the eyes of a policeman, leave alone talk to one as Seema had just done.

'That was something,' Harish said, trying hard to contain his laughter.

'Don't laugh,' Seema snapped. 'Why, don't you have a problem with what was happening?'

'Of course, I do, but that thing about putting the Jarawa woman's photo beside his wife's, Seema, that was really funny. I'm sorry, but I didn't mean to offend you. Good what you did.'

'Harish,' Seema started in exasperated explanation, 'I know these bastards – these middle-aged Indian men from respectable families. They are the slimiest of the lot. I've met enough of them back in Delhi. When they look, they strip you instantly. Men like you don't know what women like us have to face.'

The two sat in silence for some time, as the convoy continued its journey through Jarawa homeland. It was Harish who started the conversation again. 'Seema, I was thinking, it's all very fine to blame and shout at these slimy Indian middle-aged men from respectable families –'

'You're making fun of me again,' Seema interrupted, still offended, but now also a little sheepish.

'No. Not at all. I am saying that they are part of the problem. They and many others are certainly making a spectacle of the Jarawa. But, you know, I was wondering, what about the Jarawa themselves? Aren't they making a spectacle of themselves – are they not allowing a spectacle to be made of themselves? How should they negotiate with this world of ours? The problem will have to be dealt with at both ends if a solution has to be found. Don't you agree?'

'Yes, but what can be done?'

'I don't know. But some thought has to be given to this. No?'

There was a small silence again as the two pondered in unison.

'I had no sense of the scale of the interaction,' Seema said finally, 'and this is bound to have serious implications. You know, Harish, I was wondering – that Jarawa boy in the PHC – disease and things like that, it could all be an outcome of –'

The convoy came to a sudden halt and Seema's thoughts were broken off mid-sentence.

'Arre,' somebody shouted from the front of the bus, 'there is a log lying across the road.' There was stunned silence, and dread went ripping through the hearts and minds of all the travellers. Was this a Jarawa ambush? They could be anywhere, lurking just inches away behind the line of forest that kissed the road here.

Such ambushes had been common in the past. It had been the main Jarawa strategy of opposing the relentless destruction of their forests, but things were supposed to have changed. Were the Jarawas not on the road in recent times to becoming friends? The convoy was a sitting duck, but why this ambush now? There were as many, perhaps more 'civilized' men and women in this convoy than the total number of Jarawa in the Andaman forests, but that was no guarantee against anything. Jarawa arrows were notorious for being fast and accurate. Deadly accurate.

Then four gunshots shuddered through the air and the forests – two each from the front and back end of the convoy. Fear filled the vehicles like water seeping back into a sponge just squeezed dry. Everyone crouched to ensure that no arrow, if one entered the bus, would be obstructed by any part of their precious body.

The gunshot on the Andaman Trunk Road was old practice. The armed escorts were allowed to fire blank shots in the air to scare the Jarawa at even a whiff of some danger. That need had not arisen for a while, and everyone, the policemen included, were taken completely by surprise.

For a while nothing happened. Nothing moved. The convoy waited for the next move of the unseen enemy. Nothing. Not even an indication. Then tentatively, Chandrashekhar Kumar exited the van. He knew very well that the weapon in his arm would be as useful as a toothbrush should the Jarawa choose to attack. An arrow would be through his body before he could utter 'bandook', leave alone find target, take aim and shoot – if he had had any bullets in it to begin with. Yet, he gripped the gun firmly, as if his life depended on it.

He asked the vehicle driver to get off to help.

'Bhenchod,' he screamed seeing the hesitance on his face, 'get off, or I'll put this bullet through your head just now.'

The driver also knew there were no bullets, but there wasn't much resistance he could offer. He got off reluctantly. The drivers from the other tourist vehicles, the buses and the truck joined in. Shortly, the policeman from the back of the convoy appeared, his hand also firmly gripping the gun slung on his shoulder. The group moved to the front. The uniformed men stood erect and alert for an attack they could have done nothing to prevent. The others went down to work quickly, heaving with all their strength to move the log aside.

Fortunately, it was not a very big one. They pushed it aside and darted back to their respective vehicles. The vehicles came alive and started to move ahead, one by one. The tension thinned visibly. A loud, grateful cry praising Lord Murugan rose from the pilgrims' bus. It was the final release of the fear that had been wound up tight inside.

The chanting and singing resumed. This time, however, it was not as much a collective effort. These were their individual prayers, each one murmuring their personal thanks to the almighty who had just saved them a brush with their ultimate fate. Seema and Harish too exchanged relieved smiles, grateful that nothing untoward had happened.

The convoy would make one more stop on the road where there should have been none at all. This was not far from the barrier on the other end at Jirkatang. Here, in a vast clearing on either side of the road, right inside the so-called boundary of the Jarawa Reserve, was sprawled a huge religious fair. The pilgrims' bus emptied here and the devotees sauntered off slowly, merging effortlessly with the huge crowd. The typical bustle of a village fair filled the air around. Small groups of people were gathered under the many small tents that had come up here. Some sat and chatted while others were fast asleep. Further ahead was one huge shamiana, where a large group sat listening to devotional songs blaring from loudspeakers. To the right was a long queue of people going up the steps to the temple atop a small hillock – the shrine of the revered Lord Murugan.

The bus Seema and Harish were in waited here for a while too. Some of the passengers got off to relieve themselves, others for a snack or a glass of tea. The barrier was eventually lifted, and the convoy passed through. 'Boundaries that are mere lines on paper are meaningless.' SK's words came right back to Harish as he saw the barrier go up. It was a completely irrelevant line, lost in the sea of humanity – as worthless indeed as the paper the lines had been drawn on.

A relieved Chandrashekhar Kumar and his colleague alighted at the police outpost just beyond. Their duty was done, and the convoy was not their responsibility anymore. They would have many tales to tell; another layer of mystery would be added to the fables around the Jarawa.

21

IN THE BALANCE

Harish was happy to return to base. It's not like he missed the place, but he liked the sense of security and the familiarity it had come to represent.

Seema decided to visit her family for a day, so Harish had the entire campus pretty much to himself. He went straight to his room. It was 2 November, but the big calendar on the wall still showed a dolphin diving out of the October 2004 sheet of the A&N Administration's 'Spectacular Marine Life of the A&N Islands' offering. The creatures shown here were found in the island waters, but the pictures were clearly from elsewhere – either the Caribbean or the Great Barrier Reef of Australia. Circled in red was 22 on the October leaf of it, the day the boat journey along the western coast had begun. In some senses, Harish had completed one full circle – a parikrama around the Jarawa Reserve – one way by sea, the other by road. 'Just ten days,' Harish thought as he turned the page of the calendar, 'and what a learning this has been.'

Montu called out that tea was ready and Harish headed for the dining table. Piled up in the corner was a small bunch of letters, some local newspapers and a few news magazines. He picked up the letters and sifted through them uninterestedly. There was nothing for him. Sonia Gandhi smiled from the latest cover of *Frontline*. Manmohan Singh, India's new prime minister, did the same from a recent issue of *InFocus*, while the two together graced the cover of the slightly older, 30 August 2004 issue of *India Today*.

These were the reflections of the country's historic general elections in May just a few months earlier. The electorate had stunningly rejected the Bharatiya Janata Party-led incumbent government's India Shining campaign. The excitement had not died down yet.

But Harish was not presently inclined to educate himself about the happenings in Indian politics, or anything else, for that matter. He was completely occupied by the experiences of the last couple of weeks and the just-concluded bus ride in particular.

He now knew a little more about the islands, of the Jarawas, the settlers, about David, Uncle and Seema and, most important of all, himself. He had been on a parikrama both of the islands and of himself. If his emotions had betrayed him, they had also brought him a measure of acceptance – of his faults and his failures. Very importantly, however, he had a sense now of the direction his compass was pointing.

The fate of the Jarawa, as far as he could see, had been sealed and he wondered if there was anything he could do about it. All he had learnt of the Jarawa was only from the fringes of their lives, society and land – from the people occupying these fringes and the changing landscape around their forests. This fringe was now threatening to overwhelm the core, the original people were on their way to becoming the had-beens.

'Something has to be done about this,' he thought, 'something can be done.'

He didn't know what the Jarawa wanted, but did it matter? There was a fundamental reality to be acknowledged: that the Jarawa could not be asked, at least not for now. There was no language for that yet.

The world around the Jarawa, that of the settlers, the outsiders, was itself changing so rapidly that it too was bewildered. It had been trying in its own way to deal and engage with the Jarawa, with their much smaller, more intimate and ancient world, one that was mysterious and unwilling to yield with ease. Two worlds existed alongside each other, but they inhabited time zones and realities so distinct, they could have been on different planets. There was little, if anything at all, in common. When one did not know even how to communicate with the other, where was the question of a fair negotiation?

'How would the Jarawa negotiate with this world?' Harish had asked Seema on the bus journey back. This, he now realized, was not about the Jarawa anymore. It had perhaps never been about them – it was about him and the world that he came from. How could this world negotiate fairly with the Jarawa? That was the question and therein lay the challenge. Did it have the inclination? Did it even have the capacity and the understanding – the world that he belonged to, the world of Uncle Pame, Felix of Ranchi Basti, Pintu the boatman, Shiva the other boatman, Chandrashekhar Kumar the policeman, Michael Ross the British photographer, the balding middle-aged Jarawa tourist from a respectable middle-class Indian family, Basu the politician, Seema, David, Justice Singh . . .

This world knew, but it was refusing to see. The other original islanders, the Onge and the Great Andamanese, who had cohabited these forests with the Jarawas, had all but gone. The Jarawa were now being dragged down the same path. There was the evidence and the weight of history – the Jarawa would be pushed down the road to annihilation – that was the word David had used in their first meeting. What do the annihilated feel? That was not the question Harish wanted to ask. What does the annihilator feel? How would he, himself, feel when the Jarawa were no more? Not because he wanted them to be vanquished, but because he could do nothing about their slide into oblivion. The world he belonged to did not want to annihilate the Jarawa, but it did not seem to know better. That was the tragedy and Harish felt he had some idea of what could be done, at least what he wanted to do, of where he could perhaps start.

A few days ago, the immensity of this responsibility would have overawed and perhaps paralysed him. But this was a different Harish.

Seema came in late the next afternoon.

'Any letter for me?' This was her first question, when she saw Harish sitting in the quadrangle. Harish said nothing as he handed her the bunch of letters lying on the table. There was nothing for her.

'I know what you thinking, Harish,' she started in explanation.

'No,' Harish protested, 'I am not thinking about anything in particular.'

'I understand,' she continued, ignoring him, 'but is it that easy? You tell me, it's taken you so long to forget Usha? I might have to eventually do just that, but I can't just give up so easily. Can I, Harish? Should I?'

'But I never said anything.' Harish protested feebly. 'I'm really sorry, Seema. That outburst that evening in Mayabundar,' he continued, 'was not about you, it was about me, my failure and my loss. I agree you can't give up. You know best, I know that. If there is anything I can help with, do let me know.'

Harish feared she would break down again. Her wound was too recent, too raw and he was not sure he had helped in any way.

Seema, however, had thought this through herself, and was very much in control.

'I'll be okay Harish, and no, you don't need to be sorry about anything. I have to find my own way forward and I think I know what I have to do.'

'You've not brought your bags or any of your stuff?' Harish asked, both to change the topic and because he had just noticed she was empty-handed. 'Are you not coming back here?'

'I might have to actually go to the mainland for a few days,' she replied. 'There was an urgent message from my professor. He wants me to come at the earliest, within a week if possible. There is a seminar at the university that I had planned to skip. He insists it will be good if I come and present something. There are some scholars visiting our department from the UK and Germany, and he says I should use the opportunity to meet them as well. We are trying to get a ticket on Friday's flight to Kolkata through the Local Borns quota. I'll know for sure only tomorrow.'

'And,' she said, with a wry smile that dissolved the calm veneer off her face, 'I have to meet Amit . . .'

Harish knew instinctively that this was the real reason; the seminar and the visiting scholars only an excuse. Seema too gathered that Harish had realized this.

'It's important, Harish. I have to. Don't worry. I'll be okay. And,' she said, not wanting to continue the discussion anymore, 'what did you make of the journey yesterday?'

'Phew!' Harish exclaimed, 'that was something. I've been thinking about it. I've seen a lot in the last few days, Seema, and yesterday's journey brought it all together. There can be only little hope for the Jarawa.'

'And what is that little hope?'

'The Jarawa have to be taught to negotiate with the outside world, and the outside world that lives around their forests has to be taught to negotiate with them. This is not happening in a hurry, if at all, and while we wait for that, we need some drastic surgery.'

'And what is that Harish?'

'There is no option,' Harish braced himself, 'because this is the biggest threat – the Andaman Trunk Road, Seema. The Andaman Trunk Road has to be closed down.'

'The Andaman Trunk Road closed down?' Seema's eyes grew wide, at what sounded like an extremely bizarre suggestion. 'Do you even know what you are saying, Harish? It's a road, goddammit. You can't just shut down a road like that.'

'Yes,' Harish replied, 'I know it's a road. I'm not a fool, and I am saying that if the Jarawa have to have a chance, the road has to be

closed down. If the traffic on the road and what we saw happening
yesterday continues, forget a future for the Jarawas. How will you
stop your middle-aged slimeballs from doing what they are doing?
How will you stop Chandrashekhar Kumar from taking that bribe?
How many such slimeballs and Chandrashekhar Kumars will you
deal with anyway? How will you stop tobacco packets being thrown
out from passenger buses, how will you prevent a hundred labourers
from working in close proximity to a Jarawa habitation? And,'
Harish had become quite animated now, 'what about disease – you
told me about it, didn't you? What about changing food habits?
What about Basu's ideas – naked people on the road are not good
for the image of this country; do away with them? The road represents
everything that is wrong for the Jarawa, Seema. That is what I am
saying. I am saying it needs to be closed down, precisely because it is
a goddamned road.'

Seema was not convinced. 'But Basu also said other things – the
road is the sign of the islands' development, it's a vital lifeline, it
connects thousands of people. What about these people? And, in
any case, who do you think is going to close the road because of
some fancy idea that you have?'

'That's not the point, Seema. Not yet. It's not even the complete
solution, but it can solve a part of the problem, at least for now.' He
paused, gathering his thoughts. 'You think I don't realize that this is
a difficult suggestion, almost an impossible one? I am not talking
about its implementation. That can be discussed later. The solution
can come only if we identify the problem and accept it – if we ask the
right question. That is what I have done. I am saying the road is one
of the biggest, if not *the* biggest problem. It is also the symbol of all
that we have done wrong to the Jarawa – it is like a public amenity
being thrust into someone's private property, is it not? I can't think
of any other way to deal with this.'

'Why not?' Seema had a quick answer. 'Traffic can be regulated,
people can be educated, police can be given strict instructions,

heavy penalties can be imposed – it's too late to close down the road. Solutions of the either-or kind don't work, Harish. We have to find middle ground.'

'You really believe all this can be done? Will this prevent a spectacle being made of the Jarawas? How will you stop the Jarawa tourists? Or is it okay by you that the Jarawa should be so degraded? You,' he stressed, 'who took such strong exception to a judge talking of Jarawa sightings?'

'That's not fair,' Seema responded a trifle annoyed. 'Questioning your idea does not mean I support the degradation and violation of a people. In any case, the road is no more the only place of interaction and interface. Even if the road was closed, they would still come to the villages and what about all the other things that happen on the coast?'

Harish had thought this through. 'These are all problems Seema, I agree. But that does not take away the culpability of the road, does it? You can't deny it. No one can. The road is the most important vector, bringing in all kinds of influences upon the Jarawa from the outside world. They just cannot deal with it. Don't you see that? The road is the biggest influence. Let me repeat – I am not saying this is the entire solution, but it is an important part of one, and,' he paused for effect, 'I'm surprised you're resisting this suggestion. I thought you, of all people, would understand.'

Seema was getting angry at Harish's tone now. She decided to counter in a similar vein.

'What do you know about the islands and the islanders?' she retorted aggressively. 'It's easy for people like you to come from outside, make suggestions, take decisions and leave. Your life does not depend on the road. Does it? Those who will suffer will be my people, people from my islands.'

The discussion was sliding into undesirable and even unrelated territory much too quickly, and Harish, though aware of this, found himself unable to prevent that slide. 'Look who's talking. My people, my islands!' His words were laced with sharp sarcasm. 'Don't talk like Basu now. Where were you all these years? What do you know about these islands? You are an islander only as long as you want that ticket from the Local Borns quota. Everything else, everyone else be damned. And what islanders are you talking about – what about the Jarawa?'

Seema was now extremely upset, 'I didn't know you could be so nasty.' She got up and walked away in a huff.

'This is not fair,' Harish also mumbled, not sure whether it was addressed to Seema or to himself. 'It was stupid to allow the discussion to go that way,' he chided himself. 'And if someone like Seema is so resistant to this idea, what chance that I can convince anyone else?'

Seema made a short round of the campus and walked up to the little plateau. Here, she stood in silence for a while, watching the small fishing boat bob up and down in the bay below. About ten minutes later, she returned to the quadrangle, where Harish's sheepish, apologetic smile awaited hers.

'Sorry,' they both said simultaneously. Then stopped, waiting for the other to say something.

'That was unnecessary,' they both blurted out at the same time. Stopped again, and then simultaneously burst out again into nervous, childish giggles.

'Let's leave it,' Harish said finally, 'and get some tea.'

'Yes,' Seema smiled, 'and then I'll check out of my room. I need to gather a few things to take with me to Delhi.'

'Haan, and how long will you be away? Are you sure you're coming back?' Harish asked.

'I am the islander, Mr Harish,' Seema said with pride and mock indignation, 'and I shall be back.' She giggled. 'But seriously,' she continued, 'I'll be back before Christmas, and there is a promise you have to make to me now.'

'Promise? Me? Now? Why?'

'Oh come on – it's no big deal, and you have already agreed to it.'

'Agreed to it?'

'Nothing to be worried about, sir,' she laughed. 'You've to only take me to Great Nicobar, to Galathea. I want to see the giant leatherback turtle. Remember?'

'Ah, that's all?' Harish sighed. 'No problem. I was myself planning a trip in the first week of December – maybe the second week. But,' he raised his eyebrow in doubt, 'you are sure you're coming back?'

'Why, you don't want me to?'

'No no. I didn't mean that. Your islands, you are the islander,' he said playfully. 'Who am I to decide whether you should come back or not?'

Seema did not have much stuff of her own, only a few clothes and a whole bunch of papers. She emptied all of it into the one suitcase there and dragged it to the quadrangle.

'I'm sorry to bring this up again, Seema,' Harish said, as they sat down for tea, 'but do think about the road with a cool mind. It's not that I'm going ahead tomorrow and closing it down, but really . . .'

'See, Harish,' Seema responded calmly, 'I see the point of what you say, but for once, I'm not thinking about the Jarawa. What will happen to the thousands of others? If nothing else, this will only create a greater dislike for the Jarawa in the minds of the settlers. This is their sole means of transport and communication. Think of their discomfort and the huge inconvenience caused.'

'These are all important points, Seema,' Harish said earnestly, 'and there might be other issues that will also crop up. I am aware of all this. What I am saying is that the Jarawa have to be kept uppermost in our minds. I also agree that thousands will be inconvenienced, and it is unfair. But Seema,' he paused, 'look at it this way. The Jarawas have no chance if this is merely about numbers. No Basu will ever campaign for a Jarawa vote even if there was one, and look at what we have in the balance.' He took a deep breath as he raised his palms in front of him, like the two plates of a weighing scale. 'The inconvenience and the discomfort of these thousands on one side,' his left palm went down with the weight of the thousands, 'against the very survival of a vulnerable few.' The right palm had gone correspondingly up. 'It's their extinction. Their annihilation. There will be nothing after that.'

'That's too dramatic, Harish.'

'No. Listen to me. It is the convenience of one against the survival of the other. It is not an easy choice, but that is what it is. A choice that has to be made.'

'We'll see Harish, and I must get going now or I'll miss the bus,' Seema replied, wrapping up the conversation.

The two walked down to the road head in silence, except for the sound of the suitcase wheels screeching along on the rough, pebble-strewn path. As they waited for the bus, they exchanged a couple of embarrassed, self-conscious smiles. For the rest of the time, they were either staring at their respective feet or at the small mountains in the distance.

It was when the bus appeared at the faraway bend in the road that Seema suddenly broke into action. She took a step towards Harish and gave him a tight hug.

Harish patted her back. 'Take care of yourself.'

'Thanks, Harish,' Seema replied in a voice gone soft with emotion. 'I don't know what would have become of me if you had not been around. And many sorrys for all that I inflicted on you. You take care too. See you soon.'

The rattling red and yellow State Transport Bus had arrived. Seema grabbed her suitcase and climbed in.

Life at the Institute continued as it always had but as the days passed, Harish began to miss Seema's company. The long discussions, the endless glasses of hot tea, the occasional walk along the coast, the sharing of notes and questions, the intermingling of the personal and the not-so-personal – he realized only now how much she had become part of his life in the islands and at the Institute. He wondered if she might have felt the same.

The postcard from her that came about a month after she had gone was, therefore, a pleasant surprise. She promised to return on the 20th of December, and reminded him of the Great Nicobar trip. It also set off in Harish a flurry of thoughts. What had happened? Had she met Amit? What might she have told him? Him her? Was she coming back because matters had been reconciled, or because a final parting had indeed been effected?

Seema returned to Port Blair a couple of days later than her postcard had promised. She had stayed on at home in town, and made just one short trip to the Institute to meet everyone.

'There's a ship sailing from Phoenix Bay, day after tomorrow, 24th afternoon,' she said to Harish. 'Hope we are going.'

Harish thought she looked tired and anxious, but also relieved. 'Yes, sure, I'm all ready,' he said, thinking all the time of the many questions he had wanted to ask her.

A couple of days later they were on board the *MV Chowra* to Campbell Bay; it was one of the oldest ships in the islands and one that had made these inter-island journeys innumerable times. It was making its first voyage in about half a year, having been in the dock for repairs for the last few months. The seats had been upholstered anew, the floor was carpeted afresh and a new canteen had also been added. It was a gleaming, freshly painted white vessel that greeted its passengers at Phoenix Bay early in the morning on Christmas eve. The captain proudly welcomed the passengers aboard the refurbished *MV Chowra*, and there was loud cheering as the anchor was lifted and the ship started to move. For two days, they sailed – first past Little Andaman, then Car Nicobar, a brief halt at Kamorta, then past Kondul and Meroe and finally to Campbell Bay. Most of the people on this journey were the Nicobari tribals from Nancowry and Great Nicobar, heading home for Christmas, and there was as a consequence, much drinking and merrymaking on board throughout the journey.

Harish and Seema were the odd couple out; in contrast to the others on board, theirs was a quiet voyage. They may have had many things to ask and say, but neither was sure, and both were waiting for the other to start the conversation.

BOOK THREE

22

NESTING TURTLES

MV Chowra docked at Campbell Bay, the administrative headquarters of Great Nicobar Island late on Christmas evening. The Range Forest Officer, Mr Das, was waiting for Harish and Seema at the jetty and they set off straightaway for the turtle camp at Galathea Bay forty kilometres away. The road hugged the coast for the most part, riding over muddy brown creeks, cutting through coconut plantations rich with large fruit, and past settlements with large houses made of timber and corrugated tin sheeting. Shastrinagar at the 35 kilometres mark was the last settlement along this road, and it was just as they passed the last house here that Das slowed his vehicle, pulled aside and stopped by a small shop with a huge areca plantation behind it. Potatoes, onions, biscuit packets, slippers, towels, coconuts, packets of grain and spices, all lay together in the few shelves on display in the front. The shop was dimly lit and rather empty otherwise. A kerosene stove buzzed incessantly outside and a small kettle hissed vapour in an unintended duet. The only exceptional feature of the shop was its name, which seemed to have been freshly painted on a big board by the roadside:

Southern Most General Store of India

(6½°N Latitude)

Shastrinagar, 35 kms, Great Nicobar Is.

Proprietor – Balbir Singh

This was an accurate rendering of the shop's geography; nothing indeed lay beyond Balbir Singh's little entrepreneurial venture. Everyone who came here for the first time found this amusing and Seema smiled too as she saw the Board. For researchers going into the wilderness beyond, this was the last outpost of modern life.

Harish had been here a few months ago, and immediately recognized the old man sitting on a stool by the stove – the seventy-year-old proprietor with a long, flowing silver beard. He said a polite namaste, and sat down on the bench. The old man appeared to recognize Harish too, and returned his greeting with a pleasant smile.

'Can we have some tea, Sardarji?' Das called out from his vehicle, 'and Harish,' he continued, 'please pick up the provisions that you want. You know you won't get much at the camp. I think you should take some basic stuff – rice, dal, sugar, tea, pickle, some potatoes, onions and maybe . . .' he scanned the shelves to see if he could find something interesting, 'yes, take that tin of Haldiram's rasogollas, but first check how old it is.'

Tea and shopping done, the visitors started off again. From here, the road went winding up a gentle gradient, then descended sharply and moved along the coast for a little before it cut more deeply into the forest. When it finally emerged, they found themselves at Galathea Bay. Here, at the mouth of the river Galathea, a wide beach of silver sand extended into the distance like a graceful arc of the waning moon. This was one of the best places to watch endangered sea turtles as they came out to nest.

The turtle camp of the Forest Department here was only a small bamboo shack, holed up in a small forest clearing by the beach. Camp Officer Winbrite Guria saluted Das, and said a big hello to Harish. He too had recognized Harish from his last visit. 'If you need anything, tell Winbrite,' Das said to Harish, and then turned to Winbrite, who had just unloaded the bags from the vehicle. 'Ok, Winbrite? I'll come back tomorrow afternoon.'

'Yes, sir.' Winbrite saluted again as Das returned to his vehicle.

The sun had retired for the night, and as was the practice here, the staff had already had their evening meal. Some dal and rice was now set to cook for the visitors. As they waited, Winbrite explained with an apology, 'Hope you can manage somehow tonight. There is no sleeping place inside the hut, but first thing tomorrow morning we'll organize something. Madam has come here for the first time, I'm really sorry.'

Harish had been here earlier and knew the forest staff quite well. He had been in these islands for only a little more than a year, but had already travelled quite widely and wildly, covering almost its entire length – from Landfall in the north of the Andamans to the Nicobars in the south, even into parts of the Jarawa Reserve that very few had visited. Improvising had become a way of life; be it shacking up in a police station in a remote village, spending a rain-filled night alongside cows in an abandoned bus shelter, being out at sea for over a week on a dungi or sleeping on the jetty because the evening boat had left ten minutes before schedule, he'd endured it all. Sleeping on a pristine beach like this one, with a starlit sky for a canopy was better than most other situations he'd encountered. He would be fine. He looked at Seema. She seemed pretty alright too.

'We'll be fine, Winbrite,' Harish placed a hand on his shoulder. 'Don't worry.'

'Yes, yes,' Seema quickly added. 'Don't worry, Winbrite. I'll be fine. I'm an island girl.'

It was about quarter past seven by the time the two had their simple meal for the night. Harish now unfurled a huge blue tarpaulin sheet and spread it out on the beach some distance from the turtle camp.

'Hopefully,' he said to Seema, 'we'll be beyond the high tide line and won't have to run when the tide comes in. The tide's beginning to rise, but it's still a couple of hours from being full. That's when the turtles will start to climb.'

A cool breeze had started to blow, setting Seema's long hair aflutter. This was always a very pretty sight and Harish was lost for a moment. He was quickly brought back to the present, however, as the wind picked up speed and the tarpaulin started to flutter. 'Help me,' he called out to Seema, 'before this damned thing flies away.'

They placed their haversacks on two corners and a couple of largish logs on the other edges, to hold down the blue sheet and then settled down on it themselves. It was Seema who broke the silence after a while. 'You were so quiet, even contemplative, throughout the journey. Something on your mind? Is everything okay?'

'Things are fine,' Harish smiled and went quiet again.

Seema waited a while, hoping Harish would say something but there wasn't a word. Finally, she cleared her throat deliberately, to gain his attention. 'Harish, I,' she paused, 'I was wondering, if you got my letter?'

'Letter? You wrote me a letter?' he asked in a tone with genuine surprise.

'Yes. Why are you surprised?'

'No, I mean . . . yes. I got it. Of course I did.'

'You did!'

'Yes,' Harish continued, 'that postcard from Delhi with the dates of your arrival in Port Blair, and those too were wrong.'

'Oh, that. Not the postcard . . . It was after that, a much longer letter.' Seema paused and Harish waited for her to say something else. 'Okay,' she said dejectedly, 'let it be then!'

'Arre, what happened? '

'No, Harish, it's okay. I'll just stroll along the beach for a while. You sleep now. Goodnight!'

She got up and walked away before he could say anything.

Harish was intrigued. 'Seema's written me a letter, and a long one? What could it have been? And why did she walk away like that? I'd better ask her tomorrow – don't want so much hanging in the air,' Harish thought as he sat staring at the sky and the ocean. In a while, he pulled out the mosquito net from his sack and tucked it under his head, zipped open his sleeping bag, snuggled in and closed his eyes. Seema, meanwhile, had reached the far end of the white sands. She stood here for a few minutes watching the waves before turning to walk back.

Seema had no immediate intention of going to bed. She sat at the edge of the tarpaulin staring at the coastline, mesmerized. Like many others her age, particularly women, she had seen little of the islands, and almost nothing of the Nicobars. Till recently there were many 'island-things' she had not done, and for that reason alone, she had found the last few months to be exceptionally exciting and adventurous. They had, at the same time, also been full of turmoil and pain. There were many discoveries she had made, and now she felt she was finally beginning to find her peace, her place and her purpose. One of the biggest decisions she had made was to come back home to her islands. This was the place where, she was sure, she wanted to finally be.

The land and the sea were bathed in the soft light of the moon, which was just a few phases away from turning full. Seema looked up. Delicate filaments of cirrus frilled the night sky and the strip of white sand she sat on glowed a burnished silver. The Milky Way streamed across the heavens and a million stars dotted the canopy that engulfed everything in sight.

'The stars of Fatima's buffalo,' Seema smiled with fond remembrance. 'Must catch up with her when I get back,' she promised herself.

The moist breeze from the sea lovingly ruffled her hair and there was a soft whiz in the air as it drifted past her. In the distance, she could see the surf breaking as the waves hit the bottom of the beach. Each time a wave hit, the ocean roared in protest; the waters then receding gently, but not before leaving behind a transitory signature on the sand that had blocked their onward progress – the broken surf sparkling in the light of the gentle moon. And then the next wave would come. This was the eternal play of land and ocean, nature's rhythm of the sun, the moon, the stars, the oceans, the land, earth, life . . . 'Everything seems so much in harmony here,' Seema felt a huge calm descend on her.

'What,' she wondered, 'does Harish think? Does he feel the same as I do?' She turned around to look at him. She wanted to talk to him. Now. He appeared to be fast asleep, however, and she just about resisted the deep urge to wake him up. The moon shone directly on his face, and there was a certain quietude on his countenance. And then there were those eyes – sharp, attractive, almond-shaped. She had noticed them for the first time when they were closed, only a couple of months ago, that afternoon in Mayabundar, with tears streaming down from them.

A powerful gust of wind blew some of Harish's hair onto his face, obscuring the eyes she was looking at. He normally kept his hair short, but since their last meeting he'd allowed his locks to grow till his shoulders. 'Long hair looks nice on him,' she thought. Then another thought occurred to her. She considered it for a brief moment, tiptoed her fingers to his face and pushed back his hair as gently as she could. Her fingers lingered a little longer above his face before she became aware of what she was doing. 'What the hell do you think you're doing Seema?' she chided herself, and quickly pulled her hands back. 'Thank god, he's fast asleep.'

She looked at him for a while longer, thinking, trying to interpret the tentative silences of the past two days on the ship. Was it any different from the usual? 'What has he been thinking? What does he think of me? Did he really not get my letter? Did he not have anything to say? I sent it so many days ago!' There were many questions but no answers were forthcoming. She finally rested on the tarpaulin, some distance from Harish. Sleep crept in quickly and quietly.

It was at least a couple of hours later when she was stirred from the deep sleep she had sunk into. Somebody seemed to be tugging hard at the tarp they were sleeping on. Only semi-conscious now, she struggled with her sluggish mind. She turned to her right, to the side that Harish slept on, and barely managed to lift her head to inspect their arrangement. Harish lay still and fast asleep. She felt the strong cool breeze in her face, and beyond Harish, a little flapping of the corner of the tarp. It's only the wind she told herself as she collapsed again, closing her weary eyes and drifting back immediately into sleep.

A couple of minutes later, however, she experienced the tug again. The tarp jerked harder under her. A little more awake and clearly annoyed, she turned her head to look at Harish again. He was still fast asleep! She reluctantly turned to her left and jumped, instantly awake. Only an arm's length away on the sheet of plastic she was sleeping on, was a massive lump of black, a huge dark creature nearly five feet long, trying desperately to cross over to the other side. The movement of the front two flippers, desperately trying to push at the earth, looked much like the efforts of a drowning man desperately flailing his arms in a slow effort to stay afloat. The turtle was stuck on the smooth surface of the tarpaulin and the jerks that Seema had felt were the efforts of the helpless creature as she tried hard to come unstuck.

Seema dragged herself towards Harish and nudged him awake. He opened his eyes reluctantly, in sleepy disapproval. She pointed in the direction of the turtle, instantly banishing his sleep too.

He quickly rolled over to the other side and Seema joined him as they lifted the edge of the tarp and pulled at it. Gently at first and then tugging hard, they were able, with some effort, to drag it entirely from underneath the turtle. Then, quickly, they replaced their bags and weights on it to prevent it from flying away, and turned to look at the struggling creature. 'Keep your distance or you'll spook her,' Harish whispered to Seema just as she was thinking of walking up to the animal. 'This,' he said, in a voice full of reverence and awe, 'is what we came here for – the Giant Leatherback turtle, one of the greatest travellers of the world's oceans, the gentlest giant if there ever was one and amongst the most vulnerable.'

Seema watched intently as the turtle dragged herself a couple of feet and stopped for rest. She was panting heavily. With every bit of air she inhaled, the bottom of her neck swelled like a small balloon. She exhaled, an equally laborious process, and then inhaled again. Then her whole body, nearly 400 kilograms of marine muscle, shuddered as the front flippers came into action. She dragged her body a couple of feet more and then stopped again to rest.

'What effort,' Seema thought to herself. She remembered seeing on the *National Geographic*, just a couple of weeks ago, an underwater film on corals that had some significant turtle sequences as well. The camera had followed a green sea turtle gliding gracefully and effortlessly amidst the incredible shapes and colours of that beautiful coral garden. To now see another turtle struggling so on land was a jolt. The turtle, however, was here of her own volition, the immutability of her instinct, of the timeless process of evolution. She was here to lay her eggs, she had to undergo this labour – she had no choice.

Three quarters of an hour of laborious digging, now with her rear flippers, created a perfect excavation, a cylindrical hole about a foot and a half deep. She then positioned herself on top of the nest hole and readied herself. Harish shone the light of his torch into the nest as the eggs started to pop out in a continuous succession. Sparklingly white, perfectly spherical, a little smaller than a tennis ball. Coated in a sticky, slimy fluid, they fell slowly in ones and twos.

Winbrite and his team had also arrived, careful to approach from behind and not anywhere in the line of sight of the huge creature. An error here and she'd be spooked; all the labour wasted as she followed her instinct and returned to the safety of the sea, her eggs unlaid.

The team were an experienced lot. As the eggs began to fall, one of them sprawled on the sand, stomach down. He stuck his hand into the nest and began to bring out the eggs. These were then carted away immediately to the fenced hatchery further up the beach, where they were laid back into pits similar to the one the turtle had excavated. This had to be done to protect the eggs from being poached, particularly by the feral dogs that had proliferated here in recent years. By the time the turtle had finished laying all her eggs – a total of 101 – Winbrite's team had successfully carried all the eggs away, to a safer place.

Unaware of the benevolent designs of the people standing behind her, the turtle began the reverse process. Using her rear flippers, she began to pull sand back into the nest hole that should have held the eggs. The nest hole filled up in a few minutes and then she began her laborious crawl back towards the ocean, leaving her eggs to their fate. This is where the sea turtle was different from the crocodile. It was not in her code to be the protective, aggressive mother. She'd done the best she could, and the rest was to be left to nature and the elements.

So far, Seema had been completely engrossed in the activity of the turtle. She had taken notice of every flick of the flippers, every breath, every single groan that emitted from somewhere deep within the creature. Now, as the turtle headed back, Seema was overwhelmed. She stood for a moment, tilted her head up a little to look at the sparkling sky, opened her arms to embrace the heavens above and took a deep breath, then another, and yet another. On this remote beach of soft white sand, on this magnificent, mysterious night, she had just had a rare privilege. An ancient creature, the renewal of life, an extraordinary event; she was grateful to be alive.

'Seema,' Harish's voice came wafting through the moist breeze, from the direction in which the turtle had just headed. 'Come here quickly.'

She trotted across to a point just above the waterline, where the ocean waves thrashed tirelessly at the bottom of the beach. At the water's edge here, the turtle had sensed that extra bit of moistness in the sand below her. This seemed to bring additional life into the tired body – very much the traveller who was now in sight of her destination. She waited for the next offering from home, another gently lapping wave that just about reached her neck. It was precisely the vitalizer she needed. There was extra energy in those tired flippers as she vigorously hauled herself down the final gentle slope. She'd covered a few feet by the time the next wave came in. Her pace quickened, aided perhaps by the fact that she was now on sand that had gone soft and gooey with the water that was churning underneath her. She was completely engulfed even as this wave withdrew, and was much deeper in the water by the time the next one came along. Harish and Seema walked as far as they could into the water, trying to keep pace with the turtle, holding hands to keep their own balance in the midst of the tireless waves. Finally, they could go no further. They stood silently, watching the retreating hump of the turtle's wet back as it glistened in the white light of the soft moon. Then she was gone.

It had been an exceptional night that was now finally turning to day. Seema and Harish had spent the entire night walking up and down the beach looking, spending time with each of the turtles that had come ashore to nest. Seema now knew the mother turtle's entire routine, but did not mind spending some more time looking at yet another one perform the miracle all over again.

She was standing beside turtle number thirteen, completely engrossed, when the earth started to rumble under her.

It took her a moment to realise that it was an earthquake they were experiencing. Even as she gathered her wits, the rumbling quickly turned into a violent shake. She felt she was atop a coconut tree, swaying like a pendulum under the force of a fierce gale.

For a moment she felt scared. What was she supposed to do? Should she sit down on the sand, lie down, or just keep standing? Or run? But where? In another moment, she had an answer. There was nowhere to run to, there was nothing to fear. The sky, surely, would not fall on her head. The idea of clouds from a fallen sky floating around made her giggle. Too much was happening in the span of just a few hours.

Harish was as astonished as Seema. This was his first experience of such an earthquake, and he felt completely disoriented. Not for him the exhilaration that Seema felt. He sank to his knees and sat for a minute while the earth settled down.

What surprised Winbrite, on the other hand, was the severity and the vigour of this shake. He'd lived through many such, but none had been as intense as this. It was all over as suddenly as it had begun, and the world appeared to go back to normal. Turtle number thirteen, however, had been spooked. She stopped her digging, turned around and headed back. She would come back again, maybe the night after or maybe a couple of nights later. The eggs would have to be laid.

Dawn, meanwhile, began to dissolve the dark inky blue of the sparkling night. Surprisingly, a fourteenth turtle was emerging onto the beach. This was exceptional. Not just the number of turtles, but also that a turtle was emerging now, so late, it was early morning. This was much later than had ever been recorded at Galathea, later than Winbrite had ever seen in his decade as camp officer here. The largest number of Giant Leatherbacks he had counted in a single night was eight and never, never had he seen a turtle on the beach after four in the morning. Another first in a night of unusual events.

'Let's go,' Harish said as this fourteenth turtle finished her laborious crawl and went to work on the soft sands. 'Maybe we'll get a cup of tea and come back in time to see her crawl back. Then I'm going to crash. It's been a long, long night.'

Seema gave a tired smile and nodded in agreement. 'Some tea would be great. I feel so dead I would sleep right here. But,' she continued after a brief pause, 'I don't care! Life can't get more exciting than this!'

23

26 DECEMBER 2004

'Turtle nesting on the beaches is essentially a night-time activity,' Harish explained to Seema, as they headed towards the camp. 'But occasionally, exceptionally, the activity can spill into the early hours of the morning.'

Seema was walking a little ahead, listening to him but also reliving the earthquake she had just experienced. She looked at her watch, stopped and turned around. 'Harish,' she said, 'it's been twenty minutes since that earthquake, and I feel I am ...' She stopped abruptly, mid-sentence, her words stuck inside her.

Harish waited a couple of seconds for her to complete what she was saying. 'Yes, Seema? You feel what?'

Seema stood still, frozen like a photograph, her eyes reflecting a strange mixture of fear and fascination. Harish didn't know what had hit her. 'Why is she looking at me like that? I've not done anything wrong, have I?'

Seema, however, was not looking at Harish. He only happened to be in the way. She was looking through him; held captive by something behind him. Further. Much beyond.

Harish turned. It was a strange sight indeed. There was a greyish haze on the early morning horizon and the sea had withdrawn into the distance. The gently sloping seabed, that was otherwise always under water, was now clearly visible. And in the distance the water was beginning to rise. Everyone on the beach had noticed this strange happening. People stood where they were, rooted to the ground, transfixed by the extraordinary sight. Winbrite quickly set off towards the sea. He'd spent a decade working here, and he'd always wondered what the earth was like under the waters of the sea. He wanted to walk on firm ground, where earlier he'd seen only water. Two of his staff followed him, and were already some distance in. Seema too had started off in the same direction, and was quickly moving further. The scene pulled them like a magnet, but Harish held his ground. He was concentrated on that building wall of water. Something told him all was not right.

All the water that had withdrawn appeared to have gone up to a point and had started piling up, as if it did not want to go any further – a wall of dark, grey, angry water.

And then Harish sensed an ominous movement. The wall of water, even as it kept building up, started to move – towards them. He thought he heard an angry hissing. It was an irate, petulant sea that was coming back.

'No!' Harish screamed to himself as he realized what was happening. 'Bhago! Run!' he screamed at the top of his voice.

Only Seema seemed to have heard. She stopped and turned around to look at Harish, who was now wildly waving his arms, trying also to catch the attention of Winbrite and the other two men. Seema responded to the panic in the voice and urgency of those flailing arms. She hurriedly walked towards Harish. 'What's the matter Harish?' She admonished him. 'Have you seen such a sight before?'

'Run, Seema, run. The sea is coming back.' Harish had already turned and was now running.

Seema followed, quickly. They'd gone a few metres when Harish stopped. He turned around, hoping Winbrite and the others had got the message. They had, but it wasn't his. They'd now seen the wall of water closing in themselves, and had turned to run. 'I hope they make it,' Harish prayed as he watched them run desperately from the approaching water. They couldn't get very far, though. The water thundered in swiftly; Winbrite, the two men and the still nesting fourteenth turtle were engulfed, swept away in less than a minute.

Harish and Seema had not covered much ground themselves, and they ran now with renewed fervour. They ran past the small bamboo structure of the turtle camp and onto the road beyond. They should have taken the path to the right, where about 300 meters ahead, a narrow trail went steeply up a small hillock. It would have helped them gain valuable altitude, but time was precisely what they did not have. The water would be on them before they could manage the short distance to the foot of the hillock.

On the path to the left, Harish had, on his last trip here, discovered an incomplete single-storey concrete structure that was meant to become a forest camp. The local forest officer, the one before Das, had siphoned off the money meant for the construction and all that he had come up with was the framework of the pillars and a roof.

Harish made a quick calculation. This structure was now the only possibility of gaining some height in the short time that was available. 'Follow me,' he said to Seema as he darted to the left. The ground was overgrown with vegetation, but there was a clear narrow pathway through it that led to the stairway of the bare concrete framework.

The wall of water, meanwhile, continued to rise and was moving towards land at a speed that appeared to grow exponentially with the decreasing distance. Harish had kept a close watch on the wave, or what he could see of it through the forest. 'Slow down, slow down,' he tried hard to instruct it, as he clambered up the stairs.

From up on the roof now, about fifteen feet above terra firma, the movement of the ocean was clearly visible. There was no time. The wave would be upon them in a few seconds. 'Hold tight to the pillar,' Harish screamed to Seema, who had just reached the top. The sight from up there took her breath away. A huge, solid mass of grey water came rushing in, engulfing the forest camp, lifting it and then ripping apart the fragile construction as if it were a house of cards. Seema panicked and just about managed to hold on as the wave rushed over the building they stood on. The wave reached a height of about twenty feet and, fortunately for the two, the water hit them only at their knees. Even then, the current and the power was such that they would have been swept away had they not been clinging to the pillars.

The water gushed deep into the forest beyond. There was a couple of moments' stillness, and then it hissed viciously as it turned back, withdrawing with a force and a vengeance that made the incoming wave appear benign in comparison. There was a flurry of action, of sound and movement. The swirling of the waters, the roaring of the winds, and the most frightening of them all, the snapping. Snapping of the trees around as the water first hit and then pulled away with unforgiving energy. Right before them, a giant evergreen tree went soaring into the sky – once unshakeable, resolute, now gone in a split second, snapped like a matchstick. It came crashing down, not very far from where Harish and Seema stood, hitting the moving water surface with a loud thud; then another tree and another and another and another . . . Seema tried to keep count of these loud thuds in a feeble attempt to divert her mind from her fear and panic. It was futile. She could neither keep count nor make out the thuds anymore – there were too many, too quickly, too loudly.

The entire landscape before them altered dramatically even as they watched. The thin strip of the coastal forest, about twenty metres wide, had been flattened. Not a tree was left standing and the sight before them had turned even more ominous. Just a couple of hundred metres from what might have been the earlier coastline, another wall of water had begun to build. Harish sensed it was definitely an angrier wall, and one that would come crashing in with even more vengeance.

'Quickly!' he called out to Seema, who was hugging the pillar about ten feet from him, 'Remove the stuff you're wearing. Take off your jacket, your shoes too. Quickly, before the water comes back!'

Both stood clinging to their pillars, now staring at the wall of water with macabre fascination as it closed upon them in only a couple of minutes. This was a much bigger wave and as it reached them, it appeared to deliberately hover above their heads for a moment, just for a split second . . . and then went crashing past – this time way above them.

Both Harish and Seema held tight, but they stood in the wrong direction – they had placed themselves between the moving water and the column of solid concrete. Not that they had a choice. The column prevented them from being washed away, but there was a price to pay. The wall of water knocked them hard against the concrete.

Harish was lucky that the damage caused to him was minimal, but Seema was badly hit. At just the moment the water came in, she had tilted back a little and the water had cracked her head hard against the column she held. She felt an instant numbness and barely managed to hold on as the water went deep inland again, and then began to withdraw. In the few seconds that Seema had lost her bearings, she'd swallowed a lot of the salty and murky water that was all around her. Her feet began to tremble as blood began to flow down, off the right side of her forehead.

'Seema!' Harish called out and rushed to her side as she slid down on her knees and vomited violently.

He knelt down beside her and held her hand. Helplessness engulfed him. What was he to do? What could he do?

Harish looked towards the sea. He had no more opinions on either the ferocity or the vengeance of the third wall of water that had begun to amass.

'Seema,' he called out, wondering if she had lost all consciousness, 'don't worry, things will be alright.' He was trying more to convince himself.

This was evident even to a semi-conscious Seema, whose mind even in the face of this huge adversity was now sharply focused elsewhere. 'It's okay,' she stammered softly, 'It's okay. Harish, really,' she asked slowly, 'did you not get my letter? I waited and waited for your reply?'

'Letter, Seema? No. There was that postcard and that was all.'

'No,' she said with a sigh, and continued in what was a barely audible murmur, 'the one I wrote a few days after that.' She was putting in a huge effort into what she was saying, but it had now become completely unintelligible. Harish could decipher nothing.

'No, Seema, honestly. There has been nothing but that postcard.'

'But . . .' she said, and that was all she managed before the third wave came, screeching as it approached.

The big, grey-brown mass of water thundered in with uncompromising power, scooping up Harish and Seema and sending them swirling into the vast, now empty, waterscape beyond.

Harish got only a glimpse of Seema's red kurta – like a little red dot on a monochrome photograph gone sepia before its time. Then, she quickly dissolved into the vastness around them. The swirling waters didn't spare Harish either – he bobbed on the waves for a few seconds, then was dunked forcefully into the dark depths, pulled out, then dunked again. The water was a twirling mass of grey and brown; leaves, vegetation and huge logs, the fallen trees, that continued to bang against each other with thuds that roared beyond the sound of the crashing waves and the swirling waters. But he was lucky. The water pulled him deep inland. Here, the movement of the water was relatively limited, the swirls less menacing, and the logs hit each other with marginally less force. Had he come in the way of any of these logs, he would still have been smashed instantly. He was lucky, but only just.

The second time he was dunked, his foot was caught underwater in a mass of entangled vines and rainforest lianas. They held him under for a minute, and in panic, he gulped down many mouthfuls of grainy saline water that nauseated him immediately. There was at least a five-foot water column above him, the roof of which appeared to have darkened. Even through his turmoil and nausea, Harish realized that his chances of survival were grim. There was a carpet of logs that was forming on the water surface, banging against each other as they came together; it was only when they parted that an occasional beam of light came shining in furtively.

He had to fight for it. Harish shook his leg vigorously, taking off his shoe. The rapid movement of the water helped him further untangle his foot. He quickly pulled himself towards a beam of light that was sneaking in from his right. This gap in the carpet of logs was his only chance of getting out. It was only a couple of feet across and closing in fast. Harish mustered all the energy he had, and pushed his battered body through. Holding tenuously to a small moving log, he hauled himself above the surface of water. He took in a big gulp of air and lay stomach down on the adjoining log that had now moved in and closed the crevice through which he had just emerged.

Harish lay on the log, devoid of all energy and incapable of any emotion. Only then did he realize that he was nearly naked – the moving water had torn away his shirt at some point and his trousers too were tattered. He knew where he was and at the same time he didn't. He could not have moved much, but the view before him was so different that he could have been in an entirely different place.

But the immediate threat was over. The third wave was the last wave, and while the water kept moving, its viciousness had subsided. There was no land in sight, however, and the log was to be his home for now. The water was gentle as it lapped at the debris, and the log rolled continuously in response to those continuous caresses.

As the water settled further, Harish felt a piercing guilt. Where was Seema? Could he not have done something to save her, Winbrite and the others? Had he made the right decision to run like he had? Had he not been selfish?' The thoughts came and went as they liked, tormenting Harish. If he could have slept, he might have escaped the agony of those questions, but that too was not possible. It would take only a split second's carelessness, and he did not want to slip back into the water again.

The vigil was relentless, long and sapping. With no food or water, he lay on the log, hot and sweaty, under the unsparing glare of the tropical sun. He crouched like a monkey would do – legs pulled in but a little apart to maintain his balance, hands embracing his knees and head tucked in. This was the most comfortable position he could find, and as the stars lit up his first night on the log, exhaustion managed to drag him into a few peaceful moments of genuine sleep. As the night progressed however, it started to rain; first, a needle-thin drizzle that quickly roused him, then a violent burst accompanied with strong winds and thundering skies.

As the wet night turned to a crisp morning and the sun rose from the horizon, Harish could feel his skin crack and peel away. The second day had begun. He had no choice but to stay put on the floating log; there was nothing else in his power.

Passing involuntarily in and out of a strange consciousness, Harish spent almost the entire second day like this, now baked dry by the unyielding heat and thirst. He had picked up some water from around him and splashed it on his face once. That had given him momentary respite, but the salt of the sea burnt fiercely into his cracking skin and he didn't try that again. Then, as the day was drawing to a close, suddenly, he heard what he thought was a whirr in the skies above – it sounded like a helicopter on the move. Was he dreaming? Or was he awake?

Harish splashed himself awake with the sea water, wincing at the fresh explosions on his tired skin, and straining his tired eyes towards the north. This was the direction he thought the sound was coming from, hoping that he was right. And he was!

Entering through the curtain of a clear blue sky was a little object that appeared to be moving in just his direction – growing bigger as it moved closer – a white and orange helicopter!

His hopes soared. He wished he had some cloth that he could wave to catch attention. He pressed his left hand onto the log to keep his balance and waved as wildly as he possibly could with the other.

'Please see me. Please see me,' he prayed silently, his eyes fixed on the moving machine in the skies far above.

Flight Lieutenant S.L. Shetty had indeed seen the wildly gesticulating human being below. He, however, had a serious problem on hand. He had far overflown his range and was seriously short on fuel. If he did not turn back immediately, he would get into grave trouble. Attempting a rescue in this situation was out of question. His watch showed 4 p.m. It would take him at least half an hour to get back to base and some more time for refuelling before he could start back. By then the sun would be over the western horizon; the rescue mission would have to wait until the following day.

Shetty swung his helicopter around, sending a wave of disgust, anger and despair through Harish. The second night was about to begin.

'Why did they not come to fetch me? Did they not see me? What hope can there be for me now?'

He wanted to let himself loose, flip over and drown in the misery of the placid water he was now floating on. Just then, the sight of Seema and her red kurta dissolving into the vastness around him filled his senses. 'I'm glad she's fond of bright colours,' he thought to himself, 'she too must be floating on some log somewhere. Maybe she's already been found.'

Harish held himself together, somehow, counting on his last reserve of hope and courage.

'They must have seen me,' he assured himself. 'They were really close. Surely, they'll come back. They have to. And maybe Seema'll be there too when they get me.' He resigned himself to his fate, and settled down to wait out another night.

Morning of day three brought Harish eerie human company – a lifeless body lodged between two logs only a few feet away from him, a grim reminder of what his fate could have been – could still be. Harish looked away, but kept turning around, almost with morbid fascination, to see what was happening to the slowly decomposing body. It floated till the tide filled in and was then sucked out by the withdrawing water. Harish continued to stare, however, following the meandering course of the retreating body. It could not have gone far, but he soon lost sight of it.

He was, in fact, so focused on it that he missed the initial whirr of the helicopter, which was headed straight in his direction.

In about five minutes, the helicopter was hovering right above him and within the hour it had landed at the Air Force base at Campbell Bay with a completely dehydrated Harish. He told his rescuers about Seema, Winbrite and the others. There wasn't much to say. 'Washed out.' This was the first sound of his own voice in two days; it held a comforting familiarity amidst a world gone alien and hostile. 'They were all washed out,' he said, was all he could say, before he passed out himself.

Until the helicopter had reached him, Harish had held out. He had felt almost no pain, no thirst, and appeared to have conquered hunger. His mind and body had gone into autopilot mode, driven fiercely by the instinct to survive. When he was finally assured of a rescue, his will buckled and his energy simply drained away.

Harish himself did not realize until he finally landed in Port Blair, a couple of hours later, just how weak he actually was. He wanted to walk out of the plane, but could barely manage to sit up.

As his mind relaxed, he began to feel pain and giddiness. He felt tired, nauseated and sick. His left shoulder hurt so much that he started to cry. He was immediately taken to the special ward of the GB Pant Hospital, located just behind the Cellular Jail in Port Blair.

Detailed check-ups revealed that Harish had been extremely fortunate. From where he had emerged, it was nothing short of a miracle. A couple of thousand people had already perished in the waves that had struck, and many thousands were still missing. Harish was among those lucky few who had survived and more importantly, had been located and recovered from the vast wilderness of these remote islands. He had only been severely dehydrated and broken his left collarbone.

Harish tried hard but could not recall the point at which this significant rupture had happened. 'A bone in my body broke,' he thought to himself, 'and I never got to know of it?'

Treatment was simple – saline for two days, complete rest for another week, a tight bandage around the neck and shoulder to help the collarbone heal, and no heavy activity or lifting of weights for a couple of months.

The special ward Harish lay in was not a very large one. It held ten beds, five of which were occupied by people like him who had been impacted in the immediate aftermath. Two in particular had been badly hurt when their roofs fell on them as the earth shook. One had a serious head injury, while the other had fractures in three limbs. Only the right hand had escaped unscathed.

Early in the morning of Harish's third day in the hospital, there was hectic activity and rearrangement in the ward. The four empty beds were pushed into a corner and a makeshift curtain was put in place. Two senior-looking officials came in for a quick inspection, and a little later Harish also saw a police constable posted at the entrance of the ward.

A curious Harish asked the nurse about this when she arrived with his breakfast.

'How should I know?' she shrugged. 'Must be some VIP. Is coming in the afternoon, I am told.'

Harish dozed off and it was around noon when another flurry of activity woke him up. He had, in the meanwhile, missed the bringing in of the VIP patient. When the nurse arrived with his lunch, Harish had the same question for her. She stepped closer to him and whispered softly.

'I am not supposed to tell anybody, but because you are in this ward . . . I don't know why they had to bring these people here . . . they have brought in those junglees . . .'

'Junglees! You mean the Onge or the Great Andamanese? What happened? Were they caught in the waves as well? How many are there?' Harish asked, all in one breath.

'No, no,' the nurse responded, a little flustered at Harish's excited response. 'It is those junglees from Kadamtala area, three Jarawas, brought in by a boat.'

'Jarawas!?' Harish was taken aback. 'But they don't live on the coast. Are you sure they are Jarawas? And by boat? They were washed out too?'

'Washed out? What washed out?' The nurse was beginning to get a little agitated now. 'They were not washed out or washed away anywhere. They are down with measles.'

Fear and concern surged through Harish. He was shocked. 'Measles? Now? But how were they found? Do we know how many have been affected? Where are the others? How are they? When -'

'You ask too many questions,' the nurse snapped. 'I have work to do.' She turned around and left Harish grappling with the questions that were now racing through his mind.

'This is a disaster,' he said to himself. 'A complete disaster . . .'

24

AT A CROSSROADS

Harish's third day in hospital had been full of activity. The Jarawa had been brought in around noon, and David and Uncle too came visiting in the afternoon.

Harish learnt from them of the chaos at the Institute; the mighty waves had come in and washed away the entire kitchen block. Fortunately, there was no other damage, and most importantly, no loss of life, not even an injury. The two had managed only now, two days after Harish had been hospitalized, to make their first visit. Accompanying them were visitors Harish dreaded – Seema's parents. What would he tell them? Was it fair that he should come back like that, when the other who was with him, their daughter, should not? How would he face them? What would he say? What could he say really?

The loss and shock on Seema's mother's face was visible. She had met Harish once before, and broke down into inconsolable sobs the moment she saw him. She had to be helped to the bench in the corner, where she sat quietly with a blank look on her face.

Seema's father was more composed, but there was no doubt that he too was stunned. He gently enquired after Harish, and sat down on the chair beside his bed. There was no sense of anger or accusation in his manner.

Harish narrated the entire sequence of events as he remembered it, and saw tears well up in the eyes of all the three men. It was a strange experience for him, because in that moment he felt no emotion, he felt no urge to cry, his eyes had no tears.

'And Harish,' Seema's father asked softly and finally, a question he did not want to ask. 'Do you think, beta, there is any chance they can find my Seema? Any chance the waves spared her?' he choked. 'Like they spared you? Any chance she . . .' he could barely speak, 'might still be somewhere in those forests? Any chance, Harish,' tears now flowing freely, 'that my Seema is still alive? My Seema, my Seema . . .'

'Sir . . .' Harish had no consolation to offer Seema's father. He reached out and held the distraught man's quivering hands in his own. David was also crying now, as was the unflappable Uncle Pame.

'Sir,' David said after a while, 'let's not lose hope. The Air Force is trying its best. They have agreed to take me on a search mission tomorrow morning. I have hope. We'll try our best. Anything is possible. Believe me, anything is possible. We might still get our Seema back.'

How could David say otherwise? But if someone had asked him for an honest answer, he would have said nothing was possible. There was no hope. Harish was one miracle. It was unrealistic to expect another.

'Come, I'll drop you home. Aunty also needs some rest.'

The beleaguered company of visitors left, and now Uncle Pame came and sat next to Harish. The old man's sad, blank face twitched with a range of emotions. He held Harish's palm with both his hands, and pressed them tightly together. The surface of his palms were sandpaper-rough, solid with the weight of life and experience, yet reassuringly gentle. 'Even I've not lived through anything like this,' he said with affection and admiration.

The two sat in silence for while and then Harish spoke, his voice deliberately lowered. 'Uncle, do you know who is there in the other part of the ward over there? They came in just a while ago.'

'Who?'

'Three Jarawa. With measles.'

'Really?' Uncle's small eyes had grown wide. 'But how did they get them here? At least two bridges on the Andaman Trunk Road have broken.'

'Ah! Now I understand. That is why they were brought by boat. It didn't make sense when the nurse first told me. Do you think, Uncle,' he changed tracks as he spoke, 'Seema can be found? Do you think she might be alive?'

'I wish so Harish, I wish with all my heart, but what can be said? The destruction has been unprecedented. You can't imagine the stories that we are hearing and the pictures that we have been seeing on television.'

'If I could come back, Seema also can, Uncle, can't she?'

'Yes, she can. She can . . .'

'And Uncle,' Harish was suddenly reminded of the most important thing he was forgetting to ask, 'is there a letter for me from Seema? This was the last thing she asked me before those waves took her away. It might have been a long letter, an urgent letter. She said she had sent it many days ago. Has there been anything for me?'

Uncle tried to recollect. 'No Harish, the last lot of letters came two or three days ago. There was nothing for you. But I'll check again, maybe there was some something that Montu put away in your room.'

'I have to get that letter, Uncle', Harish said, pleading as he lay back and closed his eyes.

'It is the first thing I will do,' Uncle assured, 'the moment I get back.'

Uncle did indeed find the letter that evening – a letter postmarked Delhi, which had negotiated the Great Indian Postal enterprise with some delays, and arrived, ironically, just the day Harish and Seema had sailed for Great Nicobar. It had been lying in Harish's room at the Institute, and reached him finally the next morning with other papers and magazines that Uncle sent across.

For a moment, Harish was excited, then he felt deeply saddened. This was what Seema had been talking about, that last moment they had spent together, her hands held tightly in his . . . He felt a strange anxiety holding that unopened envelope, his hands trembling. 'What should I do?' Many minutes passed before he could bring himself to finally tear it open and pull out the letter.

December 3, 2004
Lodhi Gardens, New Delhi.

Dear Harish,

Where should I begin? What am I doing in Lodhi Gardens? I love this place. I come here regularly and came here today specifically to write this letter to you. There is a lot to tell you, and lots of different things.

Hope you got my postcard of last week. I should be back on the 20th and I hope you are going to take me to Great Nic with you. I am looking forward to that trip, Harish. I really am.

I guess you are wondering what I have been doing and how I have been. Coming to Delhi, Harish, I told you, was important. It was good I did. Things had to be settled, they had to be cleared. The distances were too much and it could only be done face to face.

And you were right Harish. Dead on. 100%. Amit was a bastard, is a bastard. I had never imagined he would turn out to be such a big one. You won't believe it; he refused to meet me even once. I called and pleaded on the phone, just to meet up, talk about things once, just once, and go our own ways. He promised and never kept his promise. Not once, not twice, but five times. Then he stopped answering my phone. One evening I decided to go and confront him at his home. I returned halfway – realising that I would only be humiliating myself further.

*It was painful Harish, very painful, but I made the break in
my mind and in my heart. I am through with him and I am
finally at peace with myself.*

*I feel like I have suddenly arrived at a crossroads. Have you
ever felt like that?*

Harish paused to take in the full meaning of what Seema had
written. He lifted his gaze a little. 'What had she been thinking?
What did she want to do? What if . . .'

He was about to return to the letter when he noticed that there
was no one preventing access to the Jarawas in his ward. It was
teatime and everyone had disappeared to the extreme end of the
corridor. It was difficult to tear himself away from Seema's letter,
but this was an opportunity Harish could not resist. He got out of
bed with considerable difficulty and walked across slowly.

Three dark bodies lay, almost lifeless, amidst the bone-white
hospital sheets. A little boy lay asleep in the bed closest to where
Harish stood, and Harish's heart sank the moment he saw him. He
had a runny nose and there was a red rash on his forehead. This was
exactly what he and Seema had seen in the PHC in Kadamtala just a
few months ago. 'If this is measles,' he thought to himself, 'then
surely that had been measles too. But Dr Bandopadhyay? And that
thing about the heat rash? Did he not know or had he been lying? He
had said something about orders from the top – that they should be
sent back into the forest at the earliest. Why would anyone do this?'
Harish's head was now spinning. 'What a disaster that would have
been, to send a measles-affected Jarawa boy back into his community.
What a disaster it indeed was. Seema was so very right. The story of
the Great Andamanese was being replayed here, with criminal
callousness.'

Harish felt a huge rage building up inside, but it collapsed
immediately and completely as the Jarawa man in the middle turned
on his side. Harish felt his knees go weak as their eyes met. A
shudder ran down his spine. He felt feeble. Helpless. Impotent. This
was now their third meeting. The same pair of big, proud, even

arrogant eyes that had breathed fire once confronted him again. The fire was still there, and so was the pride. There was everything that Harish had experienced in those eyes before. And there was more. Much more. The man stared at Harish for a while, and then, tired and defeated, lowered those intense eyes – a tragic surrender. What an unequal fight this had been. What a way to bring down a man, his life spirit, to make him abandon his freedom. Was this the beginning of the end?

The nurse walked in just then.

'Harish, what are you doing?' she asked sternly. She noticed the lost look on his face, and her tone went immediately soft. 'Sad situation, no? Poor chaps! But why are you so interested in these people?'

Harish did not answer. He turned around, and the nurse helped him hobble back to his bed, where Seema's letter lay waiting.

He sat down, his eyes shut, his mind disoriented. Why was all this happening? What should he feel? Angry? Sad? Or despondent? How did it matter?

He sat still for a few moments, then opened his eyes and picked up Seema's letter again.

And Harish, as I write this, I think of the Jarawas and what you said about the Andaman Trunk Road. You know, I just realised the ATR is like a line that just keeps going. Metaphorically, even literally, it offers no crossroads. You have no choice but to keep moving, going where the road takes you. Even if you turned, what lies ahead is probably no different from what has just gone by.

The Jarawa are on a road, at the end of which they are awaited by the Great Andamanese. If I were them, I'd be grateful for some crossroads, for an option, for a change in direction. Will the march of history allow for that?

Harish felt like he was drowning, in a hopeless surge. Why this letter, now?

What is history tomorrow is the moment in my hands today,
now. Maybe we can discuss this in more detail when we meet.
Perhaps there will be others who support us. Maybe we could
try and establish contact with Justice Singh. Never know who
might help and there is nothing to lose anyway.

I'm with you, would like to be with you in this journey and
the others too.

'It's over, Seema,' Harish murmured to himself. 'It's over. Everything
is over. There is only a dead end. Nothing else. It's late Seema, it's
too bloody late . . .'

And Harish if you ask me, beyond a point I don't think it's
about the Jarawa anymore. It's about me. About us. It's about
what we believe in, what we do, and what we want to do.

And finally Harish, I don't know how to say this to you.
Don't get me wrong . . . I want to ask if, from these crossroads,
we can possibly make a journey together, a personal one, you
and me? I thought about it really hard. You might say I am on
the rebound, but I have thought about it, and I really mean it.

We can perhaps talk about it on the ship to Great Nicobar,
maybe once we get there – we have a lot of time ahead of us. I've
said what I wanted to. I'll wait for you to say what you have to.

I feel it deep within, I feel something very special for you
Harish. I . . .

Harish could not read on any more.

'Seema . . . Seema!' He felt overwhelmed by a sense of tremendous
loss. He closed his eyes and his mind drifted back to their last night
together on the beach by the Galathea. He had lain on the tarpaulin,
and turned to where she sat beside him, staring into the heavens
above. Through eyes that were only just open he had looked and
looked at her. Since the day she had returned from Delhi, the
attraction that had gradually developed over the months had, all at
once, grown stronger. He had wanted to tell to her about it. He had
wanted to ask if she felt the same. But how could he? There were so

many things she was dealing with, so many emotions she was trying to settle. Their journeys had been closely parallel for a while, but he had not as yet seen the intersection. Maybe it was coming – he was waiting, hoping. In any case, she had just returned, and there would be a lot of time to talk. He had continued to lay quietly, pretending he was fast asleep.

Just then, she had turned towards him on that beautiful starry night. She looked at him for a long while, then slowly stretched out her hand and pushed back his hair. Then her fingers had delicately lingered over his face for a few moments . . . 'What was she thinking? What was she going to do?'

She had actually pulled her hand back immediately, but in the faraway, sanitised environs of the Port Blair hospital, Harish now created in his mind a world of his own desire. He willed only a minor deviation in the script that had already been played out a few days ago. In his mind's eye now, Seema stretched out her hand and slowly placed her delicate fingers on his lips, caressing them and gently tracing their outline . . .

'What stopped you, Seema? Why did you stop? Why did you pull your fingers back?' He now wished he had opened his eyes then, and told her how deeply he felt for her. 'If I had known then what I know now, would it have been different, Seema?' His soft tears were asking unanswerable questions. 'Could it have done anything for you,' his thoughts paused for a moment, 'if such big waves were destined to come anyway?'

He opened his eyes, and forced himself back to the last of her remaining lines.

I feel something very special for you Harish. I have perhaps drifted into love with you, quite unknowingly, quite unexpectedly and yes, quite quickly. What more can I say?
See you soon.

Love,
Seema

EPILOGUE

The letter still in his hand, an exhausted Harish dozed off into an uncomfortable slumber, only to be woken up in a few minutes by the sound of shuffling feet near his bed. He opened his eyes and felt a stab of instant fear – towering above him was the tall, thin Jarawa man from the other side of their common ward. As Harish sat up, he pushed himself away a little, towards the wall. A little space between them seemed necessary.

The Jarawa man recognized his fear and smiled a resigned, barely visible smile that flickered for only an instant. 'Erema,' he said, pointing a finger at himself. 'Erema.'

'Erema?' Harish repeated after him.

'Erema,' the man said again, tapping his chest. Then he turned his finger towards Harish.

'Tera,' he paused to take in a breath. 'Naam?'

'Ah! Harish,' he replied, sighing with relief.

'Harr . . .' Erema paused. 'Harr . . . Harish,' There was an awkward pause.

'Tumhara,' Erema paused again, 'aurat?' He pointed to the empty space next to Harish.

It took Harish a moment to understand.

'Ah, Seema? Seema . . .' Harish said shaking his head, not sure how he would explain; what could he say that this man would understand?

Erema, however, needed no explanation. He slowly lifted his arm and placed it on Harish's shoulder. 'See . . .' he stammered, 'Seema.' There was a sympathetic grimace on his face, and he asked in a tone that was measured and slow. 'Seema wash . . . Seema wash out?'

He lifted his right hand to his broad, creased forehead and drew two imaginary lines in the air. 'Naseeb,' he tried to console a now stunned Harish. Erema had not only noticed Harish and Seema together, he had deciphered what had happened in the aftermath and he even knew what to say. He'd figured out in its entirety the language and its meanings from the fringes.

Now, as Erema paused again for breath, he became visibly wistful. 'Mera ladki washout,' he said in one quick breath, almost as if allowing a pause would give him a chance to change destiny. 'Washout,' he repeated, flicking his wrist at the same time, suggesting she was gone. He paused. 'Aur ladka,' he said, nodding even as he dropped eye contact with Harish. 'Mera ladka, garam bukhar.'

'Garam bukhar,' he insisted, as he settled himself on the edge of Harish's bed, pointing towards his side of the ward.

He looked up at Harish, and as he re-established that firm eye contact of the old, the head was still nodding, and the desolate smile of a grieving father flickered fleetingly.

Harish felt a moment of unexpected liberation. His pain and his loss felt humbled in those few moments. How could he compare his loss to that of Erema's, the loss of his family, his way of life, his people?

Harish had been struggling the last couple of days with a decision he had to make. Everyone around was trying to convince him that he had to go back home to the mainland – that the islands were not the place for him anymore. Going away, even if for a while, they were arguing, would help him. He was coming around to accepting that, but something he couldn't quite place a finger on was still disturbing him. How many times could he run away? Where would he go anyway? And where would the people of these islands go? Now, as a grieving Erema sat beside him on his hospital bed, Harish knew he had found the answer. There was nowhere Erema could go. There was nowhere, anymore, he was himself going. There was nowhere to go. He would stay – at these crossroads, in these islands. So, he hoped, would Erema's people.

THE JARAWAS: A HISTORICAL SKETCH

1789: The British East India Company decides to set up colony in the Andaman Islands; Lt Hyde Colebrooke visits the islands, meets native islanders and records some of their language – it is found out later that it belongs to the Jarawa; the colony that was set up was abandoned a few years later

1839: Earliest known exploration of flora of the Andamans by the Russian scientist, Dr Hefler; he lost his life to the hostility of the local inhabitants

1857: Sepoy mutiny, also known as the first war of Indian independence

1858: Establishment of the penal settlement in the Andamans by the British

1860: A track cut from Port Blair in the east to Port Mouat in the west by the British; Jarawas were occasionally met in peaceful interactions and reportedly took away some useful metal articles

1863: First reported attack on the British by the Jarawa; Rev Corbyn undertakes an expedition to the Jarawa area

1869: One of the first records/accounts of timber extraction from the Andaman forests

1873: First record of Syphilis among the indigenous peoples of the islands

1875: First record of deaths in conflict with the Jarawa; six convicts and two Jarawas killed

1878: One Jarawa woman and two children captured during an expedition near Constance Bay

1880: Jarawas kill an Andamanese man at Port Campbell

1886: Epidemic of measles in the Andaman forests

1890s: Onges of Little Andaman Island contacted through gift giving expeditions by the British; also believed to be the time when the Jarawas first started occupying Middle Andaman Island

1891: Jarawas first occupy parts of Baratang Island

1896: Construction work of the Cellular Jail starts

1901: First census in the islands. Total population of the Andaman Islands: 18,138 Jarawa population estimate: 585; Onge estimate: 672; Sentinelese estimate: 117; Great Andamanese actual count: 625; the Aka-Bea-Da, one of the ten groups constituting the Great Andamanese community go extinct

1902: Punitive expedition against the Jarawa by the British

1906: First Working Plan for the forests prepared by F.H. Todd; construction work of Cellular Jail completed

1911: Jarawa population estimate: 114; Onge estimate: 631; Sentinelese estimate: 117; Great Andamanese actual count: 455; total population of the Andaman Islands: 17,641

1921: Jarawa population estimate: 114; Onge estimate: 346; Sentinelese estimate: 117; Great Andamanese actual count: 209; total population of the Andaman Islands: 17,814; clear felling system for extraction of timber introduced in the Andaman forests

1925: Establishment of the Karen village of Webi on Middle Andaman Island; the Moplahs were also settled in the Andamans around this time

1931: Jarawa population estimate: 70; Onge estimate: 250; Sentinelese estimate: 50; Great Andamanese actual count: 90; total population of the Andaman Islands: 19,223

1941: Total population of the Andaman Islands: 21,316

1942: Occupation of the Andaman Islands by the Japanese

1947: India's Independence

1950s: Remnants of Great Andamanese community (estimated to be a total of nineteen individuals) settled on Strait Island

1951: Jarawa population estimate: 50; Onge estimate: 150; Sentinelese estimate: 50; Great Andamanese actual count: 23; total population of the Andaman Islands: 18,962

1952: Chengappa's Working Plan for the Andaman forests

1956: Notification of the 'Andaman and Nicobar Protection of Aboriginal Tribes Regulation (ANPATR) by the Government of India

1957: Creation of tribal reserves in the names of the Jarawa, Onge and

Sentinelese communities under the provision of the ANPATR; the Nicobar islands are also declared a tribal reserve; Bush Police outpost set up at Louis Islet

1961: Jarawa population estimate: 500; Onge actual count: 129; Sentinelese estimate: 50; Great Andamanese actual count: 19; total population of the Andaman Islands: 48,985

1971: Jarawa population estimate: 250; Onge actual count: 112; Sentinelese estimate: 82; Great Andamanese actual count: 24; total population of the Andaman Islands: 93,468

1974: First contact mission by the A&N Administration to establish friendly contact with the Jarawas along the west coast of the Jarawa Tribal Reserve

1977: Two Jarawa men, one with an old bullet wound brought to Port Blair and then returned to the forest in the hope that they would carry the message of trust and goodwill

1979: Denotification of parts of the Jarawa Tribal Reserve to facilitate timber extraction, construction of the Andaman Trunk Road and clearing of forests for settlements, horticulture and agriculture

1981: Jarawa population estimate: 250; Onge actual count: 97; Sentinelese estimate: 100; Great Andamanese actual count: 26; total population of the Andaman Islands: 1,58,287

1988-89: Construction of the Andaman Trunk Road completed

1990: Master Plan 1991–2021 for Welfare of Primitive Tribes of Andaman and Nicobar Islands by S.A. Awaradi

1991: Jarawa population estimate: 280; Onge actual count: 95; Sentinelese estimate: 100; Great Andamanese actual count: 45; total population of the Andaman Islands: 2,41,453; Jarawas attack the Bush Police Camp at Jirkatang and kill one policeman

1992: Jarawas attack the Bush Police Camp near Tirur

1996: 60–70 Jarawa surround timber extraction party at Puttatang killing some labourers and injuring some

1998: Petition filed by three NGOs in the Kolkata High Court, Port Blair bench, regarding timber logging in the Onge Tribal Reserve on Little Andaman Island

1999: Another petition filed by Port Blair-based lawyer in the Kolkata High regarding the well-being and protection of the Jarawa Tribal Community; Measles epidemic amongst the Jarawa

1998-99: Jarawa hostility to the outside world comes to a gradual end

2000: Jarawa raid on the settlement of Sippi Tikry in North Andaman Island

2001: Jarawa actual count: 240; Onge actual count: 96; Sentinelese estimate: 39; Great Andamanese actual count: 43; total population of the Andaman Islands: 3,14,239

2002: Supreme Court of India orders for the closure of the Andaman Trunk Road in those parts that run through the Jarawa Tribal Reserve

2004: A 'Jarawa' Policy asking, mainly, for the Jarawa to be left alone formulated in response to an order of the Kolkata High Court seeking a policy related to the Jarawa; area of Jarawa Tribal Reserve re-notified and increased to about 1,000 sq km; earthquake off the Sumatra coast, followed by the tsunami

2005: Eruption of volcano on Barren Island

2006: Another outbreak of measles reported amongst the Jarawa; Sub-group of experts on the Jarawa constituted by the Planning Commission submits its report. The group is chaired jointly by Dr Syeda Hameed, Member, Planning Commission and Mr Jairam Ramesh, Member, National Advisory Council

2007: A&N administration notifies a five kilometre buffer zone around the Jarawa Tribal Reserve

2010: Boa Sr, the 85 year woman believed to be the last speaker of the Bo language (in the Great Andamanese group) dies; expert committee formed to review Jarawa policy of 2004

2011: Jarawa actual count: 383; Great Andamanese actual count: 54; Total population of the Andaman Islands: 3,80,581

2012: A controversy breaks out as the British newspaper *Sunday Observer* releases a short video showing six 'naked' Jarawa women dancing on the Andaman Trunk Road at the insistence of unseen male voices; A&N administration issues a modification diluting the buffer zone notification of 2007

2013: Amendment to the ANPATR; buffer zone modified again; SC orders closure of the Andaman Trunk Road for tourist traffic but allows for it to restart a few weeks later; establishment of the Andaman and Nicobar Tribal Research Institute

REFERENCES

Chandi, M. (2001). *The Dug Out Karen Dinghy ['Khlee'] of the Andaman Islands* (pp. 12). New Delhi: Madras Crocodile Bank Trust/Andaman and Nicobar Environment Team and WWF India.

Dhingra, K. (2005). *The Andaman and Nicobar Islands in the 20th Century – A Gazetteer*. New Delhi: Oxford University Press for the Andaman and Nicobar Administration.

Lal, P. (1976). *Andaman Islands – A Regional Geography*. Calcutta: Anthropological Survey of India.

Mazumdar, R.C. (1975). *Penal Settlement in Andamans*. New Delhi: The Ministry of Education and Social Welfare, Govt. of India.

Pandit, T.N., & Sarkar, B.N. (Eds). (1994). *People of India – Andaman and Nicobar Islands* (Vol. XII). Madras: Anthropological Survey of India and Affiliated East-West Press Pvt Ltd.

ACKNOWLEDGEMENTS

For being part of the journey of this book at different times, in different capacities and in different places . . .

. . . Aarthi Sridhar, Ajai Saxena, Allan Vaughan, Aniruddha Mookerjee, Annapurna Mamidipudi, Anuradha Arjunwadkar, Anvita Abbi, Asad Rahmani, Asha Krishnakumar, Ashish Fernandes, Ashish Kothari, Bhuvneshwari Devi, Bittu Sahgal, Christelle Chapoy, Colin Gonsalves, Dharama Sundaray, Debi Goenka, Deepak Dalal, Denis Giles, Dhananjay Kakde, Durgalakshmi Venkataswamy, Douglas Nakashima, Falguni Sheth Sekhsaria, Geetanjali Acharya, Gita Ramaswamy, Gouri Dange, Govind Khalsode, Harjit Singh, Harry Andrews, P. Jacob, Janaki Lenin, Janki Andharia, Joanna van-Gruisen, John Robert, Junuka Deshpande, Kalpana Sharma, K.B. Saxena, Kanchi Kohli, Kanchan Mukhopadhyay, Kanishka Gupta, Kaustubh Moghe, Kiran Dhingra, Kranti C., S. Lakshmanan (Srikant Anna), Madhumita Mazumdar, Madhusree Mukerjee, Madhuvanti Anantharajan, Mahesh Rangarajan, Manish Chandi, Manju Menon, Meghali Senapati, Milind Wani, Montu Bhowmik, Nandini Sundar, Naveen Ekka, Neema Pathak Broome, Neeraj Vagholikar, Nimesh Ved, Nina Subramani, Pradip Prabhu, Pratibha Pande, Pronob Sircar, Rainer Hoerig, Ramanujam Venkat, Rasheed Yousuf, Rauf Ali, Ritwick Dutta, Romulus Whitaker, Rosemary Vishwanath, Rustam Vania, Samhita Acharya, Samir Acharya, Samit Sawhney, Sanjeev Gopal, Saurabh Dani, Saw John, Saw Agu, Saw Pambwe, Saw Paung, Seema Bhatt, Shantha Bhushan, Shekar Dattatri, Shekhar Singh,

Sheema Mookherjee, Shivakumar Iyer (Anna), B. Syama Sundari, Simronjit Singh, Sita Venkateshwar, Smitha Rao, Sujatha Lakshmanan, Santosh Mathews, Sophie Grig, Sudarshan Rodriguez, Sujatha Padmanabhan, Sumitro Sen, Sunita Rao, Syed Liyakhat, Syeda Hameed, Tara Gandhi, Tarun Coomar, Theodore Baskaran, Tom Mathew, Vishvajit Pandya, Vivek Gaur Broome, Vijaya Sankar, Wiebe Bijker, Zubair Ahmed . . .

. . . and then, those who are not there with us anymore – Ravi Sankaran, Deepa Sankaran, Govind Raju, J.C. Daniels . . .

And finally my editors, Rajni George, for prodding me gently but firmly to chop and cut and polish, and Ajitha G.S. at HarperCollins India for ensuring I kept chopping and cutting and polishing till the end; but much before we could even get there, for believing in this book, thank you Ajitha.